Praise for *In*

"Infused with . . . fresh detail. Between ~~the sweet~~ and the summery beach setting, romance fans will find this a warming winter read."

—*Publishers Weekly*

"Fans will love the frank honesty of her characters. [Beck's] scenery is richly detailed and the story engaging."

—*RT Book Reviews*

"[A] realistic and heartwarming story of redemption and love . . . Beck's understanding of interpersonal relationships and her flawless prose make for a believable romance and an entertaining read."

—*Booklist*

Praise for *Worth the Wait*

"[A] poignant and heartwarming story of young love and redemption and will literally make your heart ache . . . Jamie Beck has a real talent for making the reader feel the sorrow, regret and yearning of this young character."

—*Fresh Fiction*

Praise for *Worth the Trouble*

"Beck takes readers on a journey of self-reinvention and risky investments, in love and in life . . . With strong family ties, loyalty, playful banter, and sexual tension, Beck has crafted a beautiful second-chances story."

—Starred review, *Publishers Weekly*

Praise for *Secretly Hers*

"[I]n Beck's ambitious, uplifting second Sterling Canyon contemporary... Conflicting views and family drama lay the foundation for emotional development in this strong Colorado-set contemporary."

—*Publishers Weekly*

"[w]itty banter and the deepening of the characters and their relationship, along with some unexpected plot twists and a lovable supporting cast... will keep the reader hooked... A smart, fun, sexy, and very contemporary romance."

—*Kirkus Reviews*

unexpectedly
hers

ALSO BY JAMIE BECK

In the Cards

The St. James Novels

Worth the Wait
Worth the Trouble
Worth the Risk

The Sterling Canyon Novels

Accidentally Hers
Secretly Hers

unexpectedly *hers*

A Sterling Canyon Novel

Jamie Beck

Montlake
Romance

This is a work of fiction. Names, characters, organizations, places, events, and incidents are either products of the author's imagination or are used fictitiously.

Published by Montlake Romance, Seattle

www.apub.com

Amazon, the Amazon logo, and Montlake Romance are trademarks of Amazon.com, Inc., or its affiliates.

ISBN-13: 9781503942240
ISBN-10: 1503942244

Cover design by Shasti O'Leary Soudant

Printed in the United States of America

This one is for my MTBs—plotting partners extraordinaire—Jamie Pope, Heidi Ulrich, Denise Smoker, Jane Haertel, Katy Lee, Tracy Costa, Gail Chianese, Jen Moncuse, Linda Avellar, and Jamie K. Schmidt. Many thanks for your unwavering support and for the encouragement to go out on a limb and make Emma's story a little sassy and surprising.

Chapter One

Straddling her hips, Dallas smeared a handful of whipped cream across Ella's breasts.

"Like a sundae." He bent over and licked her, then looked up with a lusty smile as his hand found the red curls at the top of her inner thighs. "This bit of red is the cherry on top."

He licked her again as she writhed with pleasure—her arms still tied to the bedpost—then his head disappeared between her legs.

Bang!

Emma flinched at the sound, then shoved the advanced review copy of her debut novel under her pillow before her mother marched in and caught her with smut. That's what her mom would call it, anyway. She imagined everyone's shock if they ever discovered that she was Alexa Aspen, the author of *Steep and Deep,* which many would deem "mommy porn."

Of course, no one would ever learn her secret. When her agent had negotiated her publishing contract, Emma had chosen to avoid the brunt of Sterling Canyon's small-town scrutiny by assuming a pen name.

It'd been so easy that, except at the moment she'd signed the contract, she hadn't even winced. No one would ever believe quiet, conservative Emma Duffy would read a book containing smokin' hot sex, much less write one.

Emma smiled to herself while remembering one night in Aspen three years ago when she'd been checking out a recently renovated Victorian B&B. After a couple of single, sexless years, she'd taken advantage of her anonymity there and abandoned all caution. Donning new clothes and a fake name, she'd had her first and only one-night stand. That tryst had inspired the idea for her book and its hero, Dallas. To this day, she couldn't explain what had possessed her to be so brazen . . .

Bang, bang! A quick glance over her shoulder confirmed no one was entering her room. Actually, the noise sounded too distant to be her bedroom door. Grabbing her green, cable-knit cardigan, she went to investigate. Hopefully the porch posts weren't cracking apart.

Bang!

She trotted down the staircase of her family's ancient bed and breakfast, The Weenuche, named for a Ute Indian tribe that had once inhabited Southwest Colorado. Emma's presence marked the third generation to run the inn, although technically, her mother ran the business while Emma managed the kitchen and concierge desk. The worn carpet beneath her feet sadly announced to the world that it had been decades since the place had been refurbished.

She'd wanted to copy some of the upgrades she'd seen at that inn in Aspen, but who had money to splurge on redecorating when ancient plumbing, sagging roofs, and other emergencies cropped up every month? The unusual spate of monster-sized October snowstorms hadn't helped, either. And while El Niño snowfall should bring more tourists to town, it also inevitably would cause more wear and tear on her battered inn.

Jogging across the small lobby, she shoved open the front door, which creaked against a strong early-November wind. Had the gust not set her back, she might have crashed into the unfamiliar young men in skullcaps and combat boots who were nailing flyers to the posts on the front porch.

"Excuse me." Emma approached them with caution, tightening her cozy sweater to buffer against the frigid air. "Who are you, and what are you posting on my property?"

The one with the blond goatee and short ponytail smiled. "Disclaimer notices, so we don't have to get specific waivers for people to be included in the documentary."

Documentary? She scanned the sheet of paper, which read:

REEL DRAMA, INC.

IS CURRENTLY VIDEOTAPING AND
CABLECASTING SCENES AT THIS
LOCATION FOR POSSIBLE INCLUSION
IN TELEVISION PROGRAMS.
IF YOU DO NOT WISH TO BE
PHOTOGRAPHED OR TO APPEAR ON
TELEVISION, OR TO BE OTHERWISE
RECORDED, PLEASE LEAVE THIS
LOCATION DURING OUR
VIDEOTAPING.

BY REMAINING IN THIS IMMEDIATE
VICINITY, YOU ARE GIVING REEL DRAMA, INC. YOUR
CONSENT TO PHOTOGRAPH, FILM, RECORD,
AND CABLECAST YOUR PICTURE,
LIKENESS, VOICE, AND STATEMENTS.

Oh, good Lord. What the heck had her mother gotten them into now?

"I'm sorry, will you please hold on a second? Don't post anything else until I speak with my mother." She turned on her heel and entered the lobby, calling out, "Mom!"

"Don't shout, dear. It isn't very ladylike." Her mother emerged from the back office with a large suitcase in tow. Freshwater pearls complimented her best twinset and wool slacks. She would've looked quite elegant if not for the Velcro orthopedic walking shoes. "I was just coming to say good-bye. I'm leaving now to pick up Vera for our cross-country trip. You're in charge, angel."

The overwhelming scent of her mother's beloved White Diamonds perfume enveloped Emma, making her cough.

"You told me this would be a quiet month," Emma accused, remembering when her mom had first informed her of the plans for Aunt Vera's month-long sixty-fifth birthday vacation. She'd been happy to learn of it, because it would leave her more privacy to prepare for the book launch. "You said I'd only be dealing with a private party of five while you were away."

"That's right. Apparently the freak October blizzards have made Sterling Canyon an ideal spot for that skier's training."

Skier? Training? As usual, Emma had a hard time following her mother's train of thought.

Emma raised her arms toward heaven. "So why are there men outside posting notices about filming a documentary?"

"It's wonderful." Her mother's eyes lit. "People love a comeback story, so this film should be quite popular. The free publicity will bring all kinds of attention to our inn. When it airs, it'll put us on the map so we can compete with Wade Kessler's new hotel."

"What?" Her pulse beat hard at the base of her neck. The lack of communication astounded her. "Why is this the first I'm hearing of it?"

"I'm sure I mentioned it." Her mother patted her arm.

"I think I'd remember if you mentioned a documentary."

"Emma, your head's been in the clouds lately—perhaps you just weren't listening."

Emma couldn't deny that possibility. These past several weeks she'd lapsed into thoughts about her impending book launch, its early reviews, and her next story—the one on deadline. Perhaps her mother *had* mentioned it and Emma had just not heard it amid all her nattering.

"Now that I have your attention," her mother began, "all the paperwork and permits are on my desk with a big list of items they need. I took care of most things, although you should double-check the list from the nutritionist before you grocery shop this week. Also, I forgot to arrange for a yoga instructor, but you used to teach at YogAmbrosia, so you can do it."

"Me? Then who'll be preparing breakfast, Mom?"

"Oh, yes. That. Then call there and arrange for one of the instructors to come give private lessons here in the morning." Her mom smiled and patted Emma's cheek. "It's lovely to know I can count on you, perfect girl. You always make me proud."

Normally Emma would bask in the glow of her mother's praise. But the last thing she needed now was to be dodging a camera crew while juggling her duties to the inn and her burgeoning writing career. And what made her mother think The Weenuche could compete for the same customers as Wade's soon-to-be-completed Bear Lodge—a five-star, state-of-the-art boutique hotel?

The entire situation robbed Emma of her good manners. "So you're taking off scot-free while I'm going to end up on camera at all hours, with flour on my clothes and wearing a hairnet?"

"Don't be so dramatic, Emma." Her mother smoothed her own faded red hair. "Neither of us likes it when you act like your father."

As always, a chilly two-second pause followed any mention of her father, who'd left them both almost twenty years ago to chase fame in Hollywood. The fact that he'd only ever made the D-list pleased her mother, who'd never wanted to see him rewarded for his philandering and abandonment. Emma herself felt the sting of the comparison, because she disliked any part of herself that resembled someone who'd caused so much heartache.

"Think of the film as a little adventure." Her mother cleared her throat. "I spoke with the producer, Mari, who sounds like a very nice woman. You aren't the subject of this movie, dear, so just smile and make the place inviting." She pinched Emma's cheek. "Maybe put on a little makeup, just in case you end up on film."

"You're really something." Emma rolled her eyes.

"I'll take that as a compliment." Her mother waved dismissively and popped up the suitcase handle. "Now help me load this into the car. It's parked out front."

Emma strode out the door, rolling the bag behind her while trying not to be insulted by her mother's assessment.

"Can we continue?" Goatee Guy asked as she and her mother breezed past him and his cohort.

"Apparently." Emma heaved the bag down the few porch steps. "Careful, Mom, there's still some ice."

"I see, Emma." Her mother *tsked*. "You really must get on this sooner."

"Andy will be here soon to clear it."

"Well, you and Andy have to clear all the snow and ice in a timely fashion so we can impress our guests and look good on camera. Remember, perceptions are everything—in life and in business." Her mother kissed her good-bye. "I'll send pictures and gifts from each city. I can't wait to see Chicago, Washington, DC, and New York. Did I tell you we have tickets to *Hamilton*?"

"Only thirty times." Emma hugged her ridiculous yet lovable mother good-bye.

It'd been just the two of them for a while now. Several years after her father had bolted, her beloved Grammy had died right here in the dining room. Choked on chicken, of all things. Aunt Vera lived in Denver, so they only saw her a few times a year.

Emma and her mom had nursed each other through broken hearts and broken dreams. Although the woman could verge on the absurd, Emma loved her mom and would never, ever want to let her down, so she would bite her tongue now and do her best to make her mother happy.

"Drive safely, Mom."

"I will." Emma's mother hugged her again. "This reminds me of the first time my mother left me in charge of the inn so she could go to Santa Fe for *her* sixty-fifth with her book group ladies. Do you remember that? You were so dependable, even as a teenager. I trust that the inn is in good hands with you, sweetheart. Hopefully this month will pass without a major incident."

"Yes, let's do hope." Emma smiled as she helped her mother into the car, thinking about her mother's trust. Emma was dependable, yes. But trustworthy? She'd been deceiving her mom for the past few years, so maybe that word no longer applied.

Her mother waved good-bye just as a van pulled into the parking lot. Emma assumed that it was ferrying more of the crew, possibly even the star of the dreaded documentary. Hopefully he wasn't a prima donna.

Another brisk wind blew a cloud of snow in Emma's face, forcing her to seek warmth. She hustled inside, past the guys on the porch, and scampered up to her room to run a brush through her hair, knot it into some kind of lumpy bun, and hide the box of her books under her bed.

She drew a breath, enjoying a rare moment of freedom. Her mother didn't crowd her, per se, but her presence could turn suffocating now and then.

Emma had grown up well aware of her mother's and Grammy's expectations. She'd been privy to more than one lecture about the dangers of loose morals. Not that she'd needed it. She'd seen firsthand how lust and temptation screwed up people's lives—from politicians' to her own father's.

Having helplessly watched her mom spiral into a major depression right after he left had certainly changed Emma's perspective on life and love, and on her mom's ability to cope with disappointment. Faith in God and Emma's endless acts of appeasement had pulled her through, but Emma never wanted to see her mom tested again.

So she'd clamped down on any part of herself that resembled her father, even though sometimes the bottled-up passion simmering beneath her skin burned like fingers caught on an oven rack. Her secret fling in Aspen had been necessary to avoid spontaneous combustion.

On her way back downstairs, she heard the murmur of voices and the scuffle of bags coming into the lobby. She dashed around the corner to the welcome desk and then froze. *It. Can't. Be!*

Dallas, er—Wyatt. Wyatt Lawson—famed slopestyle snowboard International Games and Rockies Winter eXtreme Games gold medalist, among other titles—stood in her lobby.

She vaguely registered other people, too, but her gaze locked on Wyatt's exotic face. Although born and raised in Vermont, he looked Brazilian with his wild, wavy black hair that hung to his jaw, his bronzed skin, his dreamy hazel eyes set deeply beneath straight, thick brows. She couldn't actually see those eyes while staring at his profile, but she still remembered them from their one incredible night together. The one she'd relived over and over while writing and editing her book.

Her heart lodged itself in her throat. *Please, God, don't let him recognize me.*

Emma had never told a soul about that night, and would be mortified if her mother or friends ever learned about her brief walk on the wild side. If they knew she'd acted like some kind of cougar, picking up a guy six years her junior. Even she still couldn't believe she'd done it.

Of course, Wyatt wouldn't associate Emma with Alexa—the alter ego she'd adopted for a few hours to break free from being Emma Duffy.

Unlike Emma, Alexa had no qualms about her sexuality. Alexa had confidently worn a silky black dress that barely covered her chest and butt. Alexa had rocked high-heeled, knee-high boots, had had her thick, red hair professionally styled, and had worn smoky makeup and loopy earrings. Yes, Alexa had been a bona fide siren that night.

Wyatt had been celebrating his victory when she'd spotted him in the bar. Targeted him, truthfully. Carefree, happy, drunk Wyatt—young and proud and on the prowl. He'd been the perfect man for her singular one-night stand. And they'd had quite a night, until she'd woken at five o'clock and ducked out of his hotel room without a trace.

But she couldn't quite regret it because that night had given life to a story, and naturally, Wyatt's image—and certain other things— remained the inspiration for her hero's character. For three years, she'd thought of him as Dallas. Thought, fantasized, spent way too much time filling Pinterest boards with his image . . .

Wyatt now turned those greenish-brown eyes her way and smiled at her—the kind of smile he'd give a friend's little sister. Her hot cheeks meant her fair skin had turned almost as red as her hair.

"Good morning. I'm Wyatt." Wyatt stepped aside to make room for a young guy with a cane wearing a baseball cap and sunglasses. Wyatt patiently followed him to the check-in desk. "This is my brother, Ryder, and that's the film crew, Jim, Buddy, and Mari. Looks like we've all descended at once."

Emma remembered briefly seeing Ryder that night in Aspen. He'd been an up-and-coming snowboarder, although he hadn't hit the podium. Sadly, the following year he'd finally made headlines when a snowboarding accident caused a traumatic brain injury. She'd read that Wyatt had left competition to help his family, and that Ryder had spent a few months in the hospital following his accident.

Looking at Ryder now, she sensed he hadn't fully recovered— physically or otherwise. A pang of empathy for the brothers settled in her chest.

But surely neither he nor Wyatt would connect her to Alexa, assuming Wyatt even remembered that night. No doubt he'd had many such meaningless encounters on the competition circuit.

For the briefest moment, sadness gripped her, forcing her to acknowledge that a major turning point in her small life had been a mere blip in Wyatt's. She shook off the wistful musing before anyone noticed.

"Welcome," Emma said, her gaze roaming the group without making direct eye contact with Wyatt. "We're so glad to have you. I'll be at your disposal during your stay, so anything you need, just ask."

Wyatt playfully cocked an eyebrow and smiled, this time a little less brotherly. A memory of him wearing that identical look—and nothing else—passed through her mind and shot straight to her girly parts. Goodness, his look had made her innocent statement somehow sound naughty. How on earth would she survive an entire month living under the same roof with Dallas, er, Wyatt, without giving away her identity?

The statuesque blonde, dressed entirely in black, approached the desk. "Hi. It's nice to finally meet you in person. I'm Mari."

Emma shook Mari's hand, thankful for a distraction. "Oh, you must be the director who spoke with my mother. Unfortunately, you just missed her. I'll be the one taking care of you while you're here."

While Emma spoke with Mari, Wyatt's lazy gaze ogled her body, unnerving her. Thank God she'd thrown on a bulky sweater. He might be hot as heck and the perfect sexual fantasy, but a man like him—a player like her dad, obsessed with fame—wasn't the kind of man she wanted or trusted.

"I know we're a bit early, but are the rooms ready? You should have all the credit card information and other things. All we need now are the keys." Mari said. "We'd like to unpack and then get some things set up."

"Of course." Emma averted her gaze again and focused on Ryder. His injuries and cane might make the old stairs a bit of a hazard. "We have a lovely room with a park view here on the main floor for you, Ryder."

"Fine," came Ryder's lifeless reply.

Wyatt leaned close to his brother's ear. "How about a 'thank you,' bro'?"

"Oh, no, please. I'm sure you're all travel-weary." Emma glanced at the clock and then the door, expecting to see Andy walk through it. She snatched a handful of keys and handed them out. "Everyone else will be on the second floor. I typically serve breakfast from six to eight, lunch from noon to two, and dinner at six thirty. If there are allergies, intolerances, or just things you don't like to eat, please let me know."

Mari's brows snapped together. "I sent a very specific list of things we'd need, including a meal schedule, specific dietary needs to suit Wyatt's training schedule, a therapist for Ryder, a private yoga instructor, and so on. Your mother assured me Wyatt would have everything he needed."

"Oh, I'm sorry, I wasn't thinking. Of course we'll accommodate all of your requests." Emma felt another flush race to her face. Hopefully she'd pull it all together before lunch.

"Wyatt requested someplace private and quiet, so we're here," Mari glanced around disapprovingly, "for four weeks. I certainly hope we haven't made a mistake."

"I promise I'll meet all of your demands. Anticipate them, even," Emma added with a ready smile, hoping to soothe her. Emma'd spent most of her life accommodating the demands of others in order to keep things running smoothly. She much preferred peace and harmony to confrontation. "Including the privacy I assume you want," she finished.

Thankfully, Andy walked in at that moment, paying no immediate notice to the guests. "Hey, Em. I need to get the ice off that walkway." Then his gaze fell on the small group. "But I can take the bags first."

Andy's twin sister, Avery, had been one of Emma's best friends since kindergarten. There had been a brief period when Emma had had a little crush on Andy, but like with the other guys in her long history of unrequited crushes, it had more or less passed. He might as well be her brother, too. As such, when his drunk driving accident last winter cost him his job as a ski pro, she'd hired him to help her around the inn.

"Everyone, this is Andy. Andy, this is—" Emma began.

"Holy shit! You're Wyatt Lawson." Andy's eyes twinkled and his jaw dropped. "Dude, you're awesome. What the hell are you doing in Sterling Canyon?"

"Andy, I think Mr. Lawson would like some privacy." Emma shot him a "back-off" look.

"It's cool." Wyatt waved at Andy. "I'm here to train."

"Gentlemen, we really need to keep to a schedule. We have a lot of ground to cover today to set things up," Mari broke in, laying her hand on Wyatt's arm, effectively yanking him away from Andy. "If you could please see our bags to our rooms, that would be perfect. We'll leave the cameras and other equipment down here." Then she addressed the film crew. "Let's meet in the front parlor in an hour to go over the shooting schedule and get some establishing shots."

Andy winked at Emma. "This is gonna be the best month ever."

Wyatt glanced at his brother while uttering, "It better be."

"Andy, could you please see Ryder to Room 101 while I take the others upstairs?" Emma asked. "Then you can come grab these other bags and bring them to their rooms."

"No problem." Andy took the key and slowly went off with Ryder. In the meantime, Mari and the cameramen had already headed upstairs, leaving Emma alone with Wyatt, who appeared lost in thought as he watched his brother walk off.

"Shall we?" Emma gestured toward the stairs.

She should be worried about Mari's demands. But with Wyatt on her heels, all she could think about was whether or not her butt looked okay in her sweatpants. Good grief, she was her father's daughter, which meant she was in trouble.

Wyatt had chosen Sterling Canyon as the training location for his return to competition because its off-the-beaten-path location would likely make it more private. He needed a distraction-free environment.

The enormity of his task left no room for complications—or women, which tended to be the same thing.

Normally he wouldn't notice a girl like Emma. Buried beneath such boxy clothes, he could barely make out her figure. At least, not until he followed her up the stairs and got a perfect view of her heart-shaped ass.

He'd always liked red hair, too, although she'd pulled hers into some kind of knot, so he couldn't tell if it was straight or wavy, shoulder- or waist-length. Not that it mattered.

Yet it did. Why'd she stiffen whenever he caught her eye? Unlike other women who threw themselves at him, this one seemed almost determined to repel him. He should let her keep her distance so he could maintain his priorities.

Nothing like the pressure of a film crew documenting his every move—and potential mistakes—to keep him focused. He needed to stay focused if he wanted to achieve his goals without ending up in a hospital bed like his brother had.

The very thought sent a shiver down his spine.

"Is it too cold in here?" Emma asked, apparently having noticed his reaction. For a second, he caught a glimpse of something warmer shining through.

"Maybe a touch," he lied. Glancing around, he noticed a bunch of Native American artifacts. Although clean, everything about the place looked old and run-down. At first glance, he'd have said Emma, with her absence of makeup and oversize clothing, perfectly matched the surroundings. But on closer inspection, a little spark of something glimmered from her lively green eyes. And Wyatt had never been one to discriminate against older chicks.

Out of nowhere, Emma let loose a whopper of a sneeze, then promptly flushed. "Excuse me."

"Bless you." He grinned as a piece of trivia popped into place, as usual. "Did you know that people exhale at up to one hundred miles per hour when they sneeze? It's why they can't keep their eyes open."

Oddly, she smiled with a faraway look in her eyes and murmured something about his trivia quirk. Intent on chipping away at her armor, he asked, "I suppose you live here?"

Just like that, her starchy demeanor returned. "You mean here, at the inn?"

He grinned, wanting another peek beneath the surface, and if possible, beneath her ugly sweater. "Mmm hmmm."

"Yes, on the third floor." She cocked her head. "Why?"

"Making sure you'll be nearby twenty-four seven. You never know if I might need you for something." He'd purposely lowered his voice and leaned closer to see how she'd respond to subtle flirtation.

Her shoulders pulled back, her eyes avoided his gaze. "I'm at your beck and call." She blushed again, clearly having not considered the innuendo in her words until they'd tumbled out.

Her bashful manner surprised Wyatt, who hadn't met a shy woman in years. He found her attitude refreshing . . . and challenging. He'd always had a hard time backing down from a challenge.

She finally, if briefly, made eye contact and then handed him the key to his room. "Shall I wait to make sure you like your room?"

"I'm sure it's fine." He noticed a light smattering of freckles across the bridge of her nose. A cute nose. Thin and straight, perhaps a little on the small side. He repressed the urge to touch it, as well as the urge to stare at her full lips. Shit, he had to stop. He might be a healthy twenty-five-year-old guy who'd gone too long without sex lately, but he couldn't let his dick hijack his goals.

"There are extra blankets in the closet." She nodded tersely, punctuating her thought. "Sometimes the old windows can be a little drafty when the wind kicks up."

"If it gets too cold, I might need something more than an extra blanket to keep me warm." Okay, so his dick didn't give a shit about his goals, although he didn't have any real intention of pursuing Emma.

He'd pushed because he had to get some reaction from Miss Prim and Proper.

She snorted. "Mari seems intent on satisfying your every whim, so I doubt you'll have to go far to get what you need. Now if you'll excuse me, I really must get to work."

She turned, scurrying away like a mouse that'd just been spooked by a tiger. He watched her trot down the stairs before he went into his room and collapsed across the bed.

Scrubbing his face with his hands, he thought about the task at hand. He had much to accomplish. Much to prove. Much to make up for.

Ryder's healthcare costs had pretty much wiped out the bulk of Wyatt's former wealth. His mom's arthritis left her unable to hold a full-time job, either. Wyatt had to win back his former sponsors, because he never wanted his family to return to the days of his youth, when food stamps barely fed him and wearing shoes with holes in their soles was a way of life. When he'd had so little power.

This comeback plan was his last-ditch attempt to right the ship and erase the condemnation he'd seen in his mother's eyes every day since Ryder had nearly died. Even more critical was helping his brother learn to enjoy life again. They'd loved working together in the past, so having Ryder with him now should be the ticket. Ryder's help should also ensure that Wyatt made a big splash in the qualifiers. He needed to get past his own mental hurdles regarding the transition—from man-made, groomed slopestyle courses to the unpredictable freeriding terrain—pronto.

Hopefully a twenty-minute catnap would prepare him for dealing with Mari. He usually flirted because ladies liked it, and it made him feel more comfortable. With Mari, he couldn't afford for her to think of him as the party boy of yesteryear. He had to train without falling into his old patterns with women.

With his eyes closed, the first thing that popped into his mind was the image of Emma's ass swaying side to side as she climbed those stairs. He smiled in spite of himself and drifted into oblivion.

Chapter Two

Wyatt woke from his nap, momentarily confused by his surroundings. Branches tapped against the antique window at the corner of his room. He stood, stretching with a yawn, as he took a minute to observe his temporary home.

The room contained timeworn furniture and assorted knickknacks, including a cross on the wall near the bed. Perhaps he should pray for a guardian angel to help him conquer "big mountain" competitions. He could use all the help he could get, and it had been a while since he'd prayed for anything. After all the prayers he'd offered on his brother's behalf, he'd figured other people needed God's attention for a while.

His phone alarm beeped, reminding him that Mari would be waiting downstairs. Did she have his interests at heart? Last time he'd trusted a journalist, she'd betrayed him and reprinted things out of context. Made him look and sound like a misogynistic asshole with an ego the size of Montana. Neither was true, not that the public believed him.

He went to the bathroom to splash water on his face and laughed when he saw the old-fashioned separate hot and cold spigots. Between the cross and the antiquated inn, no wonder Emma and her straitlaced attitude seemed to come from some other era.

He patted his face dry and finger-combed his wavy locks, then jogged down the creaky stairs. The parlor was still empty, so Wyatt went to fetch a bottle of water. He wandered through the dining hall—a cozy paneled room with four round tables—into the kitchen.

Emma's space, he thought. Like the rest of the inn, it looked tired. The stainless steel industrial appliances appeared newer, but the yellowing, unadorned oak cabinetry didn't, nor did the checkerboard vinyl flooring. At least the large window above the huge sink let in ample natural light.

God, he'd hate to be stuck inside cooking for and cleaning up after people. Such a lonely, stifling way to spend day after day. What made her choose this life? Shaking away the stray thought, he grabbed a water bottle and closed the refrigerator.

On his way out, he heard a shuffling noise and humming coming from around the corner. Then a feminine voice broke into the chains-and-whips refrain of Rihanna's "S&M." It must be Emma, although that would be the very last song he'd imagine her liking. Intrigued, he crept around the corner and peered into a sizable walk-in pantry to find Emma—back turned to him—dancing while taking inventory.

His brain simultaneously took in a few things. One, Emma had the music turned up so loud that, even from a distance, he could hear the tinny beat pulsing from her earbuds. Two, it had been ages since he'd seen anything as erotic as the contrast between her prudishness and the sensual swivel of her ass as she danced by herself. And three, if he closed the door, this pantry would become a dark, private cocoon.

A smile tugged at his mouth. Before he even considered the consequences, he stepped behind her, wrapped one arm around her waist, and tried to dance with her.

"*Whaa!*" she screeched, springing into the air like the cats in those cucumber Vines. Adrenaline gripped her hard, as evidenced by the tremble rippling down her body.

"Sorry!" Unable to help himself, he chuckled. "Really sorry. I didn't mean to scare you."

She yanked the earbuds from her ears. Her indignant expression somehow made her look sexy, despite that hideous sweater. Damn if he didn't want to grab her by that stupid knot in her hair and kiss her. Who knew? Underneath the ugly clothes and prudish attitude, she might be a little bit fun. Might even yield to him and enjoy things like handcuffs and other sex games.

Then, like a chameleon, she transformed before his eyes, shuttering her emotions and resuming control over herself. He admired control. Ruthlessly strove for it in his own life, although not always with success, as his impulsive attempt to dance with her just proved.

She smoothed the stray hairs from her face and shooed him out of the pantry. "I assume you didn't come to the kitchen to dance. What do you need?"

So businesslike. But now he knew better. Then again, it didn't matter. He couldn't indulge his curiosity. Shit, he had to meet with Mari. He had to train!

"Just this." He held up the water bottle. "I heard singing, though, so I came to investigate." And because he wanted to provoke her, he added, "Interesting song choice."

Oh, too easy. A streak of red rushed to her cheeks. He wondered how easily he might be able to make other parts of her body turn pink, too? *Stop it.* Apparently it took no encouragement to provoke him into flirting with Emma. Something about her weakened his control.

"Well, then, now that you've uncovered the big mystery, I assume you have a schedule to keep, as do I." She folded her arms in front of her body and offered him an ever-so-polite yet placating smile.

"That I do." He nodded, knowing he should feel grateful that she didn't encourage his interest. Of course, gratitude did not wash over him. He left the kitchen, going directly to the hexagonally shaped parlor near the front of the inn, where Mari and the crew were already seated and looking over the shooting schedule.

"Oh, good. You're here." Mari handed him a schedule—a gray and white grid with daily sunrise and sunset times, location designations, and other information. "It's really important that we adhere to the schedule in order to avoid cost overruns or missing certain shots and so on."

Mari smiled—a tight grin. In truth, she made him a little nervous. He could sense her ambition from a hundred yards away, which made him very aware that he was just a means to an end.

"I understand the importance of a schedule," Wyatt replied. He pointed at the words "establishing shots" on the calendar. "What's this mean? I thought we did that back in Vermont with my mom."

"Those are needed every time we change the setting." Mari waved around the inn. "I need Jim to get outside shots of this inn, the signage, maybe a few shots around town, and the view of the mountain. We should get some inside shots, too, to show where you're living, eating, exercising . . . you know, to orient people and give them a peek into where you are."

"So am I off the hook for a while?" Wyatt wanted to check on Ryder and maybe take a walk around the town to get himself oriented, too.

"Not exactly. We need your gorgeous face in the shots or it will be too boring for viewers. They'll want to see and hear your reaction to the surroundings," Mari began, one brow cocked, "such as they are."

Just then Emma strode through the lobby with a clipboard and a baggy purse. Apparently "baggy" summed up her sense of style. Naturally she didn't meet his gaze, choosing instead to look at Mari. "Excuse me. Sorry to interrupt, but I'm headed out to grab a few things. If you need anything while I'm out, Andy is around and can help you."

She smiled when she said Andy's name, just as she'd smiled at the guy earlier when he'd arrived. Wyatt wondered if they were more than boss and employee. Then he wondered why he cared.

"We're good," he answered before checking with the others.

She nodded and continued outside. He watched her through the parlor window as she skipped down the porch steps and jogged toward her car. Efficient, focused, and completely disinterested in him.

19

Mari snapped her fingers, drawing his attention, and speared him with an impatient stare. "Let's focus so we can get something more than unpacking accomplished today."

Snippy much? He'd better not get on her bad side. Unlike with past PR, he couldn't afford for this video to show him in anything less than a good light. Some guys might've loved the reputation he'd previously—if somewhat undeservedly—earned, but at heart, Wyatt didn't think of himself as a superficial adrenaline junkie. He wanted admiration for his skill and dedication, not for his looks or the women in his life. And his mother would be less patient with those antics these days.

In a backwards way, Ryder's accident had given Wyatt a chance to start over. It mattered to him that he be seen as a positive role model this time around.

"So what are we doing first?" Wyatt leaned forward to give Mari his full attention.

"While I've got you alone, let's get some of the history that we've privately discussed on film. Buddy's set to go, so are you ready?"

She'd made it sound like he'd had a choice, which he knew he didn't. "Sure."

Mari nodded at Buddy and then asked Wyatt, "Your brother's accident derailed your own career for a while. Can you tell us a bit about that time?"

He hated talking about it. Thinking about it, really. The helplessness, the panic, the ongoing worry. He'd rather someone pull his teeth out than have to publicly share his feelings, but he'd committed to this film for Ryder, his mom, and himself. He couldn't back down now.

"From the moment Ryder was loaded onto the medevac until he finally left the hospital four months later, my mom and I were by his side. I worked with him every day of his intensive rehabilitation that first year, praying he'd regain full use of his right side and his speech."

"It seems that you got your wish, for the most part."

"He's worked hard and made amazing progress. He's an inspiration to me and should be to others." Of course, Ryder wasn't the same person that he'd been before the accident. His mood swings still blew hot and cold, hypersensitivity to light forced him to wear sunglasses often, and he compensated for his slurring by speaking more slowly than normal and over-enunciating. Although Ryder had been lucky not only to survive the crash but also to regain most of his faculties, Wyatt sometimes wondered if Ryder cared about anything anymore. His brother could be invested in something one minute then lapse into apathy or anger the next.

Mari crossed her legs and smiled, attempting to appear laidback. *Ha! As if a robot could be human.* "Most people will consider your decision to switch from slopestyle to freeriding unusual, given that slopestyle not only offers a higher profile but is also what you know. Did your experience with Ryder have anything to do with that decision?"

"Yes." How much should he reveal? Not everything. Not his own doubts. "Watching him take on overwhelming obstacles only made me admire him more than ever. I want to be worthy of his respect, so I decided to tackle a new challenge in a show of solidarity. Of course, nothing I'll be facing will be anywhere near as difficult as what he's going through. His future is still uncertain. Now I'm also facing uncertainty. Hopefully, together we'll both discover that, even if life is different today, it can still be good. Maybe I'll fail, but like Ryder, I'll grow, too."

"And how does Ryder feel about being part of this journey?"

Ryder had remained relatively closemouthed since his accident, but Wyatt suspected he still missed—yearned for—his old life and the dreams forever lost to him. Those dreams didn't need to die, though. Ryder only needed to revise his role in the sport. "Ryder's injuries keep him off the competition circuit, but he can still play a valuable role in the sport as a coach, or a spokesperson, or in some other capacity." Truthfully, Ryder's enthusiasm had ebbed and flowed over the past months. The doctors had warned them all that mood regulation would be a lifelong battle now, so Wyatt did his best to discount Ryder's temper and keep him moving forward to reclaim his life. "I'm not the smartest guy, but I know, together, my brother and I can accomplish anything. He's part of my return, both as motivation and as support."

What Wyatt kept to himself was how much he missed their old relationship. Now Ryder kept everyone at arm's length. Snowboarding had always been a way for them to connect. Hopefully working together on this film would break down his brother's emotional wall and reunite them.

And if Wyatt could make all that happen for Ryder, maybe his mom would forgive him for getting his brother into snowboarding years ago. Maybe Wyatt could even forgive himself.

"I think that's good for now. Let's head outside and get those shots. Maybe you and Ryder could be walking up the steps together, tapping on the wooden sign hanging from the porch, and so on. Then I'm thinking we might get a quick sound bite from Andy, who seemed rather excited to see you here."

"Guess I'll go grab Ryder while you all get set up then?" Wyatt stood and Mari waved him off before she started talking movie lingo with the crew.

Wyatt rapped on Ryder's door. "You up?"

He heard a thump, which he presumed was Ryder's cane. Three thumps later, the door opened.

"What?" Darkened lenses shielded Ryder's eyes; his expression lacked any animation.

"Mari needs us to film a couple of outside shots. Shouldn't take too long."

"Me, too? But you're the s-star."

Wyatt didn't hear contempt, but he couldn't help but wonder. Ryder's speech now had a carefully modulated tone that made it difficult to decipher his intention and mood.

"This is our film, Ryder, just like we planned. You can raise awareness of TBI, maybe raise some research money to help others who've suffered like you."

Ryder nodded without much enthusiasm. "Okay." He closed the door to his room and followed Wyatt.

Before the accident, his brother had laughed easily, jabbed at Wyatt often, and preened for the cameras. Although Wyatt should be grateful for how far his brother had come, he couldn't help but wish for the return of his old personality.

That's why this plan had to succeed. He wouldn't give up when it came to helping restore his brother's life. To restoring some kind of happiness. So far, however, he'd seen no sign of change.

When they stepped outside, Mari called them down to the walkway. Wyatt remained close to Ryder in case the ice caused any trouble.

Mari handed Wyatt a sheet of paper entitled "Intro" containing typewritten text.

"I took the liberty of writing up a short introductory statement you might want to make while Jim films you and your brother walking up to the inn. Feel free to ad lib. We want it to appear natural. Going forward, we'll try to get as many candid shots as possible, but in this case we need to backtrack a bit. Try to be honest about your first impressions about the place, the feeling you had—in terms of goals—as we pulled into the parking lot, and so on." Mari offered an encouraging smile. "Do you need a minute or two?"

"Give us a sec to work out a thing or two."

"Oh," Mari said, eyebrows rising. "It's not necessary for Ryder to do much talking."

That message wouldn't help Ryder feel comfortable committing to the project.

"It is for me." Wyatt wrapped a protective arm around Ryder's shoulder and began speaking quietly. Once they'd agreed on a plan, he turned his attention back to Mari. "We're all set."

Her tight-lipped smile revealed her discomfort, although to her credit, she held her tongue. "Fine. Remember, although you can glance at each other occasionally, you want to look at the camera when speaking with the audience."

And thus began thirty minutes of blocking and retakes before Mari was satisfied that she had enough material to work with.

A Weenuche Inn van, worn as everything else about the place, pulled into the parking lot. From the corner of his eye, Wyatt watched Emma emerge from the driver's seat and unload bags of groceries. She strung them along her arms to the point of tipping over. He turned, prepared to go help her, when Mari snapped her fingers. "Wyatt, Ryder, let's go inside and get some more shots. We need to keep to the schedule, please."

He'd have asked Ryder to help Emma, but his cane made it difficult for him to carry things. As Wyatt turned away, he noticed Andy come out from behind the building. When Emma cast a relieved smile at him, her whole face lit.

More proof that something warmer lived beneath her polite shell of a personality. For the second time, he wondered about Andy and Emma's relationship. Body language proved they were closer than the average employer-employee relationship.

"Gentlemen?" Mari called from the inn's front door, where she'd been waiting while Wyatt had been daydreaming. Great, he'd already become distracted. In the past, he'd liked having a casual affair during training and competitions because sex relieved stress. Most of the time he'd hooked up with one of the women on the tour, like boardercross champ Jessie Taylor. Together they'd relieved a lot of stress.

He'd texted Jessie a few weeks ago about his plans to be an hour from her hometown thinking maybe something, or someone, familiar might settle his mind.

Now he regretted the impulsive move. Maybe their schedules conflicted. He didn't need to revisit that time of his life, and he had no real interest in any ongoing relationship with Jessie. Luckily she hadn't committed to a visit. Tough as celibacy might be, this time he intended to find less gossip-worthy ways of relieving tension.

The echo of Emma's laughter as she followed Andy through a back door tickled Wyatt's subconscious even as he chose to shove aside his curiosity.

♦ ♦ ♦

The straps of her recyclable grocery bags had practically gouged Emma's forearms. Wyatt's training diet called for bulky whole foods and specialty items, none of which were lightweight or cheap.

Andy whistled while helping her unload the mountain of food she'd just purchased. She watched him move around the kitchen in his loose-fitting jeans and flannel shirt. As usual, his wavy, sandy-colored hair hung around his pleasant face, brushing just above his puppy-dog, light brown eyes. Handsome in an unassuming way, looking a bit like the actor Alex Pettyfer.

Even before he'd come to work for her, Andy had been in the periphery of her life forever. Reliable, friendly, casually protective. Exactly the type of guy she should—did—want one day. A man who'd be content with the little things as opposed to the kind who always thought something better lay just around the corner. The kind who just waltzed in and grabbed a girl from behind without asking.

She hadn't expected that, no sir, even if some little part of her had secretly loved eliciting it. Even if Wyatt's nearness had made her deliciously lightheaded for two or three seconds. Of course, that carefree feeling was exactly the kind of thing that got people like her dad into trouble—that caused them to hurt and disappoint each other. Emma never ever wanted to hurt or disappoint anyone.

"Good God, Emma, there's enough steel cut oatmeal here to feed the whole town." Andy hefted another canister onto the pantry shelf.

"Wyatt's nutritionist ordered an iron-rich diet, which is why I also bought all this spinach." She held two containers of organic spinach in the air and glanced at the other two on the counter. This diet would go a long way to supporting the continued enhancement of Wyatt's already lean, muscular build. Her mind latched onto the memory of the firmness of his washboard abs beneath her fingers and lips. A lovely prickling sensation swept along the backs of her arms and up her neck. She cleared her throat. "And high protein, so we have lots of beans, seeds, and nuts."

Andy studied the array of foods as he continued helping Emma unpack. "Do me a favor and keep track of the meals you plan. I wouldn't mind getting in shape."

He frowned, pinching at his waist, which made her giggle because Andy already boasted a fit, rangy body.

"Planning on trying skiing competition now?" Emma cocked her head. She knew Andy missed being a ski instructor. He'd made a huge mistake last winter by driving drunk. Worse, he'd struck his sister's boyfriend on his way home. Fortunately, Grey's knee injury continued to be mending well. But Andy had lost his job because of the felony charge. A year from now, if he completed his probation period without incident, the felony charge would be reduced to a misdemeanor. At that point, he might be able to get his old job on the mountain back.

Unfortunately, judgments were harsh and memories long in small towns like Sterling Canyon. She'd hated watching Andy be ostracized last spring and gladly offered him her support. Truth be told, getting his help around the inn had made her days a little more fun. She'd miss him when he left at the end of his probation, although she'd be glad to see the stain of his mistake fade.

"I'm too old to start that." His grin always teased out a warm feeling in Emma's gut.

"Watch who you call *old*. We are the same age. Thirty-one's not so old."

"In the world of competitive skiing it is. Especially for someone like me, who never even took a shot." He shrugged, unbothered by that choice. "I still can't believe Wyatt Lawson is here for the month. He landed some sick-ass jumps in his heyday."

A stray memory of seeing Wyatt nail a gold-medal-winning run in the Rockies Winter eXtreme Games temporarily robbed Emma of speech, so she nodded dumbly.

Then Andy's expression turned grim as he refolded her grocery bags for later use. "Too bad about his brother, though."

She remembered watching the replay footage of Ryder's fall on ESPN the year after she'd met Wyatt and him. Naturally it became the topic of conversation in a ski town like Sterling Canyon. Wyatt had been filmed in a panic as he ran to his brother's side on the course.

Emma looked up to catch Andy watching her, waiting for some response.

"Ryder's recovery is miraculous considering the initial reports predicted a much worse prognosis." The accident occurred around the same time she'd completed the first draft of the manuscript that had since been revised at least a half-dozen times and would soon hit the shelves. The ill-fated crash had soured her sense of accomplishment at the time, but after rationalizing that no one would ever know her book's hero had any tie to Wyatt, she'd chosen to press on with her own goals.

"Wyatt sure sacrificed everything to stand by his brother each step of the way." Andy's solemn tone struck her.

"He did." That fact seemed inconsistent with the party-boy she'd met in Aspen, but having seen him and Ryder together before, she also had no doubt of his love for his brother. Perhaps he'd matured a bit as a result of the tragedy . . . although once a player, always a player. But his sacrifice, coupled with his sudden, unexpected arrival in Sterling Canyon—right when she'd been experiencing a case of second-book paralysis—could not be less auspicious. Made it seem somehow cheap and wrong to have used his image without his knowledge. "So we should do everything we can to make sure his work here goes smoothly."

"Man, I'd love to tail Wyatt for some of his training. How cool would that be, to ski alongside Wyatt Lawson?" Andy shook his head again, grinning like a young boy who'd just been offered the keys to Disney World.

"I doubt he has time to entertain you. Training must be daunting, having been out of the game for so long. Even I know how quickly the sport changes, and how aggressive the younger boarders are now with their tricks and jumps."

"True that!" Andy nodded, and then, apparently resigned to his fate of living an ordinary life, said, "So if you don't need me here, I'll go deal with that leaky pipe in your mom's room, and then I'll vacuum."

Emma shooed him away with one hand. "Yes, go do that, please. I'd better get lunch together before Mari bites off my head."

"You can hold your own with her, Emma."

"We'll see." Emma had doubts thanks to Mari's intimidating combination of elegance and power. In a way, Emma envied that presence. Men usually found it appealing. "Tell the truth. Do you find Mari attractive?"

Andy shrugged. "Objectively, sure. But she's not my type."

"Oh?" Emma chuckled. "I didn't know you were so discerning. I'm curious, now. What is your type?"

Andy's gaze wandered from hers. "Someone more like you."

The quiet admission stunned her into an awkward silence. Surely he didn't mean it literally, did he? He must be trying to boost her confidence. Before she could respond, he retreated to teasing her. "Then again, Mari is kinda hot. Do you think she's under forty, or over?"

Grateful that he'd dispelled the tension, she replied, "No idea, although she's definitely around that age."

"Getting a little lonely these days, especially with Grey and Avery always at the house reminding me of what I'm missing. Wonder if Mari's in the market for a little vacation fling."

Emma scrunched her nose. "Mari's not on vacation, and neither are you!"

"I know." Andy sighed. "But it's not healthy to be our ages and celibate."

"You got that right," interrupted a smoky voice that made Emma's skin tingle.

Her neck practically snapped in two as she whipped her head around toward the kitchen door, where Wyatt stood with a grin on his face. Heat unrelated to the ovens scorched her cheeks. First the dancing, and now this?

Andy, unaware of her discomfort, raised his hand to give Wyatt a high five. "If you want to head out any night, I'll show you the best ladies' nights in town."

If Andy was ready to troll for random women, then she must've read too much into his earlier compliment. Her shoulders relaxed, finally. She loved her friendship with Andy and would regret if anything changed it.

Relief then made room for concern, because Andy's probation required abstinence. Of course, he could hunt for women while sober. Being Wyatt's wingman would give him ample prey. No doubt there were plenty of women who'd throw themselves at Wyatt, unashamed, just as "Alexa" had done.

Wyatt shook his head. "Thanks, man, but I've got to stick to a strict training schedule. No drinks or other distractions."

He'd stared straight at Emma when he said that last part. His stare did funny things to her belly, prompting a mishmash of sensations. Sensations she didn't want to remember. And images she didn't want him to remember.

The gorgeous antique bar and crystal chandelier of Aspen's J-Bar rushed forward. She'd chosen the upscale hangout because she'd been dressed to the nines. She'd never expected to see Wyatt Lawson there, but once she'd spotted him sitting in one of the leather highbacks at the bar, she'd tapped into her courage and bought him a tequila shot to celebrate his win. Within ninety minutes and two more shots, he'd coaxed her to his room.

She'd had her fun that night and then walked away before he could make up excuses for ditching her. Emma might not have much, but she did have pride, and that meant she'd never end up losing her heart to a man dead set on fame. A man who was sure to leave.

Resolved to treat Wyatt like—and only like—an esteemed guest of the inn, she changed the subject. "Andy, can you please take care of those items we discussed?"

Once Andy exited the kitchen, she asked, "What can I do for you this time, Mr. Lawson?"

"That's the second "Mr. Lawson" of the day." Wyatt leaned his hip against the doorframe. "My dad's been dead for some years now."

"I'm sorry." He seemed young to have already lost a parent, but she'd effectively lost hers even younger, so maybe it didn't matter much.

"Thanks, but how 'bout you call me Wyatt?"

"Mr. Lawson" had afforded her the distance from "Dallas" that she needed to ensure she didn't slip up, but how could she refuse this request without appearing a total prig? "Wyatt, then. What can I do for you?"

"What are my choices?" His slow smile caused her spine to stiffen as she steeled herself against the empty flirtation. He held up his hands in surrender, somehow sensing her discomfort, which embarrassed her. "Just kidding. It's going to be a long month around here if you don't relax a little. I don't bite . . . unless I'm asked."

Just like that, she recalled his bite in vivid detail. Her nipples tightened at the memory of his teeth grazing them, and of his tongue soothing them afterward. The vision appeared so quickly she couldn't suppress her wide-eyed involuntary response.

"I'm sorry," he said, quickly. "I didn't mean to offend you. I'm not used to someone so . . . proper. I'm harmless, though."

Hardly. Emma cleared her throat, suddenly feeling old and stodgy and self-conscious. "It's fine. But I assume you came in here for a reason."

"I'm going on a run. In about an hour, could you whip up one of those peanut butter protein shakes I'd put on my list?"

"Sure, but your schedule said lunch should be served at one o'clock today. If you're going out now and want a shake afterward, shall I just serve the others lunch without you?"

"Go ahead. I'm off schedule today, but I had a big breakfast and a snack on the road, so I'll be okay." Then Wyatt tipped his head and eyed the bag of almonds on the counter. "Did you know almonds are part of the peach family?"

"More trivia?"

"Fun facts with Wyatt Lawson." Grinning, he held his arms out from his side. "It's my plan B, in case this comeback doesn't work out so well."

Emma covered a smile. He joked, but she sensed some truth, or at least some insecurity, behind the bravado. "Good luck with that, then."

"Yeah." He paused before asking, "Anyhow, where's the high school stadium?"

"About two miles south of here on Miner's Pass Road. Why?"

"I'd like to add some stair-climbing to help me adjust to the altitude."

"Oh. Sounds hard." Emma withdrew a notepad and began writing out directions to the high school. She held the paper toward him. "Here you go. Good luck."

He sauntered toward her and, when he withdrew the page, their fingers touched. A gentle touch, yet her body felt as if something had shoved her—hard. The look on Wyatt's face said he'd done it purposely. For some reason, he seemed determined to keep her off-balance. Did he recognize her? Was this a game for him? Should she confess?

"Thanks, Emma. See you later."

When he left the kitchen, she exhaled and leaned against the island for support. Two hours down, seven hundred eighteen to go.

Chapter Three

Wyatt looked over the railing toward the dimly lit parlor before descending the stairs. Apparently Emma had awakened even earlier than the ass crack of dawn and turned on some lights for him and his yoga instructor. Outside, faint stars and a see-through moon lit the last traces of night.

The sun would rise soon enough to usher in a new day. A day that—if his guess was accurate—had gifted at least ten inches of fresh powder.

His stomach fluttered in anticipation of his first official backcountry training run. Although he'd grown up on Vermont's groomed terrain parks under the watchful eye of many trainers, when making the switch to freeriding, he'd decided to follow the footsteps of other freeriders and forego a coach.

He couldn't risk his new peers dubbing him the pampered former star. The guy who couldn't hack it on his own. To be accepted—and more importantly, to win—he needed to project the same physical and mental strength as the other guys.

When he rounded the corner, he noticed that Ryder hadn't come out of his room yet. He then watched Emma heft a large glass pitcher of fruit-infused water onto a side table. She and his teacher, a hot blonde in suitably skimpy attire, had already pushed aside a few chairs and a coffee table to make room for the session.

Calm, controlled, efficient Emma. A few years ago he might've been put off by that. Now he found her maturity rather anchoring, considering everything else in his life was in flux.

Unlike the blonde, Emma had hidden herself beneath another loose-fitting outfit. The woman didn't advertise her wares, but when she laughed with the yoga chick about something or other, her freshly scrubbed face and green eyes became animated and appealing as hell.

"'Morning," he said, startling them. "You're awfully bright-eyed for five forty-five."

Emma immediately schooled her features to that damn polite librarian face she wore around him. "Good morning, Wyatt. This is Amanda, from YogAmbrosia. She's a great instructor, so you're a lucky guy."

Amanda pressed her palms together and bowed. "Namaste."

Oh, brother. Wyatt liked yoga fine. It suited a specific set of purposes: it enhanced his flexibility and balance, and helped him relax. That said, he had no interest in the goofy culture surrounding the practice. Colorado wasn't Nepal, for crying out loud.

"Hey, Amanda. Thanks for waking up so early."

"I'm excited to work with you, Wyatt. Em says you've got a strict schedule, so are we waiting for the cameras, or do we just begin?" Amanda asked.

"No cameras this morning. They'll film us some other day." Wyatt noticed Emma's brow quirk upward even as she turned her face away. "But let's give my brother another minute or two to show up. He moves a little slowly."

Wyatt shot Ryder a quick text and then filled a glass with the grapefruit mint water Emma had made. Slightly tart, but refreshing. He smiled at her. "This is good."

"I'm glad you approve." She quickly looked away again, toward her friend. Neither rude nor friendly. Definitely not fawning over him like most women he'd known. "I'll leave you to it, then."

"Oh? I thought you'd join us," Amanda said. "In fact, I'm surprised you just didn't do the instruction yourself."

Beneath that sack of clothing lived a limber body? Sudden images of her legs stretched in various positions—preferably on top of or beneath him—set him back a step.

"I haven't taught in years. Besides, I've got to get breakfast started."

Before Emma could escape—and honestly, that's the vibe he got from her every time he came near—Ryder arrived, looking wooden and miserable. "I'm not s-stretching."

"Come on, Ryder. It's good for you," Wyatt said quietly.

"I don't want to," Ryder insisted.

"Just do what you can, like we talked about in Vermont. This will help support your other therapy, and I like your company." He settled a hand on Ryder's shoulder only to have it shrugged off.

"I'm not up to it. Besides, it w-won't help you."

Wyatt cast a quick glance at the ladies. "Tell him yoga can help us both."

"Stretching won't save your ass from a r-rock or tree or cliff dive." Ryder's thick voice showcased the anger lurking behind his passive expression. He glanced out the window at the pristine blanket of snow. "This whole plan seems stupid, now. It's safer to s-stick to what you know."

The last thing Wyatt needed or wanted this morning was to be told he was stupid by the very person for whom he'd undertaken this challenge in the first place. Wyatt had no idea why Ryder had dug his heels in suddenly, but his criticism caused two years of helplessness, remorse, and exhaustion to explode from Wyatt's chest. "I'll tell you what's stupid—your bad attitude. That sure as shit isn't going to help me or my confidence, brother."

"Good, 'cause your plan sucks, and you know it," Ryder said, thumping his cane against the floor.

Wyatt stepped toward Ryder, fury pouring through his veins like boiling oil, and barked, "For weeks you've been on board with this, so what's changed? I need you to stay on point with me, dammit."

"You need, you need—" Ryder waved a disgusted hand. "I'm tired. I'm not your p-pet or project."

"Ryder," Emma's gentle voice interrupted. "If you're too tired to take instruction today, I could really use some company in the kitchen."

She flashed Ryder a friendly smile, the warm kind Wyatt had seen her bestow on Andy. The fact she didn't appear to like Wyatt much had really started to bug him.

Ryder's sunglasses hid his expression. Wyatt's gaze remained fixed on Ryder, but his brother ignored him. "Okay."

What the hell? Wyatt didn't know whether to tell Emma to butt out, or to be impressed with her for jumping in. Before he could decide, she slid him a sideways glance and cocked her brow, signaling that he should let it go. She then returned her attention to Ryder.

"Thanks so much." Emma's voice sounded sincere as she moved away from Amanda and Wyatt and gestured toward the kitchen. "I'm thinking spinach omelets, but I haven't had a chance to make fresh juice. Maybe you can help me pull it all together . . . if that's something you'd like to do."

Wyatt stood, dumbfounded, watching his brother and Emma stride off to the kitchen together—to cook, of all things. Bet she'd dance with Ryder in the pantry if *he* tried.

"Ahem." Amanda cleared her throat. "We should get started, or we'll never finish on time."

He shook his head, as if that could clear his pointless thoughts about Emma or the doubts Ryder's outburst had unearthed. Drawing a cleansing breath, Wyatt grinned at Amanda. Hopefully forty-five minutes with her would restore his peace of mind and get him prepared for the major day ahead.

Unfortunately, when he descended into downward dog, Amanda placed her hands on his hips and "adjusted" his position, dashing all hopes of concentration and peace of mind. Naturally, she acted as if that contact had been purely for his benefit. However, by the end of the session, she'd managed to make more than a dozen such corrections, none of which his male instructor back home ever seemed to think necessary. At another time and place, he might've enjoyed the hottie's hands all over him, but today they were more annoying than a swarm of mosquitoes.

Although the session had loosened Wyatt's muscles, tension still clouded his thoughts. Basically, an epic fail in terms of one of his primary goals.

Ryder's attitude sat at the top of the list of things bugging him, followed by concern about his first training run. And what was up with Emma and her weird attitude toward him? One would think she'd trip all over herself to keep him happy, given what a good review could do for her inn. Instead, she remained timid and almost . . . almost . . . wary. Spooked by his halfhearted flirtations.

"Same time tomorrow?" Amanda asked while rolling up the mats.

"Unfortunately, yes. Sorry for the early hour." He crossed his arms and kept from doing anything she might misconstrue as an invitation to touch him again.

Apparently she didn't need an invitation. She tipped her head and rested her fingers on his forearm. "It's no trouble, really. I'm an early riser."

Luckily, he heard dishes being laid out in the dining room, which gave him an excuse to walk away. "Well, sounds like it's time to eat. Have a good day."

"You, too. Tell Emma I said 'bye." She wiggled her fingers at him and sashayed out the door.

He smacked his palm against his forehead and then stormed toward the dining room to figure out what the hell had gotten into Ryder. He found Emma instead, carefully setting out napkins and silverware.

"Where's my brother?" Wyatt snapped a bit more harshly than intended.

Emma barely looked up. "In the kitchen."

Wyatt started toward the door, but Emma spoke again. "He's relaxed now and feeling productive. Before you start in on him, consider that maybe these days he needs more time to adapt to change than you do."

Wyatt glanced over his shoulder, but Emma continued working, having said her peace in that quiet but firm way that she seemed to do everything. It unnerved him even though he respected it. He couldn't decide whether she was truly stoic or if, like a glacier, bottomless layers lay waiting to be explored beneath her icy surface.

Jumbled thoughts tossed around his brain, so he kept quiet and proceeded to the kitchen without responding. Emma didn't understand his mission regarding his brother's recovery and their future.

In Vermont, Ryder had expressed interest in this project. Wyatt didn't need Emma to misread his brother's temper tantrums this month. He also didn't need Ryder to start casting doubts like darts. His pulse raced, but when he burst into the kitchen, he stopped and watched.

His brother stood in front of a cutting board loaded with apples, peeled carrots, fresh ginger, and grapefruits. With utter concentration, he grouped the items together into handful-size clusters beside the industrial juicer to his left.

"You know, you're a guest here, not an employee." Wyatt joked while sauntering over to his brother's side.

"You think I can't do it?" Ryder pulled his shoulders back.

"No, but this isn't why we're here." Wyatt watched him study the equipment, as if he'd forgotten Emma's instructions. Hell, the thing did look as complicated as one of those fancy cappuccino makers.

"I can't concentrate with you s-staring at me." Ryder's rubber-gloved palm slapped the counter just as Emma walked in.

Without skipping a beat, she came over, ignored Wyatt, and patted Ryder's arm. "I know; it's super confusing, huh? Let's go through the steps again, this time you do each step as I talk you through it."

The contrast between her warmth and physical contact with Ryder and her disinterest in him only provided more proof of her apparent disapproval.

With the patience and heart of a saint, Emma leaned in and reminded Ryder of the various steps and switches. Wyatt found himself somewhat captivated by her calm voice, her deliberate movements. Ryder nodded, listening intently, seeming oblivious to their body contact. He then placed a batch of fruit in the top thingy, pressed it down, and yelled, "Oh, sh-shit," as pulp landed on the floor by his foot.

Emma laughed, putting Ryder at ease. "That's my fault. I forgot to set the garbage can under the pulp tube. But look, there's a bit of juice in the pitcher."

After cleaning the mess on the floor, she grabbed a nearby garbage can and set it beneath the plastic pulp tube. "Now keep going. We need all of that, and we need it fast." Sparing Wyatt a brief glance, she said, "Wyatt, Mari and the crew were getting seated when I came in here. You probably should join them. We'll be out in two minutes."

Just like that, she'd dismissed him with a bored smile. Ryder didn't even look up. He kept scooping food into the processor and, wearing a satisfied grin, watching it turn into liquid. Unaccustomed to being ignored, Wyatt bit his tongue and left the kitchen, but he wasn't done with Ryder, or Emma.

Wyatt tossed his napkin on the table and laid one hand over his stomach, unable to decide whether the omelet, the fruit salad with mint, or that damn juice had been the best part of the meal.

Emma appeared for the third time, checking on their needs and stacking dirty dishes. Ryder's gaze followed her as she moved around the table. Did his brother have a crush now? Could his sudden change in attitude be the result of pent-up sexual frustration? And hell, would Emma be the right woman to change that for Ryder? For some unknown reason, Wyatt's mind recoiled at the thought.

"Wyatt," Mari said, thankfully interrupting his thoughts. "When we get to the mountain, Jim will stay below with me and operate the drone camera. Buddy will hike partway up with you and get on-the-ground action shots, too. Sound good?"

"Sure." Wyatt said. "I need thirty minutes to digest and change, then we can head out and start the ascent."

Ryder pushed his dish away and abruptly stood. "I'm staying here."

He took his cane and plate and followed Emma into the kitchen, leaving Wyatt and the others behind.

"I thought Ryder would join us on the mountain. I'd been counting on his input," Mari said.

Me too.

"He woke up with a bug up his ass. Let me go talk to him." Wyatt nodded before chasing after his brother.

Inside the kitchen, Ryder stood near Emma, arms wound tightly around his waist.

"What's going on with you today?" Wyatt demanded. "I let the yoga thing slide, but Mari needs you to come to the mountain and do some taping while I'm hiking up the ridge. And I'd like to know you're watching. I need feedback from someone who knows snowboarding."

"I'm not ready." Ryder swayed from side to side, looking off to a corner of the room.

"Do you need another fifteen minutes, half hour, what?" Wyatt asked.

"No, I'm not ready to go to the mountain today. It doesn't feel safe." Ryder scuffed his cane against the floor.

"You'll be plenty safe in the van. Just talk to Mari so she can understand what's happening, and then watch the films as they feed in so you can tell me what I'm doing wrong."

"No!" Ryder exploded, his finger jabbing Wyatt's chest. Ever since the accident, anger seemed to be the one emotion that could break through the surface of Ryder's otherwise impassive demeanor. "It's not safe for you."

"Oh, and slopestyle was safe? I think you know better than most that that's not true." Wyatt regretted the words the minute he'd said them, especially when he heard Emma's shallow gasp.

"How'd you let this happen to your brother?" his mother had yelped *when they'd arrived at the hospital to find Ryder hooked up to a zillion tubes and machines. "You were supposed to protect him."* Shame oozed through Wyatt now as a result of his snarky retort. But even if he'd mishandled this situation, he needed Ryder to cooperate, for both of their sakes. "Ryder, please. I'm counting on your support. Let's get dressed and go, as planned."

Ryder snatched his cane and thumped away, leaving Wyatt and Emma in his dust.

Disbelief and animosity consumed him. With Ryder gone, Wyatt turned his wrath on Emma. "What did you two talk about in here all morning? Why's he suddenly so obstinate? And why'd you interfere anyway, 'cause it's pretty clear to me that you didn't need his help? Shouldn't you be focused on being my innkeeper instead of my ballbuster?"

"Ballbuster." She repeated his word as if testing it on her tongue and finding it tart. Whether irked or concerned, he couldn't tell. Either way, she met his gaze with a stern one of her own. "Between my Gram and the elderly people I volunteer to work with, I've spent lots of time with people in various stages of recovery and isolation. One thing most have in common is feeling marginalized; they lack purpose. I thought redirecting Ryder and letting him help me would make him feel like he was something more than your extra baggage."

"I don't treat him like baggage!" When Emma winced, Wyatt raked a hand through his hair and drew a breath. More calmly, he said, "He has an important role in all of this, and he was on board with everything until this morning. I need him to help manage Mari and the way she chooses to tell our story. And I need his damned support when I'm out there on the slopes. What I don't need is you encouraging some kind of mutiny."

Emma stared at him in silence. He couldn't tell what she thought of him or his outburst, but she couldn't possibly think any less of him. He almost wished she'd flip her lid on him. Instead, her face filled with compassion and pity. "I'm sure you don't mean to make him miserable, but he's obviously uncomfortable."

"Because of Mari's questions? Then I'll talk to her and make sure she's more patient with his slower speech. Problem solved. I don't see what's so damn hard."

"Probably because you're totally focused on what *you* need . . . what *you* want."

"You have no idea what you're talking about, or what all's at stake here, and not just for me, but for him, too."

"I have some idea of the stakes, and he must, too. What if that's the problem? What if he's concerned you'll end up like him if you keep pushing?" Emma dropped her gaze and then turned toward the sink, reaching for a sponge.

"I've been on a snowboard almost as long as I've been walking. Ryder knows I can handle myself. Besides, this isn't slopestyle. The jumps are less acrobatic, the snow softer. No need to attempt 1440 triple corks and risk snapping my neck. Besides, if my safety is his main concern, then he shouldn't plant doubts in my head."

Emma carefully wiped her hands on a dishrag. With her hair pulled up, he couldn't help but notice the regal line of her jaw and neck, her straight, proud spine. A contradiction: quiet and soft on the outside, but firm and certain at her core. Even as his anger swelled, her palpable sturdiness tethered him at a moment when everything else seemed to spin off its axis. At another time or place, he would act on his intense curiosity about her, but not here and not now.

"Maybe you don't need the same level of acrobatics now, but you also aren't going to be on stable, man-made runs. Five people died in Colorado last year from self-triggered avalanches in the backcountry. Many others are injured from bad falls from cliffs. Freeriding has as much danger as slopestyle." Turning from him, she then muttered, "Unlike you, maybe Ryder doesn't think medals and fame are worth risking one's life."

Disdain washed over her words like acid, indicating she agreed with Ryder.

Wyatt flattened his hands on the counter, hung his head, and leaned forward for a minute, thinking. He didn't know why he'd had this conversation with Emma, but he didn't like being on the losing end of the argument. He also didn't like the way his brother had behaved during the past twenty-four hours. Most of all, he didn't like the way all of this had messed with his head. He had to silence all the noise so he could focus or he would end up hurt.

"You don't even know me, Emma, so don't judge me, or pretend to know my motives. And don't think for one second that you know my brother and his mood swings better than I do." He straightened, resolved, if also a little dejected. "You and Ryder stay here while telling yourselves that I'm an ego-driven idiot. Meanwhile, I'll go it alone."

Through his peripheral vision, he noticed Emma's head snap up to look at him, but he marched away without waiting for her to speak.

Emma froze, uncertain of whether to chase after Wyatt or leave him be. She hadn't meant to insult or undermine him. Now he sure didn't seem to be in the settled frame of mind needed to concentrate, causing her to regret throwing those statistics in his face.

She shouldn't have spoken out of turn, especially because she hadn't been completely forthcoming. And the truth was that she would be nervous for Wyatt's safety today . . . and every day for the next month. He might be a champ on the groomed competition courses he'd mastered before, but the backcountry's beauty often obscured its grave danger. Did Wyatt know how to read the layers of snow? Her gut told her *no*.

Good grief, what a quandary. And beyond the Lawson brothers' troubles, she had to sneak in time today to call her publisher's marketing team and discuss the book launch. Thank God her mom's office gave her privacy so she could avoid the tripods Mari had set up all around the first floor. If she got careless about paying attention to them, those cameras could be her undoing. Unlike Ryder, she had the option of staying out of the spotlight.

Poor Ryder. She guessed he felt responsible for Wyatt's comeback plans. The guy's fear and discomfort appeared patently obvious to her. How could Wyatt not see that Ryder didn't want to be part of the process?

Wyatt might need his brother for strength, purpose, and confidence, but that was quite a burden to foist on someone who already had enough to handle on his own. What a mess the Lawson brothers were, she thought as she prepared the snacks Wyatt had requested for his backpack.

When she got to the lobby, she found Andy staring out the window at the snow that continued to fall. All the fresh powder, plus reduced visibility, would only make Wyatt's maiden runs more challenging today.

His problem, not hers, she reminded herself. She had her own goals, for Pete's sake. Goals that left no time to get sidetracked by Wyatt, although having him under the same roof had made sleeping near impossible last night. She'd gotten used to daydreaming about Dallas—but the live, walking, talking Wyatt had pushed her over the edge.

"Those aren't self-cleaning windows, you know." Emma poked Andy in the back.

He tugged at her ponytail.

"Some days I can't deal with the way I've screwed up my life. I'd give anything to be out on the mountain today with students, or friends." He squirted Windex on the window. "Not that I don't appreciate you helping me out when the ski school fired me after my arrest, Em."

She'd wanted to lend her support, and not just because she could imagine needing it in return one day if her secret were ever exposed.

"I know." Emma laid her hand on his shoulder. "Things will turn around for you once your probation ends next summer."

"We both know the end of my probation won't make everyone in town forget how I plowed into Grey when I got behind the wheel after happy hour."

"Grey forgave you. The town will follow his lead. Be patient." She hoped she was right. Then again, many "good Christian people" like her own mother could be quick to cast judgment, and slow to forgive. It'd already been almost nine months, and some people still looked down their noses at Andy. If her link to *Steep and Deep* got out, she'd end up like Hester Prynne.

Wyatt clomped down the stairs, decked out in his snowboard apparel. While they'd been talking, the film crew had collected in the lobby. A black helmet hid Wyatt's gorgeous curls. The blue, white, and black design of his Burton jacket looked almost like ocean waves splashing across his chest and shoulders. His backpack hung on one shoulder. He carried his board under one arm, and what looked like orthopedic braces in the other.

"What's that stuff?" Emma quietly asked, nodding at the odd gear in Wyatt's hand.

"Spinal protection pads and impact shorts." Andy narrowed his gaze. "Guess he's still debating whether to put those on. Uncomfortable stuff, so I get why he'd put it off until necessary."

Emma's brain had stuttered on the words "spinal protection." How silly she'd been to lecture him about danger as if he hadn't already known. Seeing that gear drove home Ryder's concerns.

Of all the people on the planet, why had it been Wyatt who'd rented the inn this month? Not that she wouldn't care about other people's health and safety, but why did it have to be Wyatt?

The sinking feeling that karma had come 'round to kick her butt for writing erotica was weighing her down. Payback for being excited about having been a little naughty. For wanting something more than her quiet, sometimes lonely, life in Sterling Canyon.

Contrary to everything she'd been taught, she'd unleashed the little devil in her soul. Now she wondered who would pay the price for her deceit?

"What's wrong, Em?" Andy slung his arm around her shoulders. "You look upset."

"Nothing. It's just dawning on me how dangerous Wyatt's job is."

Andy shrugged. "Trip and Grey go out in the backcountry all the time. Granted, they don't have to push the jumps and tricks like Wyatt will need to, but that guy knows what he's doing. Chillax."

Emma rolled her eyes and elbowed Andy's ribs. *Chillax?*

She crossed to the group, carrying Wyatt's lunch and snacks, hoping for a truce. "Give me your backpack, Wyatt. I've got your lunch here. There's a cooler in the kitchen for the crew."

"I'll grab it," Andy called out.

Wyatt handed her his backpack. His demeanor had cooled considerably since she'd last seen him in the kitchen. This persona must be his so-called game face.

"Where's Ryder?" Mari asked, sounding annoyed.

"He's not coming." Wyatt didn't look at anyone. Before Mari could comment or question, he ordered, "Let's head out."

Andy returned with the cooler and enthusiastically helped Wyatt carry those pads. Whatever he said to Wyatt caused him to smile, for which Emma felt both grateful and envious. Maybe Ryder couldn't give his brother the confidence boost he needed, but Andy would send Wyatt off feeling optimistic.

Emma closed the front door behind them to keep out the cold. Ryder then appeared, sunglasses on and cane in hand, and approached her. Together they watched the team file into the van and drive off.

"Are you okay?" Emma asked, her heart squeezing with empathy.

"He's doing this for me. For money to help me."

Ah. Not so ego driven, then.

Ryder continued, "He thinks this will all make me happy, like before. But I never asked for this."

Neither spoke as Andy came back inside and disappeared. Emma noted the strain around Ryder's mouth. Wyatt was right about one thing: Emma didn't know Ryder or his moods. And if he had been part of the planning for this whole project, maybe he did want to be involved. Maybe today's attitude had more to do with jitters or being wiped out from a long trip than a true change of heart.

"Seeing as he has decided to do it, maybe the best thing you could do for him now is get behind his effort." Emma set a hand on his shoulder.

Ryder's forehead wrinkled, and then he pressed it against the glass. Turning his head, he plastered his cheek to the window and peered up at the sky. "All this snow. He's not used to that. Slopestyle courses are p-perfectly groomed. Known."

A muted keening colored Ryder's typically uninflected voice. His distress seeped into Emma's pores, filling her with unwanted anxiety.

"Let's move away from the window and keep busy. Worrying won't help anyone now." She tugged at his sleeve. "More cooking? Or maybe something more active? Do you like to clean? Because I'm pretty sure Andy would love a little help vacuuming the guest rooms."

Ryder shrugged. "Okay."

"Also, I'm going to try to reschedule your therapy for earlier now that you've decided to hang back. Avery—Andy's sister and my friend—is an awesome physical therapist. I know you'll get a lot out of working with her."

Avery was widely known as the town's taskmaster therapist, which meant Emma could count on her friend to keep Ryder's mind occupied for part of the day.

Ryder silently followed Emma to the supply closet. Meanwhile, she did her best to shake off Ryder's concerns about Wyatt's lack of big-mountain experience. Her phone rang then, so she answered without looking at the screen. "Emma Duffy."

Crap, her agent.

She risked a quick glance at Ryder, but he appeared preoccupied with his own thoughts. *Thank God!*

"Jill, can I call you back in five minutes? I've got my hands full at the moment."

She stalled that call long enough to get Ryder set up with Andy, who'd taken to calling him "Stevie Wonder" because he always wore sunglasses. Ryder seemed amused, so Emma didn't interfere. Maybe Ryder enjoyed being handled without kid gloves. Andy might be the perfect antidote for Ryder's mood and Wyatt's hovering.

Emma ducked into her mother's back office and locked the door before returning Jill's call.

"Hi, Jill. Sorry about that. Are you calling to discuss the marketing call later today?" Emma asked.

"No, although I can loop in to that later if you'd like. I'm calling because I read through the first half of your new manuscript. It looks good. You may need to sharpen her internal conflict a bit, but I like the playful tone and banter."

"Great. I'll go back over that while I'm finishing up the last chunk." Emma heard Andy moving around the hallway just outside the door. She suppressed the urge to whisper. "Anything else?"

"No. You'll get a good rundown of whatever marketing plans they've put in place. I heard from Kim in publicity that you got a couple of starred reviews from the trade journals, which is awesome, especially for a debut author."

Emma's face broke into a wide smile. She wished she could call her friends and share her news, but she'd never take that gamble. They loved and admired the sensible, steady Emma Duffy they knew, and she wouldn't change that for anything. While she knew they'd accept her novel, and her, after their initial shock wore off, still the "secret" would no longer be under her control. If either Avery or Kelsey told another person—like their fiancés—it would eventually make its way back to her very Catholic, very conservative mother. Not only would that result in endless prayers for Emma's soul and a stern visit from Father O'Malley, no doubt it also would reopen old wounds, and her mom would blame Emma's dad for the rotten DNA.

She hadn't exactly forgiven her dad for running off—for letting his ego and libido destroy their family and leaving her with a mother who'd fallen into a pit of despair.

Emma stood outside her mother's room listening to her sobs echoing off the tile in her shower stall. Every day since her father had left, her mother retreated to that shower to cry. Sometimes twice. And she'd been taking pills that turned her into a zombie.

"Emma, what are you doing?" Grammy stood near the top of the stairwell.

"Mom's crying again."

Grammy's brows pinched together as she waved Emma in for a hug. "Come away, dear. Let's go bake cookies."

Cookies might make Emma feel better, but they wouldn't help her mom. "Grammy, how can I help make Mom stop crying and sleeping all the time? I can't stand all the sadness. I'm scared."

Grammy patted her head and offered a wrinkly smile. "You keep being a good girl, Emma. She'll remember that you're the most important thing in her life soon enough. In the meantime, do everything you can to make her proud."

Emma hugged Grammy again. "I will. I promise."

"That's my girl. Now, here's the bigger question. Snickerdoodles or chocolate chocolate chips?"

Emma rolled her eyes. Was there even a question? "Chocolate!"

A little tingle traced down her spine from that memory. Yet, even knowing what the damage of being discovered would do to her mother, and to their relationship, Emma hadn't been able to stop herself from writing once the story began spinning itself in her head. Now she'd do just about anything to keep from hurting her mother.

Aside from the moral disappointment, her mom would be devastated to think that Emma wanted something more than a future that consisted entirely of running the Weenuche together. It would undoubtedly feel like another betrayal, just like when her dad left to chase his dreams.

No. She couldn't come clean. The pen name gave her the opportunity to explore her sensuality in a way that wouldn't harm anyone as long as she kept it to herself. It was enough for her.

Her stories were her escape. Her very personal, private escape—one she'd enjoy all on her own.

"If you have any questions or concerns after your marketing call later, let me know," Jill said. "Be prepared for a slew of blogging obligations and some directives to up your social media interaction."

Dread about that latter point consumed Emma. All she wanted to do was write. She didn't have anything interesting or funny to share on social media. Who cared about what Alexa Aspen had to say about anything real? Every time she posted anything it felt like a huge lie. Probably because it was a fiction—like Alexa—and each click reminded her that, contrary to what she wanted to believe, her integrity wasn't quite as impeccable as she'd thought.

"When will you send me the rest of your manuscript?"

Emma bit her lip, unprepared to discuss the trouble she seemed to be having now, in the middle of the dang thing. "Soon."

"The sooner the better, so I have time to give you feedback before we submit it to your editor." After a brief pause, she said, "Good luck with that call today."

"Thanks, Jill. I'll let you know how it goes."

She set down the phone and smoothed her hands over her face. Wyatt may be facing life-or-death peril on the mountain, but right now, her relative safety seemed a bit precarious, too.

Having to juggle all of these things at the same time sort of sucked. She admitted, with defeat, that the "quiet" month she'd planned on enjoying had been a pipe dream. Hopefully both she and Wyatt would make it to December without any major setbacks.

Chapter Four

Wyatt fastened the thick Velcro waistband of his spinal protection gear. He twisted and bent his torso to ensure comfort before pulling on his fleece and outerwear.

When he'd been younger, he hadn't worried overmuch about injury, but Ryder's accident had changed everything. The physical discomfort of the impact shorts and padding would be offset by the mental comfort they provided.

"Don't forget the GoPro," Mari said, pointing at his helmet.

Wyatt reached into his pack and took another minute to attach his GoPro. His pulse skipped ahead faster than normal, like it always did when he felt a lack of control.

Changing specialties forced him far out of his comfort zone, but given his age and the time he'd taken off, going back to slopestyle hadn't been the most viable option. Not to mention that panic he'd felt the one time he'd put himself on a course last year. At least in the backcountry, he wouldn't be confronted with the memory of Ryder's spectacular crash every time he approached a trick.

That didn't mean this type of competition was without danger. Or that his skillset would easily translate to the backcountry. But he forced those unhelpful thoughts away. He then double-checked his ava-lanche transceiver. "Buddy, make sure you've got your transceiver on and working."

"These Unidens have a fifty-mile range, so we shouldn't lose com-munication." Mari handed Wyatt and Buddy each a walkie-talkie. "Now, before you zip everything up, let's go outside and get a quick interview out of the way."

The van door slid open, revealing cloudy, gray skies. It had stopped snowing, which improved visibility. Wyatt peered into his binoculars and studied the face of the mountain, picking out an ideal fall line.

He scanned the field for markers to help him navigate his way toward the desired starting point, certain the landscape would all look very different up there than it did from down here. After punching a few notes into his phone as reminders—big rock here, copse of trees there—he then zipped his phone into an interior jacket pocket, right next to the inReach GPS safety device that had a direct dial to local search and rescue teams. When he turned to find Buddy, he noticed that Jim had already set up for taping.

Naturally, Mari dove straight into her questions. "Can you give us a brief rundown of what's in your pack, how you feel, and what you hope to accomplish today?"

Wyatt had never been the most articulate guy, and he didn't want to spend a whole lotta time thinking through everything. He did best when acting on instinct. Too much thinking led to worries, and worries weren't his friend up there on the slopes.

Still, this film would be a gateway to more sponsors, so he plastered a stupid grin on his face. "I'm told this is one of the better backcountry ridges in the area. As you know, most of my experience is in terrain parks, so my sole goal today is to take a few runs and get a handle on the transition . . . test my fluidity, see how I manage unexpected natu-ral obstacles like a hidden rock or tree, and so on. Despite my airdog reputation, I'm not planning on pushing hard or attempting jumps and tricks. Just getting a feel for the difference."

"What's your biggest concern?" Mari asked.

Great. Not only did he need to think hard, but he also had to discuss the very things he didn't want to dwell on.

"Honestly, I'm trying not to focus on anything negative. It's a beautiful spot with tons of fresh snow. I'm eager to get out there, and hopefully won't end up in a yard sale."

"Yard sale?" Mari's brows rose.

Wyatt took a second and really looked at her, standing there in her designer snow boots, matching snug-fit outfit, big sunglasses—all black, of course. Very New York, as revealed by her unfamiliarity with snowboarding.

"Major wipeout where you lose some gear." He wondered then if she hoped he'd wipe out. Would make for more interesting film, no doubt.

"I see you have a backpack, which is something you never wore in slopestyle competition. Can you talk about what's in there?"

Wyatt twisted the pack around and unzipped its outer pocket. "This here is called the wet room, and it's for avalanche safety gear, like this shovel and the probe. Inside the main body of the pack, I've got lunch, extra goggles and gloves, sunscreen, first aid kit, and some other stuff. Buddy over there has all the same stuff in his, too, plus camera equipment."

"Seems like you're taking on a lot—making a comeback after two years away from competition and transitioning to a sport with different terrain and dangers."

"I've always liked a challenge." Wyatt smiled, not wanting her to probe his vulnerabilities.

Mari, however, wouldn't roll over that easily. She had a job to do, after all. Like every reporter he knew, she wanted blood in the water, and she'd keep chumming until she got some.

"Some say you are getting too old to compete in slopestyle, and that the new stars have bigger, better jumps than in your day. Is that another reason you've switched to freeriding?"

Wyatt looked away for a minute, uncertain whether to bluff or be honest at this point. He couldn't guess three steps ahead to how she'd edit his comments to make him look smart or stupid, brave or foolish. He could give a simple yes or no to that question and be done with it. However, he valued honesty. "No doubt I would've considered a twenty-five-year-old competitor ancient when I won my first International gold medal at nineteen. And when I left the sport, no one had landed a quad cork yet. It wouldn't have been a cakewalk to step back into that arena now, 'though I'd like to think I still have it in me."

He paused, not able to admit that his brother's crash had spooked him. That the hard surfaces and groomed parks of his past no longer seemed safe. But he couldn't say the words—at least, not aloud. "Like I already told you, once we knew Ryder was out of the woods, it became clear that, mentally, he was struggling to accept all the changes—to see a future that excited him. So, I hope, by letting go of the old, familiar stuff, I might inspire him—and others in his shoes—to embrace change. New challenges can be exciting. Nothing lasts forever, but you keep going, pushing, growing."

He shrugged and waved a hand, signaling an end to that discussion. He'd already shared more than he'd intended and more than Ryder would appreciate. Then again, had Ryder come along as he'd originally promised, Wyatt wouldn't have needed to ad lib like that. "Let's stop talking and get moving. Visibility is good now, and I'd rather go up there before it snows again."

Without giving Mari a chance to ask another question, he zipped up his pack, fastened his board to it, and hefted everything onto his back. "Ready, Buddy?"

Buddy nodded. "Let's go."

Jim shut down the other camera and began packing it away.

"We'll be in touch over the walkie-talkies." Mari waved hers in the air. "Between Buddy, Jim, and the GoPro, we'll have some great footage today."

Wyatt gave her a thumbs-up and then began his climb, with Buddy on his heels. Once they'd moved away from Mari and Jim, Wyatt said, "Hope you don't mind if I'm on the quiet side on the way up. I need to pay attention to the terrain and think about next steps."

"No problem. I'm fine checking out the scenery and catching my breath!" Buddy replied.

Wyatt nodded before surveying craggy mountains, couloirs, and fir trees. Thick piles of heavy snow buffeted most sounds, making the rubbery squeak of boots against wet snow and the huffing of breaths the only things he really heard. Gorgeous country . . . if only he didn't need to master it.

Within thirty minutes, sweat trickled down his back beneath the protection gear. Hiking with a pack and a board wasn't for pussies. He glanced back to check on Buddy, who'd dropped about twenty yards behind. Wyatt gulped down some water, then waited for Buddy to catch his breath, too.

"I'm going to hike up to that ledge." Wyatt pointed westward, suppressing the flip of his stomach. "You could set up a little lower, on that rocky outcropping to the side there. You can catch me dropping in, film me shredding through there, then pack up your gear and follow me down. Sound good?"

"Yeah." Buddy nodded. "Let's keep going, or Mari will be barking at us about the time."

Another twenty or so minutes passed before Wyatt reached the ledge. He heard Buddy and Mari on the walkie-talkie, and knew that Jim had just sent the drone up the mountain. GPS made tracking a whole lot easier than it must've been for guys a decade ago, and sure enough, the drone appeared above Wyatt in short order.

If only Ryder had shared this with him. Wyatt would've preferred to have heard his brother's voice pumping him up before he leapt off the cornice, like he always had. *Get over it.* He took a moment to take in the 360-degree views from the ledge. Miles of mountaintops that had been here long before him and would endure long after he'd gone. Right now, though, he needed to conquer this one. One run at a time, he reminded himself, hoping to calm the nerves dancing under his skin. He depressed the walkie-talkie transmitter. "You ready, Buddy? 'Cause I'm dropping in."

"I'm set," Buddy replied through static.

Wyatt stuffed the walkie-talkie in his pocket, adjusted his goggles, and drew a deep breath. He looked down the line he planned to follow: over the cornice, jab between the stands of trees, fly over a small cliff, and then shred down the lower bowl toward the van.

Showtime. Gathering his courage, he twisted his neck left and right and then hucked over the edge.

It'd been eons since Wyatt had landed in deep pow, which felt much different from the perfectly angled, manicured landing slopes of man-made jumps and courses. He carved a few turns and began to relax when a sort of groaning sound snagged his attention. Suddenly, the face of the mountain fractured, and the snow underfoot instantly shifted. He'd known that avalanches could move up to two hundred miles per hour, but speed became more terrifying when coupled with the sensation that the earth was crumbling.

Wyatt's heart kicked against his ribs like a bronco while he attempted to board off to the left, out of the path of the avalanche, but it was too wide. When he lost control, the thundering river of snow whisked him away, pitching him in a series of bumpy cartwheels.

The rumble of tons of snow roared in his ears while shock numbed him to pain, despite being flung about like a rag doll.

Protect a breathing space. That thought broke through the panic that had seized his entire being. His tumbling then abruptly came to a halt. Somehow he landed—disoriented and curled in a ball with his board, spitting snow from his mouth—inside a muted cave of snow.

Enveloped in absolute darkness, cramped and claustrophobic, his breathing came shallow and fast in the silence. He fought the nausea caused by the echo of his breath in his ears and his relative blindness from being buried alive. At least he could wiggle his fingers and toes.

Snow cemented around his body, squeezing him with each intake of air, making it impossible to catch his breath and relax. He thought of how Ryder would react to news of his death. His mom's face flashed before his eyes, and he wondered if she'd ever forgive him. His dead father's face surfaced next, and Wyatt wondered if he'd be joining him soon and if the man's temper had followed him beyond the grave. Wyatt had spent years blaming the man for his failings and for their family's struggles. Now, however, he remembered the pride his father had shown when Wyatt had started winning local competitions.

Something broke open inside, making him wish he could see them all once more and say things he needed to say. Make apologies, tell them he loved them. Funny how the edge of death put petty angers in a different perspective. Dammit, he didn't want to die. Not here, not now. *Don't panic. Don't panic.*

A tear trickled down his cheek. When gravity pulled it toward his ear, he realized he'd landed on his back facing, generally, upward. He needed to reel in his dread and take control. Think his way to a calmer state of mind.

Fearful of disrupting the air pocket he'd created, he slowly strained to reach inside his jacket and hit the inReach device, sending out an emergency signal to nearby search and rescue workers. He then checked to make sure his transceiver was still set to send, hoping Buddy could get to him and dig him out before he ran out of air.

He didn't know whether he'd been covered by one or ten feet of snow. Feet above the head meant more blood flow to his brain—a bit of good luck. He knew, statistically, he had an 80 percent chance of surviving if he was dug out within fifteen minutes. After that, his chances plummeted. Forcing the terrifying notion away, he snatched at every breath he could. *Calm down. Think. Keep it together.*

With great care, and using as little energy as possible, he began to slowly chip away at the wall of the air pocket, desperate for light and oxygen.

This couldn't be how it ended for him. Buddy had been taping him, so he must've seen roughly where Wyatt might've landed. Buddy had a transceiver, shovel, and probe. Even if the inReach device failed, Mari would have called search and rescue already. He just had to hang on. Hang on and have faith.

When Wyatt closed his eyes in the hopes of blocking out his circumstances, he pictured his brother's face during their earlier argument. Ryder had been right—yoga hadn't helped.

Emma caught herself whistling while she managed some of the accounting. She normally hated Excel spreadsheets, but the marketing call had buoyed her spirits so much, she couldn't help but smile. Her impending book launch seemed more real than it had been up to this point.

Being unable to share this part of her life with anyone had sapped something from the experience. Of course, Emma had always shunned the spotlight. And now, if readers hated her story, at least her failure would be private.

Emma saved the updated spreadsheet, filed the receipts, and left her mom's office to head to the kitchen. The dinner she'd planned required a little extra work up front, so she had to start early. When she passed by the front desk, she saw Andy running down the stairs, pale and wide-eyed.

"Em?" Andy's gaze darted around the lobby and toward Ryder's room. She hadn't seen him so shaken since the earliest days following his arrest. "Where's Ryder?"

"At the clinic with Avery. Why?"

"I just got off the phone with a buddy on ski patrol. Search and rescue's been called over to Fork Creek Pass."

Emma frowned, slow to make the connection Andy sought.

"It's Wyatt. He got caught in an avalanche."

Her stomach wrenched before one hand covered her mouth and the other grasped the check-in counter for balance. People always underestimated Mother Nature's force, somehow believing they could "swim" their way through the fast-moving snow. Perspiration broke above her brow as she considered Wyatt somewhere out there, alone, afraid, desperate.

Once she collected her thoughts, a slew of questions erupted. "How long ago? Is he buried deep? Did they pinpoint his location?"

"The initial notification just came in."

Emma gripped Andy's arm without thinking. "How long can he survive under the snow?"

"Depends on other injuries and how he landed, how deep he is. Lots of factors, but generally 10 to 15 minutes. I bet the film crew is already on it, so maybe he's getting pulled out as we speak."

Memories from the morning rushed forward to torment her. She and Ryder had sabotaged Wyatt's confidence and concentration. What if that disagreement was the last conversation they ever shared? How would Ryder go on if he lost his brother? How much guilt would he carry into the future after refusing to accompany him today?

"Can't you find out more? Call your friend! I want to be able to give Ryder good news when he returns. Please, Andy." Her tone earned her one of Andy's cocked brows.

"He said he'd text when he had news. I'm not going to pester him with calls. We need to be patient."

58

Patient? Her head throbbed to the point of exploding. Andy's hand landed on her shoulder. "Em, I didn't mean to shake you up this bad. I just thought you should know. Let's just pray we don't have to call his mother with bad news."

"Don't say it!" She batted his hand off her shoulder. "Don't even think it, Andy. No one is dying today."

Turning on her heel, she beelined to the kitchen, needing a distraction. Needing to work and keep busy.

Once inside, she bent at the waist and grabbed her knees. *Please, God. Please bring Wyatt home to his brother. No more tragedies in the Lawson family.*

Blowing out a breath, she sent up another prayer. She'd planned a protein-rich meal of grilled salmon tacos and avocado slaw. Wyatt would be back in a while, and he'd be hungry. While the dough rested, she fetched the tortilla press for her masa harina mix and kept working.

What seemed like a century later, Andy burst through the door. "Good news, Em. Wyatt's been rescued by Buddy. I bet that was his first-ever use of a transceiver. Wyatt's lucky he was only a little more than two feet under the snow. It's not easy for a single skier to find another and dig him out on his own. If Wyatt had been under five or more feet of snow, this might've had a different ending." Andy must've seen the horror in her eyes, because he rested a hand on her shoulder. "Sorry, but cheer up. Wyatt's at the clinic now getting checked out. Amazingly, he didn't have any major injuries."

"Thank God." Emma practically fell against the counter. "I'm so relieved. So, so relieved. Ryder couldn't have handled worse news."

Apparently sensing her post-adrenaline weakening, Andy gave her a hug and kiss on the head. "Em. Always stuck in here taking on everyone's worries. Giving all your energy to others. I wish you'd invest in your own happiness now and then. How about you let me get you out of this kitchen for some fun?"

Emma frowned, her face still pressed to his chest. He meant well, she knew that. Still, is that how he—how everyone—saw her? A polite, pathetic spinster of yore—lonely and timid and hiding from the world? For the second time in as many days, she also wondered whether Andy was skirting the line between friendship and something more.

She didn't want to cross it, so she eased out of the comforting embrace. "Despite your opinion, I like being of service to others. And my heart can handle caring for a variety of people in a variety of ways. As for getting out of the kitchen, I go out with all my friends, you included, when I have free time."

"I didn't mean to offend you. You know I think you're great. I just see Avery and Kelsey planning weddings, and hate to think that you might be . . ."

Clearly, he didn't know how to finish the sentence, so Emma just snickered. "I'm glad for Avery and Kelsey. Hopefully, one day I'll fall in love. If I don't get so lucky, at least I'll have all this other love in my life."

Truthfully, a little part of her still worried about Kelsey. Things seemed rosy between her and Trip now, despite their earlier setbacks, but Trip reminded Emma of her dad. Charming, handsome, flirtatious. Hopefully Trip wouldn't miss the affection of other women the way her father had.

Andy cocked his head when he heard a car door slam. He raced to the window. "It's just Avery and Ryder."

"I'll break the news to Ryder so he's prepared when Wyatt returns." Emma bustled out of the kitchen with Andy on her heels, hoping her smile didn't look as brittle as her bones felt under her skin.

"Hey, Em!" Avery smiled, blue eyes bright and sparkling as she held the front door for Ryder. "This guy deserves extra dessert tonight. He worked hard."

"I'm glad you had a productive day. Avery, could you hang here for a bit? Your expertise may come in handy. Andy can fill you in, but I need to talk to Ryder alone for a minute."

Avery's quizzical gaze turned from Emma to Andy, who waved her over to the front desk.

"Ryder, sit with me in the parlor for a second." Emma followed him to the sofa. Once they were seated, she forced herself to look him eye-to-sunglasses. "Everything is okay, but Wyatt had an accident today."

Ryder's posture straightened, but his face gave nothing away.

"I don't have all the details, but there was an avalanche. According to the report Andy got from a friend on ski patrol, he made it out without major injury. I expect him soon, but I think he's going to need extra support tonight."

Ryder stared out the window. She imagined his blue eyes turning as gray as the dull sky outside. When he finally spoke, his voice was just that flat. "I knew this could happen."

"I know. I think, though, that he probably doesn't need an 'I told you so' now." Emma laid a hand on Ryder's knee. "I don't have any siblings, so I envy the kind of bond you guys must share. Think hard about damaging your relationship over a disagreement. Maybe being right isn't as important as getting behind him and his goals. Had things gone worse today, I doubt you'd have wanted this morning's conversation to have been your last memory."

"I should've been there." Ryder turned his face toward her, but his eyes remained obscured by the dark lenses. She'd read that some TBI patients needed to mute sights and sounds because the stimulation was too taxing. Yet even though she understood why he might wear them, she disliked the veil they created between his emotions and the world.

"There's nothing you could've done to prevent this." Emma swallowed a sigh, because she'd said that to convince herself as well. "Can I bring you some tea or coffee, or maybe more juice?"

Silently, he shook his head.

She couldn't leave him there alone with his bleak thoughts. He needed another focus. Keeping busy and moving forward usually worked for her. "Ryder, I'm guessing Wyatt may need to take a day or two off from training to recover. If you have a free day tomorrow, would you like to join me at the Canyon Care Center? I go there every Monday to visit the senior citizens. Usually I bring goodies and organize an activity. It'd be nice to have some help, if you feel up to it. No pressure."

Ryder glanced at her now, alert and thoughtful. "If Wyatt's really okay."

"Stay positive." She smiled. "I'll probably bake something tonight. You're welcome to help me in the kitchen, if you'd like."

Before Ryder could respond, they heard the van pull into the parking lot. Ryder stood and crossed to the window, his hand on the windowpane.

Emma patted his shoulder. "I'll ask Avery to give Wyatt a secondary checkup, too, just to be safe. Excuse me while I go speak with her."

By the time Emma got to Avery, Andy had already filled her in.

"I can't believe this happened on day one of his training," Avery whispered. "He probably didn't know what to look for. How foolish of him to go back there without a guide."

"You're right." Emma turned thoughtful. Avery's fiancé and his partner operated a backcountry expedition company. They'd be the perfect guys to shadow Wyatt's training. "I know Grey's still a bit out of commission for a few more weeks because of his knee, but maybe Trip could get involved?"

"I suppose, although Grey will be jealous." Avery winced. Emma knew Grey wanted to push his recovery, but Avery had kept him on a tight leash.

At that moment, Wyatt and the crew came inside. Andy went to grab some of the equipment, while Wyatt limped over to the parlor, where he and Ryder engaged in a long, silent embrace.

Emma repressed the urge to rush over and join them. Not only would it be wildly inappropriate, but also likely unwelcome. She'd wait to comfort Wyatt until everyone had calmed down and settled in for the afternoon. For now, she'd make sure that, physically, he really was okay.

When the brothers eased out of their hug, Emma tugged at Avery's elbow. "Come on."

As they drew nearer, she overheard Wyatt mutter to Ryder, "Don't say it, brother." He then slung off his coat, removed his boots, and hoisted his foot up onto the coffee table. He looked ragged, shaken. His beautiful hair lay flattened against his head. His distant gaze lacked signs of life.

"Wyatt," Emma interrupted. "This is Avery, the town's best orthopedic therapist. She worked with Ryder today. I think you should let her take a quick look at you and maybe give you a little advice about next steps or whatever."

"I'm fine. Just one sore knee. Nothing but my ego got broken." Wyatt looked like he might argue further, but then he relented. "Fine. Come have a look."

Avery spent the next fifteen minutes with Wyatt while the crew and Mari discussed the harrowing episode and then, of course, how to maximize the impact of the footage. Emma rolled her eyes, sickened by the idea of Mari looking to profit, in any way, from Wyatt's near-death experience.

Needing an escape from the crowd, she went to the kitchen and made an ice pack for Wyatt's knee. She also brewed a pot of herbal tea and made up a vegetable tray. She put everything on a pushcart and rolled it into the parlor.

To her surprise, only Avery remained downstairs.

"Where'd everyone go?" Emma asked.

"To their rooms to rest and recover. Andy helped Wyatt up the steps." Avery glanced toward Ryder's room. "Ryder's really shaken. We worked hard today on his leg strength, but from what I know about TBI, it's that inability to regulate emotions that's going to be his biggest lifelong challenge."

"I suspected as much. Maybe I can help a little this month."

"Listen, I've got to run, but are you okay? You look upset, too." Avery squeezed Emma's shoulder.

"I'm fine now that everyone is safe. Do me a favor and get in touch with Trip. I'd call him, but I have more immediate things to deal with, first and foremost convincing Wyatt that he needs help to keep this from happening again."

"Done. I'll have Trip call you." Avery sighed. "Always something, right? Tell my brother I said 'bye. See you later."

Emma paced the lobby, waiting for Andy to return. She wanted to speak with Wyatt alone. As soon as Andy appeared, she asked, "How's he doing?"

"Brushing it off." Andy's envious smile spread. "He's one tough dude."

Tough dude? No. Emma suspected Wyatt's ego demanded he pretend to be okay in front of Andy.

"I'm going to take some things up to his room. Hang here in case Mari or someone surfaces and needs anything, okay?"

"You got it, boss." Andy pulled out his phone and replied to the text that had just pinged. Emma set a cup of tea, a small plate of vegetables, and the ice pack on a small tray and ascended the stairs.

Her head ached from the heaviness in the inn. No one wanted to see Wyatt hurt or fail, least of all him, she suspected. Taking a moment outside his room to pull it together, she told herself the accident wasn't her fault. She hadn't caused it merely because she'd supported Ryder's boycott. Of course, although Emma had grown quite good at lying to the world about aspects of her private life, she'd never been good at lying to herself.

No matter. She must convince Wyatt to hire Trip, even if he barked at her.

She knocked on Wyatt's door. "May I come in?"

"Yeah."

Déjà vu caused Emma to catch her breath when she saw Wyatt stretched out on his bed. Then again, the last time they'd been alone near a hotel bed together had been quite different. Her heart pounded at the memory of him wearing only a towel around his waist. Of him dangling a robe sash in one hand with a question in his eyes. "Do you trust me?" he'd asked. Emma had been so carried away with the thrill of her adventure, she would've said *yes* even if she hadn't trusted him. As it turned out, it had been a good decision. Very good.

Clearing that thought from her mind like an unwelcome cobweb, she set the tray on the nightstand.

"I brought this ice pack for your knee." She handed it to him. "I thought maybe you'd be hungry or cold, so I prepared herbal tea and some snacks. But if there's something else you'd prefer, please let me know."

He sighed, clearly putting effort into carrying on a normal conversation. "Did you know herbal tea isn't really tea at all? Comes from a blend of all kinds of plants except for tea leaves."

"I didn't realize that." She smiled at his attempt to act normal after just having survived an avalanche. Although she had things to say, she stood, waiting for him to take the lead.

"Thanks for this." He tossed the ice pack on his knee, barely looking at her. "But I'm not hungry. Just tired."

Her gaze caught sight of his hand balling into a fist. A proud athlete like Wyatt probably hated any setback, let alone a major one like he'd been dealt today. Given what she knew about him sexually, and what little she'd seen of him this past twenty-four hours, this man preferred to control his environment. Ryder's rebellion and the avalanche had thrown him against the rocks, hard. Not so hard that he'd broken, but hard enough to rattle him.

"Oh. Then I'll take this out of your way." Before she lifted the tray, she finally looked him in the eye, needing to apologize for her role in his shitty day. "Wyatt, I'm so sorry about your day, but mostly I'm sorry if anything I did or said this morning contributed in any way to what happened. I never meant to plant doubts or break your concentration. I only wanted to help settle your brother."

"I know." He grimaced. "Relax, Emma. You and Ryder didn't cause the avalanche. That's on me."

The sound of defeat tugged at her chest. Thanks to Ryder's mutiny, he had no one he could confide in. She knew a little something about that kind of loneliness. It took all of her strength not to wrap her arms around him in comfort. "It must've been terrifying."

He nodded with a grimace. At first she doubted he'd speak, but then he gazed at her and poured out a bit of his soul. "I won't lie. I could barely think until it stopped, and then panic nearly did me in. Scariest fuckin' thing that's ever happened to me. Worse than seeing Ryder after his crash. Even when I heard Buddy calling through the snow, I didn't think he'd dig me out in time. Every second it got harder and harder to breathe. When I finally saw some light coming through the snow, I cried."

Emma's heart tightened seeing the panic arrest his features, as if he were still buried in the snow. "Does it give you pause?"

"What do *you* think?" He then seemed to regret revealing his vulnerability and yanked himself back behind a less penetrable shield. "But it won't stop me. I'm not a coward. I've set a goal, and I've never quit anything in my life—except the time-out I took after Ryder's accident."

She heard a little bluster in his tone, but she wouldn't push it. He needed to rest. He needed comfort. He needed someone to supply optimism.

"May I sit?" She nodded toward the edge of the bed.

When he agreed, she sat facing him. The proximity and heat of his body made her skin tingle. For all appearances, though, she didn't inspire any similar reaction in him. *Of course not.* He preferred girls like Alexa.

Alexa had given Wyatt one kind of bliss, but Emma could offer something he probably valued and needed more tonight: hope.

"I have two friends who operate a backcountry expedition company. They're certified in everything—know how to read the conditions and evaluate avalanche danger." She tucked her hair behind her ear. "They aren't coaches, but they'd help minimize the risks. Would you consider hiring one—Trip Lexington—to work with you this month? I think it'd be best for your safety and for your brother's peace of mind."

"Guess I proved I can't handle it on my own, didn't I?" Wyatt picked at the quilt, studying its patchwork pattern as if it mattered. "Now Mari's armed with that footage, which I'm sure will make its way onto YouTube by tomorrow, at the latest, to "drum up interest" in the film. Give people something to talk about. Make people doubt that I can pull this off."

The hollowness in his voice carved a hole in her heart. She touched his leg but then withdrew her hand, embarrassed to have shown such familiarity. Yet despite the danger to herself, she longed to do it again. He snapped his gaze to hers. For a moment, neither said anything, but her own breath fell shallow as tension-filled air pumped into her lungs.

"They say any publicity is good publicity." She smiled, hoping her teasing would break the trance. The side-eye he shot her implied he wasn't ready to joke. "Seriously, Wyatt. Please hire Trip to show you the ropes. I don't want to see something terrible happen to you."

He arched one brow. "I'd have guessed you'd come in here to tell me to pack it in and give up."

"Why would you think that?" She straightened her spine.

"Aside from the fact that you've spent the past twenty-four hours avoiding me at all costs, you pretty much agreed with my brother this morning. I know you don't respect what I'm doing."

"That's not true." Emma's cheeks grew hot. She supposed she had given him that impression, but she couldn't tell him why. "I respect your talent, Wyatt. I respect that you want to make something of your life. And I'm not avoiding you . . . I'm busy doing my job."

"Whatever." He waved one hand and stared out the window. "So this Trip guy, you trust him?"

"He's been big-mountain skiing for more than a decade, all over North America."

"Guess it can't hurt to talk to him."

"I'll see if he'll come over here tonight." She stood to go, but Wyatt grasped her wrist.

She stifled the gasp that arose from recalling that other time he'd held her wrists in his vise-like grip. Emma imagined him yanking her onto the bed and into his arms. The thought shot heat and yearning through her heart and between her legs, and she knew she wouldn't have resisted . . . at least, not right away.

"Thanks for giving a shit." His thumb brushed against the inside of her wrist and he stared at her for a few quiet seconds before he glanced at the tray. "Leave that, too, please. I'm a little hungry now that I'm more settled."

"Salmon tacos and avocado slaw for dinner in two hours." She eased out of his hold, although she could've just as easily slunk back down beside him. "Get some rest."

Hurrying out of the room before she said or did something truly stupid, she inhaled slowly through her nose and held the breath before releasing it.

How pathetic. Each time he came near, recollections of their night together overpowered her. He, however, remained blissfully unaffected. Unaware of their past. While that fact suited her present needs, it hurt to know she'd been so completely unmemorable. That nothing about the real her had stuck with him.

In her book, "Dallas" saw through the glam to the soul of his heroine, Ella.

Wouldn't Wyatt be shocked if she told him the truth? She smiled, imagining herself decked out in Alexa's sex-kitten boots and dress, with her hair wild and free. Picturing Wyatt's surprise—his eyes widening, perhaps a dawning recognition. Envisioning his heated gaze, the one that had haunted many of her dreams since that night.

Another flare of heat fired in her veins and made her breasts tingle and tighten. Something was seriously wrong with her that she wanted to arouse a man to whom she meant nothing. To whom she'd never be more than a temporary sex partner. *Stupid, stupid, stupid.*

"Em, you okay?" Andy called from the top step. "You look like you might faint."

Get it together. "I'm fine. Need to make a call, actually."

She scampered past him, down the steps to her mother's office, and closed the door.

Sitting at the desk, she pressed her forehead to the desktop and then gently banged it three times. *Cripes.* Alexa daydreams like that would be her undoing.

Chapter Five

Wyatt watched Emma light the candles on the dining table where he'd been meeting with Trip for the past fifteen minutes. The soft light flickered, reflecting in her pretty green eyes—eyes that refused to acknowledge his presence.

Her understated prettiness had snuck up on him today. Not a shock, considering she did nothing to draw attention to herself. But the more he saw her, the more he noticed how she glowed from within. He'd heard that sentimental gibberish before but had never seen it for himself. It had always sounded odd, but witnessing it affected him. Moved him somehow, even when Emma irritated him—like now, when she was ignoring him.

He watched her until she disappeared into the kitchen, then resumed his conversation with Trip.

"I'd like to get out there tomorrow, but Avery ordered me to take at least a day to rest the knee." Wyatt settled his elbows on the dining table. The avalanche had rocked him, but Trip's expertise was helping to restore his confidence. "I should probably listen."

Trip leaned all six feet three inches of his powerful body back in his chair and crossed his ankles. "Avery's conservative. She's got her fiancé—my partner—chompin' at the bit, too. Of course, I did bully him into going out-of-bounds for a quick run a couple of weeks ago." Trip winked above a broad smile, then held a finger up to his lips. "But you need to be tip-top for competition, so listen to Avery. She and I butt heads, but she knows what she's doing."

Wyatt imagined Trip butted heads with lots of folks. His big personality even eclipsed the size of his body, which meant he'd be the kind of guy people loved or hated. Wyatt liked his irreverence.

"Once I'm set, where do you recommend going?" Wyatt's gaze roamed the map that Trip had laid across the dining table.

Trip tipped back his Stetson and leaned forward again. "Day after tomorrow, we'll head up over here. Nice chutes and obstacles, but not as steep of a pitch. I'll teach you some quick tips for reading the terrain and testing the snow conditions to get a better sense for avalanche danger. We can focus around there as sort of a warm-up for the next week or so, and then shift over here," Trip's finger traversed the map, "to the backside of The Cirque. This here's about as good as you're gonna get around these parts. Steep, big cliffs, treed areas. Good practice for the qualifiers in January. If you can handle these, you can handle any gnarly conditions in competition."

The sound of Emma's muffled laughter from the other room made Wyatt look toward the kitchen door. He hadn't seen or heard her hearty laugh since he'd arrived, and now wondered how her face might light up even more when amused. When he considered that Andy was probably in there seeing that side of her, envy ripped through him. He scowled then, remembering why he was here at this inn, which had nothing to do with Emma.

Feeling the weight of Trip's curiosity, he glanced back at the man. "You're cool with being filmed, right?"

Trip's speculative gaze shifted to something mischievous.

"Just so long as you don't get jealous when I steal the show," Trip chuckled. "Is the director here?"

"Mari's always nearby, like a shadow. She's got these spy cameras all around, too. The only camera-free zones are Emma's kitchen, the office, and the guest rooms." Wyatt gestured to the small camera in the corner of the dining room. "She's paranoid she's going to 'miss' something, though it looks like that one's not running now."

"A woman?" Trip flicked his wrist and grinned. "Putty in my hands by day two."

"I thought you were engaged."

"I am. Happily so. But that status only seems to make me more attractive to other women. Go figure." Trip shifted in his seat. "Point is, we'll get Mari to lighten up."

"The key is to make her tell this story in a positive light. I need that. My family needs that, especially after today's screwup. I don't want this film to turn into sensationalist crap."

A sincere expression replaced Trip's playful demeanor. "Wyatt, you can count on me to make you look good."

"Thanks." Wyatt had to credit Emma for her good idea to involve Trip in his training. Competent, reserved, calm-in-the-eye-of-the-storm Emma.

She breezed into the dining room for the third time since he'd been sitting there, this time to dig around the buffet cabinet for some platters. As usual, she did her work efficiently without sparing Wyatt a glance. Whatever he'd thought had softened between them earlier this afternoon in his room must've been wishful thinking on his part, despite the fact he could still feel her pulse beating beneath his thumb from when he'd grabbed her thin wrist.

His heightened curiosity about her changed nothing—she still regarded him with no more affection than she did any chair in this room.

He racked his brain trying to think of what he'd done or said since arriving that had turned her off. Sure, he'd teased her and sneaked up on her in the pantry, which she hadn't liked much. But given that her attitude had been clear from the moment he'd first stepped into the lobby, he suspected his reputation had preceded him. She'd written him off as an immature, selfish skirt chaser—one she apparently thought didn't care much for his brother's well-being. Besides, a woman like her probably preferred an intellectual guy. A gentle one, too, which Wyatt definitely was not.

Gentleness hadn't factored into his life much, so he had no real road map for it. His response to the poverty and sometimes-violent years of his youth was to toughen up, unapologetically go after what he wanted, control what he could, and always try to win. It had worked well for him, although not so much for his brother.

"Smells good, Em. Reminds me of the old days, when I'd sneak out of the guest rooms before sunrise." Trip cast Emma a baiting look. "Your cookin' makes me all kinds of nostalgic."

"I'd say I miss those days, but that'd be a lie," she volleyed with a smile.

"Bet your guests miss them . . . a lot."

"Funny, haven't heard a sniffle or complaint, unlike when you were around. All those poor victims." She shook her head, proving Wyatt's theory about her opinion of casual sex. "You're lucky Kelsey is okay with your past."

"Darlin', she's more than okay with it." A glint crossed Trip's green eyes. "She benefits from my expertise."

Emma groaned. "Judging from how many women you needed for practice, you were a really slow learner."

Wyatt laughed at the comeback, a little surprised she had it in her. Sarcasm went against her nurturer vibe. Trip chuckled, too, proving that his bragging was all in jest. Perhaps that's why Emma liked him despite his behavior.

Wyatt's gaze followed Emma until she disappeared into the kitchen, at which point Trip snapped his fingers. "You got a little crush on Emma?"

"No!" Wyatt scowled, knowing he'd answered way too defensively.

"Every time she comes in the room, your attention cuts out." Trip grinned and rubbed his hands together. "Emma Duffy," he quietly mused. "This oughta be interesting."

"Trust me, there's nothing happening there. I've got to stay focused." The fact that he'd been unable to maintain that focus whenever he caught sight of her fiery hair or Grade-A ass was a secret he'd rather not discuss.

"Oh, well, then you're all set, 'cause no man has ever lost his focus over a woman." Trip raised a brow.

Okay, so maybe not exactly a secret. Given Trip's friendship with Emma, perhaps he could help Wyatt discover why she treated him so coolly. "Doesn't matter, 'cause she doesn't seem too interested in men."

Trip remained thoughtful for a few seconds then he leaned nearer to Wyatt, his playful expression gone. "Emma's quiet, but tough. She's a good girl, in every sense of the word. Not sure exactly why she doesn't have a boyfriend. But know this—when she does, Grey and I will make damn sure she doesn't get hurt." Trip maintained a pleasant grin, but the steel in his words conveyed the unspoken message—don't fuck with Emma's heart.

"What's her story?" The words popped out of Wyatt's mouth before he could help himself.

"Her story?"

"Yeah, like, were she and Andy ever a couple?"

Trip's brows rose before his face scrunched in dismay. "Doubtful. They've known each other their whole lives. Emma helped him out when he lost his job last winter, but as far as I know, they're just friends—no benefits."

Wyatt nodded, but his expression must've tipped off his relief.

Trip's lips quirked into a knowing smile. "Deny it all you want, but fifty bucks says you don't make it through the month without making a move. Fifty more says you fail."

"First you warn me off, then you dare me with a bet?"

"Pay attention, Wyatt. To win the bets, you'll have to keep your distance."

"The second bet sounds more like a challenge, like you want me to try," Wyatt said. Of course, to Wyatt, most things sounded like a challenge. "Either way, it's a shitty bet for me. Even if I win the second part, I lose the first."

"If you're any kind of man, you'll win what matters most. Now, much as I'd love to stay here and chitchat about romance, I've got to get home."

"Thanks for working with me."

"Hell, man, I get to hang out on the mountain with Wyatt fuckin' Lawson. I should be thanking you."

"We'll see how you feel next week." Any kind of hero worship made Wyatt uncomfortable. Being held up so high only meant the inevitable fall hurt more. And since Ryder's accident, he'd felt anything but heroic.

Trip lightly punched Wyatt's shoulder before walking away. "Tell Em I said 'bye."

Wyatt sat alone in the blessed quiet, happy to have a few minutes without Mari, the crew, and Ryder hovering. 'Course it only took about thirty seconds for boredom to set in, so he went to the kitchen to thank Emma for hooking him up with Trip.

"Homemade tortillas?" He pointed at the press and the fresh shells piled on a platter.

"No preservatives." She spoke without looking at him. Apparently the avocado she'd sliced open and was now dicing into a large bowl was far more interesting.

Her deft fingers worked quickly, neatly emptying the avocados without the fleshy insides getting smashed. What kinds of magic could those fingers work on his body? The mere thought strung tension through his muscles, as if his body had braced for an onslaught of sensation.

"Dinner will be ready in about fifteen minutes." She glanced at him, for a change. "Are you going to work with Trip?"

"Yes. Thanks for the suggestion. He's knowledgeable and funny."

"Funny? That's one word for him, I suppose." The dry delivery belied her little smile. Emma may not have a boyfriend, but she obviously had a tight group of friends and a lot of respect in the community. A kindhearted, trustworthy woman—something he hadn't come across too often in his adult life. It made Emma appealing in yet another new way.

He imagined she'd offer her man shelter from every kind of storm. Wyatt had never, ever known that kind of security. He experienced, then, a stark moment of deep yearning for her to unlock the doors and let him in. If only he could find the key.

"Avery grounded me tomorrow," he ventured. "Got any other suggestions for ways to keep occupied after yoga?"

Emma paused, looking uncomfortable. "If she wants you to rest, I'm happy to get you a book from the library. Or maybe you have Netflix?"

Okay, so she obviously had no interest in being his chaperone for the day. He wouldn't push. He still had tomorrow, after all. "How about something Ryder and I can do together? Any particular sights we should see in town?"

Sighing, Emma wiped her hands on a nearby dishrag. "Actually, I'm pretty sure Ryder's coming with me tomorrow to Canyon Care Center."

"What?" What was going on with those two?

"I volunteer there every Monday and Ryder's thinking of joining me tomorrow. Standard stuff—bingo, manicures, cards. Anyway, that means you'll have plenty of peace and quiet around here."

She'd made plans with Ryder behind his back? Irritation and envy caused him to step closer. Close enough to see her pulse throbbing at the base of her neck. Did he frighten her, and if so, why? Or maybe her standoffishness was an act—a form of self-protection. Maybe his nearness affected her as completely and irrationally as hers affected him. Maybe he had a shot. *Damn, Trip just might win one of those bets.* "Do I seem like a guy who enjoys peace and quiet?"

She licked her lips and backed up. He wanted to see her lick her lips again, because he could almost feel her tongue on his neck. The imagined moment pooled blood in his lower half. "Well, you don't look like a guy who wants to hang out with old people."

"But Ryder does?" Wyatt set one hand on the counter and closed the gap she'd created. He liked the way she got hot and flustered when he drew near. Those fair cheeks of hers gave everything away every time they pinked up. He had a shot. His heart knocked a little harder in his chest.

She suddenly turned pensive, looking toward the window above the sink. He could smell her light perfume despite the aroma of onion and cilantro coming from the bowl in front of her. "Ryder looks like someone who wants to feel needed. The elderly residents at the home can fulfill that longing."

In that moment, he recognized that she, too, longed to be needed—a need he could fulfill if she'd let him.

"Everyone likes to feel needed, Emma." He edged closer still, forcing her to meet his gaze. He dropped his voice to a low murmur, hoping it would sharpen her desire to match his. "Even someone like me."

A delicious tension wound its way through his limbs, and he suspected she'd been caught in its trap, too. Her head tipped back and her green eyes took on a fathomless quality, but before she could answer, Ryder thumped into the kitchen and broke the spell.

"Mari's out here." He glanced at Wyatt. "Wants you to do a voice-over for the c-clip she's putting up on YouTube tonight. Also wants to know if dinner will be on time."

Emma closed her eyes like she was praying for patience. "Tell Mari dinner will be on time, assuming you both leave me be for five minutes so I can finish pulling everything together."

Before Wyatt walked away from Emma, he muttered, "Consider this conversation on hold."

When she faced him, he noticed her gaze snagged on his mouth. That fact made his pulse, and other parts of his anatomy, jump. Trip's bet and warning drifted through his mind as he dragged himself out of the kitchen.

"Everyone likes to feel needed, Emma." His melancholy words had sounded feverish, or maybe she'd only thought so because her blood had boiled faster than water in an electric teakettle. Had the day's events affected his outlook, his priorities? He'd kept looking at her like he wanted something. Her attention? Her approval? Her touch?

A hopeful but doomed zing sailed through her heart before she took hold of herself. Wyatt Lawson desired women like Alexa, not Emma. Whatever he wanted from her, it had more to do with needing a distraction than wanting someone to burn up the sheets with, for Pete's sake.

Besides, even if she could stomach dating a highly sought-after man, she wouldn't pin her hopes on a guy hell-bent on making a name for himself—traveling the globe chasing storms and competitions. No. At best, she'd be as lonely as ever with a man like that, at worst, she'd end up brokenhearted. Been there, done that . . .

Her father placed a silver necklace with a heart-shaped locket in her hands, closing his fingers around her fist. "I know you're sad, sweetie. But when I get settled, you'll love visiting me in Los Angeles. We'll go to the beach. Learn to surf. I'll even bring you on a movie set. It'll be fun. You'll have a life here in the mountains, and one by the ocean."

He had a way of dramatizing things to make them sound exciting—of needing them to be so, too—but Emma might as well have been an oak tree for how rooted in reality she'd been.

Whatever promises he made, she doubted that he'd keep them once he left, and not just because she'd overheard her mom's accusations or sobs.

Emma'd spent her childhood desperately seeking his attention, determined to make him proud. There'd been moments when she'd thought she'd succeeded. When he'd sat in front of the fire reading to her as if fully content with his life, his family. But he was a decent actor, and apparently those moments had been just for show.

"Now give me a hug before I go, baby."

She complied, although woodenly. One thing she would not do was break down in front of him. If anything, her sadness had given way to resentment. But Emma would hide her anger. As far as she was concerned, he'd lost the privilege of seeing any of her emotions. "Bye, Daddy."

He tweaked her nose, then he stood, hands welded to his hips, and took a last look at the lobby. She knew right then she would never, ever forget the utter relief reflected in his eyes as he closed this chapter of his life. A look that proved he'd never loved her enough. "Bye."

Once he walked out, she tromped up to her bedroom. Unclenching her fist, she opened the locket to find a photo of the two of them inside. She studied his blond hair curled around his ears. His stubble and proud chin. The dimples that made lots of stupid women guests giggle, which then always made her mom and dad yell and slam doors.

With unsteady hands, she hid the necklace in the back corner of her pajama drawer, then she crawled onto her bed, pulled a pillow over her head, and cried.

Emma shook her head to break apart the unbidden memory, although remembering it might keep her in check. Setting aside a small plate for herself first, she then arranged the serving bowls on various platters to take to her guests.

When she entered the dining room, Wyatt and Mari were bent over a laptop, presumably watching the soon-to-be-released clip. Wyatt's arms wound around his body, his brow drawn low, his lower lip tormented beneath the scrape of his teeth. Emma guessed watching the footage had forced him to relive the awful event, but she couldn't be sure. Maybe that's just how he looked when he focused.

Meanwhile, Mari's ambition took priority over everything else, including giving Wyatt and Ryder no more than a couple of hours to recover from the fright. Resentment toward the woman's insensitivity coiled tiny knots in Emma's lungs. If this were a scene in a book, she might have her heroine "accidentally" spill soup on Mari, or find a way to erase the avalanche footage. But this wasn't a book, and Emma wasn't anyone's heroine.

Ryder stood to the side of the others—cane in hand, eyes hidden behind his glasses—refusing to watch the video. Discomfort and isolation surrounded him like a palpable force field, making Emma yearn to reach through it and help him reconnect with the world.

A dull ache swaddled her heart. Whatever good she might be able to do for Ryder, it would never restore him completely. Each day would present him with new challenges and struggles. She could only hope that somewhere inside he had the fortitude to press forward and grab at bits and pieces of happiness when they came. In that way, perhaps they had that in common.

"Hey, folks. You probably want to eat this while it's hot." She scattered the platters around the table while the crew took their seats. "Protein-packed and loaded with flavor. I'll be back with drinks in a second."

After she'd served them all, she retreated to the kitchen and quickly gobbled down her own meal. Any pride she might've taken in preparing that excellent dinner had been supplanted with heaviness. Not exactly the mood that would help her write another chapter of her work-in-progress, or tap into her inner wild-and-sexy to come up with a Facebook post or two tonight. She wrinkled her nose at the thought because, in light of everything that had transpired this afternoon, her book and its publicity suddenly seemed silly and inconsequential.

Seeing these other sides of Wyatt had also been making her feel more awkward about her character Dallas. Wyatt had been the inspiration for her hero, but then she'd ascribed all kinds of other attributes and layers to Dallas to mold a perfect romantic hero. It hadn't felt wrong, at least not at the time. Sometimes now, when seeing Wyatt stroll through the inn, it seemed like Dallas had sprung to life. An utterly foolish and frightening thought. Wyatt was not Dallas, and vice versa, but noticing the similarities and differences between the two only increased her discomfort.

An exhausting dilemma. Sluggishly, she cleaned the mixing bowls and taco press and then went to check on her guests.

While she cleared the table, she quietly mentioned to Ryder, "I'm going to make rum balls next, if you'd like to help."

"I have a h-headache." He turned to her.

"It's been a stressful day. You should get some rest." She touched his shoulder. "If you aren't up to going with me tomorrow, that's fine, too."

"I want to go," Wyatt interjected.

"Go where?" Mari asked before Emma could lift her jaw off the floor.

"Emma volunteers at a local eldercare place, and Ryder's joining her tomorrow." Wyatt smiled at Emma, having neatly trapped her. "Seeing as I'm taking the day off on doctor's orders, I want to go with them."

Mari's eyes lit with a fearsome mix of cunning and pleasure. "Oh, that'll be wonderful PR. The images of the avalanche juxtaposed with you turning around and helping others. Perfect."

"Hold on," Emma asserted, having finally found her voice. "I didn't agree to take Wyatt, much less consent to letting you all descend on those people."

"Excuse me?" Mari had the gall to look affronted after she'd tried to hijack Emma's plans.

"You heard me, Mari." Emma set down the stack of dishes she'd collected. "I'm here to serve your needs at the inn, but you can't barge into every corner of my life, or the lives of the people in my life. Those people trust me, and I'm not going to subject them to cameras and questions, or trot them out for entertainment's sake."

"You make it sound so distasteful. Have you considered that some of them might find it enjoyable . . . exciting, even? Naturally we couldn't record anyone who didn't sign a waiver, but why rob them of a chance to do something unique? Being in a film with an international sports figure is an opportunity most people would probably love to experience."

Emma rocked back on her heels. Could Mari have a point? Might Mrs. Marchetti or old Tom Jahns like the spotlight? It seemed unlikely. Then again, her erotica-writing career would seem even more implausible to everyone in town. Perhaps, deep down, many people would jump at a chance to experience something new, especially if they'd been confined to an eldercare facility for months or years.

"Then there's the issue of how this could help Wyatt's image." Mari raised her brow in that snotty, stuck-up way Emma couldn't stand. "But I suppose that's not important to you, is it?"

"I understand why Emma's being protective." Wyatt tossed his napkin on the table and stared straight into her soul. "I'd still like to go, with or without the cameras."

Somehow instead of Mari being the bad guy, that black hat hovered above Emma's head now, waiting for her decision. How could she deny Wyatt after what he'd confessed to her in the kitchen?

"Fine. You can come. But before the cameras show up, I need to clear it with the center's director."

"Fair enough." Mari's victorious smile made Emma want to hurl. "I'd like to be part of that call so I might be able to answer any questions and assure everyone that we won't do anything to upset the residents."

"It's after hours, so we'll have to wait until early morning to speak with her." Emma lifted the stack of dishes again and dashed into the kitchen before her good manners vanished.

Once safely ensconced in her kitchen, Emma took out her feelings on the dishes by jamming them into the dishwasher.

"Whoa." Wyatt had sneaked into the kitchen and crossed to where she fumed. He removed a dish from her hand. "Take a breath before you chip all your plates."

"I'm fine." She held out her palm, face up. "Seriously, Wyatt. Please hand me the plate and go back to your posse."

He placed it back in her hand. "I'm sorry about what happened out there. I didn't think about how Mari might react. If I had, I would've waited to speak with you in private. If it's going to be a problem, I can say my knee hurts, or make up some other excuse not to go."

Emma eyed him, trying to determine whether this was some excellent form of manipulation or simple sincerity. Having already decided some of the residents would enjoy participating in a film, she gave Wyatt the benefit of the doubt.

"As long as no one exploits the patients, I suppose it is fine. Mari's right, some of them might get a little thrill out of it. It'll certainly be a big change from a round of bingo."

"Nice to know I'm good for something." His grin seriously messed with her head, filling it with fanciful thoughts of hand-holding, stolen kisses, warm embraces.

"Imagine that," she teased, then reined herself in. For a dozen reasons, not the least of which were her secrets, she couldn't let him know her.

"What are you baking?" he asked, glancing toward the oven. "Smells good."

"I thought refined sugar is off-limits." Feeling crowded by his presence, she asked, "Shouldn't you be out there making decisions about the footage?"

"Like I have any say." Wyatt frowned and rapped his knuckles on the counter. When he looked up, his eyes glittered with fire, and his lopsided grin warned of a mood change. "As for my nutrition plan, tell me what's on the dessert menu tonight. I'm feeling naughty."

Emma couldn't think with him standing so near. Her heart relocated to her ears, its beat throbbing there, blocking out other sounds. She stepped aside to create a little distance between them before they fused together. "No wonder you like Trip. You're a junior version of him."

"First of all, I'm not that much younger than him, or you. Secondly, what's so bad about being like him?" Wyatt rubbed his jaw with one hand, and she found herself wondering if his stubble felt prickly or soft. He'd been clean-shaven the night his mouth had kissed every inch of her skin. That memory sparked a burst of goose bumps that rushed down her neck. "Seems like he has a good time and a good life . . . a happy one."

"Dumb luck. Kelsey's the only person in the world who could've looked beyond his ego and wrangled him into submission." As soon as the word submission slid over her tongue, that electric charge sparked again, knocking her into a brief daze. Judging from the way Wyatt's eyes had strayed to her mouth, she guessed he'd been struck, too.

He might not remember her or their history, but apparently a subconscious part of him had some sort of muscle memory. Emma cleared her throat and went to the oven to check on the cake. "I'm making chocolate rum balls. It's a favorite of the senior set."

He followed her, which increased her self-consciousness. "So why bake a cake?"

"It's the base for the rum balls. I crumble it up with buttercream icing, add rum, roll it up into little balls and then dunk them in jimmies."

"Let me crumble the cake. That's something my mom would've never allowed."

Emma smiled, trying to picture Wyatt as a young boy. His loose curls, begging to be tugged, dangling around his jaw. Those hazel eyes, wide and curious, seeking answers and pleasure. Whoops, another word she should avoid in his presence unless she wanted her knees to give out.

"Okay, but it needs to cool. Go finish with Mari and come back in a bit. I'll clean up and then mix the icing."

Wyatt nodded and left her alone, thankfully. Of course, Kelsey picked that one moment of much-needed solitude to call. She nestled the phone between her ear and shoulder so she could keep cleaning.

"Hey, Kels. What's up?"

"I called to thank you for thinking of Trip. He came home all wired—friskier than normal, which is saying something."

"TMI, friend. TMI." Emma smiled, glad to hear the cheerfulness in Kelsey's voice. She could only pray that Trip truly loved Kelsey and would forsake others until death. Experience told Emma it wasn't likely, but she'd keep that cynical thought to herself. "I think it's a good pairing. Wyatt's brother, Ryder, should be a little relieved, too, knowing Trip's expertise will reduce some of the risks."

"Good. Now, the other reason I called is because I have gossip."

Gossip, the grease that kept their small town running. Last February it had been all about Andy, most of it brutal. She doubted she'd handle that kind of scrutiny as well as he had. She'd never quite understood how people quickly forgot their own mistakes when throwing stones at others. Hypocrisy was alive and well in Sterling Canyon. Who was its next victim, she wondered? "Oh, really? Who are we whispering about today?"

"You."

Emma froze. Had Andy seen her books or overheard her marketing call earlier? But he'd come to her first, wouldn't he? Had someone else somehow discovered the link between "Alexa" and Emma? Heart pulsing in her throat, she tried to reply without her voice squeaking. "Me?"

"Uh huh. Apparently, you've been holding out on me. Me, the lover of all things romance! Don't bother denying it, all I want is confirmation."

Emma's vision fogged. How would she convince Kelsey to keep her secret? Kelsey would surely tell Trip, who'd never stop teasing her. And

Avery, who'd then tell Grey. Lord only knew what horrid nickname Grey would think up once he knew. And Kelsey's sister, Maura, who'd tell her husband, Bill. By morning half the town would be snickering and teasing and nosing their way into her business and onto her Facebook page, which was loaded with photos of almost-naked men.

And her mother . . . her mother would be mortified. Emma's own mixed feelings about her dual identity aside, the idea of seeing shame reflected in her mom's eyes nearly buckled her knees. What kind of dark tailspin might that send her mother into? She held the phone with her hand now so it didn't drop.

"I can't confirm anything until I know what you're talking about." Emma winced, doubting the wobble in her voice sounded carefree.

"Wyatt Lawson has a little crush on you."

Emma stared at the phone as if it had turned into a potato. The relief that the gossip had nothing to do with her writing receded while disbelief rose up in its place. "What in the world gave you that idea? Honestly, I'd have thought being in a relationship would make you less crazy, not more."

"Trip told me. Seems Wyatt has a little thing for you, but he's keeping it in check because of his training, and the fact that you don't seem to be interested. But honestly, Em, how can you not be interested? Wyatt Lawson . . . he's so darn fine."

Emma's pulse galloped ahead of her racing thoughts. *Fine? Wrong. Adorably sexy—check. Domineering in bed—double check.* "Kelsey, he's too young. And temporary. And in training, as he pointed out, assuming Trip isn't playing some colossal joke on both you and me, which I wouldn't put past him."

"Oh, no. It's no joke. He chuckled about it all through dinner. Apparently he issued a stern warning that anyone who messed with your heart would answer to him and Grey, then he baited Wyatt with a bet." Kelsey's feminine giggle rippled through the phone.

"What?" Emma slapped her hand to her forehead. "Listen, Kelsey, I know a bet brought you and Trip together, but unlike you, I didn't agree to participate in any wager. I do not want to be the subject of one, either. You tell Trip to rescind it tomorrow. I mean it. Good grief, like I don't have enough to deal with."

"You're such a party pooper. Come on, live a little. Especially this month, with your mom away. Back in July you admitted it'd been eons since you'd had sex, and I don't imagine that's changed. Why not take advantage of this golden opportunity? What've you got to lose?"

Kelsey had always jumped into everything without a moment's hesitation. It made her eminently fun and easy to be around, but it also had caused her no shortage of heartache. Her reputation had taken a few hits over the years, too. And when her and Trip's secret sex life went public, tongues had wagged all over town.

All things considered, impulsiveness didn't seem like a good plan to Emma.

"My reputation. My pride. My dignity." *My heart.*

"Fine. I won't bring it up again." Kelsey fell silent for two seconds. "Before I hang up, you still have time to bake the cupcakes for the engagement party next weekend, right?"

"Red velvet, your favorite."

"Thanks, Em." Kelsey snickered. "So, I guess you won't be bringing Wyatt as your date, then?"

Emma scowled. "You said you'd drop it."

"When have you ever known 'Boomerang' to drop anything?" Kelsey laughed, which proved how far she'd come. She'd turned that horrible nickname that Grey had coined for her former stalker tendencies into some kind of badge of honor. In a way, Emma did envy Kelsey's devil-may-care attitude, even though she didn't believe she could live with the consequences as blithely as her friend. Then again, Kelsey's bold maneuvers had led her to happiness, while Emma's caution had not.

Naturally, Wyatt reappeared before Emma had hung up. "Kels, I've got to go. I'm baking for the Care Center now."

"Emma Duffy, it's high time you consider cookin' something other than food in your kitchen," Kelsey sang before she hung up.

Emma set the phone down and stared at it, afraid to face Wyatt. She could actually feel the blush creeping up her body. Had he really told Trip he had a crush on her? It didn't seem possible. Trip must've misunderstood.

But a bet could explain Wyatt's sudden interest in coming to the Care Center. What a lame schoolboy diversion to keep him from thinking about the avalanche and the huge task ahead. Shouldn't surprise her, though, given his age.

How foolish of her, to forget all of her mom's lessons and fall for his "everyone likes to be needed" line. She could turn on him now and confront him, or she could use this knowledge to her advantage. Torture him a bit to make him pay for being an ass, and then turn him down.

'Cause if he'd made a bet, he was going to lose. She'd make sure of that.

Chapter Six

Before facing Wyatt, she unbuttoned her outer sweater and removed it to reveal the snug, V-necked T-shirt beneath. With a friendly smile fixed in place, she turned and hoped her eyes twinkled with the mischief she planned to cause.

"Sorry, I got sidetracked." She watched his gaze home in on her cleavage. To his credit, he didn't let it linger overlong before it flicked back up to her face. "I need a few minutes to mix up the icing."

"That's cool. Mind if I hang out?"

"Why would I mind?" She strolled to the refrigerator to get the separated egg whites and butter, making sure to add a tiny oomph to each sway of her hips. "There's a stool by the back door if you'd like to sit and rest your knee."

"Later." He rested his butt against the counter while she whipped the egg whites and added confectioners' sugar and vanilla.

Emma swallowed hard because, aside from the fact that he was fully clothed, he looked exactly as she'd envisioned Dallas in the kitchen scene of her book. The one where he bent her, er—Ella over the counter and made use of a rubber spatula then secured her hands on the counter and took her from behind. *Do not call him Dallas. Do not call him Dallas.*

"Did you know that confectioners' sugar actually has a little cornstarch in it?" he asked.

"Actually, that's a bit of trivia I do know!" She grinned, feeling good about surprising him.

"I should've guessed you'd know food trivia." He crossed his arms and grinned. "Where'd you learn to cook?"

Thankfully, a hundred beautiful memories of the hours she'd spent in this kitchen with her Grammy tumbled around her brain, obliterating naughty thoughts about Wyatt—er, Dallas.

Grammy had taught her how to can tomatoes and peaches, how to make the flakiest piecrust with Crisco and ice-cold water, how to pair unusual herbs for optimal flavor. Grammy had been Emma's calm in the eye of the storm, whether that had been her parents' hot-and-cold relationship, the dark months after her father left, or the awkward teen years when her mother's starchy attitude made it impossible to talk about crushes on boys without earning a lecture about keeping her legs closed.

"My grandmother." Emma smiled at the memory of Grammy's gigantic pink curlers, the paunchy gut she camouflaged beneath muumuus, her nightly bourbon nightcaps, and the stash of racy romances tucked away in her room. The ones Emma had routinely sneaked to read. "She taught me everything I know, although I can never quite replicate her recipes. She had a magic touch."

"Sounds like you miss her." Wyatt rested his elbows on the counter, leaning closer. The casual pose made her relax, too.

"I do. She was wise and kind. Helpful without being overly preachy. Tolerant, which isn't always something you see much in small towns. She had a good sense of humor, too."

"Was she Native American?"

"No." Her chin jerked inward. "Why would you think that?"

Wyatt shrugged. "The name of the inn. The artifacts. Although, you don't look like you have any of that heritage."

Emma grimaced. "I look like a relative of Casper the ghost."

"You have a beautiful complexion." His matter-of-fact tone didn't sound like a come-on or a ploy.

If not for her good manners—a reflex from her mom's conditioning—she probably couldn't have spoken. Compliments weren't something she heard often, or something she tended to believe. "Thank you."

Suddenly shy and self-conscious, she turned away, wondering if she should compliment him.

While she floundered for something safe to say, he asked, "What about your parents? What are they like?"

"My mother is . . . unique." Emma looked upward, searching her brain for a better answer. "Most people would say she's fastidious, chatty, dictatorial, and on occasion, a bit ridiculous. I suppose that's all true, but she's a goodhearted person who simply prefers order and rules. I think structure gives her comfort."

"Is your dad strict, too?"

"Hardly," Emma snorted. "He moved to Hollywood years ago to be a 'big star.' He landed some bit parts in movies and TV during those early days, but nothing that ever matched his dreams. People called him charming and handsome, but he was also a little selfish. Over the years our relationship has faded. I only hear from him on my birthday and Christmas, if that, and I haven't seen him in four years."

"I'm sorry." Wyatt fidgeted with a whisk Emma had left on the counter.

"Me, too." Emma wrinkled her nose. "Not so much for myself, though. My mom suffered more." Emma had left so much about those early post-divorce months unspoken. Those months that had changed the course of her mother's life as well as her own. "Maybe if she'd met someone new, she'd be less . . ."

Then Emma paused, because she couldn't put her finger on the words she wanted. She eyed Wyatt, a man much like her dad, and reminded herself that she'd never want to follow in her mother's footsteps and fall for a chick magnet with big dreams, no matter how flattering his attention might seem at first.

Silver screen-styled passion—the kind that steals one's breath—was fleeting. The reality was that her mother had spent most of her marriage vying for her dad's attention and resenting him at the same time. Emma had learned from that exactly what kind of husband to avoid. She wanted someone devoted to her and a family life, not to a career, and not to his own ego.

Wyatt's voice interrupted her private musing. "And you had to live through all of that here, with strangers around. Was it weird to grow up in an inn?"

Emma shrugged. "However someone grows up is 'normal' to that person, I suppose, so it didn't seem all that weird to me. And there are months when things are really quiet. November is a pretty quiet month, actually, since the resort doesn't usually open until closer to Thanksgiving."

"So I ruined your peace and quiet?" Wyatt smiled.

More like her peace of mind. That lazy smile sent her right back to Aspen and the moment Wyatt had talked her into coming to his room, when he'd tugged her close right at the bar. When he'd boldly kissed her jaw just below her ear and whispered a pleading invitation.

Heated shivers raced through her now, begging for her to act on the feelings. "Something like that."

Snap out of it! She'd been taking his friendly questions at face value, enjoying the exchange, the eye candy, the company. Now she remembered the stupid bet with Trip and her mission. My goodness, she was as gullible as her mom, letting herself wish for a kiss from a smooth talker like Wyatt.

After folding the last ingredients of the icing together, she scraped a spoonful, dipped her finger into the icing, brought it to her mouth, and gave it a lick. "Deee-licious."

His pupils widened so fast they practically exploded, which spurred her on. Smiling, she dipped her finger in again but, to her shock, he grabbed her wrist.

"Let me try." He then tugged her hand to his mouth, and closed his lips around her iced finger.

Too far. He knew he'd gone too far, but he didn't care. She'd finally shed the baggy sweater and put her awesome, milky cleavage on display. That, plus the little smile tugging at her mouth and that damn erotic icing lick had made it impossible for him to stop himself.

Now she stared at him, wide-eyed and stock-still.

"Sorry." He loosened his grip, wishing she'd dip her finger into the icing again and offer it up. "You made it look so tempting."

She slowly retracted her hand, wrapping her other hand around it and curling them both against her chest. Almost dazed, really. Very cute.

Trip was right; Wyatt would probably lose the first bet, but maybe not the second.

He watched her body quiver as she snapped back to the present. She didn't slap him, although she also didn't offer another swipe at her finger, either.

"We need to wash our hands." Emma refused to look at him. He sensed her internal battle as she crouched down and sorted through other mixing bowls. After selecting a cavernous metal one, she thrust it at his chest. "Gloves, actually. You should wear gloves before you break apart the cake."

"Okay." Wyatt's body buzzed with need, urging him to sidle up and seduce her. *Take your time.* He set the bowl down. "Where are they?"

Emma looked at him now, her brows drawn in confusion, like she hadn't heard the question, or couldn't remember where she kept them—he wasn't sure which. He'd clearly knocked her off balance. Unlike most chicks he'd known, Emma didn't play coy. She seemed entirely unpracticed when it came to flirting and men. He felt protective even as he yearned to scale those walls.

A dilemma he wished his conscience hadn't raised.

"Sorry. Over here." She walked to another drawer, retrieved two sets, and returned. "We'll wear these while rolling the balls, too."

He quirked a brow and held up the glove. "Sounds kinky."

So much for his conscience.

Her cheeks bloomed red as strawberries against her creamy complexion. That thought gave him all kinds of ideas, because few things were better than mixing food and sex.

"I didn't, you shouldn't . . ." She shook her head and peered at him. "Stop it."

Grinning, Wyatt held up his hands. "Stop what? Stop having fun?"

"Stop flirting with me. Licking my finger and playing this game." She pointed that sweetened finger at him and narrowed her eyes. "I know about the little bet with Trip, so you can just stop right now. I'm not interested in you and your little sexual diversions."

Dammit. How'd she know about his conversation with Trip already? Could he play dumb and deny it? Or should he throw Trip under the bus? *Yeah, that.* The guy had stacked the odds against Wyatt with the bet, and then gone and told her. The injustice rankled because Wyatt's interest in Emma had nothing to do with that bet.

If anything, learning a little bit about her past only made her more admirable, and him more curious. "Hold on. I never made a bet with Trip. He proposed one, but I never shook on it."

She straightened her shoulders, hands on her hips, looking bossy. "I don't really care, Wyatt. Game over. So, if you want to help with this you can, or not. If you want to come to the care center tomorrow because you really want to, not because it's part of a plan, then you can come. But this," she gestured between them, "isn't happening."

"Okay." He told her what she wanted to hear, but her rejection had essentially laid down a challenge. That meant he'd probably just exert more effort to win.

He slid the gloves on his hands and went to work crumbling up the cake. He'd be pissed at Trip, except he guessed the guy was alerting her to the chance that Wyatt would seduce her with false promises. Trip needn't have bothered. Emma had never shown any real interest in Wyatt. All the tension he'd thought he felt between them had probably been more from scorn than attraction. Even now she resumed her work, apparently unaffected by his presence, lost in her own thoughts while she finished setting up the icing.

"Tell me something," Wyatt began, unable to pretend it didn't bug the shit out of him. "Why don't you like me?"

"Did you come to that conclusion simply because, unlike other women, I'm not jumping into your bed?" Emma slid the bowl of crumbled cake toward her and mixed it together with the icing. "I like you fine for someone I barely know. I'm just not interested in being the next notch on your bedpost."

"That's a big assumption . . . about me, I mean."

Emma cast an incredulous look his way before laughing. "Are you really going to stand there and pretend you haven't been with a hundred women, if not more? Don't bother, Wyatt. Your reputation precedes you."

"Reputations are usually exaggerated." He knew it. She'd written him off because of his past.

"Whatever." She paused, looking as if she were about to lay him out with a whopper of a statement, then reeled it in and shrugged. "Point is, I don't dislike you, but that doesn't mean I want to . . . be with you."

He noticed she didn't look at him when she said that last part. Could she be lying to him, or to herself? It might not matter, but he hated the way she'd thrown his reputation in his face, even if it wasn't really all that exaggerated. He'd never forced any woman to do anything she didn't want to do.

His mood shifted, veering toward irritation. If he wanted to get laid, he could find a dozen willing partners, none of whom would try to put him in his place.

"Who says I'm dying to be with you? Maybe I'm only looking to make things friendly around here this month. The pressure on me is pretty damn intense. Ryder's giving me attitude, Mari's up my ass, and you barely crack a smile around me. All I want is for everyone to be a little more positive and fun."

Emma frowned, pouring the contents of an industrial-size container of jimmies into a baking pan. "I'm sorry you feel that way. Normally my mom's here to help run the inn. Right now I'm responsible for everything, plus I have other obligations like," she stopped, almost as if she'd stopped herself from confessing something else, "the care center, things I have to do for my friend's engagement party, and so on. Compared to you, my pressure must look abysmally small, but that doesn't mean I'm not busy or without obligations. Everything isn't about you, least of all the reasons behind my behavior."

Once again, he'd been firmly put in his place. Based on her remarks, she thought he was an ego-driven athlete. In a town like this, she'd probably seen her fair share of those guys.

Heck, her own dad had walked out on her to pursue his dreams. That alone explained why she didn't trust men. Why she chose to hole up in this inn, repressing every womanly part of herself rather than letting her hair down. "Guess it's all been in my imagination, then."

Emma measured the rum, poured it into the goopy mess of cake crumbles and icing, and started mixing. "All what?"

"The way that you've been avoiding me since I arrived."

Emma's hands went up in the air. "How many times do I have to tell you? I'm not avoiding you. I'm working, Wyatt."

"Yet you have time to cozy up to Ryder." Wyatt bit the inside of his cheek, embarrassed by the sulky tone of his voice.

Emma inhaled exactly the same way his mom had done when he was a teen and annoying her. She slid the tray of jimmies between them and started rolling the cake balls. Apparently she liked to keep busy, no matter what else was going on. "I'm not cozying up to Ryder. But you've got a purpose, with your big goals and obligations. Your brother, on the other hand, seems a little lost. My heart goes out to him. I think he might like to be something other than a planet in your orbit."

Maybe she meant well, but like the baggage comment from earlier that morning, her explanation only set a fuse to his simmering temper.

"You make it sound like I'm some kind of dick that's dragging him around to be my gofer. That's not what's going on. I've dedicated the past couple years of my life to his recovery and helping my mom. I asked him to be part of this film for his sake as much as mine."

"Asked him, or commanded?" Her damn composure remained distant and efficient. "Because from where I'm standing, it doesn't look like he's excited about being part of this production or by what you're doing."

That jab landed like a punch to the jaw. She'd known Ryder for less than forty-eight hours. He'd known him for a lifetime. What the hell did she know, and yet, she had utter confidence in her conclusion. "For a girl who hides away in this inn under baggy clothes, you sure aren't shy with your opinions, are you, Emma?"

"If you don't want them, don't ask for them. You came into my space, not the other way around." She dipped her hand in to scoop another bit of the rum ball mixture. "But before you go, has it occurred to you that maybe seeing you getting back into competition hasn't just scared Ryder, maybe it's made him jealous? Maybe watching you doing something he'll probably never be able to do—not even for pleasure— makes him feel that loss more keenly?"

Wyatt's body practically recoiled at that thought. Ryder had liked boarding, much to their mother's chagrin. He'd wanted to be part of this world back then, so why not now? Just because he couldn't compete didn't mean he couldn't still participate in a meaningful way. Perhaps Ryder didn't believe it yet, but by the end of this film he would—unless Wyatt was totally wrong. His face must've reflected the discomfort he felt, because Emma stopped working and looked at him now, her expression suddenly full of empathy.

"Wyatt, I don't doubt your intentions where Ryder's concerned. It's obvious you love him and only want to help. All I'm suggesting is that perhaps the best way to help him move forward is to let him build a new life that isn't tied to yours, or to the sport you two shared before his injuries changed his life. I know his accident changed your life, too. But his is altered in ways neither of us can truly comprehend."

Now it was Wyatt's turn to avert his eyes. Emma's perception of Ryder had shaken Wyatt almost as much as the damned avalanche. No. He knew his brother. They shared a whole life together. He'd bet everything that, deep down, Ryder still wanted to be part of it. Just like with the physical therapy, Wyatt would push his brother to surpass everyone's expectations. It worked then, and it'd work now.

He didn't want to do or say anything more to Emma, nor did he want any more of her analysis. *Enough.* All he'd wanted from this evening had been a little flirtation and relaxation. Now he felt like he'd run the gauntlet and lost.

Wyatt stripped his latex gloves off and tossed them in the trash. "It's been a helluva long day. I need to rest."

He didn't look at her face before turning away and stalking out of the kitchen.

Chapter Seven

Emma threw the van into park in front of the care center. The Old English Tudor brick structure, with its cream-colored portico, looked quite charming amid the snow-laden fir trees. Its dining hall and many of the residents' rooms were located in the rear of the building, affording magnificent, long-range views of the craggy peaks of the San Juan Mountains. All things considered, this eldercare residence had its perks.

Her mind projected years ahead, to when she might call this place home. Given the state of her life so far—no siblings, nieces or nephews, or children of her own, and no prospects—she might find herself quite alone in her golden years. Alone and patiently waiting each week for a volunteer to keep her company, to ask about her past, to offer to play a hand of cards.

A touch of despair tickled its way down her spine, which she brushed away like an unwelcome spider.

Mari's van pulled in beside Emma, toting Wyatt and the crew. Each time she recalled last night's conversation with Wyatt—the lies feigning disinterest, the secrets she kept while judging his behavior—she wished she could disappear or fast-forward to the end of the month. Anything at all to avoid seeing him.

Of course, she'd faced him this morning at breakfast. To his credit, he'd been polite. She suspected he'd wanted to beg off coming to the care center, but once Emma got the go-ahead from the center's director, Mari had been convinced it would yield documentary gold.

Mari, however, was the least of Emma's concerns. Her most immediate problem: she simply detested this version of herself.

Three days ago, she'd been a normal person. A woman who'd fashioned a quiet, respectable life around a set of values that ensured she wouldn't hurt herself or anyone else. A rational woman who'd been eagerly anticipating an exciting—if secret—new chapter in her life. Then Wyatt had arrived, and she'd turned into a freak. A wary, judgy freak who kept butting her nose into the Lawson brothers' business, which she had no right to do. Worse, she'd become a freak who suddenly didn't feel as certain about all of her beliefs.

Glancing in the rearview mirror, she noticed the cameramen and Mari unloading their equipment, so Emma got out and retrieved the two large platters of rum balls from the back of her van. Wyatt came over to where she was wrestling the van's back doors while juggling the party trays.

"Let me take these." He took the treats from her so she could lock the doors. Like earlier in the morning, his manner remained polite but distant.

She owed him an apology. At some point today, she'd offer one and then, no matter what, she'd focus on the inn and her writing. Those were her only priorities—the realities of her life. She would not screw it all up by being in some kind of warped, self-destructive thrall to Wyatt flippin' Lawson.

Without exactly meeting his gaze, she said, "Ms. Henley, the executive director, said a few of the folks are quite thrilled about being in this documentary. Mrs. Ritter asked for help with her hair. Mr. Tomlin is wearing a bow tie! Normally he's in sweatpants and a pullover, but I always suspected he'd been quite dapper in his day. He's a big flirt, that one."

Although his head was bowed, Wyatt smiled, which made Emma's heart flutter like a baby bird testing new wings. She remembered how his cheerful smile had won her attention the first time she'd spotted him in that bar in Aspen. He'd lit the room, and that had filled her with warmth, just as it did right now.

She supposed some part of her pissy attitude toward him yesterday had stemmed from a perverted resentment that he *still* didn't remember her and Aspen—even as she thanked God for that fact.

It couldn't go on, this twisted resentment she carried. She'd chosen to be Alexa. To abandon her principles for a night of pleasure. Wyatt had no way of knowing that their night together had haunted and taunted her— tempted her—ever since. Or that, like her father, those sensations whispered dangerous thoughts that made her orderly world feel unfamiliar.

Wyatt remained clueless that his *renewed* presence in her life not only reminded her of the pleasure and freedom she'd experienced with him, but made her feel guilty about using those intimate moments as inspiration for a story.

No, Emma's scorn should be aimed toward herself. But before she could apologize for last night, Mari approached them.

Without sparing a polite glance at Emma, she said, "Wyatt, let's get an establishing shot of you and Ryder out here first. Perhaps Emma can go in ahead of us with Buddy and get things set up, get waivers signed and such. That way we can keep rolling the cameras as we enter the building so we can capture realistic reactions from people when they meet you."

"To the extent any of them care about this project, it's about being on camera, not about me. I bet very few of them even know who I am, so don't expect a big reaction."

"Some might not have heard of you before this morning, but they all know who you are now. That, plus your gorgeous face, guarantees some reaction." Mari smiled at him, chilling gesture that it was. The dark plum lipstick didn't help, either.

Not for the first time, Emma wondered if Mari's interest in Wyatt was more than professional.

"Fine." Wyatt extended the trays toward Emma. "Sorry. See you in a bit."

"Good luck." Knowing a bit about Wyatt's pride made Emma aware of how much he disliked being Mari's puppet. Like her, he also hated marketing himself. Empathy prompted a sincere smile, and for the first time in days, the tight knot of worry in her chest unwound enough to allow her to breathe easily.

She then caught sight of Ryder staring at the care center. Gone were the grim lines usually bracketing his mouth. His typically rigid posture softened into a casual slouch, as if his entire being had relaxed from the relief of not having to worry about Wyatt's safety today. She suspected his eyes might even be crinkled at the corners.

If only he could remove his sunglasses, it would help others better decipher his moods. As it stood, his debilitated nonverbal communication skills kept him somewhat alienated. The urge to help him heal pulled at her heart.

Yanking herself out of her reverie, she caught up to Buddy and went inside.

Ms. Henley was waiting for them in the antiseptic-smelling lobby, smoothing her sleek, silver hair. A peer of Emma's mother, Ms. Henley also had taken to the unfortunate habit of ruining the appearance of her business attire by wearing unattractive orthopedic shoes. Perhaps for Christmas this year, Emma would scour the Internet for better options and buy all of her elder acquaintances prettier footwear.

Ms. Henley smiled warmly, as she always did whenever volunteers came to entertain the residents. "Emma, are those your rum balls?"

"Of course. I suppose you'd like to sneak one or two before I take them into the rec room?" Emma set the trays on the information desk and got introductions out of the way. "Buddy, this is Director Henley." And then to Ms. Henley, she said, "Buddy has the waivers that you and the residents who are interested in participating need to sign. The rest of the crew is still outside taking some pictures and such. Can I take Buddy to the rec room?"

"Certainly," Ms. Henley said as she quickly scanned and signed a waiver. "We've asked those residents not interested in being in the film to avoid the rec room during the next ninety minutes."

"Perfect." Emma lifted the trays and led Buddy deeper into the facility. She expected a handful of folks to be waiting. Much to her surprise, at least thirty had decided to participate. Emma noticed the extra frisson of energy pulsing in the otherwise staid room.

Mari had been right. Unlike Emma, many people craved the spotlight. No doubt some of them would be talking about this day for months or years to come. A near-weepy kind of gratitude for Wyatt's offer to come crept up on her and pressed against her heart.

"Good afternoon, everyone. I must admit, I'm wondering why I don't inspire this kind of participation on a regular basis. Do you all have something against bingo?" she chuckled as she set the trays out on two tables. "This is Buddy. He's one of the cameramen, but before the crew can record anything, they need you to sign waivers granting permission to be filmed."

Quiet murmuring and head bobbing commenced as Buddy passed around the waivers. Moments later, Wyatt and Ryder entered the room, trailed by Mari and Jim. It took Emma ten seconds to remember that the cameras were rolling, and she'd better be on her best behavior.

"Everyone, this is Wyatt Lawson, an International World Games and Winter eXtreme Games slopestyle gold medalist." Emma grimaced. "Yikes, that's a tongue twister, isn't it?"

Some of the elderly clapped to welcome him, and Wyatt waved and nodded. Emma noticed Ryder standing off to the side. "His brother, Ryder Lawson, also a former competitor, is with us as well."

Another round of applause welcomed him, earning a rigid bow of his head.

"Good afternoon, everyone. I'm Mari, the director and producer of *Xtreme Transformation*. Thank you so much for consenting to participate today. We hope you have a little extra fun with us. Before Emma begins your normal activities, I wondered if any of you might have questions for Wyatt?"

"Actually," Wyatt interrupted, "I had a different idea. There're enough details about my story out there on the Web. I'm happy to answer any questions later, but right now I'd like to turn the tables a bit. I know why I'm here in one of the prettiest ski towns I've ever visited, but I'd like to know what brought you here, and what made you stay. And any other interesting things you'd like to share. So who wants to start?"

Sounds of hearty approval swept through the small crowd. Mari, on the other hand, looked like she'd been force-fed a handful of Sour Patch Kids. Luckily, she wiped her expression clean before it got caught on camera.

Emma had to hand it to Wyatt. He'd just made her beloved elderly friends' day by giving them the spotlight. His ego, while healthy, seemed more than willing to make room for others. Selfishly, she wished it weren't true. It'd be easier to keep her distance from a jerk, after all.

About two-thirds of the audience raised their hands, including Mrs. Pellman, who tossed Wyatt a very flirtatious smile from her wheelchair.

"Let's start with you, beautiful. What's your name?" Wyatt walked over and took a seat beside her.

"Oh my, young man. You are handsome!" came her emphatic, if warbled, remark.

Wyatt laughed and cocked his head, waiting for her to speak. Emma found herself becoming a little breathless, not only in anticipation of what might next tumble from Mrs. Pellman's mouth, but also from the way Wyatt so naturally made her the center of his attention.

"My name is Florence Pellman." She folded her hands neatly on her lap and nodded, like a stern teacher. "I was born in Denver in 1922, and I married my Bernie when I turned eighteen." She paused and extended a bony finger toward him. "He looked like you."

Emma watched Wyatt suppress a look of surprise. Based on old photographs she'd seen, Bernie Pellman had looked nothing like Wyatt except, perhaps, for having wavy, dark hair. Love *is* blind.

Mrs. Pellman continued, obviously savoring every second. "But Bernie had to go fight in the war right after we got married, so I went to work at the Denver Ordnance Plant, which made ammunition. It stayed open twenty-four hours a day. We were the only plant in the country that made .30 caliber ammunition." She fell silent as if to allow the rest of the room time to pay homage to this detail. "My friends and I worked all the time, doing our part for our men. I quit once Bernie came home safely. After all that battle, he wanted peace and quiet, so we left the city and moved here. We had four kids, Bernie Junior, Steven, Robert, and Maureen. I was married for *sixty-two years*, and now have twelve grandchildren and three great-grandchildren. Maureen lives here in town, but my boys all went to college in New York and Boston and stayed on the East Coast, so I don't see them very often . . . except on the FaceTime." She shrugged—a "what can you do" kind of gesture.

Wyatt nodded in approval. "That's pretty cool that you worked in the ammunition plant. I can't imagine what it must've been like during that war, especially with your husband off in battle."

Mrs. Pellman rested her hand on Wyatt's arm. "A scary time, but also a time of bravery and pride. A lot like your snowboarding, I guess." Then she winked at Wyatt.

"You're a charmer. I can see why Bernie was happily married for so long." Wyatt patted her hand and stood to give the floor to another resident.

Within thirty minutes, he'd found a way to engage everyone in the room. Some shouted out a quick bit of humor, others like Mrs. Pellman, took their time to tell a story. Emma had believed she'd known these men and women rather well. She'd spent hours playing games with them, remembering birthdays, reading aloud. Yet she'd never seen them all come alive together in this way, reminiscing and revealing the best parts of themselves. It heartened her in the same way seeing a crocus popping through the dirt after a long winter always did.

She noticed, too, that while the residents reminisced, Ryder had meandered over to Mr. Hartley, a quiet man with a prosthetic hand. Those two men now conversed in private at a small table, somewhat oblivious to their surroundings.

Once again, Ryder had taken himself out of his brother's world and attempted to create something of his own. Emma wished Wyatt could recognize what seemed so obvious to her, then reminded herself to stay out of it.

"We forgot one person." Wyatt's voice had risen above the din of casual conversation. His gaze swung around and landed squarely on Emma. "What do you say, Emma? Care to share your story with the world?"

Instinctively her hand flew up to shield her face from the camera. "Oh, no. I've got no story to tell. Everyone here knows me. I'm the least interesting person in the room." *And the biggest liar.*

"Is that so?" Wyatt turned a skeptical face toward the crowd. "If Emma won't speak for herself, maybe you all can share some information about her with me. I've always believed that the quietest people keep the biggest secrets. So tell me, what's Emma hiding?"

"Emma Duffy has nothing to hide! She's a lovely young lady," Mr. Tomlin said. "And she bakes like an angel."

"High praise." Wyatt stared at Emma, brow cocked playfully.

Emma curtsied, hoping her knees didn't buckle. Good grief, it's like Wyatt had some kind of ESP or something. Biggest secrets indeed.

And now she'd made Mr. Tomlin complicit in her deceit simply by not correcting his assumptions. *Nothing to hide?* Oh, wouldn't they all be shocked speechless if they got their hands on a copy of *Steep and Deep*? No doubt they'd blame "that damn William Duffy."

"Emma's good people." Mrs. Ritter glanced at Mrs. Pellman.

"Very thoughtful, too," Mrs. Pellman clucked, then she peered at Wyatt. Emma could tell by the sudden, dreamy look in her old eyes that talking about her Bernie had revived her romantic spirit. "Do you have a girlfriend?"

Oh, no! No, no, no. Emma could not be subjected to matchmaking by her octogenarian friends. *My word, what a nightmare.* Of course, on the heels of that thought came another involuntary one: *This could make a funny scene in my current story.* She stifled a snort of laughter and wondered, suddenly and quite stupidly, if she'd missed Wyatt's answer.

"No time for a girlfriend." Wyatt didn't look anywhere near Emma's vicinity, she noticed. His statement should both please and relieve her, but it didn't.

Andy hadn't been completely wrong the other day. Emma *did* want what Avery and Kelsey had with their soon-to-be husbands. Unlike them, however, she'd never been sought after.

She'd been the sidekick. The girl guys would talk to about the other girls they liked. The one who'd lend her class notes to her crush to borrow or let him cheat off her on a test. Who'd bake him cookies when he was sick—cookies he'd then share with the girl *he* liked.

And yet, despite constant romantic frustration as a young teen, she'd remained steadfast in her belief that, one day, her genuine kindness and devotion would be valued. She'd been certain Mr. Right would see past her more ordinary face and body, and then he'd fall to his knees and profess his undying love.

Ha! She laughed at herself, because that romantic notion of youth had been tarnished slowly, because her life had been commandeered by her mom and her responsibilities at the inn. She'd never broken rules, sneaked out, or done any of the other rebellious things her friends had. Partly because it wasn't in her nature, and partly because she never wanted to risk sending her mother back over the edge.

Spending so much time managing her mom's postdivorce depression had seriously hampered Emma's ability to relate to and trust men, too. Worse, maybe her mom's harping on the evils of men and sex had made her a tiny bit bitter. Could that be why she'd treated Wyatt's supposed interest like a felony instead of flattery?

Wyatt continued talking about why he wasn't dating. "I'll be traveling around the world this winter, assuming I qualify for the bigger competitions. Life on the road isn't the best recipe for a relationship."

Mrs. Pellman waved a disgusted hand in his face. "Pish posh. You young people think you have forever to figure this stuff out. But before you know it, you'll wonder how life went by so fast. You'll wonder why you didn't spend more time with people and less time at work or on those gizmos everyone always has in their hands. I swear, every time my Maureen takes me out to dinner, all I see are people sitting around tables ignoring each other to look at Snapface."

"Snapchat?" Wyatt offered.

"It's all tomfoolery, no matter what you call it. It isn't real." Mrs. Pellman leaned toward Wyatt. "Why don't you want something *real*?"

Wyatt rocked back, hands raised in surrender. "I never said I didn't."

"You have a bit of scoundrel about you yet. Still wondering if the grass is greener somewhere else?" The old woman shook her head then reached for Wyatt's hand. "I gardened for fifty years, and let me tell you one thing: Grass is only green when you tend to it night and day. You remember that, young man."

Rather profound of Mrs. Pellman. Wyatt looked a little out of his depth at this point, so Emma rushed in to his rescue, thankful that the conversation had veered away from her and her secrets.

"Okeydoke. On that note, I think it's time for bingo. Today's prize is a home-cooked meal of your choice by *moi*. Who's in?"

Emma's heart swelled when everyone's hand shot into the air. She may not have Kelsey's beauty or Avery's brains, but she could cook, and she had the affection of these wonderful, wise men and women. The opinions of those who'd lived long enough to see what matters most were special to her, even if those opinions didn't keep her warm at night.

"For such a wholesome girl, I'm surprised you encourage this sinful bit of gambling," Wyatt teased, disappointed he'd failed to dig up any tidbit about Emma from the old folks.

"It's hardly gambling." She cocked a single, red brow in challenge. "More like a raffle."

"Raffles are a form of gambling. And if you need proof that gambling is a sin, consider the fact that all the numbers on a roulette wheel add up to 666." He crossed his arms triumphantly.

"Only someone very familiar with sinning would know that bit of trivia." Emma quipped, her eyes sparkling. His heart pinged when she played along, and he wished very much that they weren't in a room full of people and cameras. He shouldn't continue the banter with Mari and the crew filming, but he was powerless to stop himself from seeing where it might lead. He simply needed to know.

"Life without any sin is boring, Saint Emma." Wyatt watched her eyes narrow before he smiled and glanced around the small crowd clutching their bingo cards. "Don't you all agree?"

"I do!" exclaimed Mrs. Ritter, then she and her cronies tittered.

"You know what? I'm feeling lucky." Wyatt turned back to Emma. "Where's my card?"

"What?" Emma asked.

"Don't I get to play?" Wyatt noticed Mari staring at him while whispering something to Jim. "I'd like a home-cooked meal."

Wyatt heard Mrs. Pellman let out a little cluck behind him.

"I'm already cooking for you every night this month, saint that I am." Emma's smug expression amused him.

"Maybe I'll come back some other time to collect." Wyatt surprised himself with the comment, and then felt his cheeks heat when Mr. Tomlin muttered to someone else behind him, "Not a bad line, if I do say so myself."

Mari whispered to Jim, who then focused the camera on Emma's face.

Wyatt shouldn't continue to flirt with Emma. He knew enough about her to realize she preferred to blend into the background. He just wanted . . . something from her. Something she kept withholding. Something he suspected would be remarkable if he could only experience it for himself.

Not surprisingly, Emma played it cool and handed him a bingo card without retort, which suggested she had noticed Mari's piqued interest also. Wyatt sat beside Mrs. Pellman, who whispered conspiratorially, "I wanted to win, but now I hope you do."

He didn't win. That honor went to Mr. Tomlin, who couldn't have looked happier than if he'd won a gold medal.

"When will you make me dinner? Do I get to come to the inn, or do I have to eat it here?" Mr. Tomlin's inflection proved his strong preference for a road trip. "Will you be joining me, too?"

Wyatt couldn't blame the man. Living confined to a place like this, filled with aging, sometimes sickly, older people, must get stifling. Even without that context, a quiet meal with Emma held appeal, too. At least it would if she acted with him as she did around most other people.

Emma smiled. "Of course I'll join you, Mr. Tomlin, but let's push it off until after Wyatt and his crew leave. We'll talk later about what you'd like, and then we'll pick a date. I'll speak with Ms. Henley about getting you over to the inn. Sound good?"

"I can't wait." Mr. Tomlin sat back and adjusted his bow tie. "I need to think about what I want to eat. Something I haven't had in a long while. Something I can't get here."

"The sky's the limit." Emma collected the bingo cards. The sunlight filtered through the plate glass window, casting her in a golden glow. Saint Emma did look a bit angelic just then, goodwill flowing off her in waves, warming those in her path even more than the sun's rays. Wyatt felt himself straining toward her like a sunflower. "It looks like our time is almost up today."

"When will the movie be on TV?" Mrs. Ritter asked.

"We'll air part one in January, just before the first qualifier," Mari replied. "Then, depending on how Wyatt does, we'll follow him through the competition season and air part two after that."

Depending on how Wyatt does. A reminder of the uncertain road ahead.

He rubbed his knee absently, mind racing. With Trip's help, he should get through this month of training without being buried by another avalanche. But could Trip help him learn to read the terrain better, and quickly? Would it be enough for him to qualify for bigger competitions, or would he fall on his face—literally and figuratively—effectively ending his competition days and hopes of future film deals and big sponsor money.

He looked up to find Emma staring at his hand on his knee, her brows knitted together. Whatever part of him itched to know her better, he needed to squelch it. He'd come to this town for one purpose.

Forcing himself not to flirt, Wyatt stood and wandered off. He'd done his best to engage the seniors and give Mari the footage she needed, but now he wanted to fade away and regroup.

Earlier he'd noticed the way Ryder had disengaged from the video in order to become more involved with just one resident—a disabled man. Memories of Emma's accusations that Ryder had changed his mind about this comeback adventure, that he was being forced to relive his accident and subsequent losses, replayed.

Throughout Ryder's recovery, Wyatt had focused on his brother's physical progress. With each milestone—sitting, standing, walking, talking—Wyatt had breathed a new sigh of relief. He'd believed each step brought them closer to the way things used to be.

Now Wyatt had the chance to work on his brother's mental and emotional progress. Shadows and gaps existed now that made navigating their relationship more complicated, but no more insurmountable than the many snowboard tricks Wyatt had mastered during his life.

Surely Ryder wanted that connection back, too. They'd always connected best through this sport, this world they both loved—the mountains, the competition circuit, all of it. Ryder didn't have to lose it all just because he couldn't compete. He could still be an invaluable player. Hell, if Ryder "needed to be needed," then he needn't look further than his brother. Besides, Wyatt couldn't let go of this plan for reviving Ryder's spirit because, if this didn't work, he had no plan B. And settling for Ryder living the rest of his life so detached was not an option.

He watched Ryder's shoulders tense as he approached him. "Mind if I join you two? I'm Wyatt."

Ryder merely shrugged.

"Marcus Hartley." The elderly man gestured to an empty chair. "Your brother was telling me about the avalanche. You got lucky!"

"That's one way to look at it." Wyatt hadn't felt very lucky yesterday.

Marcus held up his prosthetic hand, grinning. "When you're dealt a blow, you learn to look for silver linings."

"Great perspective." Wyatt wondered if Marcus had made an impact on Ryder. "I've hired a guide for the rest of the month, so hopefully that won't happen again. I'm not too proud to ask for help, which is why I've asked Ryder to be part of this process. I can't do it without him and his support."

Ryder snorted. "Don't try to s-snow me."

"It's not a con, Ryder." Wyatt backhanded his brother's arm.

"Brothers," Marcus mused. "You're lucky to have each other."

"I know." Wyatt glanced at Ryder and then back to Marcus. "We always trained together. He knows my strengths and weaknesses better than anyone. I need his input. I want him to tell me what I'm doing wrong, just like he used to. I rely on him to keep me on track."

Ryder looked at Wyatt for a long moment. Did he remember the way it had been? The way Ryder had been at least as good as their coach at pointing out Wyatt's flaws—anticipating them, even? At encouraging

Wyatt to overcome them? He must've remembered something because he nodded at Wyatt, signaling an agreement.

Finally, a breakthrough. Wyatt felt a smile tug at his mouth as he wrapped an arm around Ryder's shoulder. "Thanks, brotha'."

The weight Wyatt had been shouldering since last night lifted, making him feel lighter and more optimistic than he had since he'd arrived in Sterling Canyon. He'd prove to himself, Ryder, and Emma that this was the right direction for both Lawson brothers.

Emma—a puzzle. Goodness incarnate, if these people were to be believed. But he'd seen another side to her. A testy side. And no one was perfect. So why did Emma need to project this perfect image to everyone except for him? What was it about him that brought out a prickly side?

Wyatt stopped listening to Marcus and Ryder's conversation so he could watch her now, her red hair casually hanging around her face in long layers. Her clothes were neither baggy nor tight. Neither sexy nor sexless. Dark denim jeans that clung to shapely legs. A crisp, blue-and-green striped top, unbuttoned just below the notch in her neck. Silver hoop earrings and a matching bracelet. Fresh and appealing in her own subtle way. Just looking at her stirred him deep down, where a steady hum vibrated.

He'd like to strip her down, literally and figuratively, but the timing wasn't right. He'd just gotten his brother on his side. Tomorrow he'd meet up with Trip and learn to tackle the backcountry before moving on to Crested Butte next month to prepare for the qualifier that would take place there in January.

Wyatt wouldn't trade his adventurous life for anything, although the past few days had forced him to acknowledge a certain grace in a simpler kind of life. But no matter what happened here in Sterling Canyon, he'd be cruising out of this town soon. For all of her intriguing mystery and physical appeal, Emma Duffy would become just another girl he used to know.

It'd be better for both of them if he followed her lead and kept his distance. Even as he thought it, his eyes sought her out, and he was oddly happier for a glimpse of her reading to Mrs. Ritter.

Chapter Eight

Emma worked quickly, stuffing small boxes with signed author copies of *Steep and Deep* and other goodies to send to a few of her Facebook followers in exchange for early reviews. She handwrote notes to each, thanking them for taking a chance on a new author, and then prayed that they'd enjoy her story.

If she spent any time thinking about reviews, her mouth got pasty, her palms damp. One would think that growing up with a fault-finding mother would make it easier for her to handle the idea of negative reviews. While Emma dealt with criticism better than some, it still stung. The fact that, after a day or two of curling up in a ball, she could turn negative feedback into a means of motivation didn't mean it never hurt. It always hurt.

She'd recently read advice from other authors that warned not to read reviews, or not to take them to heart, or promised any review is only the opinion of one person, not a wholesale assessment of a writer's skill. Yet, Emma couldn't quite rectify how to dismiss bad reviews as insignificant while accepting good ones as true (or using them as marketing tools). At this point, she could only hope to receive more good ones than bad ones.

And what she should be stressing about was the work-in-progress, which was going nowhere. It had become intolerable to try to create fake scenes about Dallas while his alter ego rambled around the inn, throwing off testosterone and flirty smiles.

Knock, knock.

Emma froze before she remembered she'd locked her bedroom door. "Who is it?"

"Wyatt."

Instinctively, she stretched her body to conceal the books. The cover art, which featured a shirtless Dallas, taunted her, making her question once more where the line between privacy and hypocrisy could be drawn. "Just a second!"

She shoved the box of books under her bed and placed the packages in her closet.

What could Wyatt want? Ever since the care center visit earlier this week, they'd politely addressed each other while minimizing personal contact. Contrary to her wishes, the intentional indifference only enhanced her tension and longing. Now here he was standing outside her bedroom near midnight?

Crossing the room while double-checking to ensure no visible trace of Alexa remained, she pressed her fingers to the beating pulse in her neck before opening her door a crack. "Is something wrong?"

"No." He tried to peer into her room, but she'd wedged herself into the opening. "I'm hungry, but I didn't want to use the kitchen without permission. I saw the light on under your door or I wouldn't have knocked."

"Oh." Seeing him standing in the dark hallway inspired another fantasy—one of him playfully holding up a jar of honey before forcing his way into her room and locking the door behind him. He had, after all, enjoyed using food as a form of foreplay.

Fortunately, he hadn't noticed the awkward pause caused by yet another daydream, because his gaze had dropped to her feet and stuck there. She looked down and stifled a groan. Apparently he'd never seen a grown woman wearing plush bunny slippers. Fur-lined stilettos were more likely his preference. "You can grab a snack if you'd like. I've got plenty of fruit and cereal on hand."

He shook his head and leaned against the doorjamb, crowding her. She detected a faintly spicy scent, which brought back another visceral memory of collapsing against his shoulder and nestling her face close to his neck. Her eyelids suddenly felt heavy from the heavenly recollection.

"I'm hungry." He shifted his weight to his other foot. "I want hot food, and I don't know where you keep stuff."

Midnight cooking had never been part of the deal, but Wyatt looked tired and helpless. He'd been pushing himself all week with Trip. Thankfully, the past four days had come and gone without incident.

Resigned to her fate, she stepped into the hall, chenille robe wrapped tightly around her body.

"Let's go see what I can whip up." Emma admitted to herself that she enjoyed feeding others. Food comforted. It lingered. It aroused the senses, as he well knew. She rather looked forward to comforting him in this safe way. "How about poached eggs, sliced avocados with cayenne pepper, and a little multigrain toast?"

"Sounds awesome." His hazel eyes twinkled, sending her heart aloft like a hot air balloon. What might it be like to have him look at her like that every day? The juvenile wish made her give herself a mental eye roll. *Honestly.* As if he wouldn't lose that intrigued look by week two, or sooner. "Thanks."

Unlike her, Wyatt wasn't wearing silly slippers or fuzzy pajamas. His thin sweatpants hung low on his hips. A fitted, long-sleeved shirt clung to the defined muscles of his shoulders, arms, and chest. As usual, he exuded some kind of magnetic pull, making her body whirr with yearning.

What she couldn't quite decide was whether it had to do with Wyatt, per se, or with the fact that he represented her one and only experience of breaking from societal expectations. Or maybe it was because she'd spent hundreds of hours with "Dallas." Had she now confused her book's hero with the real man, who would surely be more flawed than the fictional character? Still, she felt like the heroine in her book now, walking beside Wyatt, her pulse kicking about, her skin prickly with heat.

As they made their way along the shadowy hallway to the creaky stairs, Wyatt asked, "Would you be a little afraid to be alone in this big house?"

Suppressing a giggle, she glanced over her shoulder. "No."

"You don't think spirits hang out with all this old stuff?" He slid a sideways glance at a headdress near the landing.

She stopped, midstride. "Do you believe in ghosts?"

"Maybe. Back in Vermont there's Emily's Bridge, which is really the Gold Brook Bridge in Stowe. But people say a girl named Emily has been haunting it since the '60s." Wyatt shrugged, utterly serious. "Haven't you ever had the feeling that something else was in the room with you? Felt a shift in energy?"

Given the gravity of his hushed tone, she had to consider it. "If I have, I probably assumed it was the heat kicking on or a draft from the old windows." Emma kept walking toward the kitchen, thankful Mari's stupid cameras, which looked a little spooky at night, weren't rolling. "I wouldn't have taken you for someone who believes in haunted houses."

"You mock me."

"No. It's just . . . there's no proof they exist."

"There's no proof that God exists, either, yet most people believe in Him." Wyatt grinned. "Based on the cross in my room, I'd guess that includes you."

Emma frowned, imagining her mother's horror at the comparison. "I suppose I can see the analogy."

"They say ghost activity is more prevalent around kids and people with high energy. You're pretty calm and reserved. Maybe that's why you don't feel them."

She shot him a droll look as she punched open the kitchen door. "Are you saying I'm too boring to haunt?"

"No! Sorry, I didn't mean it that way." Wyatt stopped chuckling, his expression turning solemn. "I don't think you're boring at all, Emma. In fact, you're rather interesting."

"Yeah, right." Emma snorted and pointed at a stool, upon which Wyatt then parked his cute butt. She proceeded to the refrigerator to collect most of the items she'd need, then grabbed an egg-poaching pan. *Interesting?* Not a word ever associated with her, and she knew it. He'd say anything to get in her pants. *Men.*

"Why don't you believe me?" Wyatt yawned.

"Um, that yawn, for starters." She sliced a thick piece of bread for the toaster.

"You're not boring me, I'm just exhausted from training all week."

"Then let me feed you so you can get some sleep." Emma cracked two eggs in the pan and then quickly dissected an avocado and fanned the slices onto a plate. She could feel Wyatt watching her work, but wouldn't risk looking at him. If she met his gaze, he might see something in her eyes. Something that would tell him how much she liked his company. That would reveal how lonely she could get, and how something as simple and nonsexual as this quiet conversation could mean so much. So much that her heart fairly ached from it.

"You can change the subject, but I meant what I said. Some people have bold personalities, others create things, and a few make fashion statements." Wyatt pointedly glanced at her slippers with a grin, then his expression turned serious. "You are like an unsolved mystery. You may be quiet, but when you speak you never hold back. You're sharp and certain despite your shyness. The contrast is what's so interesting, and I'm sure there's much more I haven't even seen."

Emma clasped the opening of her robe, suddenly feeling quite exposed. She averted her gaze and checked the eggs, buttered his toast, and sprinkled cayenne over the plate. Only his gentle snicker made her look up.

"I've embarrassed you." He looked at her, handsome as ever in the still of night, his haunting, green-brown eyes glowing. "But it's true. Wish I had more time to get to know you better, Emma. Something tells me I'm really missing out."

Her chest throbbed, almost as if preparing for her to weep, which made no sense. Who cried in the face of a compliment? But the pang deepened.

"Thanks." Not trusting herself to get too close, Emma slid the plate toward him without budging her feet. Uncomfortable being the center of anyone's attention, let alone his, she deflected in an effort to resume control over her emotions. "Seems like you've had several great training days since the avalanche. I guess having Ryder participate is helping you. He's handling it all better than before, too."

"I knew he'd be fine once he jumped in. Just needed a little push to get past his anxiety."

While Wyatt cut into his meal, Emma wondered if Ryder was just putting on a good show for his brother. She kept her suspicions to herself this time, for a change.

After swallowing a mouthful of food, Wyatt glanced up with a satisfied smile. Emma's chest tightened again because she'd made him smile. Well, her food had, anyway. "This is excellent. Love the kick from the pepper."

"Thank you." Emma proceeded to clean the pan and counter while Wyatt ate. Maybe she didn't excite him quite like Alexa had, but she could give him comfort. She'd always been good at giving people that much, and she knew it to be the more lasting, reliable way to prove one's feelings. In today's Tinder world, sex often didn't mean much, but friendship still did. "How's Trip working out? I bet he loves being filmed."

Wyatt nodded. "He does. He's a damn amazing skier, too. It's easier for smaller guys like me to pull off certain kinds of tricks, but he's got no fear. Shoots right off the edge of anything. Rarely screws up, although he had a massive yard sale this week. Mari loved it."

"Why?" Emma thought about how much Kelsey would hate to see Trip tumble. Mostly because she'd worry about his safety, but also because she'd know his pride had been wounded. If Mari made Trip look bad in this film, Kelsey would be furious. In a showdown between Kelsey and Mari, Emma's money would be on Kelsey.

"I get the feeling my story isn't enough for her. She needs the film to be popular, so she craves drama to make it more exciting. Keeps pestering me for really personal information, too." He shook his head and brought his plate to the sink. "Maybe I'm paranoid. I haven't had the best luck with reporters and media."

"I always thought you were quite the media darling, with your good looks and talent." The words slipped past her lips before she'd thought about the implication.

Wyatt turned slowly and stared at her, head slightly cocked.

"Good looks, huh?" When a slow smile spread across his face, her heart swelled. If he tried to kiss her now, she'd let him. That truth shot heat to her cheeks. *Shoot.* At this rate, she'd never make it through the next three weeks without giving in to temptation. "But media darling is not near true. When I'd win a medal, all the coverage would be positive. Otherwise, people looked for controversy, and if they couldn't find it, they'd stir some up. Prod for competition between Ryder and me, hoping to uncover a rift. Or they'd paint me as a party boy, drinking and carousing my way through resorts."

Emma bit back a remark about him and partying. She'd seen him in that element, despite the fact that he didn't remember. Had it ever been fair to paint him with one brush when his entire teen and early adulthood had consisted almost entirely of significant accomplishments and rewards? After all, what twenty-two-year-old wouldn't have loved celebrating his win in a bar full of adoring women? But maybe he'd changed a bit in the three years since then.

"That kind of coverage always bothered my mom, so I really can't have it now, when she's still coming to terms with Ryder's injuries. This film has to be about the work, the sport, the comeback. Not about me and Ryder, or drinks or girls or any of that. Maybe I'm paranoid, but having Mari looking over my shoulder all the time makes me nervous."

Watching Wyatt this past week had given her another perspective. One she was glad she hadn't known before she created Dallas. Here, in real life, he'd shown discipline, a willingness to admit mistakes, commitment, and love for his brother. For a guy of only twenty-five, he seemed to be maturing. And like her, his mother mattered to him. He didn't want to be the cause of her pain, which was another thing they shared in common.

Emma suddenly envisioned a nightmare scenario where her pen name was discovered and publicized. Although that wouldn't make headlines or raise eyebrows anywhere outside of Sterling Canyon, the mere thought of being gossip fodder sent a shiver straight through her.

"You okay?" Wyatt asked, having obviously noticed her sudden stillness.

"Yes." It was time to break the spell and go to their separate rooms. Of course, she didn't really want to go back to her room alone. She could've stayed there and talked all night. Each little peek into his personality left her wanting more. She'd started to like him, and that wouldn't do. Not with her secrets. And not with the way he tempted her to abandon all caution.

And then, because he looked skeptical and she didn't want questions, she said, "Don't worry. No ghost passed through me, either. Now, if you're finished, I think we both need some rest. You've got yoga in less than six hours, and I've got a really busy day tomorrow."

"The party?" Wyatt asked, falling in beside her as they crossed the kitchen and made their way to the stairs. They weren't touching, but she could feel him anyway. Her body seemed to pitch toward him, eager for any accidental touch.

Trip must've mentioned the engagement party to Wyatt. "Yes. On top of my other obligations, I've got to finish and deliver the party cupcakes, too. Tomorrow night you'll be on your own if you get hungry after dinner."

That thought made her a little sad. She might prefer to cook Wyatt eggs than attend a loud party, except that this was one of her best friend's parties, and she truly did want to celebrate Kelsey's joy.

"Will it be a big event?" Wyatt asked.

"Depends on your definition. There'll only be about fifty guests, but it will be an all-out affair. Kelsey's dreamed of getting married since I've known her. She just got engaged on Halloween and is already moving full steam ahead."

"Afraid Trip will get cold feet?"

"No. She just wants to get on with it and start a family." Emma shrugged. Hopefully the marriage would last longer than the engagement. Truthfully, despite Emma's mother's tales of her courtship with Emma's dad, Emma had no real memory of whether her dad had ever been as wild about her mom as Trip seemed to be about Kelsey. "You kind of have to know her to get it, I suppose. She's quite the romantic. Always has been."

"Are you going with Andy?" Wyatt's casual tone caused her to pause.

"No. He'll probably catch a ride with Avery and Grey." She noticed Wyatt had begun to follow her up to the third floor. "You missed your stop."

"I'll walk you to your door so I can ward off surprise ghost attacks." He winked, so she didn't argue. He hadn't been flirting, yet the hairs on her neck tingled in anticipation of something she couldn't quite define. Might he try to kiss her? Suddenly she wished she'd grabbed the honey pot from the pantry. *Oooh, bad, bad Emma.* Then again, her mom wasn't around to notice the messy sheets or missing honey. Maybe they could be together again without anyone getting hurt.

When they arrived at her room, Wyatt said, "Trip invited me to the party. How about we go together?"

Stunned and—ridiculous as it might be—a wee bit disappointed he hadn't stolen a kiss, her mind blanked. "S-sure."

"Perfect." Wyatt flashed that brilliant, toothy smile, and for a second, she wanted to rescind her consent, sensing the growing danger of socializing with him in public. Alexa had been aloof and detached, playing a game. But Emma's soul had always been a bit like an open wound, absorbing everything and often smarting. She may put on a brave face, but her heart had no shield against Wyatt Lawson. "It's a date."

Before she could refute that designation, he added, "Thanks for the late-night snack, Emma. Sweet dreams."

Then he turned and jogged down the stairs, leaving her yearning for something she absolutely should not be considering.

She waited until she heard his door close before going into her room and collapsing on her bed. Touching her palm to her cheek, the warmth in her face didn't surprise her. In the silence, her heartbeat pounded out an upbeat tempo. Restlessly she shifted, her hands now brushing across her tightening breasts and down her stomach.

Flushed and heated, she rolled over and pulled the box of books from under her bed. After staring at the cover, she turned to page forty-two—the first of the good parts—and began reading, except this time it was Wyatt, not Dallas, coming to life.

Wyatt slid his arms into the sleeves of his brother's gray blazer. "Thanks for the loan. I hadn't packed anything this nice."

Ryder shrugged. "It's a little long on you."

Bluntness—one of the consequences of Ryder's TBI.

"You love any excuse to remind me that you're taller than me, don't you?" Wyatt teased.

Ryder shrugged. "Maybe."

"You sure you don't want to come. Trip said it'd be fine." Wyatt adjusted his shirt collar. "Wouldn't you like a night out? Like old times."

"Crowds and music give me headaches now." Ryder's mouth set in a firm line, and Wyatt immediately regretted his thoughtless remark.

"I feel lousy leaving you here alone. What will you do?"

"I'm going to a p-pottery class."

Wyatt's head snapped toward his brother. "Pottery?"

"Emma suggested it because it's peaceful and might fire up the creative parts of my brain." Ryder glanced at the platter of snacks by his bed. "She also made me some food after she got back from delivering all those cupcakes."

"She's full of surprises," Wyatt said, discomfited by the fact that Emma and Ryder still had private conversations.

"She's nice." Ryder looked at Wyatt. "Don't . . ."

"Don't what?" Wyatt's shoulders stiffened.

"You know." Ryder peered over the top of his sunglasses, something he rarely did. Seeing a hint of his brother's blue eyes fixed on him set Wyatt back a step. "Don't treat her like one of your g-groupies."

Unexpected. Wyatt almost asked if Ryder had a crush on her, but he stopped himself. He told himself he didn't want to embarrass his brother, but the truth was, he didn't want to know. Preserving his ignorance might lessen whatever guilt he would feel if something were to develop between him and Emma, which Wyatt could no longer pretend he didn't want to explore, even if it meant taking chances right under Mari's nose.

"I don't think she's the one you need to worry about. She barely tolerates me." He cocked an eyebrow. At least that statement had been truthful. Hell, for all he knew, Emma liked Ryder. She certainly took more interest in him. A scowl seized Wyatt's face.

"I didn't think you'd go out this month, w-with training and all." Ryder didn't hide the censure in his tone.

"I won't drink or stay out late. I just need to take a break from thinking about competition."

"What will you do about Mari?" Ryder asked.

"What about Mari?"

"I heard her talking to Jim. She wants s-some of this on film. 'Human interest' stuff, social life and possible romantic undertones," he finished, trying to imitate Mari's clipped voice.

"Oh, shit. Emma will freak. I've got to put a stop to that." He slapped Ryder's shoulder. "See you when I get home."

Wyatt strode across the lobby to where Mari stood with a camera-ready Jim. Holding up his hand, he said, "Stop!"

Mari tossed Jim a look that warned him not to go far. "Wyatt, you need to let me do my job."

"This documentary is about my comeback, not my personal life." Wyatt rested his hands on his hips, feeling uncomfortable in the jacket.

"This documentary is about you," Mari replied. "You are the reason people will want to watch it. Yes, the comeback story is the anchor, but you are the subject. So if you choose to do charity work, or if you go on a date with a girl you meet along the journey, like it or not, that is part of your story."

"Emma never agreed to having her life and friends exploited." He raked his hand through his hair. "Please, Mari. Besides, this isn't a date. We were both invited to the same party. We're just driving over together. That's it."

True statement, although a part of him hoped for something more, even though he knew he shouldn't.

He heard Jim clear his throat. When he glanced over, he saw the camera light on. Jim had started taping despite Wyatt's protest. Wyatt rotated further and saw Emma descending the stairs. His jaw sagged open, and Mari and Jim faded into the background as he took in the gorgeous vision in emerald green.

Gone was the nondescript clothing she'd worn for the past week. Her fitted dress had some kind of sheer overlay and sleeves, embellished with an occasional pop of beading. She'd pulled the front sections of her hair back in sparkly combs, and styled the rest into long, loopy curls that softly framed her face. The short skirt of her dress revealed toned thighs and calves that tapered into classic nude pumps.

Glossy lipstick clung to her lips, which were plump and kissable and made his body temperature spike. Her green eyes looked brighter surrounded by a hint of charcoal liner. Although everything about her still retained a demure tone, she looked sexy and womanly and very, very tempting. An odd sense of déjà vu passed through his mind, as if he'd seen her this way before, but it passed before he could pinpoint it.

"Driving over together my ass," Mari muttered for his ears only.

He shot her an irritated glance before turning back to Emma. "You look beautiful."

She did, and again he wished no one were around so he could tempt her, test her, touch her. The need raged inside, but he tamped it down.

Emma flashed a nervous smile. "Thanks. I didn't expect to see you in a jacket."

Wyatt tugged at the lapel. "Stole it from my brother."

Emma offered Jim and his camera an awkward wave. "Just don't steal the spotlight from Kelsey. This is her night."

"If it gets bad, I'll hide out in the corner," Wyatt promised, reaching for her hand. When she clasped it, his whole body came alive. For a second, he didn't move, shocked by the fact that he'd reached for her, and that she'd let him. A sweet victory indeed.

"It's fine to capture whatever you want on film here," Emma said, "but you cannot come to the party. I won't let you usurp my best friend's special night."

"Fine." Mari's eyes narrowed slightly. "It must feel rather good, going to this party on the arm of a celebrity instead of going solo."

The pointed remark appeared to bounce right off Emma. "What feels great is going out to celebrate one of the happiest occasions in my friend's life."

Wyatt couldn't help but wink at her and her deft maneuvering around Mari's loaded question. Still holding her hand, he gestured toward the door with his other one. "Shall we go?"

"Yes." On their way out, she glanced over her shoulder at Mari. "Don't wait up."

Wyatt held her elbow as they made their way around the remnants of ice and snow in the parking lot. "Look at you, taking potshots at Mari. I always suspected your 'nice girl' routine was a cover."

"Don't equate nice with pushover. There is a difference." Emma looked to where his hand held her arm and gently eased out of his grip. "That woman grates on my nerves. She's so bossy."

When they arrived at her old VW Passat, she pointed at the passenger seat. "I'll drive."

Wyatt covered a grin. Apparently Emma didn't see her own bossy streak, but he'd best not raise it now. "I've never been to an engagement party, or a friend's wedding, but I bet you don't know why people wear wedding rings on the fourth finger of their left hand."

"Tradition."

"Yes, but it started because people used to think that the vein from that finger led straight to the heart." He drew a line from his finger up his arm and to his heart.

Emma smiled in a way that suggested she thought him—with his ghost stories and fun facts—a little endearing. "Why do you know all this trivia?"

Wyatt shrugged. "I'm curious, and Google makes it easy to learn weird facts about everyday stuff."

Within minutes, they arrived at Smuggler's Notch, an upscale renovated restaurant and bar.

"So who are the key players, besides Trip and his fiancée?"

"Kelsey's the queen of the night. I doubt I even have to tell you what she looks like because you'll notice her straightaway. She's sort of a pinup girl, and will likely be on Trip's arm for most of the night. Trip's partner, Grey, and his fiancée, Avery, whom you met last Sunday, will be here, too." She paused, as if giving a moment of silence to his near miss with that avalanche, which neither of them wanted to dwell upon. "I think Trip's dad flew in this weekend, and Kelsey's family. Then some friends from town."

Wyatt opened the door for Emma, and the din of the crowd rushed out into the cold. "Lead the way."

Noise echoed off the floor-to-ceiling windows, wrought iron, and reclaimed wood of the cavernous space. Trendy joint for such a small town.

Within a minute, Trip waved them over. He'd probably caught sight of them because his height afforded him a good view of the crowd. As Wyatt and Emma approached, he noticed Trip elbow the beautiful blonde to his left and whisper something in her ear. She abruptly turned to look at Wyatt and Emma with a saucy smile. What had Trip done or said now?

Up until this point, Emma had been pleasant and familiar. But seeing Trip caused her to stiffen and hesitate, as if steeling herself against whatever schemes she must've sensed in play. She placed a wider berth between herself and Wyatt and tipped up her chin before walking straight into Kelsey's arms.

"I already had two cupcakes. After tonight you must make me stop, or I'll never fit into a decent wedding gown." Kelsey tossed her mane of hair over her shoulder. "And you must be Wyatt. Trip is having the best time with you on the mountain. Honestly, to hear him tell it, I'd think he was the costar of this little video."

Little video? Her perspective certainly put a different slant on what he considered a make-or-break point in his career.

"He's definitely made the days more fun, and safe." Wyatt shook Trip's hand.

"Glad you decided to step out for a night." Trip drank from his bottle of Red Rocket. "Need a drink?"

Wyatt shook his head. "No alcohol. I'll grab a soda water. Emma, you want something?"

"What a gentleman." Trip elbowed Kelsey again while Emma rolled her eyes.

"No, thanks." She turned to Kelsey. "I'm going to go say hi to your family. Catch you all later." Emma strode off, effectively proving to Trip and Wyatt that she wouldn't be manipulated for their entertainment. Wyatt realized his hope of using this night to get closer to Emma had been a miscalculation. She'd never let her guard down around the prying eyes of her friends.

Trip watched her go, his smile only growing broader. "Oh, it's so on, Emma Duffy."

Wyatt looked at Kelsey and then Trip. "Tell the truth, did you invite me here tonight as some ploy to win your crazy bet . . . one I never agreed to, by the way."

"Now listen up," Kelsey interjected before Trip could respond. "I'm all for fun and romance as long as no one gets hurt. So here's my one and only warning. If you toy with Emma, you'll answer to me." Then she poked Trip in the chest. "That goes double for you, so you'd better know what you're doing before you get in deeper."

"Love it when you get fired up, princess." He planted a big kiss on her lips that seemed to assuage her for the time being. Then he turned to Wyatt. "Let me introduce you to Grey. He's a big fan."

As the threesome made their way through the crowd, Wyatt noticed some people do a double take. One pulled out a phone and snapped a photo. Emma had asked him not to draw attention from Kelsey. Guess he'd need to park himself in a dark corner soon or he'd be forced to leave the party before he had a chance to observe Emma out among her friends.

Chapter Nine

"Looks like your knee is fine." Avery smiled at Wyatt after he'd been introduced to Trip's partner, Grey.

"Yeah, thanks. Lucky for me, my ego is the only thing that took a real hit."

"I doubt spending every day with Trip is good for your ego, either," Grey joked before he sipped his whiskey.

"Wyatt's not the wimp you are," Trip shot back with a grin.

"Touché." Grey raised his glass. "But seriously, the first brush with an avalanche is a crazy experience."

"Let's change the subject." Kelsey appeared to tighten her grip on Trip's arm. "Avery and I don't need to be reminded of the kind of danger you two face out there every day."

"Risks can be managed when you know what you're doing." Grey said, then he smirked and jerked a thumb at Trip. "Let's just hope this clown isn't too caught up impressing your director to pay attention to the terrain."

"Unlike you, I can multitask," Trip smirked. "Besides, yesterday's snowfall was only five inches of champagne powder. Very little risk."

Grey directed his attention back to Wyatt. "This terrain couldn't be more different from what you're used to."

"The hardest change is picking a line from below and being able to reverse it once I'm up top. Then there's accelerating out of turns in varying conditions, dealing with unforeseen obstacles." Wyatt scratched his jaw. "None of it's as showy as my old stunts, but it's every bit as challenging."

"He's being modest," Trip interrupted, laying a hand on Wyatt's shoulder. "You've got mad, natural skill out there. It's one thing to watch you on TV, another to be right there, up close."

"Wow, Wyatt. I've only ever heard that proud tone when he's bragging about himself, so you must be good," Kelsey teased, and Grey practically spit out his drink.

Trip took the ribbing with his typical good humor and then pinched Kelsey's ass while muttering, "You'll pay for that later."

"I sure hope so." She patted his cheek.

Wyatt knew a moment of envy then for the comfortable banter and affection he witnessed between Trip and Kelsey. He hadn't had a serious girlfriend since tenth grade, if one could even count that as serious.

He'd had lots of sex, though. Between the competition circuit and Ryder's recovery, love hadn't factored much into Wyatt's life. He still had plenty of time to settle down, but right now he felt a surge of envy for the way Kelsey looked at Trip. He couldn't recall ever being on the receiving end of something that genuine.

"Come on, Ave," Kelsey said. "Let's go find my sister and Emma and talk about bridesmaid stuff. My Valentine's Day wedding means we don't have much time."

Once the ladies left, Grey snickered. "I might've gotten engaged first, but you're being steamrollered down the aisle."

"Obviously my fiancée doesn't want to risk letting a good thing slip through her fingers. Don't get your feathers ruffled just 'cause Avery's taking her time." Trip gave Grey a smile and clinked his beer bottle to

Grey's glass before turning to Wyatt. "Now here's the real question, what's up with you and Emma?"

Grey, who was shorter, more reserved, but no less interested than Trip in Wyatt's answer, cocked his head, waiting. *Emma.* Well, maybe things would be progressing if Trip hadn't interfered.

"Nothing, just like you ensured when you sold me out to score points with Kelsey." Wyatt crossed his arms, feigning indignation.

"I'm just looking out for Emma." Trip set his empty bottle on a nearby table. "She's a good egg. I didn't want her to be blindsided if all you're looking for is a little action to take the edge off."

Grey laughed. "Wow, that's irony. I bet at least sixty 'good eggs' in town would shoot you on the spot if they heard that sentiment falling from your mouth now."

Trip shrugged with a broad smile. "Hey, I got no problems with any guy sowing his oats. But trust me, before Kelsey, those women knew what to expect. I never pretended my interest in any woman extended beyond the night."

"If that long." Grey shook his head. "You know, sometimes you'd be better off keeping your trap shut."

Watching Grey and Trip spar made Wyatt think of Ryder and the fun they'd had talking trash, bragging, and picking up lots of girls in bars. Now Ryder hardly socialized with Wyatt and rarely ventured out in public.

Most of the blame could be placed on the lingering effect of Ryder's injuries, but Wyatt suspected a little part of his brother had just given up, too. Had decided that he could no longer enjoy a normal life, or a beer, or flirting, or anything that most twenty-something guys did on a regular basis.

Wyatt refused to accept that fate for his brother. Hell, he couldn't live with himself if, having encouraged Ryder to compete in the first place, Wyatt didn't soon figure out how to coax Ryder into wading back into life.

The sound of laughter pulled Wyatt back to the present. He glanced around the crowd and saw Emma talking with Andy. Andy gave Emma his full attention. His eyes didn't wander the room, not even when another attractive woman passed by. Whatever he'd said had her laughing and smiling.

In one short week, Wyatt had watched Emma dedicate herself to taking care of everyone, including him. She deserved someone who made her smile. She looked happy now, but for whatever reason he couldn't explain, Wyatt's jaw clenched. He should be the guy doing that for her, not Andy.

"You're looking a little green around the gills," Trip muttered.

Wyatt snapped his head back. "How about you take care of your own love life?"

"That's what I'm doing. Kelsey wants Emma to have a little romance. I want Kelsey to have whatever she wants. Maybe you're the guy to break Emma out of her shell." Trip glanced at Emma and Andy. "Or maybe she's better off with someone like Andy."

Wyatt grunted and then grimaced, wishing he hadn't walked right into Trip's little trap.

Trip just smiled. "What I can't figure out is why you're wasting time standing here talking to Grey and me."

"Is he always like this?" Wyatt asked Grey.

"Pushy?" Grey asked.

"Gossipy, like a girl," Wyatt said.

Grey burst into laughter and Trip just shrugged, unrelenting and comfortable in his own skin.

Wyatt was about to wander over to Emma when an attractive woman joined Trip, Grey, and him.

"Hey, guys." A brunette in high heels and a skintight, waist-baring outfit sidled up with her friend. "Congrats, Trip. Still can't believe you're off the market."

"Something tells me you're going to be just fine without me, Sandy." Then he nodded to Wyatt. "Have you met Wyatt Lawson?"

"I heard you were in town, but you've been laying low. How do you all know each other?" She brushed against Wyatt, using the crowd as cover for her flirtatious maneuver.

"Trip's helping me with my training," Wyatt replied and cast a quick glance over Sandy's shoulder to look for Emma, who'd disappeared.

"Can I get your autograph?" Sandy asked.

It had been a while since he'd been asked. It felt a little awkward in this context, especially when he noticed Trip barely containing a smirk.

"Sure. Do you have paper and a pen?" Wyatt hadn't felt this self-conscious in a while.

"Hang on." Sandy strolled to the bar and reappeared with a Sharpie. "Here you go."

"Napkin?"

"How about you sign right here." Sandy pointed to her midriff. *Classy.*

"Uh, I don't know." Wyatt glanced at the guys. "This doesn't seem like the time and place for that."

"Seriously?" Sandy frowned, then shrugged and then held out her arm. "Okay, how about here?"

The temperature in the restaurant must've been turned up, because perspiration had broken out on his back. He did not want to be seen signing any woman's body parts at an engagement party, let alone have Emma catch him doing so. Sandy, however, remained persistent, her arm still dangling before him. "Okay."

As quickly as possible, he signed her forearm and handed her the pen. Behind her, he could see Trip and Grey suppressing their laughter.

"Wanna dance?" Sandy asked, gesturing toward the small area where several people, including Emma and Andy, were enjoying the music. Before he could respond, she grasped his wrist. "Come on, Wyatt. You're in Sterling Canyon. Time to loosen up."

"Have fun." Trip's low reply followed Wyatt as Sandy led him straight toward Emma.

When Emma saw them, he noticed her body tense for a second before she resumed dancing with Andy. The lights above cast a golden glow around her, making the blonde highlights in her red hair shimmer and glint just like the beading on her dress. The muscles in her legs flexed with each step.

Emma never gave off a highly sexual vibe, but she reminded him of a dormant volcano. Instinct or ESP told him that, down deep, something hot churned, waiting for release. Wyatt suddenly wanted nothing so much as to cause that eruption. He didn't know why he had a feeling it would be the most exciting thing to see, but his desire would not be ignored. He could barely hear the music or notice the crowd thanks to the voice in his head shouting *mine, mine, mine!*

He'd watch for an opportunity to swap partners with Andy before the end of the song. Andy, happily oblivious to Wyatt's scheme, raised his hand, seeking a high-five.

"Hey, man. Good to see you out." Andy then twirled Emma, who looked like she had to concentrate hard on keeping her rhythm now that Wyatt had drawn near.

"Look, Em," Sandy said, proudly baring her forearm before casting him a sultry smile. "A body brand."

Wyatt caught Emma's brow-raise before her gaze locked with his. Something that resembled disappointment passed across her sparkling green eyes before they dimmed. "Lucky you."

The sarcastic delivery seemed lost on Sandy. Wyatt contented himself to dance without saying much, although Sandy wanted to grind her ass against his pelvis. Normally he'd have played along, but with Emma watching him in her periphery, and Trip across the room laughing his ass off, Wyatt found himself counting down the final seconds of the song. Just before it ended, he clasped Emma's hand.

"Let's swap partners for the next song."

Andy looked as if he might resist, but then handed Emma over and playfully dipped Sandy. Both ladies looked less than thrilled with the switcheroo, but Wyatt stayed the course.

The tempo slowed considerably, which he couldn't have planned better if he'd tried. He wrapped an arm around Emma's waist and brought her other hand to his shoulder.

"I didn't want to sign her body, you know. I asked for a napkin." Wyatt dipped his head to get a closer look at Emma. The perfumed scent of her hair aroused him. It took a lot of restraint not to press his mouth against the sensitive part of her neck, right beneath her ear. The only way to refrain was to pull back and look at her.

"Doesn't matter to me." That tight, polite smile she'd worn at the beginning of the week settled on her face. God, he'd grown to hate that emotionless grin. Her common retreat whenever he got too close.

"Then why are you so mad?"

"I'm not." She scowled, her shoulders and arms turning rigid.

Clearly a joke or two was needed to loosen her up again. "Relax, Emma. I told you already, I don't bite unless asked."

She cracked a smile. A good start, at least. Wyatt tested the waters a bit by holding her just a little more closely. He watched her eyes widen and her lips part. Those plush lips made his heart thump a little harder—made everything in his body a little harder, actually.

Her forehead wrinkled as if she were gripped by indecision. Suddenly she glanced over her shoulder and noticed Trip watching. He tipped his Stetson with a nod, which pissed Wyatt off. The guy was determined to keep Emma on the hot seat.

Instead of retreating further, she surprised him with a steely look of determination. "Wyatt, tell me the exact terms of Trip's bet."

"I told you, I never shook on the bet." He nudged a little closer, because holding her close made his body purr.

"Just tell me the terms."

Okay, her focus was not where he wanted it to be. Best to answer her and get that out of the way.

"He bet me fifty bucks that I wouldn't last the month without making a move, and another fifty that you'd turn me down." Wyatt caught himself holding his breath.

Emma's distant gaze suggested she was thinking again, so Wyatt remained quiet, content to feel her body heat seeping through her thin dress to warm his palm. The anticipation of her possibly brushing against his torso or resting her chin on his shoulder tormented him with longing.

With her focus elsewhere, he stole a few seconds and studied her face. Her lips, full and a deep shade of pink, begged to be kissed. Her scattered freckles did, too. He'd gotten lost in the details until he glanced at her eyes, which were now staring right at him.

"So if I make a move first, he loses both bets?" Emma cocked her head.

Every hair on Wyatt's body vibrated with resounding force. Honestly, he hadn't made those bets, but right now he wanted to see what she'd do next, so he didn't reiterate that point. "I guess so."

Another three tense seconds passed while she appeared to gather her courage. His body was strung so tight, he thought he might snap in two.

"Is he still watching?" Emma leaned closer to whisper in his ear, and he felt a shiver rush down his legs.

"Uh huh." Wyatt gulped, his hand clasping hers a little tighter now.

She drew a deep breath before her hand curled around the base of his neck. "You owe me half your take," she murmured just before she pulled him in for a kiss.

Emma's sense of triumph scattered along with all other thoughts the instant Wyatt's hungry kiss consumed her. He tugged her snugly against his body as he tilted his head to get a better hold on her. His other hand threaded into her hair, and she remembered how much he'd enjoyed wrapping her hair around his hands the last time they'd been together.

Her body remembered his scent, his taste . . . the rough feel of his strength. Remembered the way he'd made her soar and shatter. She trembled from those memories, which then caused him to groan with pleasure. Tumbling into some crazy kind of ecstasy, Emma's body slackened against his. She might've let him strip her down to nothing right there if the pounding bass of a new song hadn't jolted her back to reality.

Suddenly remembering where she was—in a room full of friends' parents and her neighbors—she pushed away from Wyatt. Dazed, they stared at each other, chests heaving.

A lazy smile spread beneath his heated gaze. "Remind me to thank Trip for that stupid bet."

Heat throbbed through her limbs. Her skin must've looked like a boiled lobster. Never, never, never had she made herself a public spectacle. Damn that Trip Lexington, and damn Wyatt Lawson, too.

She staggered, and Wyatt reached out to catch her. "Emma, are you okay?"

"Yes." Shrugging out of his grasp, she straightened her spine. "If you'll excuse me for a minute."

She turned and marched toward Trip, whose usual smirk had been replaced by openmouthed surprise. "You lose. Pay Wyatt the hundred bucks." Then, as regally as she could manage, she smiled at Kelsey, Grey, and Avery and proceeded directly to the ladies' room.

Setting her hands on either side of the sink basin, she took a few seconds to catch her breath and compose herself. To adopt a laissez-faire attitude and strut back into the crowd as if that kiss had been no big deal.

Predictably, Avery and Kelsey burst into the bathroom before Emma had a chance to recover.

"Oh my God, Emma Duffy." Kelsey literally bounced on her toes, every one of her curves jiggling with excitement. "I'm so proud of you. That was *H-O-T!*"

Equally predictably, Avery smacked Kelsey's arm before turning to Emma. "Em, are you drunk?"

"Emma's never drunk, Ave," Kelsey said, as if the mere idea of Emma being anything less than sober were a fairy tale. She flashed a saucy smile. "She's just in *lurve.*"

"Honestly, Kelsey." Avery rolled her eyes, then reached for Emma's shoulder. "What's going on with you and Wyatt? I mean, you never do things like that. Then again, we are at Kelsey's engagement party, so I should expect just about anything to happen."

Kelsey didn't even take offense. Instead, her smile beamed like sunlight bouncing off the mirrors. "Emma, this fling is exactly what you need right now. Your mom is gone. You've got one of the sexiest snowboarders in the whole darn country staying at your inn all by his lonesome. It's high time for a little fun and romance. Not work, work, work all the time. Volunteering everywhere and being so . . . good."

Unlike Kelsey, Emma had never thrown caution to the wind and doubted it would work out well if she did. But that dull adjective burrowed under her skin like a Lyme disease–infected tick.

"*Good,*" Emma repeated the words flatly, staring at her reflection. "Why is that always the first word everyone says about me?"

"You're a kind, caring person. A good friend and daughter," Avery said. "Why does it sound like you don't like that label?"

"Because it's so . . . boring." Emma looked at Avery. "People call you *smart, assertive, adventuresome.* Kelsey's *sparkly* and *romantic* and *savvy.* I'm just *good.*"

Avery rubbed her hand on Emma's back. "It's not meant as an insult. You're our rock. The sane person who keeps us in check. The one we trust for the best advice."

"Well, maybe you shouldn't," Emma said, almost in tears. She knew her friends loved her, but there was an entire side of her heart they didn't know. A side no one knew. With all her secrets and repressed needs, she was the last person who should be giving anyone advice.

A private piece of her soul wondered what life might've been like had her dad not taken off and left her to prop up her broken mother. The devil that wouldn't leave her shoulder whispered subversive ideas about where she might be living and what she might've accomplished if Grammy hadn't always counted on her to keep the Weenuche legacy going. Emma didn't dislike her life, but there were times when the parts that didn't fit so well really chafed. Tonight was one of those times.

Only Wyatt had ever caught a glimpse of another side of Emma, and he didn't even remember—didn't know that she was Alexa.

Still, she wouldn't share these thoughts with her friends. Ever since her father left, she'd locked down any part of herself that might cause conflict or controversy. That might create distance or cause people to judge her unworthy.

She'd clung to being good as a way to keep people close and make them happy, even though it could make her feel fraudulent and wretched and lonely. At the end of the day, she was still afraid of doing things that could hurt the people she loved, or herself, in the future. The "good" reputation she'd cultivated had become a prison.

"Well, I don't know about everyone else, but I couldn't be more tickled than to see new romance blooming at my engagement party. You know, if something more happens between you two, I'm taking all the credit for creating an environment neither of you could resist." Kelsey swooped in and swaddled Emma in a hearty embrace. "Be happy, Emma. Let go and have a little fun. Be like me for a change and learn to get over what everyone else thinks. Just live and see what happens."

"If this gets back to my mother . . ." Emma stopped herself, realizing that, at thirty-one, she sounded pathetic to be worried about her mother's opinion. Yet, for so long, it had been just her and her mom making their way together.

Emma straightened up and smoothed her hair. "I only kissed Wyatt to make Trip lose that stupid bet and wipe the smug look off his face. Now, whatever happens, if anything happens, it will be between Wyatt and me. Not because of Trip."

Kelsey wrinkled her nose. "I don't know about that. What just happened out there got the ball rolling, and that's all because of Trip."

Her proud smile sparked Emma's laugh. "You see him through the rosiest glasses."

"God, I do love that man." Kelsey's unapologetic, big love for Trip made Emma wonder if her own mother had ever been so enamored of her dad.

Did the fact that Kelsey totally accepted Trip's nature give them a better chance at lasting? Had Emma's mother's insecurities and judgments—her restraint—driven her father away?

That last thought felt like a betrayal of her mom, who'd been so devastated when he'd left them. And he hadn't proven himself to be the most loving father since then, either. No, the fault had to be with him and his selfish, lusty nature. Lust usually wreaked havoc in people's lives. This much Emma knew.

Even so, she'd already started falling for Wyatt.

"Shall we return to the party?" Avery asked. "The longer we stay in here, the more questions it'll raise."

Emma drew a deep breath and prepared to face the consequences of her lapse in judgment. She'd have to do it with her head held high, even if her insides were fumbling like a puppet on loose strings. "Crap."

Wyatt's phone kept beeping. His Twitter feed had blown up because someone at the party tweeted a picture of him and Emma making out, along with a text that read, "Check out @AirdogLawson's latest training regimen."

Dammit. He'd become so preoccupied with Emma, he'd forgotten that something like this could happen. That the reputation he'd been trying to rebuild could take a hit. Probably best if he didn't respond. Most of the time responding only made the noise last longer.

Ryder would probably see this before Wyatt got back to the inn, too, which wouldn't lessen the tension between them. Not for the first time tonight, a dose of guilt slid down to sour his stomach. He hated the idea that he and Ryder might both want Emma. Worse, that he'd plowed ahead and tried to take her without first figuring out exactly how it could hurt his brother.

"Well, well, well." Trip pulled out his wallet and thumbed through his cash. He handed a hundred bucks to Wyatt. "I gotta hand it to Emma. Didn't think she had it in her."

Wyatt shoved the money back at Trip. "I don't want your money."

"Fair's fair." Trip thrust it forward.

"I mean it. Keep your cash. My interest in Emma's got nothing to do with you or the bet, and I don't want this on my conscience." His conscience had enough to atone for tonight.

Trip put the cash back in his wallet. "This gets more interesting by the minute."

Wyatt's phone bleeped again. "Dammit. Forty-seven retweets? Don't people have anything better to do?"

"What's wrong?" Kelsey asked, appearing out of nowhere with Avery and Emma.

"Nothin'." Wyatt stuffed the phone in his pocket.

"What retweets?" Emma asked, eyes alert and nervous. Just the sight of her got him going again, despite the many reasons he shouldn't lose control.

Maybe he should make light of the tweets so she didn't freak out. He glanced at the others. "Excuse us a second." Clasping Emma's arm, he then maneuvered her into a corner a little distance from her friends and the crowd, hopeful no one else was snapping pictures. "Some joker posted a picture of our . . . dance. Basically called me out on getting distracted from my purpose for being in town."

Emma's pink cheeks paled. "May I see?"

Wyatt grimaced, but he unlocked his phone and pulled up the tweet. It bleeped again.

"Forty-eight retweets," she said, handing him back the phone. No tantrum. No whining. No words of regret. Maybe she didn't mind so much.

"You're not mad?" He peered into her eyes, trying to figure her out. When he'd said she was a mystery, it hadn't been a lie. "I can respond if you want, but I think it's best to ignore it."

"My name isn't mentioned," she shrugged with a self-deprecating chuckle. "Not that my name would mean anything in the Twitterverse anyway. But you can't see my face in the photo. And it's just a kiss, after all. Gossip about the fallen 'Saint Emma' will travel only through town. I'll face a few snickers next week at the grocery store, and poor Mr. Tomlin will be heartbroken. Mrs. Pellman will take credit. Oh, yes, that will be a big source of entertainment for them. But it should all die down before . . ." Then she fell silent and lowered her gaze.

"Before what?"

"Nothing." Her gaze dropped to the floor.

"No, it's something." He tipped up her chin, searching her eyes for answers. "Before what?"

She sighed. "Before my mother returns."

He almost laughed but sensed it would only piss her off. *Her mother?* "Why would your mom care if you kissed me?"

Emma grimaced while looping her fingers through her hair. He wanted to do that for her, but he refrained from touching her again, intent on listening. "She has a very strict sense of propriety. The idea of me making out in public, in front of her friends, with a guy I barely know will not sit well. She'll jump to all kinds of conclusions about where it might lead."

"And that bothers you." He understood, actually, because much of his life had been about wanting his parents' affection, which always seemed frustratingly out of reach. In the process, he'd made a name for himself and earned money to improve all of their lives. Until he'd helped destroy Ryder's, that is.

Now the only way he might win his mom's approval would be to recapture his fame and, in the process, help Ryder begin to live again.

"Yes. I like to make her proud. Maybe I am old-fashioned at heart, but I respect her values and faith." Emma's discomfort from that last admission showed in her cheeks. She straightened her shoulders and immediately changed the subject. "So where's my fifty bucks."

"I didn't take Trip's money." Wyatt crossed his arms.

"Why not? He'd have taken yours. Besides, I earned it." She turned her head, searching for Trip.

Wyatt grasped her hand, unwilling to let her cut this conversation short just when it was getting somewhere. "I keep telling you, I never shook on that bet, and I don't want him, your friends, or you to think that my interest has anything to do with money or that stupid bet."

Emma's eyes widened. "Well, that's . . . that's sweet, Wyatt."

"Trust me, I'm a lot of things." He squeezed her hand, hoping her heart thumped from the contact like his did. That her blood thickened in her limbs, making them heavy, just as his were. "But sweet isn't one of them."

Emma's breath caught for a moment before she tugged free from his grasp and smoothed her hair. "Let's get back to the party. If people tease, we'll say it was a dare from Trip. Everyone will buy that, and it'll take away any speculation that something more is happening."

"Would that be so bad?" Frustration began to crowd his thoughts, sharpening the tone of his voice.

"I don't know if you've noticed, but I prefer life outside of the spotlight."

"Not the speculation, the something more." He stepped closer, determined to make her admit the fact that she liked him—at least a little bit, anyway. "Say what you want, but that kiss didn't feel like something you did just to win a bet."

She looked like she might run, so Wyatt boxed her in by settling one hand against the wall behind her shoulder. "It felt like something you wanted. I know I did."

"Please, stop." Emma's eyes darted over his shoulder, scanning the crowd. "We're in public."

He knew he shouldn't risk this type of publicity, yet he leaned closer so that his lips were near her ear. "Then let's go someplace private."

He pulled back in time to catch the flare of heat flicker in her eyes. No matter how much she protested, that kiss and the brilliant green glow in her eyes told him he affected her. Like a gambler who'd gone all in, he waited—muscles taut with anticipation—to see if his wager would pay off. Her hesitation offered no relief.

"There are at least twenty women here who'd happily hook up with you tonight, Wyatt. Why are you so intent on me?"

"I already told you, I think you're interesting."

"Because I'm not falling at your feet? Because you like the challenge? Because you think I'm quaint?"

In for a penny, he thought, as he twirled a bit of her hair in his fingers. "Because I think your red hair is almost as pretty as you. Because you dance in pantries when no one is looking. Because I love and hate the way you look out for Ryder. Because you're a great cook. Because you're patient with Mari, those old folks, and me. Because you care about your mom's opinion." He noticed the artery at the base of her neck beating faster, so he stepped even closer. "Because the upside of the fact that you turn your back to me on a consistent basis is that I get to stare at your ass, which has led to a fair number of fantasies.

And because that kiss a few minutes ago confirmed that, no matter how much you fight it, there's something between us that wants to be explored."

Her enlarged pupils practically eliminated every trace of green in her eyes. Her shallow breath told him he'd excited her. As far as he could tell, there was only one thing standing in their way. "So the question is, why not me, Emma? What's so wrong with me?"

She blinked, her brows furrowed. Her throat worked hard to swallow. "Because I know how this goes, Wyatt. Nowhere. You'll be gone like that." She snapped her fingers.

"I'm here for a few more weeks. Can't we just see what happens? At the very least, it could be a really fun memory." Truthfully, no woman had kept his attention once he'd moved on to a new location before. Then again, Emma wasn't like any of the other women he'd known.

Her green eyes dimmed like the sun ducking behind a cloud. In a low, defeated voice, she uttered, "Trust me when I tell you, I'm not that memorable."

As soon as the words were out, she slapped her hand over her mouth.

"Why'd you say that?" Wyatt demanded.

"Nothing. Please drop this. People are staring, and I'm getting really uncomfortable. I told you I didn't want the attention stolen from Kelsey, either. Let's mingle."

She'd shot him down and shut him out. He didn't like it, and not only because it never happened. He knew, however, he'd get no further with her here at her friend's party, nor should he try in front of prying eyes. That, and he'd promised not to do anything to draw attention away from her friend, Kelsey. "You know what, I'm going to catch an Uber home and spend some time with Ryder, if he's back from pottery, that is."

"Why do you sound miffed about the pottery?"

Miffed? What a perfectly Emma word. He wasn't miffed, but it sounded nicer than infuriated, so he let it go. "Because he and I had a decent week together, but you keep finding other things for him to focus on. Is he the reason you keep shooting me down? Do you have a thing for my brother?" Wyatt held his breath, regretting his question.

"No!" Emma's brows furrowed. "And I told you already, I'm not trying to come between you or suggesting that he abandon your training. But why can't he also explore some things for himself so that, once you've accomplished your goals this year, he has something of his own?"

"I don't want to talk about this anymore."

Emma crossed her arms. "Then quit bringing it up."

"I'm leaving." Wyatt waved his hand in her face, only to quickly realize it showed his immaturity.

"Fine." She bugged her eyes at him, then looked embarrassed that they'd both regressed to childlike behavior.

"Tell Trip I had to bolt, and apologize for my early exit." He felt idiotic—like a four-year-old having a tantrum because someone stole his candy. Still, he didn't even turn and look back as he made his way through the crowd.

Chapter Ten

When Wyatt returned to the inn, he walked in on Mari and Jim editing film in the dining room.

"Hey, guys." Wyatt waved from the archway of the room. He opted not to sit with them because Mari followed his Twitter handle, and he didn't want to give her a chance to grill him about the photo. At least it hadn't been video.

Mari glanced at the clock. "You're back earlier than expected."

"I never planned to stay out late. Just needed a change of scenery." Wyatt decided Mari hadn't yet seen the Twitter feed, because if she had, the cameras would be on and she'd be slamming him with questions about Emma. "Ryder back yet?"

"I think so." Mari barely looked up from the screen.

"'Night." Wyatt wandered across the lobby to Ryder's room and knocked on the door. "You in there?"

"Yeah," came his reply through the door.

Wyatt entered the room and hung up Ryder's jacket before he sat on the corner of the bed. College football played on the TV, although the volume had been turned down very low. "Thanks for the loan."

"Sure."

Emma's lecture about Ryder's future replayed in his mind. Maybe she had a small point, and Ryder could have a little something of his own without leaving Wyatt in his dust. He forced an upbeat attitude when he asked, "How was the pottery class?"

Ryder glanced at him, his expression cautious. "I liked it. The instructor said I'm a n-natural."

The faint tone of pride coloring his brother's speech caught Wyatt's attention. Since the accident, his brother's monotone voice made Wyatt question whether the brain damage had also stolen Ryder's ability to feel things. Apparently it had only made it harder for Ryder to show emotion, but not impossible.

Confirming that, lurking beneath the stoic exterior, his brother still experienced some range of emotion other than anger made Wyatt want to dance. But sadness diminished that joy because Ryder's response meant that Emma was right. Ryder was not as invested in being part of Wyatt's team as Wyatt had hoped.

"That's great, Ryder." Wyatt playfully jiggled his brother's foot. "I'm glad Emma suggested it."

Perhaps that had been a slight exaggeration, but deep down he had to acknowledge his own selfishness. When he'd picked Sterling Canyon for his early training, he'd never anticipated the likes of Emma Duffy. Who would've thought a shy, conservative, older woman would throw all of his carefully laid plans into disarray?

Ryder sat up straighter against the headboard. "Where is she?"

"Still at the party. I came back to rest up for tomorrow."

Ryder held up his phone so Wyatt could see the Twitter app opened. "After you k-kissed her?"

Wyatt shrugged, affecting a nonchalant posture. "She kissed me, but only as part of some stupid bet that Trip made. It's a long story."

Ryder tilted his head, clearly disbelieving him. His brother knew him better than anyone, maybe even better than he knew himself at times. The plain truth was that Wyatt wasn't done with Emma, but he realized he couldn't honestly pursue anything without knowing whether Ryder had feelings for her. "Do you like Emma? I mean, like, do you *like* her?"

"Not like you d-do." Ryder wiggled the phone.

Relief rushed through Wyatt's limbs. "Good."

Ryder snickered; another sign that missing pieces of his personality were bubbling back to life.

"No more lectures about her. I'm going to bed. See you in the morning." Wyatt stood and paused. Maybe Ryder did need his own life at some point, but Wyatt still liked having his brother along as much as possible. "Yoga at five forty-five?"

Ryder groaned. "Okay."

When Wyatt made his way back through the lobby, he bumped into Mari, who was on her way upstairs. The smug smile playing about her mouth told him he was in trouble.

"Wyatt, I just saw the Twitter pic." She rested her hands on her hips.

"It's nothing." Wyatt waved her off with a smile. "A dare from Trip, that's all."

"It's out there on the Web now, so it's not nothing. We need to talk about including her in the film." Mari's tone had shifted into business mode. "The good news is that a romantic angle lends another layer that people will love, especially if it can add a little conflict or tension to the story. Does she support your shift to freeriding competition, for example?"

Wyatt halted midway up the stairs. "Mari, I've told you from the outset, I'm trying to build a new image as a serious athlete, not a playboy."

"I'm not talking about painting you as some gigolo. But a relationship with a small-town woman makes you more relatable and real to people, just like seeing you connect with those old people, or helping your brother, or any of this other personal stuff does. We need to give the audience a three-dimensional view of who you are so they are rooting hard for you once the qualifiers begin. That's the momentum you want and need. That's what will get you loyal sponsors. Especially if you're choosing a girl as unlikely as Emma, with her quiet life here at this inn and the whole volunteering thing she has going on . . ."

The negative spin Mari's tone cast on Emma's life pissed him off. More importantly, if Emma couldn't stand friends at a party staring at her, she sure as heck wouldn't want to be part of a film that could subject her to much more public kinds of gossip and opinions. "Mari, there's nothing between Emma and me. You're running down a rabbit hole. That kiss happened because Emma wanted Trip to lose a hundred bucks. He never thought she'd do it."

Mari narrowed her gaze, trying to decide if he was being truthful. "Okay, but if it changes, you need to let me know."

Wyatt didn't make her any promises. If she took his silence as assent, that'd be her problem, not his. He followed her upstairs and went to his room, eager to trade the button-down shirt and slacks for sweats and a pullover.

He'd flopped into bed by ten, so he turned on the TV to find something to hold his attention. Unfortunately, nothing—not football, Tosh.0 reruns, or ESPN—kept his thoughts from straying back to that super-hot kiss Emma'd laid on him at the party. She'd shocked him, but he wouldn't complain. Her responsiveness proved she had some interest in him. A girl like her couldn't have kissed him like that if she felt nothing.

Her words drifted back to him. *Trust me when I tell you, I'm not that memorable.* Did she think that because of the way her dad had walked out, or had some guy made her feel forgettable? He couldn't imagine the latter, but she definitely had a self-esteem issue—one he'd be happy to help her remedy.

He wondered what time she'd get home, and whether he should wait up to continue the conversation she'd been unwilling to have in public. They'd have some privacy here, and if he happened to convince her to loosen up a bit, there were plenty of bedrooms available.

He felt his lower half stir a little at that thought and decided he would wait up, however long it took.

◆ ◆ ◆

Emma carefully picked her way across the walkway to the inn, bracing against the cold breeze. Her heels weren't meant for winter weather, but she'd felt pretty in this outfit tonight. Wyatt seemed to have liked it, too, despite the fact it hadn't been nearly as sexy as the getup she'd sported as Alexa.

She trembled then, but not from the cold. All those reasons he'd recited for being interested in her looped through her head again. In truth, they'd looped through her memory so many times since he'd left, they'd tied up her brain in knots.

He'd looked so earnest. A not so small part of Emma might enjoy taking advantage of the opportunity to explore a little romance while her mom remained out of the picture. If it were just Wyatt here without Mari and the crew—without Ryder—she might force herself to relax and go with the flow. It'd feel safe to let that part of her out to play for a while because the risk of anyone but her getting hurt would be low.

But Mari would be all over her if she knew. Emma had already grown accustomed to seeing the tripods and light stands everywhere and sometimes forgot to check whether the stupid cameras were running. Plus, Ryder might resent being a third wheel. The last thing she wanted to do was make him feel even more marginalized than he already did.

And then there were her secrets. If she'd reminded Wyatt about their night together when he'd first arrived—if she'd joked about it—it could've been less of a big deal. Maybe she could've sworn him to secrecy. A whole week later, though, she just felt more mortified. Mortified that he still hadn't made any connection to their past and embarrassed that she'd covered it up. She couldn't possibly reveal herself to be so ridiculous, awkward, and forgettable now. Besides, it wasn't like that night meant anything to him anyway.

Even if she did confess about Aspen, she could never tell him about her book. That secret would go with her to her grave. Knowing him better now convinced her he'd misunderstand and assume that she'd planned the whole thing. That she'd seduced him in order to get material for her story. It hadn't been that way, but given the combination of his mistrust of women and journalists (and her secrecy), he'd think her a liar.

Sighing at the quandary, she waltzed through the front door, removed her shoes, and quietly crept up the stairs, hoping not to wake anyone. As she rounded the second floor to head up to the third, Wyatt's door opened. "Emma?"

She gulped, praying he didn't want to continue the argument they'd been having when he'd left. She deflected her awkwardness with a joke. "Don't tell me you're hungry again?"

His eyes lit with mischief. "Not for food, anyway."

Okay, so he wasn't still pissy, but he was staring at her with a predatory intent she knew she'd be too weak to fend off. Especially when he looked a little sleepy, his hair rumpled, his cozy flannel pants hanging low, drawing her attention down there.

She shook her head, simultaneously enjoying and hating the flirtation. "Good night, Wyatt."

"Hang on." He stopped about two feet from her and rested his hand on the banister. He had attractive hands. Long fingers, trim nails, the lightest smattering of dark hair at his wrists. She knew from experience the pleasure those hands could bring, and that thought made her tingle. "Did Kelsey enjoy the rest of her party?"

"She did. Thanks for leaving so the spotlight stayed on her and Trip." Emma dug into her purse and pulled out one hundred dollars. "Unlike you, I made Trip pay up."

She handed him fifty, but he shook his head.

"You keep it. You earned it." His tone had flattened, playfulness gone. "I've been thinking."

"Uh oh," she murmured, half-joking, half-terrified.

"I can't decide if the real truth is that you're refusing to spend time with me because you think I'm a user, or because you don't want to end up on camera."

The fact he seemed so troubled by her rejection surprised her. At first she'd suspected his ego couldn't take the hit, but now she wondered if there was more to his persistence. "I don't think you're some jerk, Wyatt. And I do not want any part of my personal life to become memorialized as part of some documentary."

He stepped a little closer, and her body predictably responded with a shock wave of flutters. Flutters she had to admit she enjoyed. His smoky, hazel eyes fixed on hers as he lowered his voice. "What if we kept it a secret?"

Another secret. If he only knew how hard it was for her to keep the secrets she already hid from the world. Another one might do her in.

"Listen, you're good-looking, and you seem like a nice enough guy. But if we get together and it feels like a mistake for either of us, it could be uncomfortable for the rest of your stay. And if we hit it off, it will hurt when you go. Either way, it's a bad idea."

But the lusty devil whispered that it would no doubt provide hot memories for months to come.

He stood there, silently debating. His eyes scanned her from head to toe before focusing on her face, as if looking for some kind of sign. She braced for another argument, but he shrugged. "Seems I can't talk you out of your opinion. But before you go upstairs, there's something weird happening with the radiator in my room. Can you come take a quick look?"

She frowned. "I swear, I wish I'd win the lottery so I could afford to fix up this old place and make her beautiful and functional again."

"I kind of like her just as she is." He'd looked straight at Emma when he spoke, lest she missed his double meaning. A meaning she didn't want to examine too closely.

She strode into his room and went directly to the radiator. Nothing appeared to be hissing or bubbling or cracked. "I don't see anything weird."

As she spoke those words, she vaguely registered the sound of the door closing. She turned around in time to catch Wyatt slowly prowling toward her. "That's because I lied. I wanted to get you in here, where no one is listening or watching or gossiping, so we could be honest with each other."

"Wyatt . . ." She waited for a surge of anger to arise, but instead her stupid feet just froze in place, and her body buzzed with nervous excitement. She'd seen this version of him before—the guy who liked to take control. She liked this version of Wyatt, too, and doubted she'd be able to resist him.

"Emma." He came right up to her and cupped her face "Stop thinking for a few minutes. Just let go and give me control."

And just like that, she dropped her shoes to the floor and gave in to his kiss.

Wyatt had a great mouth, with full lips and a very skilled tongue. Within seconds she'd abandoned all sense of right and wrong and let herself melt against him, her arms looping over his shoulders. A fallen woman . . . but, at the moment, a very happy one.

He clasped her wrists and, backing her up to the wall, pinioned her arms above her head as he pressed himself against her while kissing her mouth, jaw, and along her neck and shoulder.

She submitted completely, because she rather loved the sensation of being overwhelmed by his powerful body. Almost as if the choice had been stolen from her, although it hadn't. She knew she had a choice, but he'd effectively maneuvered her so quickly, it allowed her to pretend she didn't.

"Emma." His ragged voice brushed across her ear as his hand found the inside of her thigh. "I've been thinking about you since I left the party. Tell me you want this."

Her body quivered from the electrifying twinges firing through her limbs and into her core. Some dirty, carnal part of her did want this. Wanted this very much. Even though she knew regret would follow.

He stroked his hand up along the inner side of her leg until his fingers found her underwear. He dipped one inside the elastic band. "Tell me it's okay."

She could feel his erection throbbing against her hip.

"Yes," she breathed, barely able to get the word out.

"You smell so good." He licked her neck and dipped one finger inside of her body. "You feel good, too. So wet and ready."

He withdrew his hand and licked his own finger. "You taste good."

Unlike her, he had no shame or embarrassment about sex, his body, or hers. As Alexa, she'd been able to handle it all because she'd been playing a role. But here and now she was Emma. No hiding. No roleplaying. The intimacy and exposure caused a hot flush to color her entire body.

He spun her around until she faced the wall, then began unzipping her dress, all the while pressing kisses along her shoulders and spine. His mouth was hot and wet and very, very seductive. His desire and attention made her feel beautiful and sexy, and that rarely happened. Stupidly, her eyes misted at the realization.

He quickly tugged her dress down around her hips until it fell in a puddle around her feet. She stepped out of it, and he immediately placed her palms against the wall. "Keep your hands up here."

She felt the warmth of his chest against her back, his rigid erection pressing against her rear. He fondled her breasts, his fingers rolling her nipples until she arched her spine. "You like that, Emma?"

He sucked at the sensitive spot on her neck just below her ear. Then his hand caressed its way down her stomach until it slid inside her underwear again, finding the spot that ached for his touch.

She gasped when he got there, which made his chest rumble with pleasure. "I want to make you explode."

She heard herself panting, which should embarrass her, except her mind couldn't focus on it for long enough to matter. Tendrils of pleasure stretched throughout her body, blotting out every one of her usual emotions. "Oh, oh, Wyatt."

"I'm so turned on right now," he growled and twisted her around so he could kiss her hard. A desperate kiss they both seemed to need like air and water and sunlight.

Emma tugged at his shirt, which he quickly tossed aside. Their breaths and bodies mingled, hands groping and pulling at remaining clothing, until neither had a stitch on. Wyatt lifted her to lay her on the bed. Then he crawled on top of her.

He pinned her against the mattress and stared at her, his breath ragged. "No more turning your back to me. No more ignoring me, Emma." Then he kissed her again before pulling back. "You're beautiful." He rose up on his knees and let his fingers trace all the lines and ridges of her bones and muscles. "This creamy, flawless skin makes me want to see it turn pink." He roughly grabbed at her breast and pinched just a little. "I knew down deep you'd pent up all this fire and heat."

He spread her legs wider with his knees before lowering his mouth to her pelvis bone and then taking it lower and using his tongue and hands to drive her wild.

Her fingers instantly tangled into his silky curls as she moaned in pleasure.

Emma trembled as waves of an orgasm racked her body. When Wyatt's face reemerged, he wore that sleepy, sexy grin again, although his lips glistened. "I told you I never bite unless asked." He paused. "Any objections?"

The most she could do was shake her head, because she could barely form words at this point. Wyatt, meanwhile, retained an unnerving amount of self-control as he licked along the centerline of her stomach up to her breasts, and then nipped at her collarbone before kissing her mouth again.

Emma forced herself to come out of the sexual haze and take part in what was happening. She reached between his legs and stroked his rigid, throbbing erection. He stammered something, his body quaked, but then he reached for her hand and held it at her side.

Lowering himself now, he glided his penis back and forth over her wetness without penetrating her. The friction made her writhe, seeking the release he held just outside her grasp.

"Are you ready?"

"Yes," she managed. He stretched to reach the nightstand and grabbed a condom, which he put on with lightning speed. Rolling onto his back, he murmured, "Ride me, Emma. Hard!"

And she did. She rode him swift and fast and fell apart almost immediately because he'd already had her on the knife's edge of bliss. He tugged at her hair and tongued her breasts until her nerves were strung so tight she thought she might pass out. As soon as she shattered, he flipped her over, raised her hips, slapped her ass, and took her from behind.

"You're so fucking hot," he said as he slammed into her. His hands and mouth were rough and aggressive, whether biting her shoulder, pinching her nipple, or slapping her bottom. Just like before, it all turned her on. A tiny part of her felt embarrassed to like it so much, but the bigger, happier, satisfied part silenced that critical voice in her head.

His rhythm increased and she could tell he was near to tipping over the edge. Rather than shout into the room, he clamped his mouth onto her neck and suckled her while his hips jerked with his ejaculation, and he collapsed on top of her.

Both of them laid there, breathing heavily, sated and, on her part, a little dazed. Some moments later, he rolled off of her and then turned her so they were lying face to face. He had the most adorable, satisfied smirk on his face, so she laughed.

"Laughing at me?" He pinched her ass. "Careful, or I might have to punish you."

She looked at him, unable to say anything. Suddenly, in the quiet, still of the night, she felt exposed. She felt ashamed for behaving so brazenly, and for liking it. For not being more truthful with him, yet feeling trapped into keeping her secrets.

"You're blushing." He traced his finger along her jaw. "That was amazing, and overdue, I think."

"Yes, well, I certainly didn't plan on it," she sighed. "We've scratched this itch, so we can go on with the next few weeks keeping our secret, right? Nothing more. That's what you said."

"I said we'd keep it quiet. I never said it'd be just one night, Emma." Wyatt frowned. "Is that really all you want?"

Emma sat up, looking for her discarded clothing. "I think it's best that we keep this compartmentalized. Nothing has changed. You're still taking off on your tour, and my life is here, with my mom and my friends. Let's just enjoy this night for what it is and let it go."

He rolled onto his back and stared at the ceiling while she slipped out of bed to get dressed.

When he didn't respond to her conclusion, she said, "I should sneak upstairs and let you rest. You've got yoga in five hours. The last thing I want is to mess with your training routines, Wyatt."

He propped himself up on his elbows, giving her a gorgeous view of his eight-pack abs and exquisitely carved chest. All lean and wiry, formidable, just like him. "I could argue with you, or I could let you go and bet that the memory of what just happened will be enough to change your mind tomorrow."

"Pretty cocky." She teased, although deep down, she knew the memory would keep her tempted.

"Gold medals do that to a guy."

She threw a pillow at him and then picked up her shoes. "'Thank you' sounds weird, but I guess I can't lie and pretend I didn't enjoy this little ruse you cooked up."

"See, it's already working." He wiggled his brows. "Tomorrow night you'll be knocking at my door."

"Don't count on it."

"I have other tricks up my sleeve." He winked. "Curiosity will eat at you."

"I've got to go." She leaned down to give him a quick kiss, hoping he couldn't see the curiosity burning in her eyes. "Sleep well."

"Oh, I'll sleep like a baby." He flung himself back against the pillows.

Emma crept out of his room and headed toward the stairs when Mari reached the second floor with a diet Coke and an apple. Apparently this group had odd eating habits, and really unfortunate timing.

"Sneaking out of Wyatt's room so late? He said that kiss on Twitter was just a bet, but now I'm not convinced."

Emma tapped into some nerves of steel and waved Mari off. "Wyatt had texted me that his radiator wasn't working right and his room was too hot. So I stopped in to check on it and fix the problem."

"And did you?"

"He should cool down now. No worries. He'll be up and out of here on schedule tomorrow." Emma smiled as if everything were perfectly normal. "Now if you don't mind, I'm exhausted from the party. See you at breakfast."

Emma jogged up the stairs and closed her bedroom door, wondering how in the hell she would interact with Wyatt without giving away their secret. Heaven help her if Mari caught on to the deception. It didn't take a genius to know that Mari wouldn't respect any boundaries, and Emma couldn't afford for a woman like that to start snooping.

Chapter Eleven

Emma kept to the kitchen while Wyatt and Ryder practiced yoga with Amanda. Images from last night kept distracting her from preparing breakfast. She placed her cool palm against the burning heat of her cheek.

All morning she'd been tottering on wobbly legs, as if the inn had transformed into a ship and set sail on choppy seas. Regret wouldn't be the right word to describe the uneasy sensations blowing hot and cold within her, although Lord knew she'd never look at Room 201 the same way again.

Sadly, she hadn't much experience with sex. Still a virgin at twenty-three, she'd finally done the deed with Tommy Feeney, whom she'd dated for several months prior, and several more afterward. Theirs had been a sweet, pleasant kind of lovemaking. One in which she'd felt some genuine, if not earth-shattering, connection. A year or so later, she'd dated a ski school instructor, Scott Heinke. He'd been a bit bolder and more adventuresome, but the relationship ended with ski season's closing. He'd never returned to Sterling Canyon, and she hadn't really missed him once he'd gone. In both cases, living with her mom had prevented her from fully enjoying the relationships. Any privacy occurred at their apartments, and only rarely did she find a way to spend the night without raising her mom's suspicions.

And then there'd been Wyatt—impossibly young, impossibly glorious, and utterly unforgettable. As much as a peculiar mix of pride and embarrassment over the one-night stand had driven her out of that hotel room in the wee hours, it had not prevented her from reliving the splendor of him over and over.

Those memories had sustained her, and then fed her story, which in turn spurred new fantasies. Never did she dream Wyatt would waltz into her life again. That she would abandon all caution again to experience the all-consuming passion he inspired. She couldn't know if her inexperience had something to do with her vaunted opinion of his skill, and at the moment she didn't care. Wyatt may be younger, but he was simultaneously adorable, sexy, and seductive.

And yet, even now, what they shared could be little more than a shooting star racing across the sky, doomed to burn out. Should she take Kelsey's advice to heart, abandon her misgivings, and enjoy the present without worrying about December, or next spring, or however long it may take after he left, for her to forget him? Would it be worth the potential pain? The lies and secrets?

Good grief, the fact that she didn't automatically say *no* only proved she hadn't learned anything from her parents' mistakes.

She rubbed her temples, exhausted from overthinking. Deep down, she knew she probably would be knocking on his door, just as he'd predicted. Oddly, she could barely muster indignity at the thought, despite knowing all the risks.

For now, she'd return to being the polite innkeeper in front of Ryder, Mari, and the crew. Friendly, solicitous, accommodating. She'd also make sure Wyatt understood that she wouldn't be subjected to Mari's questions.

Heaviness settled around her heart when forced to admit the mounting lies of omission—with family and friends—that proved her quite adept at deception. Still, her best shot at fooling Mari, Ryder, and everyone else, was to avoid Wyatt in public as much as possible.

When she heard the kitchen door swing open, her body involuntarily tensed.

"Can I help with the j-juice?" Ryder asked.

"Sure." Relief mixed with disappointment washed over her, loosening her muscles. "Do you remember how to work the juicer?"

"I think so." He crossed to the sink to wash his hands, and then looked at the fruit bowl. "What should I use?"

Emma wiped her hands on a towel before joining him at the other counter. "How about a simple tangerine and grapefruit combo. Sound good?"

"Okay." Ryder began peeling the fruit.

Grateful for his taciturn nature, she returned to stirring the steel cut oatmeal and latched onto a reason to turn her thoughts away from Wyatt. "How'd you like the pottery class?"

"It was great. I'm g-good at it."

The hint of pride caused her to glance over her shoulder in time to catch him grinning. A smile started in her stomach and worked its way up to her face. "Jack Crawford is a wonderful teacher and a super nice guy."

"He said I could come by the studio whenever it's convenient."

"That's great. Maybe you can make me a mug or something before you leave at the end of the month."

Ryder fell silent while the juicer whirred. Between batches, he finally asked, "Will you miss W-Wyatt when we go?"

The question stunned her. Wyatt surely hadn't confessed, so Ryder must've seen the stupid Twitter picture, or heard them last night. *Oh, shoot.* His voice had maintained its uninflected tone, which left her unable to guess which answer he'd prefer.

"I'll miss you both." Not a lie, yet not exactly truthful. Emma wasn't prepared to discuss Wyatt with him, especially not when the soreness from last night accompanied each step.

Ryder merely grunted, which she suspected was his subtle way of calling her out.

Wyatt then burst in to the kitchen, bright-eyed and full of energy, looking way too handsome for her to handle so early in the day. A bubbly mix of uncertainty and desire made her tongue-tied.

"Good morning, gorg—" He stopped in his tracks when he saw Ryder. "Oh, I didn't know you were in here."

"Obviously." Ryder snorted. When he pressed another batch of fruit through the juicer, Emma was glad for the disruptive noise.

She took advantage of those precious seconds to collect herself and play it cool in front of Ryder. With a cordial smile, she glanced at Wyatt. "Breakfast is a few minutes away, so why don't you go grab a seat and relax."

Turning her back, she bent down to retrieve small bowls for raisins, brown sugar, and almonds. Wyatt stepped closer and murmured, "I thought we made a deal last night. No more turning your back on me unless it's in invitation."

Emma cast a quick glance at Ryder, who was loading the last batch of fruit into the juicer. She glared at Wyatt while jerking her chin toward Ryder's back. His brother may have some clue about the situation, but they didn't need to advertise, either. "I have a bunch of toppings for the oatmeal, and I made some turkey bacon, too. I already set out yogurt, fruit, and water in the dining room if you want to get started. You have a schedule to keep."

Ryder took the pitcher of fresh juice and started toward the door. Apparently determined to keep Wyatt's priorities in check, he said, "Come on, let her work in p-peace. We should talk about using drones to pick your lines before we head out anyway."

"I'll be there in a second." Wyatt stared at Ryder without blinking until his brother shrugged and left them alone, then he turned back to her. "What's the matter?"

"Nothing." She kept chopping almonds. "I'm trying to get your breakfast on the table."

When he crowded her, she had to repress a small gasp.

"Are you seriously going to treat me this way after last night?" he demanded.

Emma pressed her lips together, feeling awkward and irrational, but still committed to her plan. "We agreed to keep things on the down low."

Without hesitation, he gripped her wrist and dragged her to the pantry. He closed the door behind them and then pulled her into a kiss. Apparently compartmentalizing meant different things to him than to her. His hands clamped around her waist and his voice became husky. "I wish you would've stayed the night. I was in such a frenzy, it went too fast."

She pretended that she was in control of the situation. Pretended her knees weren't buckling, her body wasn't blazing like a summer sunset, her heart wasn't banging against her ribs in response to his touch.

"I can't stay all night or we'll get caught, just like we could now if Mari comes searching for either of us." She laid her hands on his chest to push him away, but found herself gripping his shirt instead.

"I'll hide in here if she does." He cupped her face and ran his thumb along her jaw. The tender gesture burrowed into her heart, filling it with heat. "I'm so relaxed this morning. I have a feeling today is going to be my best day yet. You may be my good luck charm." He kissed her again, this time trailing his mouth down her neck.

A whimper escaped her throat because she could too easily be seduced and risk exposing them both. She forced herself to ease away. "Wyatt, we need to act indifferent toward each other in front of everyone. Please. Go talk to Ryder about the drones. I really would hate for you to get hurt because you're losing focus."

"I want to see you again tonight." His hand slid down her back and around her butt. "Will you sneak into my room?"

Her heart beat faster, but something—conscience, caution, self-preservation?—held her back. "Maybe."

"If you don't come to me, I'll come to you." His sexy smirk made her smile, even though she should be irked by the blackmail.

"Please go before everyone wonders what's going on in here." She pushed at his chest. "Treat me like an innkeeper, okay?"

A peculiar heat lit his hazel eyes, making the green glow against the golden brown. Her body responded in kind.

"Actually, having you be my serving wench could be a fun bit of role-playing later, too." He glanced around the pantry. "Maybe we can make use of that honey, or the chocolate sauce." He winked and then opened the pantry door.

A sudden vision of him licking either of those sticky, sweet foods off her body made her swallow hard. She willed herself to contain her whorl of emotions and calmly stroll back to the counter. Setting the little bowls on a tray, she asked, "Can you hold the door open for me?"

He did as she asked. Ignoring the gaze she felt boring through her back as Wyatt followed her into the dining room, she set out all the food while greeting Mari and Buddy. Thankfully her phone rang, giving her a perfect excuse to absent herself.

"Excuse me." She glanced at the screen, which then caused her heart to stop its banging and drop to the floor. Covering her dismay, she said, "I'll be back to check on you all in a few minutes."

Emma slipped into the kitchen and drew a steadying breath. "Hey, Mom. How are you and Aunt Vera enjoying the trip so far? Do you love Chicago?"

"We went to the art institute, the 360 Chicago building, the Adler Planetarium, and did some shopping at the Water Tower. The city is very busy, and very big. I can't imagine wanting to live surrounded by skyscrapers, although the lake is pretty."

"It sounds exciting to me. Lots to do."

A pause warned Emma that her mother was thinking of how to state whatever it was she was about to say, and that it probably wouldn't be particularly pleasant.

"Well, it seems you've found your own form of excitement, despite being stuck in a small town. In our very small town, where everybody talks, Emma." Admonition colored her words, and Emma knew right then that someone had informed her mom of the kiss. Good grief, if anyone had been privy to the happenings in Room 201 last night, Emma'd be banned from the premises.

Hoping to divert the conversation, she ignored the bait and asked, "When do you go to DC?"

"Don't change the subject. Tell me what's going on with you and our guest. Did you really maul him in the middle of Kelsey's party? I don't want to believe Connie Buckman's voice mail."

Connie? That biddy hadn't even been at Kelsey's party. Emma's mind raced, trying to picture the chain of gossips that had worked so fast that this news had already reached her mom. Annoyance didn't begin to cover the hot emotion coursing through her body. One day she'd love to find the courage to tell all the busybodies to mind their own business.

"Mom, I'm thirty-one, so please don't talk to me like I'm twelve." There, that felt good. So good, in fact, it spurred an unusual burst of chutzpah. "And yes, I did kiss him in good fun because of a bet."

Emma then frowned because that statement made the second or third half-truth of the morning, and it was barely past seven o'clock. She didn't like having to defend herself, and she also didn't like lying. No matter what, at the end of the day, Emma had always considered herself a conservative, kind, and honest person. The recognition that things were changing nettled like a burr.

Living with secrets proved everything her mom had always claimed about casual sex and lies of omission. Emma's justifications of her recent behavior corroded her integrity, a part of herself she'd always relied upon to feel proud.

"Emma Anne, honestly. According to Connie, everyone assumes you're doing more than 'kissing' our guest. Our *guest*. That's not what I meant when I asked to you to keep him happy. And Lord knows, I raised you better than to flaunt yourself in front of the whole town." Her mother's scolding stole her breath.

Of course, when she recalled the way Wyatt had disrobed her and pinned her to the wall, sheepish acknowledgement cooled her anger.

Before Emma found her voice, her mother continued, "I left you in charge of everything, Emma. I'm trusting you with our livelihood at a critical time, with an important guest and opportunity. You know the publicity from his stay could improve our future. What if this little fling you're having goes south and jades his opinion? I can't believe you'd jeopardize our family legacy for something so . . . base. Haven't we both seen how those impulses can cost people everything?"

Her mother's histrionics aside, Emma wasn't ready to be done with Wyatt and the sort of hopeful anticipation he inspired—even if it was stupid, dangerous, doomed, deceitful. At the same time, she despised herself for letting her mother down. And for the fact that her mother wasn't completely wrong. Sure, if things went south, Wyatt could use his platform to burn the inn. Worse, he could very well end up costing Emma something more important—her heart. Not that she'd confess anything now.

"Mom, don't overreact because I kissed someone. I mean, honestly, can't you hear how ridiculous that sounds? I'm not hanging out on the corner of Cottonwood and Main selling favors. I'm sorry if people are jumping to conclusions about me and Wyatt." She paused to swallow the guilt about that truth, then teased, "But maybe a little notoriety could make the inn more popular."

The dead silence on the other end of the line told her that her joke had bombed. The quiet stretched on, making Emma's eye twitch.

"Emma, if anyone knows how easy it is to get caught up in a flirtation with a dashing, larger-than-life kind of man, it's me. Don't set your sights on a boy who's always going to have women chasing him." Her mother's voice had softened and wavered, as if she'd just been nicked by the memory of her own lost love. "Trust me, honey. No matter how lonely you may feel now, taking up with someone like that athlete is not going to end well. He's probably got women in every town. I don't want to see you hurt."

"Mom, I'm not stupid. Sooner or later you have to let me make my own choices without weighing in and criticizing." Emma sighed, sorry that she'd upset her mother, and conceding that Wyatt definitely wouldn't lack for women while on the tour. "Now listen, I need to pack lunch for the crew before they head out to the mountain. I'll call you if I need anything, but just relax. Everything is fine. Tell Aunt Vera I said hi. Love you!"

Emma hung up before her mom could protest. She shoved her phone in her pocket and went to work on snacks and lunch, trying not to think too much about how confused she was about her feelings, her morals, and her mother's constant warnings.

Tension tightened her chest. Her brief taste of freedom summoned something deep in her nature even as common sense struggled to hold its ground.

Yesterday self-restraint had lost its iron grip. Perhaps Emma had been too lonely for too long to care enough to resist.

She frowned then, because as much as she might enjoy a torrid affair, the risks were sky-high. Mari's antennae had already been raised by what she'd seen last night, and Emma didn't think she was cagey enough to fool Mari for too long.

Mari could ruin her life. Her life, which quite honestly required her to set all this silliness aside and focus on her new manuscript. The one moldering upstairs despite the looming deadline.

One might think Wyatt's arrival would've have made it easier to finish her book. After all, her original encounter with him had spurred a million fun, fictional ideas. But she'd built Dallas's character on archetypes and fantasy. Getting to know Wyatt better had increased a sort of nagging guilt she had about having used him to create Dallas in the first place. That guilt paralyzed her each time she sat down to write.

Looks like her mother was right. Sex and lust were threatening to destroy her carefully tended life.

◆ ◆ ◆

At four o'clock, Emma shut down her computer, pleased that she'd accomplished sixty minutes of writing without interruption. It hadn't been easy, but she'd consciously refused to write a scene in a senior citizen center. Nope. Straight up fiction with absolutely no basis in her reality. With discipline and determination, maybe she could manage all of her jobs and identities without a colossal screwup.

She ran a brush through her hair and then slipped downstairs to prepare a snack for Wyatt and the crew, whom she expected would be back by five.

"Hey, Em, you've kept yourself scarce, today," Andy said, having been waiting for her in the kitchen. "'Fraid I'm going to razz you about last night?"

"Razz me?" She hoped her face didn't betray her discomfort. "It was one stupid kiss because I wanted Trip to lose a hundred bucks."

"Shit, that just means he'll be more aggressive at tonight's poker game so he can recoup the loss."

"Sorry," she smirked. "Honestly, it's a little ridiculous that my kissing someone causes town-wide shock waves. The rest of you do whatever you want all the time, but I go out on a limb and everyone comes down on me."

Andy fell silent, his expression chagrined.

"You have to admit, it was really out of character." Andy stepped closer, reaching out to touch her hand. But he pulled back, as if whatever he wanted to say next made him uncomfortable. "Em, all jokes aside, I'm glad it wasn't more than a dare. Wyatt's a fun dude, but he's got a reputation for flings wherever he's competing. Women are a great way for athletes to release some pressure. I don't think he's a bad guy, and I'm sure he's a lot more exciting than guys like me, but I wouldn't want to see you misled or hurt. And don't forget, we local guys will be around after next month."

Emma might've been upset by Andy's remarks if she weren't used to his telling Avery, and sometimes her and Kelsey, about the many ways that men could be disingenuous when it came to women. She might've even pumped him for more information if she hadn't once again gotten that odd feeling that he wanted something more from her.

No doubt, her chances of a stable, healthy relationship were greatly improved if she chose someone like Andy. She stared at him now, with his boyish good looks and affable smile and almost wished that the long-ago crush she'd had would return. Dating Andy would be so much easier than seeing Wyatt. But that ship had sailed, on both counts. Apparently Emma Duffy wasn't interested in easy.

"I wasn't born yesterday. I know Wyatt's not looking for love." She pretended that she could care less, but her heart dropped as the words fell from her mouth. It hurt knowing she and Wyatt had no future.

And not just because he'd have no interest. She couldn't pursue a real relationship with him and keep Alexa Aspen a secret. Emma needed to view the expiration date created by his impending departure as a silver lining, because it meant this fling didn't require her confession.

Everything would work out as long as she could convince herself that it didn't hurt at all.

"I'm glad to hear you've still got a good head on your shoulders." Andy flashed his lopsided grin before wandering out of the kitchen.

Emma shook her head. *Good head on your shoulders?* Hell, if she heard one more comment like that she might fling herself off The Cirque. Sure, those remarks were meant as compliments, but *boring* was what she heard each and every time.

For thirty-one years she'd liked being considered a mature, reliable, responsible person. Why, lately, did it chafe her like wet clothes in a rainstorm?

Emma stirred the hummus she was making, adding cayenne for a kick. She chopped veggies, and toasted some pita bread, then arranged everything onto a big platter and set it on the dining table. Anything to keep busy and leave little room for depressing self-evaluation. Then, like sunlight peeking through a cloud, a little smile tugged at the corner of her mouth. At least with Wyatt she wasn't so dull. He didn't treat her naughty, spontaneous side like a capital offense.

Taking advantage of a few extra minutes, she ran upstairs to apply a bit of lip gloss and mascara. She couldn't change her top or overdo the makeup because Andy would notice and then pity her. A quick glance in the mirror suggested she looked pretty enough, so she headed back downstairs to wait for Wyatt's return.

When she reached the lobby, she found Andy engaged in conversation with an attractive, athletic-looking young woman.

"Hey, Em, this is Jessie Taylor."

Emma immediately recognized the woman's name. Jessie was a competitive boarder and had run in the same circles as Wyatt and Ryder. In truth, her name had been romantically linked with Wyatt's for a brief time before Ryder's accident. She remembered because she'd been slightly jealous at the time.

From behind Jessie's back, Andy cast Emma a sympathetic glance. "Came to visit Wyatt."

The niggling envy from yesteryear surged forward, compressing Emma's heart into a hard little raisin.

"Em?" Andy prodded. "Did you hear me?"

"Sorry. I've got so much on my mind." Aiming for something between polite detachment and friendly demeanor, she stepped forward and shook Jessie's hand. "Nice to meet you."

"Same." Like Emma, Jessie had green eyes. No freckles, of course. Silky blond hair only enhanced the young woman's natural beauty. She looked even younger than Wyatt. Perhaps twenty-two?

Jessie tucked her hands in her jeans' pockets and smiled, unaware that Emma could not have appreciated her presence less. "Andy mentioned that Wyatt and Ryder might be back any minute."

"They usually return by five." Emma cleared her throat of the frog stuck in there. "Are they expecting you?"

"Sort of." Jessie casually shrugged, her carefree gaze wandering the lobby. "Wyatt texted me when he decided to train here. I live in Durango, so he thought we might hook up if I was around."

Hook up? Hook up as in visit, or as in have sex? The image scorched Emma's lungs like a hot poker, but she wouldn't let Jessie or Andy see the jab. She had no right to be angry. She and Wyatt weren't a couple. Of course he'd reach out to an old flame if he knew he'd be nearby. What guy—especially one who needed "to release some pressure," as Andy had so aptly stated—passed up guaranteed sex? Still, Wyatt should've warned Emma that Jessie would be coming.

Emma—apparently little more than his sexual stopgap until a younger, more compatible partner arrived to replace her. Wyatt had more in common with Jessie, another thrill-seeking competitor, than he ever would with Emma. Jessie led an exciting life and shared his dreams. Emma was too timid to reveal all of herself to her friends and family, let alone race down the side of a mountain.

Humiliation left her weak-kneed. Her nose tingled, making her want to run and hide. "Well, make yourself comfortable in the front parlor. I've got to start dinner."

Emma nodded at Andy and Jessie and then bolted to the kitchen. The kitchen that had so often brought her comfort now shrank around her like cellophane wrap. Dammit, she could not fall apart over something so utterly ridiculous. How had she turned into Kelsey in little over a week's time?

Regroup, Emma Duffy.

Methodically, she retrieved the spices needed to prepare the steelhead trout she'd bought for dinner, while forbidding herself from adding eyedrops to the Meyer lemon sauce.

◆　◆　◆

Wyatt jumped out of the van and high-fived Ryder. "Best day yet, just like I knew it would be. I can't wait to watch this footage. Did you see the sweet little jump Trip built for me with his shovel? It's cool to land in soft snow instead of hardpack. Anything about my jumps look troubling on the monitor?"

"Not really." Ryder shrugged noncommittally, and Wyatt immediately regretted his insensitivity. Ryder could only stand on the sidelines with his cane and watch Wyatt getting back into the groove. Yet pity would increase Ryder's discomfort, which left Wyatt perplexed as to how to proceed.

"When's your next pottery lesson?"

"Tonight at seven." Ryder's mouth quirked upward, which it so rarely did these days.

Pottery, of all things. Who'd have thought?

Emma had. Emma saw things about people that Wyatt missed. She cared about others, whereas Wyatt had lived a fairly self-centered life until Ryder's accident.

Looking back, he could see that he'd spent most of his time chasing his goals to make sure he'd never live in fear and uncertainty again. He'd been generous with his money, but not with his time. Until he'd met Emma, he hadn't considered that maybe time was the most valuable thing he could offer. He could probably learn a lot from her if he chose to explore that path. But that would mean giving up his other goals, which he couldn't honestly consider.

"Wonder what Emma's cooking for dinner?" Wyatt asked, searching for neutral territory with Ryder.

"Something good."

"No doubt." Wyatt slapped Ryder's shoulder before grabbing his gear from the back of the van. He'd been focused all day, heart pumping, legs burning up the slopes. Now the thought of Emma had his heart pounding and body burning in a different yet equally satisfying way. He jogged up the steps to catch up to Ryder before he opened the door. "Can't wait for a shower."

"You need one," Ryder joked, which Wyatt took as a good sign. A near-perfect day, and he planned on an even better night. He strolled into the lobby expecting to see Emma, then stopped in his tracks.

"Jessie?" Ryder's voice cracked. "Holy sh-shit."

Ryder actually smiled—a real smile—and hugged Jessie. While those two embraced and said hello, Wyatt glanced around for Emma. He wondered if she knew who Jessie was and if she knew anything about his and Jessie's past. Either way, he suddenly found himself in a tight spot and not at all pleased Jessie'd showed up without any warning.

Of course, if it hadn't been for Emma, he wouldn't have cared about the lack of notice. In fact, he might've been happy for her company. Now things were complicated. Not that Emma seemed to be all that invested in him or that he'd made any promises. Still, seeing Jessie here felt wrong.

Ryder released Jessie, so Wyatt opened his arms to greet her with a hug as well. "Hey, Jess. Why didn't you tell me you were coming?"

She squeezed him tightly and then planted a quick kiss on his lips. "Thought I'd surprise you."

Mari came inside just in time to catch them still arm in arm, her eyes lit with curiosity.

Double shit, this would be unpleasant. "Mari, this is an old friend of mine and my brother's, Jessie Taylor. One of the best boardercross competitors out there."

175

"Jessie Taylor . . ." Mari seemed to be remembering something. She'd researched Wyatt's past fairly extensively, and he saw the moment her memory snapped into place. "Oh, yes, I remember. You two were something of an item a couple of years ago, just before . . ." then she trailed off, realizing that referencing Ryder's accident probably wouldn't win her any friends. "Before Wyatt took a break from competition."

"An item? I suppose you could say that." Jessie's pretty green eyes twinkled. He'd always liked her pale green eyes. Emma's were greener, clearer, sharper . . . prettier.

Naturally, Emma walked in on the scene, her gaze briefly snagging on Wyatt and Jessie's joined arms.

"Welcome back, everyone. I've set out some snacks." She gestured toward the dining room, giving no hint of her emotions. "Dinner will be at six thirty. Should I set an extra plate?"

To everyone else, that breezy voice must've sounded normal. But Wyatt instantly detected the detached tone, the rigidity of her spine, and the slight upward tilt of her nose. She'd never admit it, but Jessie's arrival bugged her. He didn't want her to be hurt. He needed to fix this before it got out of hand.

"Jess, go catch up with Ryder while I shower." Then he called out to Emma's retreating back. "Emma, that radiator is still acting funny. Can you come take a look now so my room isn't freezing when I get out of the shower?"

Emma stopped and glanced over her shoulder, her green eyes clouded with emotion. "I'll send Andy right up."

She'd called his bluff and risked a slew of questions from Andy when he saw that the radiator worked fine. Oh yeah, Emma Duffy was pissed.

Wyatt refrained from reacting to the snub, aware that Jessie, Ryder, and Mari were all watching him. He brushed aside his own emotions and smiled. "I'll be back down in ten minutes."

He took the steps two at a time and called Emma's cell once he reached his room. She didn't pick up.

Chapter Twelve

Emma snatched glimpses of Jessie and Wyatt while collecting the empty dessert plates. All evening, she'd been forced to endure their laughter and easy banter. Even Mari had joined in and relaxed, her typically pinched expression lightening.

Jessie sat between the Lawson brothers, but her body leaned closer to Wyatt's. A hair flip here, a saucy smile there. No doubt she expected to spend the night, or maybe two. Emma could hardly blame her, because unlike Emma, Wyatt was memorable.

Wyatt's brilliant smile flashed again, only to falter when he caught Emma's eye. That made him stiffen and sit up straighter, as if Mother Superior had entered the room.

Suppressing a sad groan, Emma decided to assert herself so he didn't pity her.

"I'm heading out shortly, so if there's anything you all need before I go, please let me know. Jessie, I don't mean to presume anything, but will you need a room?"

A sudden, tension-filled hush ensued. Emma purposely kept her focus on Jessie, although, peripherally, she could see Ryder turn toward Wyatt. Pulse racing, Emma now very much regretted flinging herself into the air like a trapeze artist without first checking to see if a net had been secured below.

No net. No net at all.

Jessie cast Wyatt a knowing glance. "I don't need my own room, thanks."

Emma doubted Wyatt wanted to hurt her, but he probably didn't want to hurt Jessie, either. Even if he didn't want Jessie to stay with him, he wouldn't embarrass her in front of everyone. And wishful thinking aside, chances were he'd be happy to have Jessie stay. After all, unlike Emma, Jessie wasn't afraid to be with Wyatt. She didn't make him feel like he needed to remain a shameful secret. She'd probably even lend her name to help his documentary get more publicity.

In short, Jessie deserved him.

Emma nodded and smiled. Hopefully no one noticed how her cheeks were cracking under the strain. Or heard her heart whimper when it smacked against the ground. "Fine. I'll see you all in the morning. Enjoy your evening."

"If it's not out of your w-way, can I get a lift to Crawford's studio?" Ryder asked.

"Absolutely." Emma nodded. "I'm leaving in ten minutes, so I'll meet you by the door."

As she left the room on shaky legs, she heard Mari speak up. "We have a little time to get Jessie on film, if that's okay. Just a couple of quick questions about the old days, and what she thinks of Wyatt's transition plans."

"Great!" came Jessie's bright reply.

Great, Emma repeated in her head with a heavy dose of sarcasm.

Thank God Kelsey had agreed to meet with her this evening, because Emma couldn't have stayed at the inn much longer. She certainly didn't wish to watch Jessie and Wyatt canoodle all night. Canoodle . . . an old-fashioned word. One she'd heard her mom and Grammy say over and over. Her comfortable use of that kind of vocabulary counted among the many little things that set Emma apart from others. Made her a bit more peculiar and unrelatable, she supposed.

After wiping down the counters, she grabbed her purse off the pantry doorknob and marched through the inn. Along the way, she passed the parlor, where Mari sat in a chair while Buddy filmed her interviewing Jessie and Wyatt, whom she'd trapped on the sofa. How sweet they looked together: two young, fearless athletes with so much to look forward to.

Wyatt caught Emma watching. He opened his mouth as if he were going to call out to her, so she trotted ahead to where Ryder stood waiting by the door.

"Sorry. I went as fast as I could. Hope you won't be late." Emma opened the door and held it as he went through with his cane.

"No problem." He followed her to her car. They passed an unfamiliar Jeep in the parking lot, which Emma assumed must belong to Jessie. What did it feel like to be so independent and free? To take off on a whim and meet up with a lover, or travel, or do anything unexpected?

A swell of resentment toward Emma's mother surfaced, followed by guilt. Her moralistic mother had only ever loved her and sought to protect her from pain. Then resentment surged again, this time directed at her father and the damage he'd left in his wake. Of course, Emma was an adult. Blaming others for her choices didn't really work anymore.

An awkward silence descended after she started her car. She wanted answers about Jessie even though it wouldn't be fair to pump Ryder for details. Before she could help herself, she said, "You must've enjoyed catching up with an old friend."

He shrugged noncommittally. "Jessie's fun. Kinda ditzy, though."

"Oh?" Emma wanted to pry further, but that would be bad manners. And very obvious. "I'm surprised she's not in training now, too."

"Guess she figured she could skip a day and visit since she lives so close by." Ryder stared straight ahead.

Ryder's blasé attitude about the visit surprised her. When she'd briefly met him years ago, he'd been extroverted and silly—a flirt with a number of women in the bar, too. Now he barely engaged with anyone, preferring solitary activities like cooking and pottery. Had Jessie's return been yet another reminder of a terrible tragedy? Or had seeing Wyatt reconnect with a former flame stirred a different kind of sibling rivalry?

Suddenly Emma wondered whether Ryder had left a sweetheart behind. "Ryder, forgive me for asking, but I'm curious. Do you have a girlfriend back home?"

He snapped his head toward her, brows raised above his glasses. Finally, he snorted, "No."

"Haven't met anyone in a while?"

"I'm not exactly a p-prime catch these days." His brows dipped back beneath the rims as his head bowed.

"Oh, I don't know about that. You're young, attractive, sensitive, even if it sometimes comes out a little rough." She smiled, hoping she hadn't totally overstepped.

"So are you, but you're a-alone, too."

"An unfortunate thing we have in common. Must be one reason we've become fast friends." Emma kept her eyes on the road as if her headlights might illuminate her thoughts, which had raced ahead. "Do you think people like us—self-conscious people—are alone because we make it hard to be known?"

"Dunno. I'm not the same as before, but even back then, I wasn't trying to b-be known."

"Well, you are a guy, and young at that." She grinned before sighing. "But I'm not. Sometimes I wish I could just . . . be. Let go and see what happens."

He stared out the passenger window for a moment. "Be careful, Emma. If you 'let go,' do it for yourself, not for someone else. Don't go against your n-nature to make someone else happy or you'll end up regretting it."

Ryder never mentioned Wyatt's name, but his meaning could not have been more obvious. He knew his brother's love 'em and leave 'em history, as did she. Over the years, he must've seen other girls, like Jessie, get their hopes up only to have them dashed. She considered his concern a compliment, even though it choked off any lingering hope she might have been harboring about Wyatt.

But more honestly, she thought about whether letting go meant going against her nature, as he presumed, or running toward it. For so long, she'd cultivated certain traits while burying others. Even *she* no longer knew who she was at her core.

Two turns later, Emma pulled up in front of Jack Crawford's studio. Through the window, she saw him sitting behind one of the potter's wheels. "Do you need a ride home?"

"I'll be okay." Ryder opened the door. "Thanks, Emma."

When Ryder disappeared through the front door, Emma took a second to slap her forehead. What had she been thinking? She hardly knew the guy well enough to be dishing out love-life advice. In fact, love lives were the last thing she should advise anyone about.

Shifting into first, she pulled away from the curb and drove to Kelsey's.

"I'm glad you called. Now I don't have to spend the evening alone." Kelsey greeted her with a generous glass of red wine. As always, she looked like a sexpot, in her formfitting clothes and high heels.

Emma glanced down at her jeans and button-down shirt. Modest, clean, hopelessly plain clothes.

"Thanks." Emma set her purse down and gulped the wine.

"Oh, God. You just drank that like Trip does. Slow down! It's not beer." Kelsey plopped onto the down cushions of her sofa.

Emma loved Kelsey's condo. Rich wood floors, a big hearth and roaring fire, earth tones and comfy furniture. Best of all, privacy. Emma had never really known that particular luxury. Until recently, she hadn't realized she wanted any, either. "You're so lucky to have this place all to yourself."

"Hardly to myself these days." Kelsey smiled.

No one had suffered more heartbreak—whether exaggerated or real—than Kelsey had over the years. Since fifth grade, she'd chased love only to be told she was too clingy. Until she'd hooked up with Trip.

Had Kelsey confided in Emma about her secret bet with Trip this past summer, Emma would've advised against it. She would've listed the many reasons why Trip was wrong for Kelsey (a list that would've included half the female population in town), the many ways Kelsey's heart would be shredded—yet Emma would've been 100 percent wrong, and Kelsey wouldn't have that giant rock on her finger now.

Thank God Kelsey hadn't come to her. Emma had a lot to learn about love, and she needed to start learning from someone other than her scorned mom.

"What's with the frown? Did you come over to discuss some problem?" Kelsey swirled her wine, dipped her nose deep into the glass, and sniffed before taking a sip.

"No. I called because Andy mentioned the guys' poker night. I figured you'd be alone. Did you invite Avery?"

"She's caught up in some book about sisters in France during World War II. Sounds depressing to me." Kelsey waved it off, as if reading were a silly pastime.

Emma had read *The Nightingale*, however, and understood Avery's desire to curl up alone and finish it. She swigged more of her wine. "Well, your party last night was a success. Now on to the wedding plans."

"I'm thinking green gowns for you and Ave because the color flatters you both. And as much as I love your cupcakes, I'm ordering a traditional wedding cake from Sweet Cakes. You won't have time to bake anyway, because we're going to be busy picking flowers, bands, a menu. I really want your input with the menu, and to make sure I don't get ripped off by the caterer."

"Where did you decide to hold the ceremony?"

"I'm going to keep it intimate. I booked the Pinnacle Lodge because it has the best views, and Trip loves those mountains."

"So romantic, and a beautiful setting." Emma thought of how her friend had gone from the depths of despondency to the zenith of happiness. Honestly, Kelsey and Trip's love story would make a compelling romance novel, too, but she couldn't steal it. One "real life" inspiration was more than Emma could manage to keep secret. Besides, borrowing their whole story would be cheating. She squeezed Kelsey's leg. "It's wonderful to see you this excited and in love. You know I like to give you a hard time about Trip, but he makes you glow, and for that, I can love him."

Kelsey's pretty, caramel-colored eyes misted. "Thanks, Emma. I threw caution to the wind, and it worked out." Then she set her glass on the table and cleared her throat. "Maybe some people might learn from my example."

Emma poured another glass of wine and tucked her feet under her butt, refusing to take the bait. "This is a great wine. What is it?"

"Uh uh. I'm not letting you off the hook that quickly." Kelsey leaned closer. "Emma Duffy, I'm not as smart as Avery or as rational as you, but I know a thing or two about lust, so don't sit there and pretend that the only reason you kissed Wyatt Lawson last night was because of Trip's bet." Kelsey held up a hand to cut off Emma's protest. "Nope. Don't even bother. Now, the only thing I really want to hear from you is what happened last night when you got back to the inn." Then she giggled. "Trip said Wyatt seemed unusually loose and relaxed today on the mountain."

Emma's panicked three-second hesitation sent Kelsey into a frenzy of hand clapping while she bounced on her cushion. "I knew it. I knew it, knew it, knew it! Tell me everything. Don't even think of leaving something out, either."

"It doesn't matter what did or didn't happen, or if I like Wyatt." Emma tapped a fingernail against the nearly empty glass. "Jessie Taylor came to visit him today. She's there now."

"Who's Jessie Taylor?" Kelsey scowled.

"Snowcross competitor, former lover, super cute girl . . . a girl that he'd invited to visit." Emma set the glass on the table and then nestled deeper into the cushion, averting her gaze.

"He kissed you like that and then invited his ex-girlfriend to the inn?" Kelsey's raised voice rang out.

Emma glanced at her fired-up friend. "Easy, tiger. In fairness, I think he'd gotten in touch with her before he arrived in town. She's from Durango, so she drove up to surprise him."

Kelsey slapped Emma's arm. "What in Sam Hill are you doing here with me? Go back to the inn now so he doesn't think you don't care if he gets together with her. Have you learned nothing from me in all these years?"

She flung herself dramatically back against the sofa, causing the first laugh of Emma's evening.

"Oh, I love you," Emma chuckled.

"That's another nonanswer, Emma." She sat up again and leaned forward. "Tell me why you won't go after Wyatt. What are you afraid of?"

"Be realistic, Kelsey. He's young. He's an athlete on a mission who'll be gone in a couple of weeks. There is no possible future, so what's the point?"

"The point is that it feels good when a man makes you feel beautiful. The point is, you don't know what the future has in store, but if you never venture anything, you can guarantee your days will be spent working at the inn with your mom." Kelsey softened her voice. "Your mom's sweet, but I don't want to see you turn into her. Alone and a little bitter about love and men, rattling around that big old inn. Please take a chance and have some fun."

"I have fun, but if I set my sights on someone like Wyatt, I'll be exactly like my mom, because Wyatt's just like my dad."

"You don't know that. Look at Trip. He was worse than your dad, but now he's reformed by love." She grinned. "Besides, I'm not saying you should fall in love with Wyatt. But have some sex, for God's sake, Emma. You won't be struck by lightning. Trust me. I'm still standing!"

Kelsey sighed in the face of Emma's mute stare. "You're so private, sometimes I can't understand you at all. You know me, I have to get everything off my chest."

Emma chuckled. "Well, maybe because there's already so much of it, it can't hold anything else in."

Kelsey laughed and glanced down at her generous cleavage. "Could be."

After topping off her wineglass, Kelsey sighed. "I want to see you happy. I want to see you do something wild before you die, too. Even you seem sick of being the "good" girl . . . at least, that's how it sounded last night in the bathroom."

Emma couldn't deny that truth. She sure was sick of being held up as some pious, dull, paragon of virtue. Of course, she wasn't a "good" girl last night, and look at how that had ended. Here she sat, drinking away pangs of jealousy while Wyatt reconnected with his ex. Yet again, her mom's dire predictions about casual sex seemed dead-on.

"So maybe you don't get your crazy on with Wyatt, but promise me one day you'll make me happy and do something no one expects."

A tiny part of Emma wanted to confess all her sins right then and there. Instead, she merely said, "I promise, someday I will surprise you."

◆ ◆ ◆

Emma returned to the inn before ten o'clock, surprised to see Jessie's Jeep missing. Had she left town? Her reckless heart skipped three beats as she jogged up the porch stairs and burst into the lobby.

She heard Wyatt's voice coming from the dining room, but it sounded tinny. Quietly she crept over to its entrance and caught Mari and Jim watching film footage on the large computer monitor. Their backs were to her, so they didn't hear her. From her spot near the archway, she could see a majority of the screen, so she decided to watch.

A mature woman's voice cut in, and Emma saw photos of a much younger Wyatt drift into view. She guessed the voice-over was his mother. Emma froze, mesmerized by glimpses of Wyatt looking so young. A mass of curls and white teeth, his good looks imminent despite his youth.

"Things weren't easy around here back then. My husband got laid off a few times, and new jobs are hard to come by in rural Vermont. Sometimes he'd drink, and sometimes he'd get a little rough with the boys. We didn't have much. Wyatt always wanted more."

Some still shots of Wyatt and Ryder playing in a yard strewn with junk flashed on the screen, followed by another of an intimidating-looking man standing in front of a mountain lake with both boys. Emma's heartbeat seemed to sputter and slow as she took in this information she hadn't known about Wyatt's childhood.

"When his friend gave him some old snowboard equipment, Wyatt didn't care that it didn't fit right. He believed he could do something with that sport, and he wouldn't be stopped. He worked as a busboy at the resort in exchange for a ski pass. Teachers would call me 'cause he'd skip school to go practice. He entered local competitions and started winning, and before we knew it, he had sponsors and then a coach."

More photos flashed of him winning small trophies and medals, working his way up to the world-recognized podiums. A smile lifted the corners of Emma's mouth as she imagined his excitement, pride, and hope. His sense of accomplishment from having done it all on his own. She knew something about that feeling thanks to her upcoming debut, yet unlike Wyatt, she wouldn't be able to share her achievement with anyone.

"My boys dealt with a lot of chaos when they were young. Ryder went with the flow, but Wyatt never could. He wanted to control something, and snowboarding gave him that. Made him feel safer, if you can believe it. 'Course, we learned the hard way it wasn't safe at all, though Wyatt wasn't the one who paid the price."

The screen displayed footage of Ryder's crash and Wyatt's anguished reaction. Emma's smile vanished and a hard lump formed in her throat as the echo of his mother's final words—dripping with blame—replayed in her head. Emma recognized that tone from the way her own mom sounded whenever her father's name came up.

Wyatt must feel the weight of that blame every single day. So much so that he was willing to risk avalanches and other potentially fatal accidents in order to support his brother and mom, to restore stability to his family. Could his need to have Ryder participate in this comeback actually be some kind of apology, or chance at salvation?

Emma frowned as she quietly backed away without being noticed. She dabbed her dewy eyes. Her chest ached a little. Her mind hurt from trying to reconfigure all the pieces of the puzzle that made up Wyatt Lawson.

She stopped by the front desk to check the voice mail. While listening to a message from her mother, Wyatt and Ryder entered the lobby—without Jessie.

Ryder greeted her with a brief nod. "I'm going to b-bed."

Wyatt kept his gaze on Emma, although he managed to slap his brother's shoulder. "See you in the morning."

Emma wordlessly placed the phone back in its charger. She wanted to run to him and kiss him and let him take whatever control he needed from her if it made him feel safe and secure. But Mari and Jim were awake, and Ryder hadn't yet disappeared into his room.

"I told Jessie I didn't plan on her staying in my room, so we picked up Ryder, they had a drink, and then she went home." He approached the desk, an obvious question shone in his eyes.

"I see." Emma could feel heat traveling to her cheeks, but she didn't care. He'd turned Jessie away, and she knew he'd done it for her. Only the tiniest part of her brain rattled a warning about getting in deeper with Wyatt, like a gnat buzzing near her ear. Still, she said, "If you're hungry, I can bring something to your room."

The gold and green streaks in his smoky hazel eyes flickered. "I'm starving."

"I'll be up shortly with something to satisfy you." Emma could hardly believe her ears. It was as if Alexa had invaded her body. Her knees weren't even wobbling. If anything, Wyatt looked like he might be dizzy.

"Be quick," he finally said, reestablishing some sense of control. She let him have it.

"As you wish." She gestured toward the stairs. He walked away, still watching her over his shoulder until he couldn't see her.

She turned and strolled past Mari and Jim, straight through the kitchen to the pantry, actually. Reaching out to the third shelf, she snatched the small honey pot and then made her way up the old servants' stairs in the rear of the kitchen.

Chapter Thirteen

Wyatt's heart raced while he brushed his teeth and waited for Emma. Since Jessie's arrival, he'd been working out how to fix the situation without hurting either woman. Ultimately, he'd had to hurt someone, so he'd picked Jessie.

That hadn't been a great moment. Scratch that—it had plain sucked. Wyatt hated to disappoint anyone, especially a special friend like Jessie. If only she had called before coming, he could've spared her the trip rather than having to reject her advances to her face. Jessie had taken it in stride, but he wouldn't know how she truly felt about him until he saw her again, if he saw her again.

Wyatt laughed to himself, then wondered what, exactly, it was about the prim innkeeper that fascinated him so much that he'd gambled turning away his ex for the possibility of seducing Emma again.

He'd assumed he would've had a lot of persuading to do to get Emma in bed, given her frosty 'tude earlier this evening. Never had he expected for her to offer a repeat of last night's performance without first demanding answers about Jessie.

Wyatt paced the narrow room, his body temperature rising with each anxious step. Before long, he'd tossed his shirt aside to cool off. He sprawled out on the bed, hands behind his head, and recalled the night before, when he'd had Emma pinned to the wall.

The visceral memory made him painfully hard in an instant. How much longer until she showed up?

Following a quick warning knock, he heard his door open. He sat up just as Emma came into view holding the honey pot. Holy shit. She'd remembered his earlier comment from the pantry and was willing to play along. That kind of attention—playfulness—could make her a keeper, but he shoved the dangerous thought aside.

Wyatt shot off the bed. Emma's gaze drifted over his chest and then dropped to the bulge in his pants, where his state of arousal made itself known.

"Oh," she whispered.

"Yeah." He smirked as he took the honey from her, already imagining the places he'd taste-test it. Brushing his knuckles along her cheek, he whispered, "I love that you brought this, Emma. You're full of surprises."

"Sometimes, anyway." She grinned, and his heart galloped like a thoroughbred at the Kentucky Derby for having made her smile. He made a mental note to try to do that more often in the coming weeks.

When Emma started to unbutton her shirt, he set down the honey. "Let me."

He refrained from ripping it open, choosing to enhance both their pleasure by stretching out the anticipation. He might be locked and loaded, but Emma needed time to catch up.

Stepping closer still, he cupped her face before kissing her. He started off lazily, giving himself time to savor the feel of her smooth cheek beneath his thumb, the way her pillowy lower lip slid between his, the taste of her mouth—she'd obviously sampled the honey.

Her hands pressed against his chest, as if testing his strength, before she slid them up over his shoulders and around his neck. She threaded her fingers through his hair—her firm yet gentle touch very much like the woman herself—sending goose bumps racing across his scalp.

Wyatt had kissed enough women to know it wasn't always enjoyable. Sometimes a person could be too aggressive, making him feel as if his mouth were being jackhammered by someone else's tongue. Some women kissed like a dead cod, just opening their mouths and letting him do all the work.

Emma kissed perfectly. Together their tongues found a natural rhythm of give-and-take that foretold of things to come. Things he was all too eager to do. Things that gave his heart a vigorous workout in more ways than one.

He unfastened a second button, all the while maintaining the steady pace of their kiss. He listened for little sounds of impatience in her throat, savored the way her fingers groped at him more urgently. Even though his dick throbbed insistently, demanding release, he kept a leash on his own desire in order to stoke hers.

Wyatt didn't often do tender, yet something about Emma inspired the gentle feeling in spite of his baser instincts. She'd brought him the honey pot, after all. But moreover, Emma had overcome a childhood blow without turning bitter and hard. If anything, she showered those less fortunate than her with love and respect. She deserved to be the center of someone's attention, and Wyatt was more than happy to be the guy to do it.

Slowly, he removed her shirt, kissing her shoulders as he tugged her arms free from the shirtsleeves. He brought his hands around her back and unclasped her bra, then trailed his fingers beneath its straps and gently removed it as well.

The sight of her perky breasts, tipped up, rosy nipples every bit as hard as he was, strung him even tighter. He cupped them, enjoying the weight and warmth of her in his rough hands. He kissed her harder now, while using his thumbs to toy with her.

She moaned and arched her back slightly while pulling him closer. "Wyatt."

Her voice carried his name through the air, caressing him like a warm breeze. Patience frayed as lust became more insistent. He unzipped her pants while she stroked the length of his erection over his jeans.

God. He pressed her against the wall to keep himself upright. He reached for the honey and dribbled some on her breasts.

"It takes two million flowers to make one pound of honey, so we better not waste a drop," he murmured before covering one nipple with his mouth and sucking hard.

Her pleasure-filled moan confirmed that, for all her softness, Emma liked sex a little on the forceful side. Her gasps urged him to continue, so he moved his attention to her other breast and suckled there, too. Before long, his legs shook with need, so he dropped to his knees. "Stay still."

He yanked her pants down, removing them completely, then slowly rolled her panties down, too. A blush crept up her body, making him smile. She was a contradiction, this girl who'd submit to his will and play with props but who still got embarrassed by her body or sex or both. Maybe she just needed more practice—another thing he'd be happy to provide.

While on his knees, he kissed her stomach and used his hands to stroke her waist, hips, and legs. He sunk his fingers into the damp curls between her thighs.

Emma may be shy, but she responded with lightning speed. The slick feel of her, her musky scent, drove him wild with hunger. When her hands dug into his hair, he removed them and planted them against the wall on either side of her hips. He smeared honey across her pelvis and below before licking her skin and moving his mouth to where his fingers had previously been exploring.

Emma bucked her hips and moaned her approval, tilting her pelvis to provide him better access. His chest tightened with emotion, with the desire to please her and help her let go.

The unique taste of her juices mixed with the sweet, sticky honey had him tonguing her hard and fast, like a man who'd been deprived of food for a week. Fire raced through his blood, scorching him, shooting electric currents through his body.

He heard a little whimper and sob just before her knees buckled. He gripped her hips to keep her upright while redoubling his efforts to make her come.

"Oh, oh. Wyatt!"

He stood, holding her trembling body against the wall until she recovered, and then kissed her mouth. When her slackened muscles reclaimed their strength, she began to tug at his jeans.

"Lay on the bed, face down," he commanded.

She didn't hesitate. While he yanked off his pants, he watched her stretch across the mattress, her sweet behind exposed for his pleasure. Standing at the edge of the bed, he bent over and grabbed that ass, the one that taunted him every single time she turned away. He pinched and slapped her there until it turned a little pink.

A quick test with his fingers told him it turned her on. Now he wanted to feel her everywhere, so he climbed over her, trailing his tongue along her spine until he reached her neck and they were skin to skin. He nibbled at her ear while slowly grinding his erection against her body. "I wish we had some way to tie your hands."

"I won't move them," she promised, and he smiled. He'd meant to take her this way, but suddenly changed his mind.

"Do you want a taste of honey, too?" he asked, now certain he wanted her mouth on his dick more than just about anything.

"Yes."

He turned her over and kissed her, enjoying the way her hands stroked his back and cupped his ass. Before he got carried away, he rolled onto his back and nodded toward the honey pot. "Enjoy."

"I will." She smiled before drizzling honey over the head of his penis.

His hands groped the sheets in anticipation of her mouth clamping around him. Even bracing for it hadn't prepared him for the full-body seizure that seemed to tear through him. He wanted to watch. To enjoy the cascade of her silky red hair against her creamy complexion, the slight sway of her round, firm breasts, those full lips sucking him. Too soon his eyelids grew heavy and his head tipped back. "Jesus, Emma. Slow. Down. Slow . . ."

He longed to explode in her mouth, but he also needed to bury himself inside her body. Pressure built to a nearly unbearable point. His muscles went rigid. Just in time, he dragged her up against his chest and kissed her before rolling on top of her. He snatched a condom from the top of the dresser and quickly applied it, and then finally seated himself fully inside her.

For a moment, he propped up on his elbows and held himself still, brushing her hair from her face. She opened her eyes. So pretty, those clear eyes. So trustworthy and trusting at the same time.

A peculiar, soft emotion stole through him. A feeling of rightness, of contentment born of more than lust and attraction. A sense of comfort and stability at a time in his life when everything else was shifting unpredictably.

He eased his hips slowly in and out, all the while keeping his gaze locked on hers. He registered when her lips parted, when her heartbeat quickened, when her breath came heavier and faster. Physically, everything between them felt so damn good, yet he wanted more than her willing body there with him.

"Admit that you like me," he said, surprising both of them. Then, as if he could counteract his unexpected vulnerability, he thrust hard, hoping to somehow restore dominion.

"Isn't it obvious?" she purred. Her flirty answer didn't satisfy him. It didn't sound like Emma, either. It sounded like what Emma thought he wanted to hear.

"No. Admit that you like me, not just the sex. You spent a whole week pretending not to like me, Emma. Tell me that was all a lie." He kissed her before she replied, because a little part of him feared her answer.

Wyatt had never, ever demanded anything like that during sex before. Hell, he'd been a wham-bam-thank-you-ma'am kind of guy most of the time, although he'd had a few weeks-long relationships now and then.

In the dimly lit room, shadows made it difficult to clearly see her expression. But she brushed her hands up his arms and across his shoulders until she was tenderly holding his face. "I like you very much."

Emma's words washed through him, soothing him like the sound of a steady rainfall on the roof always had. "I like you very much, too."

Suddenly things looked more vivid, smelled a bit stronger, tasted a bit sharper. He'd gone still again without realizing it, until Emma slid her hands down to his hips to remind him to move. And move he did.

Starting with a leisurely pace, he deliberately alternated long, slow thrusts with sharp, quick ones, building steadily. When her legs wrapped around his waist, she cried out, at which point he finally allowed himself to tip over into the same state of bliss she'd reached.

Wyatt collapsed on top of her, his head turned away, blinking and dazed. Confused, yet totally sated.

Emma traced his spine and shoulders in a gentle, endless loop of caresses. She made no move to lift him off her body, or to shift uncomfortably beneath him. He might well have fallen asleep in the comforting arms of this puzzler of a woman if he didn't think she'd suffocate.

Grudgingly, he rolled onto his back, pulling her with him. It was late. He had yoga in six hours, yet he couldn't let her leave just yet. And although she hadn't asked, he said, "I'm sorry about Jessie."

Emma briefly tensed. "It's fine."

"I'd texted her weeks ago and not given it much thought after that. I had no idea she would just show up."

"Wyatt, you don't owe me an explanation. It's not like we've made any promises."

He frowned at her indifferent response. "I'd rather you not go out with some other guy while I'm here, if it's all the same to you."

Emma chuckled, nestling against his side. "I'll be sure to keep them all at bay until you go."

Her self-deprecating tone caused him to raise her chin and look her in the eye. "You're a girlfriend kind of girl, Emma. Why aren't you with someone like Andy?"

"Andy?" she laughed. "He's like family."

"You know what I mean. A local guy who'd buy you flowers and take you out, make you happy."

She looked away then, no trace of a smile remained. "Most guys our age are still looking to have fun. 'Saint Emma' isn't generally viewed as being very fun."

He heard the sting in her voice about the nickname he'd given her last week. She hadn't liked it, apparently. He remembered his initial impression of her, and how he'd dismissed her as being uptight. Of course, that impression had evaporated the second he found her dancing in the pantry. Even before that, he'd questioned whether something wilder swam beneath her calm demeanor. "Lucky for me, I'm smarter than most guys my age."

She grinned. "Or maybe you're just making the most of a convenient situation before you take off. Unlike local guys, you don't have to worry about dealing with me month after month. Living in a small town makes it awkward when things end, so it's sometimes easier not to date at all."

"I know all about growing up in a small town." He flashed back to his childhood home, which made this inn seem like a royal palace. "At least this one is pretty."

"Will you return to Vermont after competition season?" She nestled her head against his chest.

"I haven't thought that far ahead. If I can up my sponsorship money, I can make sure my mom is okay. She wants Ryder to be home with her, but I think he'll get depressed there, especially around her negativity. He needs to be with people his own age. Someplace like this town, which is friendly to outsiders."

"What does Ryder want?"

Of course she'd ask that question.

"Hell if I know. You might have noticed, he doesn't talk much these days." Wyatt heard her quiet intake of breath and knew she'd just held something in. He squeezed his arms around her. "I heard that. Whatever you're thinking, go ahead and say it."

She rested her chin on his chest. "Maybe he'd talk more if he believed you'd listen."

"I listen all the time."

"Did you know he thinks the main reason you're competing again is for his sake?"

"He told you that?"

"That first day, when you left the inn, he said that you were doing it for money for him, but that he hadn't asked you for help. So he's not only concerned for your safety, but also feeling guilty at the possibility of you getting hurt." She pressed her lips together and added, quietly, "I suspect you know a little something about that feeling, though."

Emma never failed to throw right-left-right jabs. "Wow. Give me a second while I reset my jaw."

"Sorry." She kissed his chest. "Earlier Mari and Jim were editing the opening of the film. I overheard your mom say something that made it sound like she blames you for Ryder's accident. It didn't sound like she'd ever kept those feelings secret. I hope she hasn't convinced you that it's your fault."

Wyatt shifted uncomfortably. "She's not wrong. I got Ryder into the sport."

"He knew the risks, just like you do."

"It's not the same. I loved it more than anything. No one encouraged me to get involved. But Ryder's interest didn't burn as hot. If I hadn't dragged him along, he might now be living a normal life somewhere, making pottery, with a nice girl keeping him warm at night instead of dealing with a serious disability and an uncertain future."

"What happened is tragic, Wyatt, but it's not your fault. And if you feel that way, why are you so determined to drag him back into it with you again?"

"I think he needs a goal, and I want to reconnect with him. To rebuild the bond we had. In that way, boarding was the best time for us." Wyatt snorted. "Besides, he can't get hurt on the sidelines."

"Unless the bad memories depress him, or he sees you get injured. Trust me, that avalanche rocked him."

Hell, he didn't like that remark, but he couldn't exactly dismiss it either. Emma smoothed her hand over his chest and abdomen, apparently lost in thought for a moment. He started to relax, but then she asked, "Is the guilt what's driving you back to competition?"

"Apparently Ryder's convinced you it is."

"No. You used to glow when talking about snowboarding, but now it's different. You're driven, but you don't look like you love it the same way."

"How can you say that when you just met me?"

Her eyes blanked for a second. "I've seen you, Wyatt. Interviews, YouTube videos, ESPN clips."

"Most of that stuff is filmed in the heat of the moment. I'm sure if I win a qualifier, you'll see the 'glow' again." Of course, he might be exaggerating. Ryder's accident had changed everything for him, including his love for the sport. He still enjoyed the recreation of it, but a niggling sense of fear colored his outlook on competition. Not that he wanted to admit that to anyone.

"Why'd you switch to freeriding? Wouldn't it have been safer to stick with slopestyle?"

"I like a challenge." He hoped the offhand remark fooled her. "Why all the questions?"

"I don't want to see you get hurt. I suppose I agree with Ryder—it seems like you'd be safer doing what you know."

"I'm old by slopestyle standards. The new guys have better jumps. I'd been out of training for two years, so it would've taken a lot just to get back to where I was, let alone compete at the higher level. Freeriding has a more mature pack of competitors. And I do like a new challenge."

Emma propped up on an elbow and twisted a bit of his hair around her finger. "Wyatt, do you ever feel fear?"

Normally he'd dismiss the question out of hand with a quick no. But something about her body language and tone suggested she had her own reasons for asking. That his answer would have meaning for her, and not just because she was curious about his career.

He snuggled her a little tighter until she lowered her head to rest against his shoulder, so he wasn't looking her in the eye. "I used to love those showy, acrobatic jumps, but the truth is . . . the truth is Ryder's accident spooked me. I knew there were risks, but never really believed anything bad would happen. Ryder's accident proved me wrong. And slopestyle courses aren't forgiving. So I guess fear was a small factor in my choice to transition. I won't let fear keep me out of the sport completely, but freeriding doesn't hold bad memories, so it doesn't mess with my mind. In that way, it seems safer."

"Except for the avalanche." She'd said it as a statement, not a question, and he couldn't deny it anyway.

"Yeah." He stared at the ceiling, remembering lying in this very bed that afternoon in a mild panic, questioning everything. Then Emma had introduced him to Trip and given him another chance to make things right for his family. Reliable, quiet, steady Emma.

She popped up and stroked his cheek. "Tell me one last thing. How do you make yourself go out there and face your fear every day?"

"Why do you sound so invested? Is there something you're afraid of?"

"Maybe." She tucked her head back into the crook of his shoulder.

"Now you've got me curious." He rolled on top of her and pinned her to the bed, aiming to be just playful enough to coax an answer from her. "What scares you, Emma?"

She turned her face away, keeping still and quiet, and then met his gaze. "Teach me how to overcome it and maybe I'll tell you."

He smiled at her sassy answer. "I knew you had secrets."

"Everyone has secrets. As long as they don't hurt anyone, I think it's okay to keep them."

He thought for a moment about whether he agreed. Part of him disliked the idea of her keeping a secret, but the other part knew he had no real right to demand answers. "I suppose I can see that logic."

He sensed an easing of the tension in her body, which only made him more curious. "Listen, the only way I know to conquer fear is to make yourself do what scares you most."

Her green eyes went wide. "But what if the worst thing you fear comes true?"

"For me, that would be death, in which case I won't be around to deal with the consequences." His joking way of handling things fell flat.

"Or paralysis, or TBI, or . . ."

He rolled off her again, feeling antsy. "Don't try to convince me to quit competing."

She reached across him, her breasts brushing against his chest, and dipped her finger in the honey. Then she traced her sticky finger around his lips. "Would that be so awful . . . to be like the rest of us?" She kissed him, nipping at leftover honey on his lip. "To live a normal life?"

"I don't know. I've never lived a normal life." When her eyes dimmed, he added, "But I could get used to this kind of normal. Being with you every night. That part would be nice."

She didn't say anything, and he could tell she was thinking about something. She did that—retreat inward—often. Curiosity prickled through his brain like sparklers on the Fourth of July.

"Emma, don't you have any big dreams?"

Her brows pinched together so briefly he might've imagined it. "I've always been someone who is more comfortable with my feet on the ground. Big dreams can lead to big disappointments, after all."

"So can wasted opportunities and regrets." Again she fell silent, so he pressed on. "Big dreams don't have to be like mine. You mentioned something before about wishing you had money to fix up this inn. Maybe your dream is simply restoring this place and making it a 'must stay' for tourists?"

"That would make me happy." Yet her voice didn't sound particularly happy. "I know it would ease my mother's worries, and I'd like to honor my grandparents' legacy, too."

"The way you just said that makes it sound like this inn isn't your dream, though. Fixing it up would only make you happy because it would please your mom. What about you? What do you want?"

"Pleasing my mom and honoring my family legacy does make me happy, Wyatt. That's a big part of who I am."

He didn't know why he thought she wasn't being completely honest. Whatever secret fear she had must be why she held back. Maybe he could help her meet this one goal with a few well-placed tweets about her inn and her cooking. If she realized he could be a good ally, she might let him help her with her secret dreams, too.

Emma's sad little smile kicked him in the gut, so he dipped his fingers in the honey and smeared it along her neck, determined to kiss her and hold her and make her feel good again.

He couldn't walk away from competition any easier than she could face her secret fear—the one he was now determined to discover. But that could wait until later, he thought, as his tongue trailed down her stomach.

Chapter Fourteen

"Emma!" Andy's bellow snapped her out of her daze.

She blinked in the sunlight, temporarily disoriented by the crowds and activity at the annual Adaptive Alpine Ski Day, which kicked off ski season on the mountain. Andy, a certified adaptive ski instructor, always volunteered to work at this event, and Emma supplied plenty of baked goods and helped manage the crowds.

For the past few moments, however, she'd gotten sidetracked by another bit of plotting—mentally scripting dialogue between Dallas and Ella. She had to finish the darn sequel! Her agent had been waiting for it, and Emma had been stalling.

"Sorry. Did you ask me something?" She reorganized the food trays at the table where she'd been daydreaming.

"I thought Wyatt was coming to sign autographs, but the day is almost over. Have you heard from him?"

"Why would I hear from him?" Even as she feigned casual indifference, she wished she would hear from him soon. Trip had decided to graduate Wyatt to tackling "super gnarly" runs in preparation for the qualifiers at Crested Butte. Naturally, this led Emma to envision hideous images like Wyatt hurtling into a tree or careening over a cliff wall and smashing against its face.

Andy cocked an eyebrow and shook his head. "Emma, ever since Kelsey's party last weekend, I've caught you and Wyatt giving each other hot looks. Then there was that night when Jessie visited but didn't stay over." He rested his hands on his hips. "I'm pretty sure you ignored my warnings about him." When referring to Wyatt, Andy's tone had shifted from its prior worship to something closer to disdain. Was it because of her? "So you don't fool me with this attitude."

If Andy had noticed her and Wyatt's behavior, surely Mari had, too. The fact that Mari hadn't confronted her or Wyatt with suspicions sent a chill down Emma's back.

Choosing to ignore Andy's petulance, she said, "Wyatt will be here. Settle down and have some cookies."

Andy snatched two chocolate chip walnut cookies. "Jeremy's dying to meet him, and I don't want to let him down. He's got the best attitude. I love that little dude."

Jeremy Snyder, a local nine-year-old boy with spina bifida, had first worked with Andy last year. Andy hadn't been confident that the boy's parents would let them work together again after Andy's recent legal trouble, but they had. Thank God, because Emma knew Andy's heart, and pride, would've been broken if they'd snubbed him. It had taken nine months, but some people were finally willing to cut Andy some slack. Better late than never, she supposed.

Emma wished she could tell Andy that the past couple of weeks had been among the best of her life. That her mother's absence had given her the freedom to explore a side of herself she'd needed to know. That spending every night with Wyatt had changed her life, and not just because of the intense sexual connection.

But she couldn't tell, partly because he seemed so upset by the idea, but moreover because he'd pity her. He would, and he'd be right to do so. Because Andy knew that Wyatt would leave town soon, and that

Emma wouldn't be part of his life once he'd gone. Wyatt would find a new woman by the time he got to Europe, while Emma would remain here, with her mom, at the inn.

Of course, she had her upcoming book launch to enjoy. She might even have a few fans by Christmas. This should be an exhilarating time. Sadly, the zip of pride she'd experienced when first holding her author copy in her hands no longer coursed through her.

It would be easy to blame the secretiveness for diminishing her enthusiasm, but she suspected something worse at play. When she'd created Dallas, she'd turned him into an athlete Alpha-hole. Domineering, competitive, sexy—all traits readers craved. Everything she'd assumed Wyatt Lawson to be when she'd met him years ago.

Then Wyatt reappeared in her life in the most unexpected way. Other than the superficial resemblance and career, Wyatt had real quirks, sensitivities, and worries that were nothing like Dallas. And now Dallas—until recently, her fantasy hero creation—seemed like a flimsy, clumsy version of the real man. An insult to the courageous, caring, exciting man Wyatt was. Rationally, her feelings made no sense—after all, Dallas was a fictional character. But their shared face still triggered turmoil.

Jeremy appeared and tugged at Andy's jacket. "Andy, I'm ready to go again."

"Okay, buddy."

"Where's Wyatt?" Jeremy glanced around. "Did I miss him?"

"Nope. He's still training. I bet when we get back down, he'll be here to sign that autograph for you." Andy took the T-shirt Jeremy wanted to have signed and stuffed it in the boy's coat.

"Okay."

Andy nodded at Emma and swiped a cookie for Jeremy. As they wandered off, Emma glanced at her phone. Three o'clock. No texts. The lifts would close at four. Hopefully Wyatt would get back in time . . . and in one piece.

Within fifteen minutes, Emma caught sight of Mari, Ryder, and Jim, and a welcome rush of relief coursed through her. If they were here, then Wyatt hadn't been injured.

Ryder saw her and wandered over. "Can I take one?"

"Of course." She bit her lip, like that might help her hold her question inside. It didn't. "How'd Wyatt do today?"

"Fine." Ryder barely looked up. Instead, he focused on the cookie, almost as if intentionally blocking out the crowd.

"Ryder, is this event too much stimulation for you? It's so bright, and there are a lot of people milling around."

"I'm okay." He bit into the cookie. Emma noticed him surreptitiously watch a physically disabled teen excitedly suiting up in four-track equipment.

Emma wondered whether he'd ever considered exploring adaptive equipment so he could snowboard again. For once, she kept her big mouth shut and didn't push. Ryder had his own way of handling things, and like his brother, he'd be out of her life soon. She shouldn't get too invested in his recovery.

The energy of the crowd shifted and suddenly the throng headed toward the base of the main run.

"Wyatt must've just come down with Trip," Ryder said, watching Mari and Jim hustle up through the crowd.

"All the kids here are excited to meet him." Emma smiled.

"Everybody loves Wyatt," Ryder said, giving her a knowing glance.

Ryder knew. Or if he didn't know, he had a good guess. Surely he'd been around his brother long enough to recognize the telltale signs. He must think Emma quite silly for falling for his brother, like so many others before.

"He is a showman, after all." Emma chose to make light of it all, because honestly, what else could she do? "Let's go watch."

Together they trudged, in silence, across the hard packed snow. When they squeezed through a circle of onlookers, Emma noticed Jim filming Wyatt as he high-fived kids and signed T-shirts and helmets and other things thrown his way.

The magnificent mountains and blue sky surrounding him paled in comparison with his stark beauty. His teeth were nearly as white as the snow, his dark hair and warm skin tone looked so rich in the sun's golden glow. Healthy, proud, happy.

She liked seeing him this way, which was every bit as sexy as when she saw him in private. Maybe even more so. Even Trip, who on most days was hard to miss, faded into the background when cast in Wyatt's shadow.

Wyatt noticed Ryder at the outskirts of the crowd and waved him over.

"Hey, everyone, you remember my brother, Ryder? He competed in the Rockies eXtreme Games, too. He hasn't had an opportunity to get back on the slopes in a while, but I'm thinking maybe you all can convince him to try again, just like you." Wyatt smiled at Ryder, but Emma's stomach dropped.

Ryder's face colored—an angry shade of crimson. Thankfully his glasses hid his eyes from the kids, because Emma would bet everything that his glare would be frightening.

She doubted Wyatt had intended to upset Ryder. Given Wyatt's unwavering belief that the key to their happiness lay in his brother's return to this sport, he probably thought he'd hit upon the perfect solution. Equally clear to her was the fact that Ryder might well wish his brother dead in that instant.

One oblivious preteen slapped his hand against his mono-ski. "This is fun. You should try!"

Ryder slowly faced the boy and shook his head. "No, thank you."

He turned to go, but Emma seized his arm. Torn by the desire to ease his discomfort yet save Wyatt's blunder, she murmured, "Ryder, Mari is filming all of this. Perhaps we should help make the best of it for now."

"I d-don't care." Ryder tugged free of Emma just as Wyatt caught up to them.

Wyatt winked at Emma, then called to Ryder's back. "Where are you going? I just got here. Help me mingle with these kids. You could be a real inspiration here, Ryder. Make a difference by showing these kids there isn't a limit to what they can do."

Ryder stopped in his tracks but didn't spin around. Neither brother so much as twitched. Silence descended for awkward moments while Emma waited to see what might happen next. Unfortunately, the small crowd nearby had also been holding their breath.

"Except that there is a limit." Ryder turned on Wyatt, his face ferocious. Emma stepped back in shock as Ryder's voice ground out low and firm through gnashed teeth. "There is a limit. I used to be able to fly free, to jump, to flip and turn. Do you think I can do any of that in a sled, or tethered to another person? Would you really think that sounded f-fun? Or would it remind you of e-everything you lost, of everything that would never be? And I'm not just talking about the sport, Wyatt. Be a good example, you say. My life isn't about being an example to people!"

The light on Jim's camera glowed. Wyatt wouldn't be pleased that this argument was being filmed. No one would be happy that Ryder's outburst might have inadvertently hurt some of the kids' feelings.

As quietly as possible, she said, "Hey guys, cool down. There are kids around, and Mari."

"I don't care!" Ryder barked. "I'm sick of being part of this production. I don't want to keep traveling and being t-toted out like an exhibit. A footnote in your story. I just want to choose my own life."

"You're not a footnote." Wyatt's crestfallen expression pricked at Emma's heart. All his yearning to put his brother back together—to put their relationship to rights—blazed in his beautiful eyes. "We're in this together. You and me, like always."

"It can't be like before. It just can't. I'm d-done." The terseness in his voice had fled, leaving room only for exhaustion. "Do what you want, but don't do any of it for me. I'm not coming to Crested Butte. I'm out."

"Just like that." Electrifying anger gathered like thunderclouds in Wyatt's eyes. He crossed his arms and arched a brow. "Giving up and going home to Mom?"

"Only you see quitting this as giving up. I'm changing course. Maybe I'll get good at pottery and open a studio. Maybe I'll let someone ghostwrite my story my way. Maybe I'll stay right here in Sterling Canyon. The p-point is, I have options."

Wyatt cut Emma a harsh glance. "You didn't offer him a job, did you?"

Before she could answer, Ryder interjected. "Leave Emma out of it. I don't have a job. I haven't made any decision beyond the one to quit following you around."

"You're going to bail on me before the first qualifier?" The ache in Wyatt's voice tied Emma's stomach into a wad of knots.

"You don't need me." Ryder gestured toward Trip. "Take him if you need a security blanket."

"Screw you, Ryder. I don't need a security blanket. This is about us. This has always been about us. About our family coming out on the other side of everything and being whole again. Don't you dare throw any other crap in my face now."

"Wyatt, the kids!" Emma noticed Andy tugging Jeremy away.

When Wyatt finally remembered their surroundings, he whirled on Mari. "Stop recording. Stop recording, dammit."

Jim looked at Mari, who nodded.

Wyatt then glared at Ryder. "You know what, you win. I'm sick of worrying about what you're thinking and how you're feeling. Trying to make up for what happened. I'm done. You want out, you're out. Have a nice life. Just tell me where to send the checks."

Emma gasped, but Wyatt didn't seem to notice or care. He tossed his board and helmet to the ground and stormed away from the mountain, the fans, and her. Far from his finest moment, but she'd give him a pass because his pain had broken through the surface and hijacked his good sense.

"Ryder," Emma said, but he ambled toward the van without glancing back. She whirled around. "Trip, will you please take Wyatt's things to the van. I'm going to catch up with him."

Before leaving the venue, she strode over to Andy and Jeremy. "Hey, Jeremy. If you give me that T-shirt, I promise I'll get Wyatt to sign it later."

Jeremy reluctantly handed her the shirt. "Why's he so mad?"

"Oh, grown up stuff, honey." She avoided Andy's gaze. "Tell you what. How about you ask your parents to bring you to the inn tonight around six. Wyatt will be there for dinner, and you can pick up the shirt and meet him then. I promise."

"Emma!" Andy said.

"I promise." She stared at Andy, even though she had no business making a promise she might not be able to keep. In fact, she went ahead and made another. "And I promise he won't be angry."

She tucked Jeremy's shirt under her arm and then chased after Wyatt. Fortunately, there weren't many streets in the small town, so it didn't take her long to spot him.

"Wyatt!"

He glanced over his shoulder, then stopped and waited for her. Red-rimmed, raw-looking eyes stared at her defiantly, as if he expected a lecture. She reached up and set her palm against his cheek while glancing around for someplace more private.

"Come with me." She walked ahead one block until they came to the entrance of her small stone church. "There's a little room in the back where moms take crying babies during Mass. It'll be empty now, so we can sit and talk."

Head bowed, he followed her inside.

An instant calm settled over Emma in the solemn space. Colorful light poured through stained glass and spilled onto the altar. The scent of incense and the faint echo of their footsteps reminded her of a thousand Sundays spent here with her mom. She'd often come here to think or ask for forgiveness. Today she asked for help with Wyatt. Of course, she didn't mention that little prayer to him.

Emma half expected to burst into flame, having brought her illicit lover into this sacred place. Instead, standing there sharing it with him gave a new depth to her feelings, as if merely being here together lent sanctity to their relationship. It reminded her that, aside from the sex, she felt a genuine, loving connection to this man. A man who was helping her come to know herself better. Who'd been encouraging her not to be so ashamed of her needs and desires.

Of course, she hadn't quite conquered her fears, but maybe someday.

As she'd predicted, the baby room was empty. She guided Wyatt there and then promptly wrapped her arms around him. They stood in an awkward, stiff embrace for several moments while Emma waited for him to speak. When his hands slid down to cup her butt, she realized he'd resorted to sex to release his emotions.

He nuzzled her neck and then kissed her forehead, her nose, and finally her mouth. She recognized his pattern now—his need to control something in order to reset his balance. She surrendered for three, maybe five seconds, but they were in church, and she needed to get him to open up before he returned to the inn and confronted his brother again.

"Wyatt, stop. Let's sit and talk."

"I don't want to talk," he protested, kissing her neck. "Let's do this instead."

"We're in a church!" She pushed away.

"I forgot, Saint Emma wouldn't think of fooling around in church."

"Most people wouldn't." She flinched at his mockery. "And there's no need to be cruel. I'm on your side."

"Sorry." He scratched his neck and then pulled her close. "That was an asshole thing to say."

He let her go and paced the small room, his expression somber as a judge.

"Ryder's outburst shocked you. How can I help?" Emma clasped her hands together, waiting.

Wyatt studied her. "Don't act surprised. Ryder's attitude is exactly what you've been claiming he's been feeling all along."

Emma hung her head, quietly replying, "That doesn't make me happy."

But Wyatt hadn't heard her, probably because he'd gotten absorbed by his own thoughts. At least, that's how it appeared. His mind wouldn't let go of what it wanted. Perhaps that ability to focus—to will something into being—is what made him a great athlete, but right now, it wasn't helping him be a good brother.

"I don't know what to do." Wyatt's arms stretched heavenward before falling to his sides. "He refuses to cooperate and engage in life again."

"He is engaging in life. He's just no longer interested in snowboarding."

"Because he's afraid or he thinks he can't be part of it. But look at all those kids today. Many of them are worse off than Ryder, yet they get out there and have fun. Think of all the athletes who overcome disabilities and compete, too. Why can't he be like them and try instead of sulking and withdrawing? God, his attitude reminds me of our dad, and I hate that."

Emma stilled. He didn't recognize what he'd admitted—how, subconsciously, his attempt to control Ryder had been his way of making up for the things he hadn't been able to control as a boy. If she could get him to see that, maybe he could accept Ryder's decision. "Why do you say that?"

"Because my dad always gave up. When he got fired, he'd complain about why he couldn't get a job instead of actually trying to get one. He'd drink and sit around watching TV. Yell at my mom. Blame others. I worked all the time as a kid, and my dad took most of my money to pay bills while he moaned about unfairness. He never took control, never manned up. Now Ryder's following right in his footsteps and retreating. It's killing me, 'cause I know that path leads nowhere."

When she touched Wyatt's arm, his tension radiated through her. "I think you're drawing parallels that don't exist. After all, Ryder didn't ask you for money. He doesn't gripe about his injuries. And he is trying to solve his problems . . . without your help, actually. Give him some time to figure out his new place in the world, adjust to his disability, and learn what he can and can't handle. I'm sorry he's hurt you, but quitting your film doesn't mean that he's giving up on life, or on you." She rubbed his back. "It doesn't mean he doesn't love you."

"If he loved me, why won't he sacrifice something for me, the way I have for him? Why's he sabotaging this film?" Wyatt pressed the palms of his hands against his temples. "God, now Mari has this blowup recorded. I've totally lost control of the process. Who knows how I'll look when she's done."

Wyatt squeezed his temples harder and closed his eyes. Sensing some kind of breakdown, Emma wrapped her arms around him.

"If it helps, I have a T-shirt from one of the young boys who wanted to meet you today. I told him you'd sign it and he could meet you tonight before dinner." Emma looked into Wyatt's sad eyes. "Let's go home so you can shower and relax. I'll make sure Mari knows to have the cameras rolling when Jeremy shows up. We'll convince her to use the positive footage instead of your argument with Ryder."

"Yeah, right," Wyatt scoffed. "You're being naïve if you think Mari will cut the sibling rivalry shots. She wants conflict. Conflict sells.

People like to watch tension. Good deeds bore people, as you well know."

His last words landed like a slap across her face. He must've seen it, because he immediately cupped her jaw. "I didn't mean that I think you're boring. I was only referring to when you said other people do. My point is, controversy is more entertaining."

"Well, then, maybe the argument should be part of the film. The clash between Ryder's injuries and your goals is part of your journey." She gently pushed some of his bangs off his forehead. "Maybe if you realize Ryder isn't turning into your dad, you can ease up. He just wants to make his own choices, like you. Can't you understand that?"

"But I don't even know if he can hold a regular job yet. He gets headaches from overstimulation. He'll be broke, living in a hovel, with food stamps and secondhand shoes."

"Think you're overstating a bit?" It dawned on her that Wyatt had more fears than he realized.

"Here's some relevant trivia, Emma. Fifteen percent of our country lives in poverty, and you've got no idea how quickly that can happen. I've lived it, and I never want to go back there. I can't believe he would, either. That life sucked."

Like a quart of milk spilled on the counter, Emma's thoughts ran everywhere. Of course no one wanted to live in poverty, but lots of people created happy lives from humble places. Sighing, she stepped back. "Not everyone needs what you do to be happy."

"Don't say it like I'm some jerk who needs to be famous. Have you any idea what it's like to be so poor you're actually hungry? To never know if the lights will turn on that day, or if you could go to the doctor when you were sick? You've never been that vulnerable. Let me tell you, it's a scary fuckin' thing, Emma. I wouldn't wish it on anyone, let alone my brother. So don't downplay my concern like it's nothing, when your big fear is probably a lot less serious."

Well. Yes. Shame and insecurity were less grave than starvation, abuse, and a disabled brother who seemed determined to strike out on his own without a plan for success.

She'd never understood exactly what had driven her dad to ditch her and her mom in order to chase his dreams, so she'd blamed his ego and lust. In contrast, it seemed Wyatt's need to succeed came from a deep-seated fear of uncertainty. A sympathetic motive, perhaps, but like her dad, he'd never be content with a normal life. He'd always strive to do more, to be more.

She'd known this relationship would be brief, but these reminders struck little blows to her heart. And given his current attitude about her and her secret, she certainly wouldn't spill it now.

"I don't want to argue. Maybe you'd prefer to be left alone to work this out for yourself."

"No." He grabbed her, pulling her close. "I don't want to be alone. I don't want to argue with you, either. Let's stay here for a few minutes. I'm not ready to face anyone else just yet."

Wyatt held Emma close. Gentle, sweet, kind Emma, who let him bark at her to work out his bullshit. She deserved better than him, that much he knew.

He'd had fun with other women, but he'd never been this honest and exposed. Never trusted someone enough before her. On paper, they didn't match up, with the age difference and her traditional attitudes. In real life, though, he'd never felt so content.

He'd miss her when he left town, but he didn't want to think about that too much. Couldn't afford to, really. His mission hadn't changed despite the surprising intensity of his feelings.

Emma's face remained plastered to his chest. "Thanksgiving's around the corner. If you can make peace with Ryder's decision, it might be nice to fly your mom here for the holiday. If she sees you both moving on and happy, maybe your family can heal."

Her optimism surprised him, given her own family dynamic. It'd be awesome to live in a world that worked that simply. As if a good meal and a holiday would magically bring everyone together. "What are you doing for Thanksgiving?"

She looked up and smiled. "My mom is away until December 3. I could go to Kelsey's sister's house, but I'd rather spend it with you, unless you'd rather be alone."

"Why would I rather be alone than with you? I may be slow, but I'm not stupid." He kissed her then, because her lips were so close and plump, and he felt safe and secure in her arms. "So I won't meet your mom?"

"No. But that's probably a good thing." Emma grimaced.

"She wouldn't like me?"

"You'd remind her of my dad, with your good looks and big dreams. It'd scare her, and my mom's no fun to be around when she's scared."

He noticed her avert her eyes. "Do you think I'm like your dad?"

"Only in the good ways." She kissed him lightly, but her playful answer didn't sit well with him.

"Seriously, do you think I'm the kind of guy who'd ditch my family for fame and money?" His sense of self suddenly rested on her opinion.

"I doubt you'd do that."

"Of course not." He squeezed her tight. "Hell, I'm doing it for my family. So my mom has a roof over her head, and so Ryder can get the therapy and other stuff he needs."

"I know. You're a good man, Wyatt."

Coming from her, that compliment meant something. If they hadn't been in the church, he would've laid her down on the floor and made love to her right there. "I wish . . ."

He wished they were someplace else. Some other time, even, when he didn't need to worry about Ryder, or the qualifiers, or Mari.

She squeezed him. "What's your wish?"

"I wish my life was less complicated." He eased away. They had to get back to the inn before Mari started spinning new theories about them.

She looked up, but her gaze drifted off with her thoughts. Finally, she said, "When you mean that, it'll happen."

"Just like that?" Chuckling, Wyatt snapped his fingers.

"Yes, actually. I've never met anyone as goal-oriented as you, so when you choose a quiet life—if you ever do—you'll have one." She snapped her fingers. "Just like that."

With that remark, she crossed the room, flung open the church doors, and strode straight into the rosy glow of a Colorado sunset. When the warm sun's rays lit the dim vestibule, he could almost hear a ghostly whisper urging him to follow her into that light.

Chapter Fifteen

"Ryder!" Wyatt called when he and Emma entered the inn's lobby.

Naturally, Mari appeared before his brother, arms crossed, one finger tapping her elbow. "We need to talk."

Pressure gathered behind his eyes, but exploding again would only further alienate Mari. Then he'd never persuade her to dump the footage from earlier that afternoon. "I know, but first let me talk to Ryder."

"That's what we need to talk about. Ryder's role in this film is already publicized. Now he's threatening to pull out? Meanwhile, you continue to keep me at arm's length." Mari pointedly glanced at Emma before returning her attention to Wyatt. That look told him that he probably shouldn't have been spending so much of his free time hanging out in the kitchen, or at the front desk, or wherever else Emma happened to be. "You're not letting me do my job. I'm supposed to tell your story, which includes more than how well you can transition from one sport to another."

Wyatt sensed Emma's discomfort almost as strongly as if she'd reached out and touched him. "Excuse me, but I'd better start dinner." She handed Wyatt the T-shirt. "Don't forget to autograph this for

Jeremy. He's coming around six o'clock to meet you." She then smiled at Mari. "Won't that be a lovely moment for the film, Mari?"

"Of course," Mari capitulated, although her eyes stayed locked with his, even as Emma walked away.

Aw, hell. Weariness robbed him of the will to argue. To his dismay, he chose to beg. "Mari, please don't include the footage from today's argument in the film."

Mari closed her eyes and sighed. "If Ryder is serious about quitting, then that has to be in the film. It's a turning point in this story, Wyatt. Surely you see that. Don't assign a good versus bad value to what happened. It's simply an honest look at his injury's impact on both of your careers and your relationship. That's important stuff."

"No, it's exploiting personal conversations. I don't see how that makes this film better. I thought we would focus on my career and comeback. Not on my family."

"Like I've explained to you from the outset, this kind of bio-documentary has to be three-dimensional in order to be interesting. Fans can watch short YouTube clips of you on the slopes if all they want to see is the actual snowboarding. The movie must be personal and give fans the sense that they are getting to know the real you. Show them what it's like to live your unique life. That means you need to let me, and them, in. Show us who you are—the good and the ugly, what you really want, who matters to you, and why. All of it, Wyatt."

"My outburst in front of those disabled kids makes me look bad." Wyatt raked his hand through his hair, knowing his anger should be directed at himself instead of Mari.

"It makes you human. People make mistakes, especially when confronted with unwelcome news. We'll offset that with footage tonight of you and the boy who's coming. And of you and Ryder making up. This is the kind of human drama that people relate to. It's all good. You have to trust me or this won't work."

Mari looked sincere. Her two prior documentaries hadn't been overly sensationalized. But he'd been burned before, and it could happen again, even though he couldn't argue with most of what she'd said. No matter what, he'd promised to keep Emma out of the film, so he wouldn't go back on his word.

Why even consider it, really? Fans didn't expect him to be getting involved with a woman while training. Hell, he hadn't expected it. It wasn't the smart move. Yet, he couldn't help himself. He wouldn't give her up until he had to leave town, either.

"Fine. Go get Jim or Buddy if you want to record me and Ryder, because I need to fix things with him right now."

"Thank you." She touched his arm before jogging up the stairs to grab the crew.

Wyatt scrubbed his hands over his face and then went to knock on Ryder's door. "Ryder, please come out so we can talk. I know you don't want to be part of this project anymore, but if you could please let Mari record this last thing, I'd appreciate it."

He waited, listening for the sound of Ryder's cane. When he heard movement, he backed up a few steps.

Ryder opened his door. "Hey."

"Hey," Wyatt replied. "Can we talk in the front parlor or dining room? It'll be the last time I ask you to be on camera."

"Sure." Ryder followed Wyatt to the parlor, where they sat opposite each other and waited for the crew.

His brother sat, spine erect, hands on top of his cane, apparently bracing for another argument. How had they gotten here when all Wyatt wanted was the brotherly rapport they used to share? "I know the sunglasses help you, but can we have this conversation eye to eye?"

Ryder paused, then reached up to remove his glasses, revealing the blue eyes Wyatt had known his whole life. It had been so long since he'd looked into them, Wyatt's breath caught. Although the color hadn't changed, they somehow looked different. Less mischievous. "It's good to see you again."

Out of nowhere, his nose tingled and his own eyes misted. He'd forgotten how much he missed seeing his brother's eyes. How did Ryder handle living behind those shades in order to cope? Did he miss the vivid colors of the world? Another thing stolen from him, thanks to the accident.

Emma had been right about so much. Wyatt couldn't possibly comprehend the hundreds of ways that Ryder's life had been altered. The countless losses he reexperienced on a daily basis. And Wyatt had thought making him confront the sport that had robbed him of so much would be a good thing? He hung his head in his hands, tugging at his hair with his fingers.

Mari and Jim arrived before Ryder said anything else. It only took them a minute or two to set up because the tripods had been in place for weeks.

"The videography would be better if Jim worked one of the cameras by hand, but you two might be more open if we're not present, so let's go with the two cameras on the tripods and hope for the best." Mari gestured for Jim to follow her into the dining room to do whatever it was they did behind Wyatt's back.

Once they were gone, he absently stared at the floor for a moment, unsure of where to start. Finally, he opened with, "I'm sorry."

"Me, too." Ryder fidgeted with his cane.

"No, you've been trying to get me to listen, but I've been determined to do it all my way. No surprise to you, I'm sure." He paused, his heart aching, beating at half speed. "I'd convinced myself you'd be happier in this environment. That you'd remember what we loved about it and would find a new way to be involved. That you'd be psyched not to give it all up. I never meant to make you feel like a footnote in my life, Ryder. I just wanted you back *in* my life. I thought it would break through this barrier between us." Wyatt slouched back into the chair, unsure of what else to say.

"There's no barrier." Ryder leaned forward, eyes squinting even though dusk left only lavender-tinted haze streaming through the windows.

"I feel a distance. We used to be together night and day—on the slopes, out on the town. Joking, teasing, all of it." Wyatt rested his elbows on his knees, closing the distance between them. "When you were in that hospital, hooked up to machines, fighting for your life, I wanted to jump inside your body and fight for you. I couldn't stand the thought that you might not make it, or to see you suffer. The relief I felt when you slowly started coming back—I can't even tell you what that meant. But it's like we got 80 percent of the way, then it just plateaued. There's this gap now. I'd thought this project would bring us all the way around."

Ryder sighed and tapped his cane, his brows drawn thoughtfully. "You want it like it was, but I'm different now. I can't handle loud bars, snowboarding—it's not going to happen. I don't j-joke around and find things funny like before because it takes so much effort just to get through the day. Things are different, but that's got nothing to do with you, even if you think it does. You think I blame you, but I don't. I don't blame you, so quit hovering and expecting me to love what you love. I never loved it as much as you did. Never."

"I know. That's why I feel responsible for what happened in the first place."

"That's d-dumb. I could've quit at any time. And it could just as easily have been you who got hurt. Everyone out there on those jumps could be me. I just got lucky." Ryder smirked and his twisted humor lodged another lump in Wyatt's throat. "I know you need to win to feel in control. But every time you go out and make me watch, I think you might get hurt. I can't stop you from doing this, but I can't be part of it, either. I need to get out. And don't make me the reason you stick with it. I get d-disability money, and I can get paid to talk about TBI. I'm not saying I don't need any help or support, but I don't need you to risk your life to give it."

A little voice whispered for Wyatt to heed his brother's warnings and walk away. But he had never quit anything, and he wouldn't start now. Not with his reputation in the balance. With his family's financial security at stake. "I love you. I'd do anything for you. I've committed to this comeback, and I won't quit. So, if you don't want to be part of the journey, I accept that, but please stop getting in my head and trying to talk me out of it, okay?"

"Okay."

"Thanks." Wyatt tapped his hand on his thighs. "One last thing. Emma thought it might be nice if we brought Mom here for Thanksgiving in a few days. What do you think?"

Ryder's brows rose. He tipped his head, like he might probe about Emma, but then his expression settled. "I'd like it. I don't think she should be alone."

Ryder's empathy for their mom didn't surprise Wyatt, although he'd never felt quite the same way. As a kid, the amount of shit she put up with from their dad had pissed him off. She'd never stood up to their father, or on behalf of Ryder and Wyatt. He didn't love her less because of it, he just didn't understand her at all. Then again, she never understood him, either.

"Okay. Can you set it up with her? Have her fly into Montrose and we'll figure out how to get her from there. I'll pay for the ticket." Wyatt rose from his chair, arms outstretched, going in for a bro' hug.

Ryder put his sunglasses on before slapping Wyatt's back, but Wyatt jerked him tighter. This was a good-bye of sorts, and even if he pretended he was okay with it, he wasn't quite ready. Emma was heading to the front desk at that point. Wyatt saw her smile and place her hand over her heart.

"I'm glad to see this." She approached them, carrying a Sharpie. "Looks like you've come to an understanding."

"Ryder's off the hook, but I'm still going forward with my plans." Wyatt hid all traces of disappointment from his voice.

Ryder rubbed his temple. "I need to lie down before dinner."

Emma grabbed him into a quick hug. "Go rest. I'll knock on your door when dinner's ready."

She watched him shuffle off and then faced Wyatt, her brow knitted, eyes filled with concern. She laid her hands on his chest. "How do you feel?"

Wyatt shrugged. "I've been better."

When Emma wound her arms around his neck and hugged him, he held her tight. She nestled her head against his shoulder. Her body and scent worked its magic, relaxing him almost instantly. He bit his lip and closed his eyes, stretching out the moment for as long as he could.

"I'm proud of you." She gave him an extra squeeze before easing away.

Before he let go, he kissed her. "Thank you, for everything. Even though you never agree with me, you always make me feel better. How is that possible?"

"It's my special gift." She grinned and handed him the Sharpie so he could sign Jeremy's shirt.

He tugged her back for another kiss, but she held him off, glancing around as if only now remembering where they were. "Not here! Everyone's in the next room."

"Later, then," he purred and swatted her ass, forgetting all about the fact that the cameras were still rolling.

◆ ◆ ◆

Three days later, Emma responded to the twentieth inquiry she'd received about the inn in the past ten days. Historically, her inn relied on repeat bookings for most of its business, so the flurry of new interest had perplexed her. This one, however, gave her the key to the mystery, because it referenced a tweet about her cooking. A tweet from @AirdogLawson.

She scrolled through his Twitter account and noticed he'd been posting pictures of the inn and town, and praising her cooking. All these days he'd been trying to build up her business without once taking credit. It would thrill her mother, but not nearly as much as it melted Emma's heart. He'd been determined to help her, and she hadn't given him the respect of honesty about her true dreams.

Shame sifted through her mind as she replied to the email. Unfortunately, Mari approached her, interrupting her musings.

"Do you have a few minutes?" Mari asked. As always, her sleek blond hair framed her hard, chiseled face. Piercing eyes added weight to her air of authority.

"What do you need?" Emma fixed her best innkeeper smile in place to ward off the command Mari projected over everything in her path.

"I'd like to speak with you." Mari gestured to the sofa. "Let's sit."

Emma opted for the chair opposite the sofa. Although Mari might only be eight or ten years older than she, the woman's confidence could make Emma feel like a child.

"I'd like your help with Wyatt." Mari folded her hands in her lap, spine erect, body pitched forward.

"Help with what? He and Ryder settled things, haven't they?"

"Wyatt is determined to keep parts of his life private, preventing me from painting a full picture. I understand his trust issues with the media, but I'm trying to make a compelling and engaging documentary. Every influence on his life and each decision during this comeback are relevant and important, including you."

Emma's pulse throbbed in her ears. "You overestimate my influence on Wyatt and Ryder."

Mari sat back, her eyes drifting upward as if searching for patience.

"Let's drop the pretense, Emma." Mari fixed her intelligent gaze on her. "I know."

"Know what?" Emma weakly attempted to forestall the inevitable.

"I know that you and Wyatt are involved in a relationship that extends beyond innkeeper and guest. Beyond friendship."

The word "how" nearly leapt off the tip of her tongue, but Emma restrained it by pressing her lips together.

Mari didn't wait for a confession. "I'm trained to observe people, settings, situations. Wyatt, in particular, has been less careful lately, openly wearing his feelings for you. I've also overheard Trip making overtures to Wyatt to settle here after competition and join him and his partner at Backtrax. Trip's shrewd enough to realize Wyatt's name would drive business in their direction, but the fact that Wyatt didn't outright dismiss him suggests he has other reasons to consider returning to Sterling Canyon. As if that weren't enough to convince me, I caught an exchange between you two on camera the other day right here in this room. So let's not pretend that you don't know what I'm talking about."

Trapped, like a firefly in a jar, with no escape. Nonetheless, her heart floated inside her chest as if it'd been filled with helium. *Wyatt might return to Sterling Canyon?*

Mari cleared her throat, bringing Emma back to reality.

"Wyatt's entitled to some privacy. Maybe being behind the camera has made you forget how too much scrutiny can suffocate a person." Emma gestured toward the equipment strewn about, while privately acknowledging her own mother's scrutiny had been equally overwhelming. She should be an old pro when it came to evasion, but right now she felt as transparent as glass. "Would you want to shine a spotlight on a relationship that had no real future?"

"Wyatt knew the deal when we entered into this project. Despite his misgivings, he agreed to be subjected to the scrutiny in order to further his own goals of attracting major sponsorship money. He and I have a symbiotic relationship. What's good for him is also good for me. So I'm not the problem. If anything, you're the problem. You don't want to be part of this, and he's trying to protect you." Mari leaned forward, her expression as earnest as Emma had ever seen it. "If you care about him, help him reach his goals. Be part of this project and help make this film a success. Help him get what he needs for his ego and for his family."

Oh, well done. Mari had neatly trapped her in that jar again, except this one contained no air holes. How could Emma refuse to help Wyatt when he'd been trying to salvage her beleaguered inn?

Emma's gaze dropped. She couldn't admit the entire truth behind her reluctance, so she latched onto the most obvious sliver. "Wyatt hasn't mentioned Trip's offer, so I doubt he's giving it any real consideration. He probably didn't turn it down outright to spare Trip's feelings. And you know my 'relationship' with Wyatt won't last beyond next week. He's young, he's got years of competition ahead of him. He'll have a dozen girlfriends before he settles down. Mari, there's no need to draw attention to me because I am not, nor will I ever be, a significant factor in his life."

Mari shook her head. "But you have been a factor during this part of his training. You've been an influence on his relationship with his brother. I suspect you're behind his mother's arrival in two days, too. Like it or not, you are a part of this story, Emma." Mari sat back, eyes narrowing speculatively. "I can only guess that your reluctance to cooperate means you've got something to hide."

Panic flooded her mouth with a metallic taste. Emma locked her fingers together to settle the tremors and tried brushing aside Mari's accusation with a laugh. "You have quite an imagination. No wonder you love filmmaking."

Mari heaved a sigh and then abruptly stood. "I'd hoped your feelings for Wyatt would persuade you to help. It seems I've been wrong about you. Maybe you're just using him for your own purposes. Isn't that ironic? He doesn't trust me, who has his interests at heart, yet he fully trusts you, and you either care too little or are engaged in some kind of deception. Either way, I suppose it is a good thing that you're not in this film and that he'll be leaving soon."

Emma's throat tightened, cutting off her air supply. Mari turned on her heel and left the room, leaving Emma to stew in a sea of unflattering accusations.

Emma didn't care too little for Wyatt. She cared entirely too much, which meant she'd be hurt no matter which path she chose.

She could come clean. Go to Wyatt today and confess all—Aspen, Alexa, the book. Her conscience would be clear, but he would be hurt, angry, and ultimately, resentful. When he left, his memories of her would not be pleasant or welcome, and that thought clawed at her heart.

If she stayed silent, their relationship would never be completely honest, but when it ended, which it must inevitably do, it would be with fondness. Emma couldn't bear to see the light in his eyes go dark on her. Surely, after a lifetime of doing nearly everything right, she was entitled to this one small wrong. A lie of omission hurt no one but herself.

Her mother's warnings rattled around her brain. Unwelcome reminders of how she'd put herself in this position and only had herself to blame for any misery. How did someone arrive at this place? How had she arrived here? Then she suddenly wondered if her father had ever struggled with a similar conflict before he'd left? Had he been confused by his conflicting desires, or felt guilty as hell?

A pleasant hum reverberated throughout Emma's body, even as she groggily opened her eyes. Four forty-five in the morning. Last night she'd thanked Wyatt for his help with the inn by letting him call all the shots. Her body now lay heavy with lingering pleasure and exhaustion.

She should get moving, but she only had another six nights to spoon with him.

Since her conversation with Mari, her moods had swung from delight to near depression on an hourly basis. She'd dissected this relationship from its inception. At the outset, Emma had convinced herself she could enjoy Wyatt just as she'd enjoyed that one night in Aspen. A discreet event that hadn't touched her heart yet had temporarily set her free. Allowed her to safely explore a side of herself she'd always deemed dangerous and not altogether good.

It had started out that way, that night earlier this month when he'd tricked her into coming into his room to check on the radiator. Perhaps she could've remained on the sidelines, cheering her body on, if she'd restricted their interludes to sex. But by the third or fourth night, she'd started staying longer. Sometimes they'd slept a while and then had had sex again, other times they'd talked into the night. They never discussed their futures—both were smart enough to know *they* didn't have one—yet she didn't feel alone in her disappointment that everything would very soon, and very abruptly, come to an end.

But facts were facts. He had to go compete, and she couldn't indefinitely keep *Steep and Deep* a secret from him if things continued beyond next week. Ironically, Wyatt would probably get a kick out of the fact that she'd written erotica, but he'd also want to read it. That would be a disaster.

If her pen name didn't trigger his memory, surely one or two of the specifics in the sex scenes might. The combination . . . well, surely the déjà vu would grip him until he figured it out and then he'd feel used. And Mari would eviscerate her if she found out about her past link to Wyatt and its connection to her book.

A slight shiver passed through her.

"You cold?" Wyatt's sleepy voice brushed across her ear as he snuggled her closer. His hand cupped her breast then, and his warm mouth kissed her shoulder.

She reached up behind her to stroke his cheek and thread her fingers through his hair. Boy, she'd miss this. Miss the way he smiled at her, touched her, whispered in her ear. Miss being part of a couple, even one as secret and screwed up as this love affair.

A slight purr rumbled in his chest and before long she felt his hard shaft against her hip. She twisted within his arms to face him. To kiss him.

Dark shadows hung like drapes around them. In the quiet, she could hear her heartbeat thudding in her ears. Beneath her hands, his muscles tightened as his body reacted to desire, excitement, and need.

Their minds were always in sync in bed, knowing just how and when to stroke, tease, touch, or kiss. A perfect fit, she thought, as he glided into her with lazy thrusts.

"Emma," he murmured, the weight of feeling he attached to her name settling over them like a thick, down blanket.

At night, they were playful, experimental, and he always seized control. But when they made love like this, her heart came alive with tenderness almost to the point of pain. Despite the lack of light, the room glowed from pure emotion.

The strongest urge to confess everything pressed on her chest. Her secrets tarnished what otherwise had been the most beautiful few weeks of her life. Other words wanted to be let out as well. Words like *love*. Rationally she knew that love didn't happen so fast. That lasting love took time and honesty and everything else she and Wyatt didn't have.

Nonetheless, her heart beat out those four significant letters like a drum, reminding her of all the things she admired about him: his strength, his loyalty, his ability to apologize, his generosity, and the way he accepted and desired the parts of her that she'd always feared.

She'd repressed her needs and curiosity for years, but how would she return to hiding it all when he left? Having soared for weeks, how could she lock it all away again without suffocating?

When their bodies were sated, Wyatt stroked her cheek. "Are you crying?"

She felt her other cheek, not realizing tears had leaked from her eyes. Oh how she wanted to laugh, she wanted to cry, she wanted to hide.

"Emma?" Wyatt's solemn face looked so beautiful she felt new tears springing forth. "What's wrong?"

"Nothing," she lied. She cupped his face. "I'm being emotional."

"Because I leave next week?"

"Because . . . because I'm not used to this, to someone like you. You've burst into my life and changed me. I didn't expect . . . I didn't expect all of these feelings to surface. It caught me by surprise."

"I never meant to make you sad."

"You haven't. This month has been the best," she chuckled. "That's why I'm sad. It'll be hard to say good-bye, even though I've always known it had to be this way."

He frowned and pressed his lips together. "I'll miss you, too. We'll keep in touch, though, right?"

She nodded, although the words sounded empty. Of course, she'd rather he not make false declarations. He'd already shouldered enough guilt about Ryder, so she wouldn't add to it by pressing him for promises he couldn't keep. Promises she couldn't allow herself to consider because of her own deceit.

Wyatt buried his face against her neck and held her. "Don't think about next week. Let's make the best of the time we have and figure out the rest later."

"I agree." She kissed the side of his head. "And now you have to roll over because I've got to shower, start breakfast, and do a million things before I drive up to Montrose with Ryder to get your mom this afternoon."

He rolled off Emma and grimaced. "I'm sort of dreading seeing her. When we'd left Vermont, I'd planned on Ryder being excited about everything, not spending hours each day making pottery. Not going off without any kind of plan. His random behavior will be another thing she'll blame me for. Another way I failed him." He threw one arm over his eyes.

Emma kissed his chest. "Ryder's been much happier since you let him out of the project. She'll see that. I'm sure all she really wants is to see you both happy. Besides, you can't control him. And frankly, from what you've shared, she should've done a better job protecting her sons when she had the chance. Glass houses, you know."

Wyatt's megawatt smile burst through the shadows. "True enough."

"See you later." Emma kissed him once more before slipping out of his room, determined to get a grip on herself and make his final few days with her as perfect as possible.

Chapter Sixteen

Emma stood at the door, waving good-bye to Wyatt and his crew as they loaded up their van to hit the slopes.

"What time should I be back here to go pick up my mom?" Ryder asked.

"Noon should give us plenty of time to park and greet her at baggage claim."

"Okay." Ryder's ride to Jack Crawford's studio pulled up to the curb. "See you later."

She closed the door and hustled to the registration desk to scan her lengthy to-do list. When she heard the door open, she assumed Ryder had forgotten something.

"Emma?" Andy asked, surprising her into looking up.

Smiling, she asked, "Hey, what are you doing here? I thought Avery wanted to hit the road early so you'd get to Arizona before five."

"We're leaving soon, but I wanted to swing by first . . . make sure you were all set for the holiday. Will you join Kelsey's family?"

"No, I'm preparing everything for Wyatt's family and crew, but don't worry. I'm fine." More than fine, actually. Her first holiday shared with a love interest in many moons, sad as that was to admit. Not that

Andy knew it. "It's hardly the first Thanksgiving I've prepared for guests. Just the first without my mom."

"How's her trip going?" Andy ran a hand through his hair.

"So far, so good. They're heading in to New York City as we speak." For a moment, she envied her mom's mini-adventure. She projected decades ahead, imagining taking off with Avery and Kelsey on an adventure longer than the four days they'd spent in Cabo in September and smiled.

"You've really been enjoying the break from her, huh? Gets a little tedious working and living with a parent, I bet?"

"It can be." The burden of being the main focus of her mom's life sometimes wore thin. She'd stepped into that role as a teen to help lift her mom's depression. Complacency, timidity, and love then conspired to keep Emma forever locked in the role.

Andy kicked his toe against the carpet a couple of times, hands in his pockets. Then he glanced around, making sure no one was listening. "Em, the truth is, I'm concerned about how you've gotten attached to Wyatt. Now you're hosting his family holiday, like you're in a serious relationship. Like you've forgotten he's leaving here next week. Maybe I'm wrong. Maybe you've got all this under control, but if you don't, I'll be here for you once he's gone . . . if you need someone to lean on."

Andy's candor set her back. The vague reference to being there for her neatly brushed along the edge of friendship while also preserving it. His feelings both touched and embarrassed her.

"Thanks, Andy, but I'm honestly fine. I know what I'm doing." *Liar.*

He stared at her, brow cocked, unable or unwilling to hide his doubt. "Okay, then. Have a happy Thanksgiving. See you on Monday."

"'Bye." Emma watched him go. Off to be with his family, unlike her, who was playing house with a secret lover who would soon be out of her life. A little bout of blues surfaced as she thought about her own family. Picking up the phone, she decided to call her mom. "Just checking in. How's it going?"

"We're getting close to the George Washington Bridge. Lord, the traffic around here. I don't know why people live like this."

Emma smiled, imagining her mom and Aunt Vera amid the sophisticated, fast-paced crowds of New York. "Remember to be careful, Mom. New York can be dangerous."

"We'll be fine, honey. How about you? Will you be going over to the Callihans' for dinner tomorrow?"

"No. I'm cooking for our guests." Emma doodled flowers on the nearby notepad.

"Oh, of course. Sorry."

"Don't apologize." She set the pencil down. "It's the job."

"You sound sad. What's wrong?"

"Nothing."

"Emma, I know you. Something's on your mind."

"Can't I just call to say hi? Maybe I miss having you hovering over my shoulder." Emma smiled to herself because, despite her complaining, a tiny part of her did.

"And here I assumed you were enjoying my absence . . . perhaps a bit too much."

Rather than take the bait, Emma opted for sarcasm. "I won't lie. The wild parties have been a blast. I've redecorated, too. Red and purple velvet all over the place. Wait until you see it."

Her mother sighed. "That's not the tone I expect from the girl I raised. Honestly, Emma, what's gotten into you lately?"

Emma frowned. She couldn't say *nothing* because that would be a lie. She had been changing, little by little. But now wasn't the time for that discussion. "Sorry, Mom. I was only kidding. Have a good time at the Macy's Thanksgiving Day Parade tomorrow. I'll speak with you later."

"Love you."

"You, too." Emma hung up and glanced around. Despite the vast, empty spaces, the walls seemed to be closing in on her. Rather than sink into a funk, she set her mind to being productive.

Given her long list of tasks—addressing matters related to her book launch while also preparing the pork tenderloin marinade and afternoon snacks—she'd brought her laptop downstairs to save herself multiple trips up and down two flights of stairs.

Less than two weeks from now, she'd officially be a published author. A twinge of energy tickled her nerves. If a similar sensation consumed Wyatt every time he soared off a jump, no wonder he flung himself into the air on a regular basis.

Setting up her computer at one of the dining tables, she opened her website and studied it. Against the advice of pretty much everyone in the industry, hers didn't contain an author photo.

Although she'd been told readers like to put a face to their favorite writers, Emma wouldn't risk creating any link between herself and Alexa Aspen. She'd purchased a photo of a silhouette of a woman in lingerie to use as her avatar on social media sites. She'd set up a Gmail account under her pen name.

The only tricky part of her plans had been her P.O. box. Everyone at the local post office knew her, so she'd traveled ten miles to Ophir to preserve her anonymity. Kind of a hassle, but it made her feel better. So far she'd been able to slip things past her mother, although the box of advance review copies had been a challenge. She'd been slowly depleting her supply by sending them to bloggers and a few readers who'd started to follow her on Instagram and Facebook.

Emma scrolled through some photos she'd saved for her prelaunch countdown post, proofread a blog post one last time, and published it. Glancing at her watch, she then hustled into the kitchen to prepare the apricot glaze for the pork and pull together the black bean and quinoa side dish. After those tasks were complete, she went back into the dining room and logged on to Facebook to post the link to her blog and engage with her author friends for ten minutes.

Her phone buzzed on the table.

"Hi, Jill," she answered, noting her agent's name on the screen.

"Emma, I'm checking in because I was expecting your draft manuscript by now. I need time to read it in case you need to make revisions before its submission deadline."

"Sorry. I got a little hung up, but I promise you'll have it within a week." In order to separate Dallas from Wyatt, she'd scoured Pinterest until she'd found a suitable replacement image—Marlon Teixeira—that freed her to write Dallas as she wanted without feeling like she was somehow using Wyatt.

"Great. I look forward to reading it. I assume you're getting geared up for the launch now, too?"

"I am. I admit, I still love staring at the *Steep and Deep* cover. The title font is perfect, and the black and red is really sexy. I've scheduled a bunch of fun posts and a Facebook party with some giveaways. I'm almost finished writing all the blog posts publicity requested for the blog tour they set up. Things look good."

"They're putting a lot of promotion behind this project, so I'm feeling confident it will make a nice showing."

"Thanks, Jill. I hope readers fall in love with Dallas like I did." As she said those words, she frowned, because in that moment Dallas's face had become Wyatt's again. A Freudian slip of sorts, she supposed. Not a good thing, because one-sided love would likely be more painful than the loneliness she'd learned to live with.

People say it's better to have loved and lost than never to have loved at all, but having watched her mom suffer from lost love, she wasn't looking forward to feeling even a fraction of that kind of pain.

"I did, and I suspect others will, too. He's a memorable hero." Jill's words were reassuring.

"Thanks."

"Have a great Thanksgiving. I'll speak with you soon."

"Have a good holiday, too." Emma hung up and shut down her computer, satisfied with her productivity.

She pulled out two platters for the afternoon snacks, checked Mrs. Lawson's room to make sure Andy had prepared it before he'd taken off, and then tied back her hair and put on a little hint of makeup. What little she knew of Mrs. Lawson didn't warm her heart, but Emma still wanted to make a good first impression. She laughed at herself then, because the odds of Emma ever seeing Mrs. Lawson after this visit were longer than those on the Colorado Rockies playing in the World Series.

◆ ◆ ◆

Emma unloaded Mrs. Lawson's luggage from the van and followed her and Ryder into the Weenuche. The woman couldn't be much older than fifty despite the cracked-leather texture of her skin. She must've been a smoker, or spent a lot of time outside in the harsh Vermont climate. Her petite frame and graying hair lent a hint of vulnerability to her otherwise rugged appearance.

The woman had hung on Ryder's every word since they'd collected her at the airport. Love and concern shone from her hazel eyes, which were similar in color and shape to Wyatt's.

Emma hoped Mrs. Lawson would shower Wyatt with that same degree of attention when he arrived. Although Emma couldn't bring herself to be honest with him, she'd worked hard to help knit his family back together. That feat would absolve her sins of omission—or so she hoped.

"How old is this house?" Mrs. Lawson asked once they entered the lobby. Her even tone didn't disclose whether she liked or disliked the aging Victorian.

"It was built in 1900. Survived the 1914 flood, actually."

"So much history. Is it haunted?" When Ryder snickered, his mother playfully tapped his arm. "These old places can be, you know."

Apparently Wyatt's interest in the spirit world had been fostered from a young age. She supposed all parents, not just her own mother, had a way of brainwashing their children into adopting their belief systems. Emma's mom had instilled one set of values and fears, Wyatt's mom another.

"Wyatt mentioned the same thing, but I've never yet seen a ghost here. Let me know if you sense any. Perhaps my grandfather will appear. He grew up in this house and absolutely adored it, so I could imagine him hanging around." Emma went to the front desk to retrieve Mrs. Lawson's key. "I planned to put you beside Ryder here on the first floor, in Room 102. Is that okay, or would you rather be upstairs?"

"Next to Ryder is perfect." She cast him another fond gaze and pinched his cheek, as if he were still a kid. "It's good to see my beautiful boy."

Acid pitted Emma's stomach. She'd expected Mrs. Lawson to dote on Ryder because of his injuries, but the woman hadn't asked a single question about Wyatt since they'd picked her up ninety minutes ago. Wyatt, the son who'd paid for her ticket. Who was working hard to provide his mom and Ryder some measure of security. "Wyatt should be back soon. He planned to cut his training short today to spend some time with you."

Mrs. Lawson nodded thoughtfully, but said, "I'm glad Ryder took the whole day off. I appreciate the greeting."

Emma's eye twitched. She glanced at Ryder, wondering if he enjoyed the disparity of his mother's affection for her sons.

"I didn't take the day off for you, Mom. I'm not working on the film anymore." Ryder tugged at his ear. It surprised Emma that he hadn't yet told his mother of the change in plans.

"Did your brother fire you?" Mrs. Lawson's eyes lit with indignation.

"I quit," Ryder admitted. "Wyatt wanted me to stick with him, but I'm not interested in that w-world anymore."

"Who could blame you, honey? After what happened, I thought you were crazy to come in the first place." Mrs. Lawson linked her arm with Ryder's. "Why don't you come home with me after the holiday?"

That was it. Emma did not like Mrs. Lawson. Wyatt had already been hurt by Ryder's decision, now his own mother would deprive him of what little time he had left with his brother.

Ryder shrugged noncommittally. "We'll see."

Doubts about her plans for the Lawson family reunion trickled into her consciousness, but she bit her tongue. "Let me show you to your room. You'll probably want to freshen up after such a long trip."

She hefted the suitcase and escorted Mrs. Lawson to her room, where she gladly left her. When she passed through the lobby, Ryder was still there.

"Is she always like that?" Emma huffed.

"Like what?"

"So uninterested in your brother." Emma's fists settled on her hips.

"They've always butted heads. He blamed her for letting my dad get away with so much, and she blames him for my accident." Ryder leaned against the front desk.

"Why can't you get her to quit blaming Wyatt so they might get along? The most important thing you three have is each other."

"It's not that simple, Emma. She thinks Wyatt doesn't respect her. In a way, she's not wrong. You've seen how Wyatt shoots off his mouth when he's mad, and he was m-mad a lot back in Vermont because my dad was . . . difficult." Ryder shrugged. "They love each other. They just don't trust each other."

Trust. Always difficult to regain once lost.

"I guess he'll never get what he needs from her." A shiver passed through Emma because she worried Wyatt might very well end up dead in his quest for salvation from whatever sins he believed he'd committed.

239

"Which is what?" Ryder crossed his arms defensively, obviously protective of his mother.

Emma softened her voice. "For her to look at him like she looks at you. I bet this comeback attempt has more to do with some twisted kind of atonement to the two of you than with his desire to be back in competition."

"Maybe." Ryder frowned.

"Sorry. I don't mean to judge." She frowned, reflecting on her own family. "Heck, I haven't talked to my dad in seven months. Tomorrow is one of the biggest family holidays of the year, and I'll be spending it without either parent."

Ryder cocked his head. Even though his darn sunglasses hid his eyes, she felt his intense gaze. "Maybe you should take some of your own advice and call him."

Call her father. A novel idea.

Emma didn't respect some of her father's choices, but she'd never intended to cut all ties. His departure had devastated and angered her. She'd wanted him to miss her so much he'd come running back, so she'd refused to initiate contact.

Her mother—pleased to see her ex punished however possible—hadn't discouraged that behavior. Once her mom recovered from her depression, Emma'd refrained from reaching out to her father, afraid her mother would view it as a betrayal and slip back into darkness. The sad truth was that her father accepted the loss pretty easily, and his calls became less frequent each year.

Still, the cumulative effect of her decisions deteriorated the relationship so slowly, she didn't recognize it until it was too late.

At thirty-one, she understood how exaggerated her parents' reactions to their own divorce had been. If her mother had moved on instead of wallowing and blaming and praying, maybe Emma's whole life could have been more of an adventure.

Now Emma faced her own romantic dilemma. One she knew her mother would not understand. But what about her father?

He might be the only person who could empathize with her desire to ignore caution. Who wouldn't judge her for how she'd barreled ahead into a highly sexual, gratifying relationship with Wyatt. Who might even applaud her decision to press forward with her books even though, somewhere in the back of her mind, she feared she could never indefinitely hide behind a pen name.

◆ ◆ ◆

Wyatt exited the van and braced himself to see his mom. He knew Ryder hated being their mediator. Considering how his plans to help his brother had backfired so far, he was determined to do this one thing right. They'd all be parting ways soon, and Wyatt needed to leave for competition on a mental high note.

Voices coming from the dining room beckoned, so he went there before changing out of his gear. Ryder and his mother were drinking tea and eating some hummus concoction Emma must've prepared. Emma, however, was nowhere to be seen. *Smart girl.*

"Hey, Mom!" When his mom remained seated, he brushed off the insult and bent down to offer an awkward hug. "How was your flight?"

"Fine, thank you." She flashed a stiff smile and gestured toward a dining chair. "Sit down and have something to eat. Your brother has been filling me in on the past few weeks."

If Ryder mentioned the avalanche, his mother either didn't care or chose not to ask. Wyatt didn't know how to feel about that, so again, he pushed it aside. He couldn't start an argument within minutes of seeing her, could he?

Mari and Buddy were chatting as they strolled into the dining room. Upon seeing his mother, Mari quickly donned a polite expression. "Hi,

Mrs. Lawson, it's nice to see you again. I hope you had a good flight. This is your first trip to Colorado, right?"

"Yes." His mom spared Mari a placating glance. "It's quite dramatic. The mountains are quite different from those at home."

"You should see them up close." Mari cocked her head. "Perhaps you'd like to come out with us on Friday to watch Wyatt train. You can watch live feed from the video monitor in the van. It's quite exciting. Your son's an exceptional athlete."

"No, thank you." Her mouth settled into a firm line. "Danger doesn't appeal to me, especially after what happened to Ryder."

"Of course. I'm sorry." Mari shifted gears and pointed at the small camera in the corner. "Buddy, grab that camera so we can upload the video."

Video?

"Why'd you film the dining room all day?" Wyatt asked, wondering whether Emma had noticed.

"To get footage of your mother's impressions when she arrived. I assumed we wouldn't be here on time. Had one rolling in the parlor, too. Most of it's probably useless, but we might've caught something worthwhile. Ah, the fun job of editing," she joked, although it didn't strike Wyatt as being very funny.

Then again, Emma had probably spent the majority of her day in the kitchen and the office. He couldn't imagine her passing through the inn would merit any interest, so she was safe.

Wyatt pulled off his jacket. "Let me grab a quick shower and change, then I'll be back down to visit."

"Take your time. I'm not going anywhere." His mother dragged a carrot stick through the hummus.

Wyatt nodded at this brother, then trod through the inn wishing his skin didn't itch every time he interacted with his own mother. On his way up the stairs, he bumped into Emma.

"You're back." Her welcoming smile made the itching stop.

"Safe and sound." Just the sight of Emma lifted his spirits.

"Thank God." She peeked down the stairs, muttering, "Did you see your mom?"

"Briefly. Thanks for getting her, and for making snacks. I've got no idea how the next few days will play out, but it's nice to know you're here to talk to if things go south." He reached for her hand and flashed a devilish smile. "In fact, got a few minutes now? My shower isn't working great."

"Nice try." She tugged her hand free. "I think I'll pass given that everyone is awake and milling around."

Normally she'd say those things to him with a worried look on her face. Right now, however, she looked calm and confident.

Wyatt narrowed his gaze. Her hair looked normal, smooth and tucked behind her ears. Her clothing looked comfortable and fresh as usual. Yet something seemed markedly changed. "You look different. What's going on?"

Her eyes widened. "Wow. Who knew you could be so perceptive?" She wrinkled her nose. "I called my dad today."

The few times her father had come up, she'd sounded melancholy, so her happy expression threw him. He noticed her fingers toying with a heart-shaped locket he hadn't seen before. "Really? How'd that go?"

"He was surprised, but it went well. A good first step." She glanced around, possibly concerned about someone overhearing them. It felt like the wrong time for him to press for all the details, but he needed to know one thing.

"Just tell me, what made you decide to reach out?"

She shrugged. "Your mom's arrival. The holiday. Watching your family struggle with the past, all of it made me realize I needed to revisit my own relationships with my parents. To start making decisions that suit me instead of worrying so much about how they might perceive me."

"Is that the secret fear you've been worried about?" His chest filled with warmth, thinking maybe he'd played some role in helping her.

Emma glanced at her feet for a second. "Not exactly, but it's a step in that direction."

"Good for you, Em. That deserves a reward." He nudged closer, only a little disappointed she still wouldn't share all her secrets. "Sure you don't have time to come check out my shower?"

"Stop!" She pushed at his chest, laughing. "I've got to take care of some things for dinner. Clean up and go spend some time with your mom and brother. I really want to see you all settled before you leave here."

Wyatt heaved a sigh. "Wish me luck."

Wyatt, Ryder, and his mom had been hanging out in the parlor for the past ninety minutes, digesting another excellent dinner. He hadn't seen Emma since she'd cleared the dishes. Mari had gone to her room to review the day's footage, and Jim and Buddy had hit town for a drink.

Every few minutes, Wyatt glanced at the clock, wishing his mother would go to bed. It should feel like eleven o'clock to her. Why wasn't she sleepy?

Ryder rubbed his temple. "My head hurts a bit. I'm tired."

Their mother brushed his bangs away from his forehead. "That's okay, honey. We understand. Actually, I'm a little wiped out myself."

Thank you, God.

"Me, too," Wyatt lied. "Trip and I pushed hard today, so I could use some Z's. Looking forward to a day off tomorrow, and no doubt dinner will be amazing."

"Emma's an excellent cook. I'm surprised neither of you has gained weight this month." His mom surprised Wyatt then, by finally acknowledging his generosity. "Thank you for buying my ticket and bringing me here for the holiday. That was very thoughtful of you."

"You're welcome." Wyatt would've given Emma credit, except he thought that might ruin the rare moment with his mom.

The three of them said their goodnights and meandered to their rooms. Wyatt closed his door and then stretched out on his bed. Emma usually slipped in sometime after ten, but tonight he didn't feel like waiting that long.

He'd been melancholy all afternoon, especially after his mom asked Ryder to return to Vermont with her on Sunday. Although that would only be a few days before Wyatt would be moving on to Crested Butte, he hated the idea. It still hurt when he thought about Ryder bailing on this journey.

Worse, he didn't like thinking about saying good-bye to Emma so soon. He wished she could come on tour with him for a while.

Glancing at the clock for the thousandth time, he decided to take matters into his hands. With so little time left to share, he didn't feel like wasting any of it. After making sure no one saw him leave his room, he dashed up the stairs to find Emma. He knocked before turning her knob, but her door was locked.

"Hold on!" she called from inside amid a tumble of noise. Several seconds later, she opened the door. "Oh, is everything okay?"

"It will be," he grinned, nudging his way into her room.

"Did you ditch your mom and Ryder?"

"They went to sleep, and Mari's been in her room for the past hour. I realized I've never been in your room. I want to see where you live."

Oddly, she drained of color. Her shyness still surprised him, especially after all the things they done with each other this month.

Her room dwarfed his guestroom. A queen-size bed and dresser took up one side of the space. Across the room, a sizable nook housed a seating area with a sofa and a coffee table decorated with eight or nine pillar candles. An antique standing lamp with a fringed shade stood beside the sofa, and a vine-patterned area rug covered most of the floor. On a blank wall between the two spaces sat a large desk.

Her taste in décor matched her wardrobe. Clean, simple patterns in soft greens, yellows, and whites.

It smelled faintly sweet, like her body lotion and spice-scented candles. However, the windows were smaller up here. Although the pale palette helped brighten the space, something about the attic settled heavily in his gut. Emma lived like a princess in a tower, locked away with too little sunlight and no adventure.

He couldn't change that, except perhaps for providing a little more adventure here and now. He gathered her in his arms. "Light the candles."

"You want to stay here?" she squeaked.

"Yeah. I want to have you in your bed so you'll think about me when I'm gone and you're here alone."

She stroked his cheek before curling her arms around his neck. "I'll think about you regardless, Wyatt."

Wyatt knew he'd remember that softness in her voice for a long, long time.

"Good." He kissed her, feeling suddenly restless and needy. Screw the candles, he couldn't wait. "I assume living with your mom means you haven't had many men up here?"

"You're the first." She blushed at the admission like it was shameful, when actually it turned him on.

"So tell me, what kinds of fantasies have you spun up here, and how can I make them come true?"

Her eyes widened before turning mischievous. No matter how introverted Emma could be, when it came to sex, she always opened up to him. She eased away and crossed to her closet. Seconds later, she returned, dangling a robe sash from her hand.

He'd always loved these games, but with Emma they were even better. The girl who retained supreme control by day handed it over to him at night. She trusted him enough to let go, which meant everything. "I suggest you get undressed and lie on the bed."

While she disrobed, he decided to light those candles after all. He brought one to the nightstand. Holding the sash between his teeth, he took off his shirt and pants and then straddled Emma and tied her hands to the wrought iron headboard.

Golden light flickered from the nearby candle, making her creamy skin glow. She raised her knees to cradle his hips, but he pushed them open and lowered himself so he could kiss her.

He hadn't forgotten the feel of her tears on his fingertips this morning, or the sound of her wavering voice as she'd explained her flurry of emotion. He'd replayed the scene throughout the day because no one had ever reacted to him that way. Had ever made him feel that important. That needed. That wanted.

Sure, women had wanted him before for superficial reasons. But Emma actually cared. She saw something worthwhile in him that had nothing to do with his medals or even his face. She kissed him as if everything in the world depended on it. As if he made her come alive, which is exactly how he now felt in return.

"Emma, I know I promised you this fantasy, but I really want your hands on me. I want to be closer than this." He registered her surprise, and the warm green glow that shone from her eyes.

"Untie me, then."

He loosened the knots until she slipped her hands free and ran them along his spine. "Don't stop."

And she didn't. Neither did he. Not for a long, long time.

An hour later, their sweat-soaked bodies lay snuggled together sideways on her bed. The candles still burned, casting shadows all around them. Wyatt found himself wishing he could live two lives: one that allowed him to stay here longer and another that went off to compete.

He combed his fingers through her silky hair, staring at the ceiling. "Do you ever take vacation time?"

"Not often." She propped her chin up on his chest. "I did go to Cabo in September for a few days." She mirrored his sudden grin. "Why'd that make you smile?"

"Because I'm glad you get out of here once in a while. Maybe you'll come visit me this winter. Maybe you'd even come check out Switzerland in April."

"I've never been to Europe." Her voice filled with a wistful sort of wonder, but her brows pinched with doubts.

"If I make it to the finals, say you'll come. Come for the competition, and then we can stay a few days afterward. I'll be done, one way or another, and we can explore the area."

She kissed his chest, but her eyes weren't dancing with anticipation. "Part of me wants to jump at that invitation. But when we started this . . . thing . . . we both knew it would end. Maybe we're better off not making plans."

"Is that really what you want?" He sat up slightly to counteract the tightness in his chest.

"It's complicated." She rolled away.

"What's so complicated? We're two adults. We're not doing anything wrong."

"I'd rather not talk about it." She pulled the blanket up to cover herself, and he could feel her withdrawing into that hard shell she'd hidden behind when they'd first met.

He wriggled back down to get closer to her. "Is this about whatever it is you're afraid of?"

She fell silent. His heart pounded, demanding more of an answer, but he waited.

"The important thing, the only thing that matters, is that you leave here knowing this month has been wonderful for me." Her eyes watered, just like this morning. "You've made me see a lot of things differently. But before you came, I made some choices that might inadvertently hurt some people, and I haven't yet figured out how to untangle it all and go forward."

"You could never hurt anyone." He kissed her forehead.

"Not intentionally." She snuggled closer. "Until I'm able to sort it all out, I don't want to make promises."

Her serious voice caught him by surprise. It almost sounded like a warning, although he couldn't envision any scenario where she'd disappoint or hurt him, unless—"Is there someone else?"

"No!"

"Good." He pulled her back into his arms and stroked her hair. "I hear you, but think about coming. I'd love for you to be there cheering me on."

"I'll be cheering you on wherever I am."

He stroked her arm and continued down her hip until he cupped her ass in his hand. "The celebration would be much better in person."

"Then maybe we should celebrate right now." She kissed his neck.

"I suppose there's no such thing as too much celebrating." He glanced at the corner of the bed. "Gimme that sash back. I still owe you a fantasy."

Chapter Seventeen

Emma lit the gold candles on the table, which she'd decorated with a magnolia-leaf garland, persimmons, and white roses. Eggplant-colored napkins lent a pop of unexpected, rich color, while the candlelight caused the pale green water glasses to sparkle. Mari, who'd been treating her with tempered disdain lately, had already turned on the blasted cameras. At least these shots of the inn would be flattering, pleasing Emma's mother.

The house smelled of turkey and stuffing. She'd baked homemade rolls. Butternut squash soup simmered on the stove. She'd glazed the turkey and made mashed potatoes and her Grammy's gravy. To top it off, spicy pumpkin pies with homemade whipped cream. A smile bubbled up, knowing Wyatt might have special plans for the leftover whipped cream later.

The murmur of conversation coming from the parlor drew her attention. Throughout the day, she'd witnessed a slow thawing between Wyatt and his mother. God willing, her suggestion to gather his family would have a lasting, positive effect. But families were dynamic things, and one never knew what new challenges might crop up in the future.

Her recent conversation with her father still replayed in her mind. She'd asked him whether he might do things differently now that he'd had the benefit of hindsight. He'd admitted to some regrets, mostly about their relationship, but said he couldn't have lived his whole life pretending to be someone he wasn't. He couldn't have set aside all his dreams just to make her mother happy. He believed he would've become a resentful, bitter man if he'd stayed, even though he'd been torn about leaving. Even though he never achieved the success he'd dreamed of.

She knew exactly how it felt to stifle herself in order to be someone people—her mother in particular—expected her to be. Already, at thirty-one, tendrils of resentment had begun to twist through her thoughts, causing discomfort and unhappiness. Not that she admitted any of this to him.

Emma fingered the locket she'd dug out of the corner of her dresser drawer yesterday. She'd never worn it before then. It would've upset her mother, but that wasn't an issue today. Right now it made her feel a little closer to the stranger she called *Dad*. A man she wanted to know better.

She'd stopped short of sharing her own dilemma with him, having not known him well enough to trust him with explosive information. But hearing her father say, *No decision is ever perfect—everything in life comes at some cost*—had given her something to chew on when deciding how to handle her future.

She could choose to write something less erotic down the road, or to come clean with everyone instead of acting ashamed of writing the kind of fiction that people devoured. That second option still made her stomach clench, but she needn't make a choice this minute. Only Wyatt's departure loomed in the foreground, tempting her to lay everything on the table and hope he understood why she'd kept quiet.

She blew out the match and glanced at the clock. Her mom and Aunt Vera had attended the parade and were probably enjoying the final course at La Pecora Bianca, a restaurant that "re-envisioned the traditional Thanksgiving menu," according to Aunt Vera's research.

Although Emma'd enjoyed her freedom this month, Thanksgiving felt odd without her mother. How could it not, when they'd been so bound together for so many years? For all of her rigidity, her mother had also been loving, proud, and steadfastly in Emma's corner. How many hours had her mom spent drinking tea while keeping Emma company in the kitchen, or snuggling under a shared blanket while watching their favorite shows?

"Emma," Ryder interrupted her musings. She looked up to find him standing near her with a tall paper bag in his hand. She assumed it might be a bottle of wine until he said, "I made you something at the studio. A thank you for helping me, and for being there for Wyatt, too."

A small lump lodged in her throat as she accepted his gift. She removed a twelve-inch-high clay cylinder from the bag—a smoky-merlot glazed vase with deep, horizontal grooves and an intentionally imperfect column. "Ryder! Did you come up with this design, or did you copy something you'd seen?"

"A little of both. I altered some c-concepts I'd seen in other people's work." A touch of color invaded his cheeks.

Emma set the vase on the table and grabbed him into a hug. "I absolutely love it." Stepping back, she lifted it again, her hands caressing the grooves and unique shape. "I wish I had some long-stemmed, fresh-cut flowers. For now, I suppose I'll just set it here on the buffet for everyone to admire, like a sculpture."

Wyatt and his mother came into the room, followed by Mari, Buddy, and Jim. Wyatt nodded at the clock. "You said six o'clock. It smells so good, I'm starving."

"Did you all see Ryder's work?" Emma gestured toward the vase, still astounded by its quality, and the spirit with which it had been given.

Wyatt's brows rose. He crossed to the buffet and raised the vase for a closer inspection. "You did this?"

Ryder nodded, but Emma could see tension in the firm set of his mouth.

"In just a couple of weeks you learned to do this?" Wyatt's incredulous expression seemed to annoy his brother.

"I told you the instructor said I had natural t-talent." Ryder crossed his arms.

"Hell, yeah, you do. This is awesome." Wyatt set it down and smiled. "What'd you make for me?"

"Nada," Ryder snorted, then he softened. "Not yet, anyway."

Wyatt cocked a brow over a playful grin. "I expect something when I'm done with this year's competition circuit. But right now, I just want to eat."

"Emma, do you have a preference for seating, or should we select for ourselves?" Mari asked, angling for the head of the table.

"No preference." Emma waved at the table. "Seat yourselves while I set up the buffet and serve the soup."

"Aren't you eating with us?" Wyatt asked as he pulled out a chair for his mother, whom he sat between himself and his brother.

"I'll join you all once I get everything else set." She smiled.

Wyatt pointed at the empty seat on his right. "Sit here, then."

Mari shot Emma an arch look. Wyatt had grown increasingly less guarded this past week.

"Thank you." A flush rose up Emma's neck. "I will."

It took several minutes before Emma finally sat down, at which point Mari spoke again: "If you'd all indulge me, I grew up with a Thanksgiving tradition where all of us share something we've been grateful for during the preceding year. May we do that this evening?"

"That's lovely, Mari." Mrs. Lawson piped up. "Why don't you start us off?"

"Certainly, and then we can go clockwise." Mari sipped her wine. "I'm always grateful that I earn my living doing what I love. This year my job has given me the chance to watch a gold medalist in training.

We've butted heads now and then, but it's been a privilege to see Wyatt's discipline in action. More than that, he's shown himself to be someone capable of deep passion and commitment, to his family, his sport, and others. Someone deserving of success, and of being surrounded by honest people worthy of calling him a friend." Her gaze skidded to Emma before settling back on Wyatt. "I'm grateful to play some small role in helping you achieve your goals this year."

Emma had never seen Wyatt blush before, and the sight stole her breath. More importantly, Mari's speech momentarily caused his mother to look at him through fresh eyes. At least, it appeared that way, judging by the way they glistened now.

Ryder cleared his throat, knowing his turn had come. "This time last year, I still needed a wheelchair and walker to get around. I'm walking and talking better now, and I owe a lot of that p-progress to Wyatt. He left competition at the height of his game to be by my side. That cost him medals, fame, and money, and even though he'd never admit it, it had to be a h-hard choice. I'm grateful for that, and for him now letting me choose my own future without making me feel obligated to repay him."

Emma watched Wyatt shift uncomfortably in his chair. "Let's not make this the 'Praise Wyatt Hour.' You're making me feel like you're boosting me up 'cause you think I'm doomed to fail, or worse."

"Don't talk like that," his mother muttered. She clasped both of her sons' hands. "I'm grateful to my boys for bringing me here for the holiday. And for being there for each other all these years. Life was never easy for our family, but you're both strong, strong boys with big hearts, so I must've done some things right."

Wyatt slipped his arm around his mother's shoulder and kissed her head. "Thanks, Mom."

Emma's eyes watered, and she held her breath, waiting to hear what Wyatt would add to this discussion.

He swallowed a spoonful of the soup first and flashed a satisfied smile. "I'm grateful for Emma's awesome cooking all month."

Buddy interrupted with a quick, "Me, too!" and the others chuckled.

Wyatt then reached for her hand. "I'm grateful for the way she's been like the calm in the middle of a storm. For the kindness she showed Ryder right from the start, to the way she's helped me accept certain things beyond my control. And for organizing all of this tonight. I've never met anyone who gives so much to so many people and doesn't ask for anything in return. If anyone here deserves a medal, it's her, not me."

Now tears spilled down her cheeks. Her skin flashed hot and cold, and her voice cracked a bit when she said, "Thank you, and you're welcome."

She fell silent, overwhelmed by a rush of mixed emotions and the six pairs of eyes staring at her.

"Your turn. What are you grateful for, Emma?" Wyatt asked, squeezing her hand.

"I have a guess," Mari said in a lighthearted tone Emma knew couldn't match the woman's feelings.

"Oh, that's a fun twist," Mrs. Lawson added, oblivious to the alarm coursing through Emma's veins.

"Isn't it?" Mari's mouth curled into its slick, city-girl smile. "Of course, perhaps I should frame my guess as more of a congratulatory comment."

"Well, now I'm curious." Wyatt's eyes darted from Emma to Mari, apparently unaware that Emma's blood had run cold, freezing her in place. "Don't leave us in suspense."

"Emma here is about to become a published author. I know that's a highly competitive industry, so she must be very grateful to have a publisher's support." Mari raised her wineglass as if she were toasting Emma.

Bile rose in Emma's throat. Perspiration broke out along her hairline. She couldn't look at Wyatt or anyone, her gaze fixed somewhere over Mari's shoulder.

"What?" She heard Wyatt's voice as if she was hearing it under water. "Is it true?"

Mari *tsked*. "I'm surprised she didn't share it with you, Wyatt, considering what close friends you've become. I'll admit, I was surprised. Not by the pen name, of course, considering the subject matter. But the sample pages are quite titillating. I preordered a copy last night."

"What's it about?" Mrs. Lawson asked, her interest clearly piqued.

Emma couldn't move. Her mouth wouldn't work. Words wouldn't form. She closed her eyes like a two-year-old playing hide-and-go-seek, wishing herself invisible simply because she could no longer see anything.

"It's a super-sexy erotic romance." Mari grinned. "I like the pen name. Alexa Aspen. Rolls off the tongue. Perfect for the genre."

Emma felt Wyatt lean closer. "Is this what you've been afraid of? You're embarrassed because you wrote a sexy book?"

She opened her eyes and saw him still smiling. He hadn't put it together yet, thankfully. Maybe she could salvage this if she could get her body to respond. If she could stand up and get him to follow her so she could explain it all in private.

"Here's the crazy part," Mari continued. "The premise of the story involves a champion snowboarder. Obviously it was written long before you two met, but it's quite a coincidence. Starts off with a wild one-night stand in Aspen. Guess I'll have to wait a couple of weeks to read past chapter one."

Emma's gaze now fixed on Wyatt. He'd been looking at her, but then his eyes wandered off, brow drawn in thought.

"Alexa Aspen." He faced her again, this time his gaze traveled her features, starting and ending with her hair. "Alexa . . . Aspen." He sat back, clearly off-balance. "Was it you? Was she you?"

"Wyatt . . ." Emma trailed off. What could she say? She wouldn't now add to her sins by denying the truth. Thankfully she hadn't eaten yet, because if she had, it would come right back up. She'd deal with Mari and this stupid film later, but first she had to talk to Wyatt.

"Was. She. You?" Gone was the playful grin she'd known all month. His eyes had cooled, his mouth grim, like Ryder's.

"Yes." Emma reached for his hand, but he withdrew it. "Wyatt, it's not what you think."

"Isn't it?" His jaw clenched. "So that wasn't you in my hotel room? Wasn't you who snuck off without a word? Wasn't you who exploited me to make money off some book?"

A beat or two of razor-sharp silence settled in the room, defying anyone to breathe, much less talk.

"Oh, Emma, you're not at all who you seem to be, are you?" Mari interjected. "At least now we know why you didn't want to be part of this film."

The tension in the room had become unbearable, pressing in on Emma from all sides, finally propelling her from her chair. She could barely see clearly from the tears clogging her eyes. "Excuse me."

The words came out choked, but she managed to cross the dining room without stumbling. As soon as she was out of sight, she fumbled toward the stairs quickly, panting as she groped the railing for support on her way up to her room.

She locked the door and flung herself across her bed, muffling her tears in her pillow. She could blame Mari, that vicious bitch. Surely this news would do nothing to help Wyatt's state of mind or his comeback. Its primary goal had been to humiliate Emma, but even Mari hadn't realized the full scope of the truth. Hadn't known about her and Wyatt's past.

No, as much as Emma wanted to scratch that woman's eyes from her face, she had only herself to blame for the web of lies and omissions that had led to the look of disdain on Wyatt's face.

She curled into a tight ball on her bed, clutching her pillow, unable to stop the tears from flowing, or the remorse from consuming her.

A heavy knock rattled her door.

"Emma, let me in," Wyatt ordered.

She bolted upright and wiped her face, sniffling.

"Emma!" he hollered. "You owe me an explanation, dammit."

Reluctantly, she slid off the bed and unlocked the door, then crossed to her sofa, sat down, and hugged her legs to her chest. "I'm sorry."

"For which part? For lying to me when I first showed up here?"

"Why would I humiliate myself and remind you of who I was?" Emma glanced up. "Imagine how I felt to have been so completely unmemorable. You can't blame me for not saying something. You should be grateful I didn't hold it against you."

At least he had the grace to look away for a minute. "Even so, you didn't have to spend that first week treating me like there was something wrong with me. And once we got together again, you couldn't find a way to be honest about that, or warn me you'd written a damn book about me?"

"It's not about you," she defended. "It's fiction."

"Sounds like this fiction has an awful lot in common with reality." Color had returned to his face.

"It doesn't. I spun a story around the night we met. Dallas is nothing like you, though. Aside from the snowboarding stuff, at least."

"*Dallas?*" Wyatt rolled his eyes. "You named me *Dallas?*"

"It's not you."

"Was it my face you saw when you wrote about him? Did you use things I did and said to fill in some of the blanks in this fiction?"

"I was there, too. I'm entitled to use my own experience as inspiration for a story. This wasn't a conspiracy to get you, Wyatt. Your name is never mentioned in anything connected to this book."

"Neither is yours, apparently."

"No, neither is mine."

"Who are you, Emma? Not the person you pretend to be—not Saint Emma. My God, I honestly can't believe you're the same woman I met in Aspen. Was that just some big game to you?"

"No. I never did anything like that in my life before that night or since. Not until you came here, at least."

"Like I have some magical power to transform you into a different person." He shook his head in disgust. "All this time I've thought you were so strong and composed. I admired you. But it's all an act to cover the fact that you're dishonest. A coward who's too afraid to be yourself. You sure as hell duped me."

"If you want to call me a coward because I like to please people, go ahead. I like the way the people at the care center think of me. I like being involved with my church's youth group. I like knowing that my community respects me. Those things matter to me, especially living in a small town like this. Men's reputations soar when they sleep around, but women are still slut-shamed. You didn't grow up here. I'm not about to upset my mom just to prove a point, either. You weren't here when my mom sank into a major depression and flirted with bottles of sleeping pills. I was the one thing standing between her will to live or die, so don't judge me for learning to keep her happy. To not risk doing anything that could send her into a dark place.

"Have I repressed part of myself? Yes, but not just for her. My dad let temptation wreck our lives, and I didn't like that. I also didn't want to risk pregnancies, abortions, and other things that could happen if I trusted the wrong guy or treated sex so casually. But in Aspen, something snapped. I had an opportunity and urge to unleash everything—just one moment to be free. You gave me that. And that experience opened up something inside that I couldn't suppress anymore. Still, I didn't want to upset my mom or take those other risks, so I poured all those feelings and desires into the book.

"That's how I got to this place. I didn't mean to lie to you and everyone, but I also don't owe the world this private part of my life. And honestly, I can't think about what this will do to my mother if my link to this book gets out. Will you help me convince Mari not to include it in the film?"

Wyatt slowly shook his head. "Even if that's all true, you still could've trusted me—the guy you were screwing—with the truth. Justify your double life any way you want, but you had no good reason to keep the secret from me." He raked his hands through his hair. "For all I know, these past few weeks have just been about getting new material."

His eyes went wide as that thought took root. "Was that what you've been doing? Have you been toying with me this whole time, taking every private thing between us and putting it in a new story?"

Emma rose off the sofa and stepped closer, her body aching for his forgiveness, for his touch. "No, Wyatt. I swear, that's not true."

"So there's not another book?"

Shoot.

"There's a sequel, but I haven't put anything that happened this month in that book."

"Sorry if I find it hard to believe you." His resentful glare made her insides ache.

"Don't believe me, then. But you can't want this kind of gossip to end up in this film. It's exactly the kind of publicity you've been determined to avoid. Please. Please help me convince Mari it's not good for you."

"Or for you and your reputation. Try to be honest—for a change—about your real motives."

Emma withdrew, her own anger now rising. "This is why I didn't tell you. I knew you wouldn't believe me."

"Don't start with the cop-outs. You didn't give me a chance, and now I can't believe a single word that comes out of your mouth." He waved his hand at her in disgust. "I'm outta here. I'm going to go to

Crested Butte ahead of schedule, 'cause I can't be in your company any longer. We'll be gone first thing in the morning."

"I wish you wouldn't, Wyatt. Please take the night to think about everything. Think about what we've shared. You must know how much I care. Don't end it this way. Please don't hate me."

"You should've thought of that before you lied to me."

"I didn't lie." She stomped her foot. "You said we could have secrets."

"If they didn't hurt someone." He smacked his chest. "This fuckin' hurts, Emma."

"So did the fact that you didn't recognize me, but I got over it. And if this had stayed a secret, it wouldn't have hurt anyone. It was my secret, and it really has nothing to do with you."

"It has everything to do with me . . . from the night in Aspen to this tell-all book." He shook his head, his expression a mixture of sorrow and rage.

"Wyatt," she called, but he'd stormed out of the room. She stood there for an indeterminate length of time staring at the spot he'd vacated, as if she could will him to reappear. To reconsider and think about everything they'd shared.

She shook from the loss of his affection, so she slipped beneath her comforter and stared at the ceiling, tears trickling from the corners of her eyes.

Hours later, when the house had fallen silent, she slipped downstairs to clean the kitchen in private. When she rounded the corner into the dining room, she was surprised to find the table cleared.

A light glowed from under the kitchen door. Hesitantly, she pushed it open, unsure of who'd she'd find, certain she couldn't handle another confrontation.

Ryder was wiping down the counters, having already finished cleaning the pots and wrapping whatever leftovers there were.

"Ryder." She stopped and held her breath. "You didn't need to clean up."

"I figured you'd be too t-tired to do it." He folded the dishrag and laid it over the faucet.

Emma's eyes watered again. At this rate, she'd be dehydrated before dawn. "I don't think I deserve that kindness from you."

Ryder leaned against the counter. "Wyatt's mad, but that's between you two. You've been my f-friend. Whatever your reasons for what you did, I don't think you meant to h-hurt anyone."

"I didn't. No one would've ever known anything if Mari hadn't told." Emma frowned then. "How did she find out, anyway? I've been so careful."

"Those cameras were rolling yesterday to catch my mom's arrival. She caught you talking to your agent on the phone."

Only her hurried state of mind yesterday could explain why she'd been so careless. So unaware of those damn cameras.

"Will you be going back to Vermont with your mother?" Emma asked, searching for neutral territory.

"Yeah. It's the best place for me right now. I'll finish my therapy and then see where life points me."

"I hope you keep up with your pottery. I think you could really do something with that, Ryder. Sell it, show it, I don't know."

"Maybe." He shrugged. "Maybe."

"I'm sorry things ended so badly here, but I'm glad I got the chance to know you." She wanted to hug him, but in light of the circumstance, she held back. "I wish you the best of luck."

"Same here, Emma." He crossed the kitchen. Before he left, he said, "Don't let anyone make you feel bad about your b-book. I hope it sells well."

She smiled at the little smirk on his face. "So do I. Actually, it feels kind of good to be able to say that to someone, finally. Thank you."

"You're welcome." And then he disappeared.

Emma stood in the quiet kitchen where she'd spent a majority of her time this past decade. The comfort it had always given now cloyed.

Her father's advice replayed. She slid to the floor, as if being pulled down by the heavy weight in her heart, and hugged her knees. The thought of going back to business as usual with her mom, of keeping her writing a secret, of repressing her sexuality out of fear or shame (or some mix of those two) bore down on her with unbearable pressure.

She wanted a solution. A way to fix everything and make Wyatt understand why she'd hidden the truth.

After some time, she gave up her hopeless search for an answer. She shut off the light and meandered back through the inn. The tripods were no longer scattered in the corners of the rooms. Apparently Wyatt had wasted no time in forcing the others to pack up to hit the road.

Moonlight filtered through the transom windows, casting long shadows on the old carpet. Her shadow looked like a ghost, which prompted her eyes to sting again. She hesitated at the second-floor landing, glancing at Wyatt's door. No light shone beneath it. He wouldn't welcome her slipping into his bed tonight, as she'd done every night for the past couple of weeks. If she'd known this morning was to be their last time together, she'd have stretched it out a little longer.

Her nose tingled, but she forced back the tears. Enough crying for one day. What was done was done. She couldn't change the past. Her only choice now was how she'd live out her future.

Chapter Eighteen

Wyatt's eyelids felt glued to his eyeballs when he woke up. Woke up? That'd imply he'd slept. He'd caught a few catnaps throughout the night, but nothing restful. His bones hurt. Hell, his whole body ached, and not only from the lack of sleep.

Last night he'd looked up Alexa Aspen's website and read that sample chapter. Fiction my ass! Dallas looked just like him, or at least a striking approximation. Emma might've gifted Dallas an extra inch or two of height, but everything else she'd described would lead a sketch artist to draw a perfect replica of Wyatt's face.

She'd written their whole whipped-cream sundae thing into the story, too. He might not remember everything from that long-ago night—considering he'd been drinking—but he sure as shit recalled that particular part.

He also recalled waking up to an empty bed that next morning, feeling mildly disappointed Alexa had left without any fanfare. Not that he'd have followed up. He'd been on his way to the International Games within weeks of that night and had no time for anything more than quickies on the sly.

He wasn't proud of that, or of the fact that he hadn't recognized Emma. Of course, Alexa had dressed in barely there clothes and worn lots of makeup. A far cry from the frumpy version of Emma that had greeted him the day he'd arrived in Sterling Canyon. Honestly, how did she expect him to make the connection?

Then again, he didn't even put it together after they'd slept together again, which seemed inconceivable to him now. That must've have stung her pride, too.

Wyatt supposed, if he were in a generous mood, he could understand Emma's decision not to remind him of their past. He wasn't, however, feeling generous.

No. Hard to be generous when one felt used. Deceived. Foolish.

Emma presented herself as one kind of woman—thoughtful, helpful, honest. In reality, she was a whole other person. Someone capable of lying to everyone every day. Someone who could pull off publishing a book without her own mother having a clue. Someone who still might leak his name to sell that damn book if it didn't do well enough on its own, and who might've used their recent "experiences" for another damn book.

Well, he wouldn't help her use him to make money. He'd played upon Mari's disdain for Emma to keep her from giving *Steep and Deep* free publicity through the film. However, Ryder, his mother, Jim, Buddy, and Mari all knew the truth. It didn't take long for gossip to spread. If each of them only told one or two people, surely it would multiply, especially if he did well in competition and got more media attention. Even Mari could change her mind if she decided the link to the book could bring the film more publicity.

He winced, already conjuring explanations he could offer if cornered by the media. Then he cringed thinking about what Emma might've made up in that book that might then be attributed to him. What kinds of things did Dallas do and say, and would people think that Wyatt and that character were one and the same? Just thinking about the cheesy name *Dallas* caused his hands to fist into tight balls.

The whole situation made him sick. It had been the absolute last thing he needed or expected from this holiday. The only upside to the whole disaster was that his mother suddenly had shown him a little empathy. Oddly, Emma's plan to help his family come together might succeed, even if it did so in an ass-backward kind of way.

He sat up and rubbed his hands over his face. He'd packed most of his things last night, so he only needed to shower and dress. Shouldn't be a problem, but his body felt like he'd gained four hundred pounds overnight.

Rolling off the bed, he lumbered to the bathroom, practically stomping on a note that had been slipped beneath his door. Emma must've slid it there sometime in the middle of the night.

His last memory of her wasn't pretty. Ruddy, tear-stained cheeks, eyes as red as her hair, trembling body, choked voice. He shook his head to clear away the image. He hadn't been too hard on her. Her lies deserved every bit of his scorn.

Ignoring the letter, he stood beneath scalding-hot water to ease his sore muscles before dressing and making a final sweep of the room to ensure he hadn't left anything behind.

He'd instructed everyone to be ready to go by eight. Fifteen more minutes and he'd be gone from this old inn for good. He hesitated, mentally preparing himself to remain stoic when he saw Emma. He didn't expect her to make a scene, but just the sight of her was sure to rock him. Inhaling slowly, he grabbed his things, opened his door, and rolled his suitcase right over her note.

Once in the hall, he hesitated. Glancing over his shoulder, he stared at the crumpled envelope with his name written across it. He went back and stuffed it in his small duffel bag. Maybe he'd read it later, or not. He didn't know, but he decided to preserve the choice until his mind stopped bouncing around like a basketball in the Final Four.

When he reached the bottom of the stairwell, he heard everyone in the dining room. Had Emma made everyone breakfast even though he'd been pretty clear that they wouldn't be lingering?

Again he paused, wondering if Emma was in there waiting for him, or if she planned to corner him near the office or in the kitchen. With cautious steps, he crossed to the dining room. Apparently Emma had set out a light breakfast buffet with fresh fruit, bagels and lox, juice, and yogurt. Irrationally, her gesture filled him with resentment. He didn't want to be reminded of her thoughtfulness.

"'Morning." He gripped the back of a dining chair, uncertain whether he wanted to give her the satisfaction of eating, but knowing he had a half-day drive ahead of him.

Mari must've sensed his tension. "Emma isn't here, Wyatt. We spoke briefly and settled the bill, then she left the inn to afford you the space she assumed you wanted. She won't be back until after nine, so you can relax and eat before we hit the road."

"Good." Even as the word fell from his lips, he didn't mean it. Just like Alexa, Emma had slipped away without saying good-bye. That ache he'd hoped to ease with the hot shower flared back to life, making itself at home in his chest. "Pass the yogurt, please."

It seemed no one knew exactly what to say, so they kept their thoughts to themselves. Wyatt didn't know which was worse, hearing the scrapes and pings of the silverware break the silence, or listening to the rattling of his mixed-up thoughts.

After everything that had happened—the way Emma'd betrayed him—how dare she steal his chance to decide how or if to say good-bye. Obviously she didn't care about him at all. If she'd cared, she couldn't have let it—him—go so easily.

He speared a strawberry with his fork.

"Mom and I decided it might be best if you all drop us in Montrose and keep going to Crested Butte," Ryder said.

"I can hang in Montrose for a day or so," Wyatt objected.

"You'd planned to train today and tomorrow. With everything that's happened, maybe it's best if you press on and get back on the mountain." He drummed his fingers on the table. "You need to focus, not b-babysit Mom and me."

"Hell, I need to call Trip." In his hasty anger last night, Wyatt hadn't stopped to think about all the plans that needed to be adjusted.

"It's done," Mari said. "Emma took care of it."

First she made breakfast, then she handled Trip? Well, if she thought those little gestures made up for anything, she had another think coming.

"I'd booked him for the next few days. He's going to be out that money now." Wyatt set down his fork.

"Wyatt, it's handled." Mari offered a tight smile. Her demeanor suggested she might have some regrets this morning about the way she'd blindsided Emma. When he'd questioned Mari last night, she'd claimed she'd been worried that his misplaced faith might detract from his training. At the time, she'd had no idea of their former connection, so she hadn't anticipated it being so explosive.

That had made sense to him last night. In the cold light of day, Wyatt now wondered if Mari hadn't been a little jealous, or a little pissed. Either way, he sure didn't feel more focused and relaxed today than he had yesterday morning. Mari's plan had backfired in a major way.

Still, he couldn't blame her. If Emma had told him the truth, none of it would've mattered. Or, at least, it wouldn't have mattered as much.

"I'm sorry this holiday got so messed up." Wyatt set his chin on his fist and looked at his mom. "I'd hoped we would've had a few days to catch up."

"It's fine, honey." His mother patted his arm. "You didn't do anything wrong. I think you're smart to get away from someone who took advantage of you."

"Thanks." His robotic reply sounded hollow, and a small chamber of his heart rebelled against that characterization of Emma. But he wouldn't sit there and second-guess himself. He had his first qualifier in a few weeks. He needed to keep his head on straight and continue the work he and Trip had started. Maybe Trip would come up to Crested Butte with him for a week or so, although he couldn't count on that.

After all, Trip's fiancée was Emma's best friend. Wyatt could only speculate about how Emma would spin what had happened. Given her gift for words, and her desire to keep her own secret, he didn't imagine she'd paint him in a flattering light.

Where the hell was she, anyway? Probably at church, praying for forgiveness. His thoughts strayed to that little room where she'd soothed him after his recent argument with Ryder. When he'd stumbled and acted like an ass, she'd been there to help him. Then again, he hadn't hurt her, so she shouldn't expect him to return the favor now. "Guess we should load up the van and push off, then."

"We're ready." Mari wiped her mouth and set the napkin on the table.

Fifteen minutes later, they pulled out of the parking lot. Wyatt glanced out the window and watched the inn fade away as they drove down the street. He suspected his memories of Emma would not vanish as easily. Meanwhile, her note remained stuffed in his duffel bag, waiting for him to decide whether he wanted to read anything she had to say.

Except for the night she'd cooked for Mr. Tomlin, Emma had done little more than think and cry those first few days after Wyatt had left.

She'd dodged Andy's questions—his concern—by blaming Wyatt's mom for the early exit. She'd told everyone that he'd decided to take a brief respite from training in order to spend a few extra days with his family before they all split up again.

It hadn't been quite as easy to pass that story by Trip, who'd been more involved in Wyatt's training schedule. She knew he and Kelsey had their suspicions, but they graciously let Emma slide without pressing for details. Kelsey wouldn't let Emma's silence go on forever, though. At most, Emma would get ten or so days before Kelsey would march to the inn and demand the truth.

The truth. Something Emma had lost sight of for a while. Depending on how one viewed it, she hadn't been truthful in decades.

Wyatt had accused her of pretending to be someone she wasn't. At first, she'd accepted that assessment. But the quiet, lonely stretches of time and self-evaluation made her realize it wasn't quite accurate.

She was kind, considerate, caring, and generous. She loved her mother and wanted to make her proud. She enjoyed giving back to the community in all the ways she'd done for years. None of that had been a lie. None of it had been pretense.

The only pretense involved everything she'd repressed in order to keep her mother happy. To retain the good opinion of the townsfolk. To keep herself from making the kinds of mistakes that hurt herself and others. It hadn't been a small thing to bury that part of herself that wanted more. That craved adventure. That liked sex and flirtation and independence.

And yet, even though her one shot at setting it free had blown up in her face, she knew in her heart she could not go back to the way she had been before Wyatt came to town. She didn't really want to, either.

At thirty-one, Emma Duffy had grown up, finally. Wyatt had been right to call her a coward. At least, a little right. However, her time with him had helped her embrace the parts of herself she'd feared—the things that had made her feel ashamed or nervous. He may not have any kind thoughts for her now, but she'd always be grateful.

And so, when her mother finally returned from her trip, Emma had allowed her two days to settle back in before she decided to drop the bomb.

Her book launched in two more days, and she wanted to share the milestone with her mother, Kelsey, and Avery. She'd trust them to keep her secret, but would take whatever came her way if they failed. She'd told Wyatt not to feel guilty for Ryder's accident, or responsible for his choices. Now she realized she couldn't continue to accept guilt for however her mom would respond to her choices. Or allow the opinions of others to dictate her future happiness.

At the same time, she didn't want to be like her dad and show no concern for whether her actions would hurt her mom or others. She'd have to walk a fine line, but she was ready to be more true to herself. Another step in the right direction, she hoped.

She finished frosting the red velvet cake and set it on the dining table. Everyone would be here soon. Her stomach tipped and turned like a Tilt-A-Whirl ride, but she kept breathing slow and steady.

"Are we celebrating something?" Her mother bustled into the dining room. "Let me guess—you have a reel of the film to show us? You know, our bookings are up this month. We owe that snowboarder some gratitude. Too bad he had to leave early."

Emma didn't react to the mention of Wyatt, or tell her mom why he'd helped secure some of those bookings while he'd been here. That thought wrenched her stomach, just like the white lie she'd told her mom about why he'd left early.

While she'd decided to come clean about some things, there was no reason to give her mother a heart attack. If her mother envisioned Mari's ambush and Wyatt's outrage, she honestly might have a stroke. Most importantly, Wyatt wanted no association with this book, so she couldn't betray him again by telling anyone of his role in its inception now.

Revealing her own link to the book would be more than enough for her mom to handle. The personal relationship she'd had with Wyatt was, ultimately, nobody's business but hers . . . and his.

Avery and Kelsey arrived together, chatting as they came into the dining room.

"Mrs. Duffy, welcome home!" Avery hugged Emma's mother, as did Kelsey. "Emma kept us up to date on your travels. Sounds like you and your sister had an amazing adventure."

"We did!" Emma's mother took a seat, as did her friends. "You girls ought to plan a cross-country road trip, too."

"I'll drive," Kelsey offered.

"No!" Avery and Emma said in unison, then they laughed while Kelsey scowled.

"Okay, let's change the subject." Kelsey folded her hands on the table. "Pray tell, why did you call us here, Emma. And I thought I told you, no cake before the wedding. Are you trying to sabotage my dress fittings?"

Emma cleared her throat and sat down before her knees gave out. "Sorry. I called you three here to celebrate something. You only have to take one bite for good luck."

They all looked at each other, possibly thinking another might know what Emma would say next. Within seconds, their attention returned to Emma.

"I admit, I'm curious!" Avery tucked her hair behind her ear and leaned forward. "What's the occasion?"

Drawing a deep breath, she plunged ahead.

"I wrote a book, and it goes on sale in two days," Emma began, but before she could say more, Kelsey yelped and Avery beamed at her.

"I had no idea you were interested in writing. What an accomplishment." Avery's smile stretched across her whole face. "I can't wait to read it."

"Oh, Emma. An author!" Emma's mother clasped her chest. "I'm so impressed. No wonder you've been so scattered lately. I can't wait to brag to my friends, and that dreadful Connie Buckman."

"Slow down. You may not want to share this with your friends. In fact, I'm publishing under a pen name."

Avery's brow rose and Kelsey's eyes widened. Her mother frowned. "Why on earth wouldn't you want people to know you're an author, Emma? That's absurd."

Emma withdrew three signed copies of her book from the paper bag on the table. The cover, which featured a woman in lingerie and a black lace mask being fondled by a shirtless man, captured everyone's attention. "Mostly because I worried it might embarrass you, Mom. And having watched Andy suffer from this town's judgment last winter, I thought prudence might be the best choice. I'm still the same person I've always been, but I can imagine small-minded people reacting badly."

Her mom stared at the book, her face pinched as if she were looking at a steaming pile of dog doo.

"*Steep and Deep?*" Her mother's voice wavered.

"Emma Duffy, when I begged you to surprise me someday, I sure didn't expect this," Kelsey laughed and turned the book over in her hands, oblivious to the fact that Emma's mom might faint right into her lap. "I love it!"

Although Kelsey's immediate acceptance heartened Emma, she couldn't tear her gaze from her mother.

"Mom?" Emma noted the dismayed heartbreak written all over her mother's face. She'd expected it, of course, but the sliver of hope she'd clung to now stuck her like a knife, sending a sharp pain to her heart.

Her mother shoved the book toward Emma with tears in her eyes. "You cannot publish that book."

"It's too late. It's already been shipped to bookstores."

"I can't believe you wrote this! I raised you with Christian values. My word, Emma. I'm glad my mother isn't here to see you now."

"Grammy read books like this, Mom."

"No she didn't. Not like this! Not kinky books. She read some cowboy romances. Hardly this kind of trash." Her mom's voice warbled with pain and anger. "How do you know about these perverted things? Don't tell me you've done these things."

"Mom!" Emma knew her whole body had flushed, because her shirt now stuck to her back.

Avery interrupted, "Perhaps Kelsey and I should leave you two alone?"

"No!" Emma said, defiance and disappointment collecting in her gut, forcing her to stand up for herself. "I want to celebrate. This *trash* took hundreds of hours to craft. I suffered dozens of rejections before landing an agent. This book sold at auction, which means a few publishers wanted it, and was a top-pick review by a respected trade journal. I worked really hard. I know it isn't *The Grapes of Wrath*, but I'm still proud of it."

Her mother's hands rose in the air. "Oh, for goodness sake. Proud? Proud of being a pornographer? Because honestly, Emma, that's all this is."

"It isn't porn, Mom. It's fiction. There are themes of redemption and acceptance. There are layers to the characters. Sex is just one part of the story. Yes, it's an important part. But—news flash—most people think sex is an important part of life. Maybe you've just been so angry for so long that you forgot about the benefits of a healthy sex life!" She slapped her hand over her mouth. "I'm sorry! That was out of line. I didn't mean it."

"You sound like your father, always with some justification." Her mother rose slowly with as much dignity as she could manage under the circumstances. "I will not be a hypocrite and celebrate this depravity." She turned to go, but then looked at Avery and Kelsey. "I beg you girls not to tell anyone in town. I don't want Emma to be known as a smut peddler. And I don't want the inn's reputation to be linked with this kind of thing, either. We don't rent rooms by the hour!"

Without another word, her mother hurried from the room.

"I'm sorry, Emma." Avery reached across the table. "I hope she didn't completely ruin this for you. Regardless of her opinion, this is an amazing accomplishment. I'm so proud of you. But of course, I'll respect your and your mother's wishes to protect your privacy. I like the pen name, by the way."

That pen name—initially a cute nod to her secret past—now served as a horrible reminder of her broken heart. She wished she could share that with her friends, too, but Wyatt had been very clear about his wishes not to be associated with this book. The least she could do for him was respect that.

"Thank you. I'm not ashamed of this book, but I know others will judge me. Judge my mom. I also wouldn't want the people in charge of my volunteer positions to feel pressured to let me go because of public backlash. If someday I get caught, so be it. But for now, I'd rather stay under the radar."

Kelsey sat back. "I suppose we shouldn't tell Trip and Grey, either?"

"Spare me one of Grey's nicknames and years of ribbing from Trip, please." Emma tried to joke, but even she could hear the heaviness in her voice.

"What if it becomes a bestseller? Might you come out of the closet then?" Avery asked. "Give me a piece of cake, by the way."

Emma sighed, doubting she'd ever be a bestseller of anything. Still, she'd proven she could let her fantasies run wild, so why not go with this one. "If I become a bestseller, then I'll have money to fix this inn. Maybe that will finally convince my mom that my writing isn't shameful. I'd still keep the pen name, though."

"Give your mom a break. She's always been so conservative, and you've shocked her." Kelsey then stared at Avery's slice of cake. "Dang it, give me a slice, too."

Emma started to cut a thin section when Kelsey barked, "Oh, come on. You know me better than that."

"But you said—"

"I know what I said. Since when did you ever listen to me anyway?" Kelsey gestured for a bigger slice, then snatched the plate and dug in.

"Emma, this book's about a champion snowboarder," Avery interrupted, having now read the back jacket copy. "But you only just met Wyatt."

"It's fiction." Emma couldn't tell the truth out of respect for Wyatt's wishes. "We live in a ski town, so I chose a familiar kind of athlete-hero. You both know the type, don't you?"

Because both of her friends were engaged to professional skiers, they chuckled. Avery conceded. "Fair enough, but quite a coincidence."

Crisis avoided, for now, anyway.

"Speaking of Wyatt, have you heard from him?" Kelsey aimed yet failed to reach a casual tone.

"No." The thought of him, as always, made her chest tighten.

"Trip is going up to Crested Butte for a few days in early January before the first qualifier." Kelsey watched Emma for a reaction.

"I'm glad. Trip helped Wyatt a lot, especially after Ryder stepped away. I think Wyatt likes having a wingman to help point out his weaknesses."

"Will you go watch the competition?" Kelsey asked.

"Maybe," Emma lied, hoping her indifferent attitude would stop Kelsey's probing. She'd love to go, but Wyatt would rather stick pins in his eyes than see Emma in the crowd. "First, I've got to focus on my book launch. You two could help if you leave reviews on Amazon and Goodreads."

"Consider it done," Avery said. "I'll also tell some of my clients about this hot new romance they just have to read."

"Me, too, although a lot of my clients are men." Kelsey licked a bit of icing from her finger. "I'll be honest, it's going to be hard to keep the secret, but I promise, I won't crack."

"I think the only thing that will keep my mom from kicking me out is the fact that she'd have to come up with an explanation." Emma glanced toward the entrance of the dining room, as if her mom might reappear. "I knew this would be hard for her to accept. But I can't keep holding a part of myself back. And I wanted to be able to share this part of who I am with the people I love and trust."

"I may skim the sex scenes you've written so I don't imagine you in them," Avery laughed.

"Skim away." Emma grinned and ate a bite of cake. "You don't even have to read the book if you don't want to. I just wanted you to know this about me."

"I'll read the sex scenes, and if they're good, I might even force Trip to act them out." Kelsey punctuated her declaration with a quick nod, and Avery shook her head.

"Let's get going so Emma can go talk to her mom in private." Avery stood and tucked her copy of *Steep and Deep* in her purse.

"Okay. Can't afford to wolf down another piece of cake anyway," Kelsey sighed while staring dreamily at the cream cheese frosting.

Emma showed her friends out and then marched upstairs to her mother's room. Facing her mother's anger should be easier to deal with than her former depression. It would take time, but hopefully her mother would accept Emma and her writing, even if she never embraced it.

For tonight, Emma would suffer though her mom's ranting and pray that, in time, she would realize that Emma was still the daughter she'd always been proud of. But as she approached her mother's room, she heard the shower running and froze. In an instant, she'd been transported back to being that frightened thirteen-year-old girl, except this time she, not her father, had devastated her mother.

She waited, expecting guilt and panic to consume her. Instead, the unmistakable heat of anger began bubbling through her veins. Anger that her mother couldn't be proud of her accomplishment. That she'd stooped to emotional blackmail and name-calling to manipulate Emma and ruin her joy. That this dynamic had cost Emma so much over her lifetime, and more recently, had cost her Wyatt.

Rather than walk inside and placate her mother, she turned away and went to her room. No longer would she repeat old patterns and repress herself just to keep her mom happy. Happiness was a choice people had to make for themselves. If her mother chose to overlook all of Emma's finer qualities because of one point of disagreement between them, then that would be her choice. From now on, Emma planned to live her life by her own compass.

Chapter Nineteen

New Year's Eve had come and gone. All the talk about resolutions had only left Wyatt feeling more conflicted about his future.

His mom and Ryder were back in Vermont. Ryder had become an apprentice with some artisan pottery group. He'd discovered a real passion for pottery and possibly for a girl named Cindy, whose name Ryder casually brought up more than once when talking about his day. Apparently she belonged to this collective. Clearly another inspiration for his brother's commitment to the art. Between that and therapy, Ryder had been keeping busy and sounding better.

Being on tour without Ryder had been hard, but at least seeing his brother move forward had tempered the loss.

Their mom had landed some kind of work-from-home Internet job that generated a little extra income. Since Wyatt had paid off her mortgage three years ago, she and Ryder were getting by just fine without him. They were happy. Only Wyatt floundered, unable to find joy doing the thing he'd always loved most.

Even now, as he shot down a chute, carving perfect, tight turns, he didn't feel the rush that used to come from mastering the mountain.

When he and Trip finished the run, Wyatt unlocked his bindings and grabbed his board. "Sorry you can't stay another week, but thanks for coming up here to help me get used to this mountain's terrain."

"You didn't need me, Wyatt." Trip hefted his skis onto his shoulder and started walking off the slope toward the parking lot. "You got this. I wouldn't blow sunshine up your ass, either. I know they've roped off the competition course until game day, but we covered a lot of similar terrain. You shouldn't have any major surprises. Keep loose and have fun. Hopefully they'll get some fresh pow this coming week so the course is soft."

"They're calling for snow, but you know those guys get it wrong as often as they get it right."

"Mountain weather's never predictable." Trip tossed his skis in the back of his van. "So, I have to ask. Any chance you might consider my offer to partner with Grey and me once this is all over? 'Cause I think you ought to consider how long you want to live this life. Take it from me, eventually you'll want to settle in to something more stable. I used to love not knowing where I'd end up next, or what woman might be with me. But in a few years, that'll change. With your name, we could really build a world-class mountain expedition business. And Sterling Canyon's a perfect town for guys like us. Even if you only came for a few months a year until you're ready to walk away from competition, we could work something out."

Wyatt couldn't think about Sterling Canyon without thinking about Emma. And that gave him instant heartburn. "I don't know. I'd always assumed I'd move on to extreme ski films or what not."

"I never had the spotlight you do, so maybe that's hard to give up." Trip unlocked his door. "Maybe it's none of my business, but that's never stopped me before, so I'm just going to ask: What happened with you and Emma?"

"What do you mean?"

"You both play dumb, but no one believes either one of you. And let me tell you, you both seemed a lot happier back in November than you do now."

Wyatt should be plenty happy. He'd been kicking ass on the slopes. The publicity surrounding his arrival and preparation for the competition had been mostly positive. One or two of the established freeriders talked a little trash about his ego, but he kept a lid on his temper and let it go. He'd learned that from Emma, he supposed. She'd always maintained her dignity, even in the face of disaster. Even in the face of heartache.

"Helloooo . . ." Trip waved his hand in front of Wyatt's face. "Where'd you go?"

"Nowhere." Wyatt hoped to avoid talking about Emma, but Trip wouldn't let it go.

"Here's my parting advice. All this," he gestured back to the mountain, "is awesome. The beauty, catching air, the element of danger—it's a helluva rush. But it's a solo kind of high. Now that I have Kelsey in my life, everything, even this, is better. I'm here to tell you, you can find a life that gives you all this, and everything else. Maybe you can have it with someone like Emma, or maybe not. But don't think it's an either-or proposition, Wyatt."

"Old man, you're so whipped!" Wyatt joked because he wasn't ready to have a serious discussion about Emma or the future. "Get on out of here before I throw up."

"Okay, I'm going home. Unlike you, I've got someone eager for my return." He slid onto the front seat. "The offer's always open with Backtrax. Grey's camped out at Avery's, and I've moved in with Kelsey while we build our house, so the apartment is pretty much empty. You'd have a cheap-ass place to live until something better comes along."

"Thanks, Trip. I'll keep in touch."

"Good luck, buddy. I'll be watching you on ESPN, so don't let me down."

Wyatt waved Trip off and then strolled to the condo he was sharing with Mari and the guys.

He dumped his equipment in a locker and then went up to the unit to shower and rest. Once he'd dried off and stretched out on his bed, he pulled a copy of *Steep and Deep* from the nightstand drawer and withdrew the wrinkled envelope from its pages.

> *Wyatt,*
>
> *I imagine someone like you can't fathom how someone like me could get to be my age and still be plagued by insecurity and fear. How could you, when you fear almost nothing? You, who turned family hardship on its head and became a world-class athlete—who pushes past fear to pursue your passions—couldn't possibly relate to me, who allowed myself to be swallowed up by everyone's mistakes and expectations. Whose desire to be liked ranked higher than my need to be truly honest with anyone, including myself.*
>
> *My weakness has cost me your regard, which was a high price to pay. I hope one day, when you look back on the weeks you spent here, you might remember me for more than my mistakes. You might remember that, in my own way, however pathetic and one-sided it might be, and even though I never found the courage to say it aloud, I loved you.*
>
> *Emma*

He folded it for the umpteenth time, tucked it back into the book, and shoved it in the drawer.

He'd thought back on that last conversation many times. Of the desperate look in her eyes when she'd talked about her past and her mom. Of the fact that she'd made him breakfast even after he'd said some truly awful things to her.

He'd been following Emma's book since it launched, convinced that she'd planned to leak his name in order to sell it. She could've thrown him under the bus without revealing her real name, but she hadn't. Even her Pinterest board had some male model posing as Dallas. That silly name still irked him, but not as much as it had at first. The character might physically resemble Wyatt, but the similarities pretty much ended there, thank God.

Her book had earned a bunch of positive reviews in a short time. Readers loved Dallas. Emma's sex scenes were damn hot, too. It made him feel a little weird to think of how many people might be getting a charge out of those scenes that had been more or less ripped from his life. Then it made him smile to think of how people would be shocked to meet Emma in person. No one but him would believe she had it in her to write those things.

So far, Mari had kept her promise not to tie him to the book. If any of the crew had whispered the truth to anyone, it hadn't gone anywhere. It seemed Wyatt would not be caught up in some kind of embarrassing sex scandal, and Emma would continue to live two lives—the public one and the private one.

He couldn't deny missing her. He could even admit he'd overreacted that night when Mari spilled the beans. Could admit that, although Emma had been dishonest about some important stuff, it didn't erase all the good she'd done for him and his brother. For his family, and for so many other people in her life.

Lies or not, she still was one of the kindest people he'd ever met. One of the sexiest, too, despite her uptight clothes and attitudes.

But he couldn't imagine investing more time, more of his heart, in a woman who lived her life in fear. She'd been wrong in her note. Wrong to say he didn't understand fear. He understood fear just fine. But he wouldn't buckle to it. It wasn't in him, and he couldn't partner with someone who let fear dictate her choices.

So he'd let go of Emma.

◆ ◆ ◆

Emma made her way toward the competition fences. She'd overheard others guessing the larger crowd today was due to Wyatt's presence. Freeriders never achieved the same level of fame as gold medal slope-style boarders, mostly because freeriding wasn't part of the International Games. Apparently, Wyatt's former fame followed him and cast a bigger spotlight on this event.

Some speculated that he wouldn't have it in him. But Emma knew Trip believed otherwise, and Trip wasn't a guy who'd overestimate another man's ability.

She scanned the crowd, wondering if Ryder and Mrs. Lawson might have come. Given Mrs. Lawson's negative opinion of the sport, and Ryder's desire for distance, she wasn't surprised when she didn't see them there. She did see Mari, Buddy, and Jim, who'd taken a position higher up on the slope, with their cameras aimed and ready.

Emma hadn't warned Wyatt of her decision to come, so she stayed down near the announcers rather than risk a run-in with Mari.

Truthfully, the pros and cons of coming still banged around in her head. He'd been furious with her, but six weeks had passed. Part of her hoped his anger had softened, at least enough to say good-bye with less ferocity. Another part hoped he'd even be glad to see her in the crowd. That maybe her coming here would show him that what had happened between them wasn't a lie at all.

Emma watched other competitors tackle the course while waiting impatiently for Wyatt's turn. She'd only ever seen him compete live that one year in Aspen, but he'd always been fluid on video. In contrast, many of the guys here lacked his finesse. She suspected this would bode well for Wyatt's score, but then again, she knew little to nothing about this sport.

A flurry of activity and raised voices told her Wyatt was up next. She edged closer to the finish line in order to get a better view. With binoculars in hand, she found Wyatt up at the starting gate. His helmet and goggles hid his gorgeous face, but she recognized his jacket.

Her pulse hammered beneath her skin and her mouth went dry from anticipation. She sent up a quick prayer for his safety and then held her breath when he hucked over the edge of the first cliff.

Bouncing on her toes, her jaw clenched as she watched him tackle the terrain. Near the top, he kept things controlled and straightforward, sailing over cliffs and threading through chutes with clean landings and razor-sharp turns. As the pitch became less severe, the old Wyatt started showing off for the crowd with some acrobatic jumps that a few others had tried but not executed as well.

He flew past the finish line and swooped into the corral near where she stood. Her cheeks hurt from the huge smile that broke across her face. He'd done it. He'd done exactly what he'd planned on doing, and her heart soared. She hugged herself, so glad she'd come and been part of this exciting moment in his life. He might not care, but it meant everything to her to share in it with him, even from afar.

Wyatt whipped off his goggles and waved at the onlookers and judges, his signature smile in place . . . until he saw her.

His hand stilled above his head and his smile faltered, almost as if he'd seen a ghost. For a minute, she regretted coming. He certainly didn't look pleased. Stunned, perhaps, but not happy.

She wouldn't cry. She'd told herself not to expect him to be happy to see her. Told herself that he'd probably view her arrival as another ambush. Still, tears clogged her throat. But she wouldn't let fear or doubt make her turn and run either. That old Emma was dead. New Emma would face the music, one way or the other. Uncertain of what to do, she gave him a thumbs-up.

Wyatt seemed to remember that all eyes were on him, so he smiled as he spoke with the reporter waiting at the staging area. Within another two minutes, he walked off the course and ditched his equipment by the fence.

Standing still, she watched him approach. "You did an amazing job. I don't know anything about scoring, but I can't imagine you not ranking in the top three."

"Why are you here?" No friendly greeting. No hint of any emotion other than surprise. No interest in discussing the competition.

"To support you. I didn't . . . I know you . . ." She sighed and glanced at the ground. "I couldn't not come. I wanted to see you take this step. I didn't mean to upset you."

He stood still, but even with his gloves on, she could see his hands clenching and unclenching.

Seconds stretched on. Wyatt saw Mari and the crew coming their way. "Mari's going to need a quick interview for the film."

"Of course. I'll let you go. It's good to see you again. Congratulations on a fantastic run." She yearned to touch him, hug him, hold him tight and not let go. Instead, she tucked her hands in her jacket pockets.

He hesitated, looking torn. "Can you hang until this is all over?"

"I'd planned to wait and see if you qualified."

"Don't leave until we have a chance to talk."

"All right." She watched him amble away and let out the breath she'd been holding.

A little while later, Wyatt's triumphant smile dominated the podium when he took second place at his first-ever freeride competition. He'd done it. He'd transitioned from one sport to another and was on his way to the next round of competition.

That thought made Emma both joyful and sad. He'd be traveling all the way to Europe if he kept up this level of performance. That meant more chances to get hurt or worse, and less opportunity for them to be anything more than a memory.

Mari sidled up to Emma before Wyatt got off the stand. "I'm surprised to see you here."

"Not sure why. As you know, I'm full of surprises." Emma folded her arms, bracing for an onslaught.

"Yes, you are." Mari glanced over to where Wyatt was being interviewed. "He looks happy now, and I suspect it isn't only because of his success today."

Emma had thought about Mari often over the past several weeks. Her feelings had run the gamut from hatred to, well, dislike. Yet Mari had respected Wyatt's wishes and kept Emma's secret. She'd been looking out for Wyatt, and maybe wasn't quite the self-centered bitch Emma had pegged her to be from their first meeting.

Emma aimed to be gracious. "Thank you for keeping the truth about the book out of this film."

"I didn't do it for you. I did it for him. The media fallout from that could've distracted and derailed him." Mari stared at Emma. "There aren't any more skeletons, are there, Emma?"

"None. At least, none that affect Wyatt." Emma smirked, enjoying toying with Mari.

Wyatt caught up to them then and quickly dismissed Mari. "Emma, I'm starving. Can you meet me at Django's in forty-five minutes? Find us a quiet table while I shower. We can eat and talk."

Dinner? Dinner had to be a good sign, didn't it? Her heart skipped a beat. "Sure. I'll see you in a bit."

An hour later, Wyatt joined her just as she was finishing a large glass of Cabernet. She'd grown a little braver in the past few weeks, but she hoped the wine would give her a little extra courage tonight. Wyatt hadn't seemed like he wanted to lay into her earlier, but she also had no idea what to expect.

He looked handsome now, showered and shaved. Around the inn, he'd mostly worn sweatpants and hoodies. Tonight he wore dark denim jeans and a moss green sweater that set off his hazel eyes. His wavy hair was combed rather than tangled.

Wyatt's gaze roamed her face for a minute. Perhaps he, too, was a little nervous and uncertain.

"I read the book." Wyatt's gaze continued drinking her in.

"Oh?" She bit her lip. Now it was her turn to be shocked. He'd read her book. She couldn't imagine what he'd thought of it, or her. Rather than allow anxiety about his disapproval keep her quiet, she asked, "Did you like it?"

"I was glad to see that Dallas isn't much like me after all."

"No, he isn't." Oddly, calmness settled over her. He knew the full truth about her and the books. Her worst fear had come to pass; yet here they were, conversing like grown-ups. Now there was nothing between them, at least, not from her side of the table. A giddy sort of relief shot through her, or maybe it was just the wine. In either case, she was finally free to be completely herself with him.

"But Ella . . . she's a lot like you."

He'd noticed. That surprised her. "Not a lot. Just a little."

"Enough." Then, as if he couldn't help himself, a crooked grin emerged. "Especially in some of those sex scenes."

If he could joke, maybe he didn't hate her. Maybe he would finally forgive her. Her heart swelled with hope. "Write what you know, or so I'm told."

He chuckled, then the waiter arrived to take their order. Once he'd left them alone, Wyatt leaned forward, his expression chagrined. "I owe you an apology for some of the things I said that night."

"You had a right to your anger. I lied." She shrugged.

"Yeah, but I went too far. I felt cornered."

"Let's agree that we both made mistakes and call it even. The important thing is that you believe I never intended to hurt you."

"I can see that now." He cocked a brow and smiled. "I almost feel bad that you didn't use my name to help sell more books. Although it looks like you racked up a bunch of nice reviews on Amazon, so maybe you didn't need my help."

Emma laughed. "Well, had I pimped your name, maybe I'd be a *New York Times* bestseller already." Then she leaned forward, her words weighted with sincerity. "But what happened in Aspen, and at home, was private and personal. Not for public consumption."

"Agreed." He fiddled with his napkin.

An awkward silence ensued, so she filled it by deflecting. "How's Ryder?"

"He's good. He's all in with the pottery thing. I think he even has a girlfriend, although he doesn't give her that label."

"And your mom? Are things better there, too?"

"A little." He sat forward and spoke in low tones. "That's all thanks to you. I see that now. All those little disagreements we had in November changed me for the better. You made me look at things differently. Made me see the bigger picture. I want you to know that the time we spent together meant something to me. It wasn't just some fling."

Her pulse beat wildly. She couldn't have wished for much more than those powerful words, and yet he'd said it all in the past tense, meaning tonight must just be a sweet good-bye. Swallowing the tiny lump forming in her throat, she said, "I'm glad."

He smiled and shook his head. "I still can't believe you came here today. Where are you staying?"

"I'm not."

His eyes widened. "You're not driving all the way home tonight, are you?"

"I'd planned on it. Of course, now it will be a late drive home."

His mouth fell open. "You made an eight-hour round trip just to watch me?"

"It was worth it." Emma smiled, glad for the fact she'd acted boldly, even if this would be their final good-bye. "Besides, I needed a break from the inn."

He stared at her, his hazel eyes warming. "And here I was thinking I kind of missed it."

"Were you?" Emma's pulse kicked up again.

"It has its charms." He winked.

Flirting. Flirting was good. Emma could flirt.

"Such as?"

Wyatt brought his hand up to his mouth, as if he were whispering a secret. "The innkeeper's sweet and helpful. Almost perfect."

"Only almost?"

Wyatt shrugged, now looking a little wistful. "She's afraid to really live her own life."

Emma shook her head. "Not anymore, actually."

"No?" He came fully alert, dropping all games.

"No. She learned a tough lesson recently. Even told her mom and a few friends about these naughty books she writes on the side. I think you'd be surprised by how she's changing."

A slow grin spread across his beautiful face. "That sounds like something we should celebrate."

"Like your victory here today?"

He reached for her hands and squeezed them. "If I remember correctly, you're pretty good at celebrating my victories."

"And here I thought I wasn't memorable at all."

"To the contrary, you're rather unforgettable." He tugged her hands to his mouth and kissed them. "I think we have some unfinished business and a trip to Switzerland to plan."

Her heart nearly burst at the renewed invitation. "You seem pretty sure of yourself on several fronts."

"I've never failed to reach any goal I've set. If that makes me cocky, so be it." He kissed her hand again. "Stay with me tonight?"

"Why not." Emma leaned across the table and kissed him, right there in front of everyone. Proving to him, and herself, she'd no longer run from love.

Epilogue

A stunning June sunset hung low in the sky, casting an orange and purple glow over the patio where Grey and Avery's wedding reception was being held. Everything about the afternoon and evening had been so romantic, Emma didn't want it to end.

Avery and Grey were making their way around to all the guests. Kelsey's small baby bump was concealed by the flowing bridesmaid's dress Avery had picked for her and Emma.

Her friends were happy and settled. While Emma couldn't claim to be quite so settled, she had been very happy these past few months, thanks to Wyatt.

"Your mom still doesn't like me much," Wyatt whispered in Emma's ear while they danced, and she knew she'd never get tired of being in his arms.

Emma peeked at her mom, who was sitting with the Callihans and Randalls. It had taken several weeks postpublication for her mother to really look her in the eyes without getting emotional, and another month before she'd reluctantly accepted that Emma wasn't going to stop writing.

Since then, the fact that Emma offered to use her royalties to help update the inn had helped, as did the fact that her friends had kept their promises and, so far, no one in town knew a thing about Alexa. Between the renovations and Wyatt's continued efforts to promote the inn, business was better than it had been in years. One would think her mom would feel indebted.

Of course, her mom's suspicions about Wyatt extended beyond the "coincidental" nature of his being a champion snowboarder and Emma's books involving one who resembles him.

"I'm sorry. She worries that you're going to take off, like my dad." Emma snuggled closer, grateful that he'd not only survived the Freeride International Tour, but placed second overall. Since then, he'd visited often, but had continued to travel all over the world shooting extreme ski videos. Whenever he came to town, she savored every second of their time together. "She'll relax someday, I promise. In the meantime, I like you a whole lot. Love you, even."

"Love you, too." He spun her around and pulled her close again, his one hand resting low on her back. He kissed her temple. "Still, I think she blames me for your books."

"Well, you did inspire them." She rested her head on his shoulder and breathed in the scent of him.

His husky voice rumbled over her. "Must be why they sell so well."

"Cocky as ever."

Wyatt shrugged. "Some things never change."

"Good to know. I wouldn't want you to change." Then again, she did wish he'd take fewer risks with his life. She never pressured him about it, though, or asked him to move to Sterling Canyon. Trip badgered him enough on that score.

But she wanted him to settle down here with her. She couldn't deny that, at thirty-two, she'd started to think about marriage, of starting a family of her own. One she'd raise in a guilt-free environment, of course.

"I have been thinking about changing one thing."

"What's that?"

"My address."

This caught her attention. She raised her head to look him in the eyes. "Oh?"

"Turns out I have an inside track on a truly ugly apartment." He grinned.

Emma's heart leapt. "Backtrax?"

Wyatt nodded.

"Really?" She tried not to let her excitement overwhelm him or call too much attention to them. Rather than press him or push him, she waited.

"Trip's a pain in the ass. Wants my name on the door in the worst way. I'm thinking it might not be a bad gig." He smirked, watching her work hard to control her emotions. Then he brushed his hand along her jaw and kissed her. A long, slow kiss. The kind she wrote about in her books. When he eased away, he said, "But you're the real reason I'd come here, Emma. I'm tired of missing you for weeks at a time. So, if I come, do you think your mom could handle that?"

"Honestly, I don't care." Emma tightened her arms around his neck. "I love her, but I love you more."

"That's all I needed to hear." He kissed her. "Consider it done."

Acknowledgments

I have many people to thank for helping me bring the Sterling Canyon books to all of you, not the least of which include my family and friends for their continued love, encouragement, and support.

Thanks, also, to my agent, Jill Marsal, as well as to my patient editors Chris Werner and Krista Stroever, and the entire Montlake family for believing in me, and working so hard on my behalf.

A special thanks to Brock Butterfield, a former freeride competitor, who answered all of my questions about the sport and even suggested some great plot points. Also, I need to thank Abbi Nyberg of the United States Ski and Snowboard Association for teaching me a bit about the ins and outs of the Olympics and the X Games and about pro ski sponsorship. Of course, for the sake of fiction, I modified some of what I learned from these two, but their input was invaluable and appreciated. Also, many thanks to documentary filmmaker and producer Megan Smith-Harris. She taught me a lot about that process (notwithstanding my fictitious interpretations), and is much, much nicer than the character I created in this story!

My Beta Babes (Christie, Siri, Katherine, Suzanne, Tami, and Shelley) are the best, always providing invaluable input on various drafts of this manuscript. Also, thanks to Heidi Ulrich for the hours she spent critiquing the story. Finally, thanks to my real-life hero (dearest hubby), who gave Emma's fictional book its *Steep and Deep* title.

And I can't leave out the wonderful members of my CTRWA chapter. Year after year, all of the CTRWA members provide endless hours of support, feedback, and guidance. I love and thank them for that.

Finally, and most importantly, thank you, readers, for making my work worthwhile. With so many available options, I'm honored by your choice to spend your time with me.

About the Author

Photo © 2013 Lora Haskins

Jamie Beck is a former attorney with a passion for inventing stories about love and redemption. A recent inductee into the Romance Writers of America's Honor Roll, her popular stories include her sassy Sterling Canyon books and emotionally complex St. James novels. In addition to writing romantic women's fiction, she enjoys dancing around the kitchen while cooking, and hitting the slopes in Vermont and Utah. Above all, she is a grateful wife and mother to a very patient, supportive family. Visit her on Facebook at www.facebook.com/JamieBeckBooks.